REBELLION.BOOK THREE

TIDES OF WAR

M.R.FORBES

Quirky
Algorithms

Published by Quirky Algorithms

Seattle, Washington

Cover illustration by Tom Edwards

http://tomedwardsdmuga.blogspot.com

1

LEX'EL DUR RORN'EL CROUCHED behind an outcropping of broken masonry. He lifted his arm, checking the levels in his oxygen tanks, and then turned his attention to his quarry.

The humans and the un'hai had found a hiding place beneath the twisted metal of one of their simplistic structures, a place marked by a pair of overlapping, symmetrical red lines. It had been destroyed by one of the gur'shah at least a dozen years ago, probably more, the floors collapsed, leaving a small area where the same gur'shah could now remain out of view of the sky.

The hunter had seen the battle that had won the mechs for the humans. He respected them for their victory, at the same time he despised them for his kind's defeat. It was all well. They would be removed from their so-called rebellion soon.

Today.

Nine days had passed since he had set out to track them. Nine days since he had access to more than a taste of fresh oxygen, as he sought to stretch himself to the limits of his genetic capabilities. Their speed had made following difficult, but their need to hide from passing gi'shah had given him the time he needed to catch up.

And he had caught up. Every daybreak for the last six days. It had meant moving at full speed and barely pausing to rest, but that was the investment required of a hunter if it wished to catch its prey. It was an investment too few of his pur'dahm brothers were willing to make, choosing the easy kill instead of the true challenge.

It was the reason he was the best of them.

It was the reason he had lived when the others had not.

He moved slowly, methodically, shifting from one position behind the wall to another beside it, peering out at the makeshift camp. Every day had been the same for the humans. They would set up their camp at dawn, finding a place to hide in the ruins of their former civilization. Then they would vanish into the ped'ek, all except a guard, to eat and to sleep. Occasionally, one of them would evacuate the transport to void somewhere nearby, usually before they assumed the guard's duty.

He had never considered attacking them while they did. Perhaps other hunters might have, but he believed it to be dishonorable. A disgrace. No. He wanted the advantage, as any good hunter would. But he also needed the humans to have a chance to fight back. There was no glory in killing something that had no means to defend itself.

That was why he had waited so long, watching from a distance for hours as the humans made their camp. He had tracked them hundreds of kilometers as they traveled north. He wasn't completely sure where they were headed, but he had an idea. While the Domo'dahm had been shattering bands of resistance in the north for weeks, there were still reports that a few of the larger groups had managed to evade them, hiding below the ground like druk'kek.

He believed their intent was to rendezvous with these forces, to lend the strength of the bek'hai weaponry to their cause. If the humans were half as intelligent as he was, they would begin attacking other smaller bek'hai outposts from there and work to capture more and more of their technology to use against them.

It was a plan he was going to enjoy ruining. Considering it now, he couldn't help but smile. That was the glory of the hunter. His glory. The Domo'dahm would surely move him near the front of the cell for singlehandedly ending the largest threat the humans had ever mounted.

His father was certain to be doubly pleased with the death of Ehri dur Tuhrik. The un'hai had always been more willful than the other lor'hai, but her actions were beyond willfulness. It was treachery and disloyalty, with no room for argument. She had betrayed her people, and she was directly responsible for the deaths of his fellow hunters.

He would be sure to kill her last.

He scanned the camp one last time. The guard posted outside was an older male. Lex'el had seen him during the battle. He had led the charge into the compound, and if his fellow hunter's deaths were any indication, he had comported himself well. His courage was respectable. Yes. He would be a good one to begin with.

He ducked back behind the wall, reaching down and sliding his lek'sai from his back. He eyed the blades thoughtfully for a moment, before looking out from behind the wall once more. The man was looking away from him, toward another line of destruction, apparently intrigued by something he saw there.

He looked in that direction as well, curious to know what it was.

Then he began running back to the ped'ek, opening the hatch and vanishing inside. Lex'el raised his arm and checked his sensors, hissing as he recognized pur'dahm Fior'el's sigil.

Nine days. That druk'shur had nine days to find the humans and make his attack. He was certain Fior'el's resources must have happened on their position by accident. He had watched how the humans hid from the sorties. It was simple and effective, and no doubt guided by Ehri.

Unless...

He put his other hand on the display, moving his fingers to change the screens, cursing at himself for his stupidity. He tapped the screen violently, shutting down his own transponder.

He hadn't expected any of the pur'dahm would be capable enough to think to track his movements instead of the enemy's.

He leaned back against the wall, closing his eyes. There was nothing for him to do now but wait. He opened a valve on his tank, taking a long breath of pure oxygen, feeling the tingle as it moved through his system. He could only afford to give himself one.

"Do not disappoint me, Ehri dur Tuhrik," he said as he listened for the attack to begin.

It was his glory on the line.

2

"GET YOUR LAZY ASSES up and moving, people," Kroeger shouted as he entered the confines of the transport. "We've got not-very-friendlies incoming, and I don't really feel much like dying today."

Major Donovan Peters' eyes snapped open, and he turned his head to where the older man was standing, his neck muscles taught as he released a spew of curses while reaching for one of the bek'hai rifles.

"Don't just lay there like a sack of shit, Major," Kroeger said, noticing him. "Get your tail over to that ugly ass hunk of steel and go kick some tail."

Donovan pushed himself up, shaking the sleep away. He couldn't have been out for more than a few minutes. Had the Dread been following them and waiting for them to settle down for the day?

"Kroeger, take Thompson and Mendez and find some high ground," he said as the rest of his team came alert. "Ehri, Soon, you're with me."

"Yes, sir," they all said, gathering themselves.

Kroeger tossed a rifle to both Thompson and Mendez. "Let's go, ladies and gents. We aren't getting paid for this, which means it's our asses on the line."

Then Kroeger was out the door, with the others right behind him.

"They were following us?" Donovan asked as Ehri moved beside him.

"It seems that way," she replied, though something in her expression gave him the feeling she wasn't convinced. "It can't be a large force, or we would have noticed."

"If they call in air support, we're going to be in trouble in a hurry."

"They won't."

Donovan nodded. He had learned a lot about how the bek'hai waged war over the last couple of weeks. Their system was an odd mix of both caste and meritocracy, where the elite caste, the pur'dahm, fought one another for positioning and power while at the same time seeking to fulfill the Domo'dahm's directives. What that meant for them was that any attacks against them would come from a single pur'dahm looking to gain rank and glory within that system. While the bek'hai elite would use whatever resources he had to achieve the objective, the last thing he would do would be to ask another for assistance. It was a major weakness on the part of the Dread.

A weakness they had exploited during their raid on the smaller bek'hai compound.

A weakness he hoped they could exploit again now.

They spilled out of the transport with Donovan in the lead. A plasma bolt struck the side of the ped'ek a meter from his head when he did, and he turned to see a return bolt vanish into the line of distant rubble as one of their infantry fired back.

"Move faster, Major," Kroeger shouted from somewhere out of sight.

Donovan pushed himself harder, breaking around the back of the transport, using it as cover as he reached the stolen enemy mech. He scaled the side of it, making it to the chest and putting his hand on a small, hidden control there. The cockpit swung open, and he pulled himself inside.

He leaned back, quickly activating the toggles that would start the vehicle's power supply and get it moving. In front of him, alien text surrounded a view of the world outside. He didn't know what most of it meant, and he didn't need to. The important part was universal - a blue reticle in the center of the HUD that showed him where his weapons were going to hit.

He flipped another switch, and a brace dropped over him, securing him to the rear of the cockpit and lowering a pair of joysticks. Each one was attached to rotating joints that mimicked the arms of the mech and provided all the controls for both upper body rotation and offense. His legs were kept free, tracked by sensors that would translate their movement into the bipedal motion of the mechanized armor.

It was all fairly rudimentary; primitive compared to other bek'hai technology. The Dread evolution had forced them to abandon the original control system that utilized a gel-filled capsule and a symbiotic neural network to transfer commands. They had replaced it with manual controls that could be used by the more human drumhr, who had lost the ability to communicate with the symbiotes.

It was nowhere near as efficient, but combined with invincible shields, it was just as effective.

"Rebel One, online," he said, activating the mech's comm system.

He continued to be grateful that the three mechs they had taken from the Dread compound had all been linked together, giving them the ability to coordinate their defense.

"Rebel Two, online," Ehri said a moment later.

"Rebel Three, online," Soon said.

"Let's keep an eye out for targets and stay cautious," Donovan said. "We need to know what we're up against before we do anything stupid."

"Yes, sir," Soon said.

The plasma bolts continued raining in, slipping harmlessly past the mech's shields and burning away at the armor below. Each of the mechs was already pockmarked from what amounted to small arms fire and would be able to take a lot more damage before it succumbed to limited attacks. Donovan knew instinctively that the trailing edge of the offensive would be clone soldiers, heavy in numbers and highly expendable. If the

Dread in charge of the attack had any intelligence at all, he would use them as a diversion while he tried to flank their position with his armors.

"Okay, Rebels. We're heading north together. We don't want to get caught in a crossfire."

"Roger," Soon and Ehri replied.

Donovan started moving, walking as though he were standing outside on the ground. The mech began to move the same way, its lefts shifting and coming down, pressing him forward into an even gait as he moved the machine out from cover and around the hospital, with Ehri and Soon right behind him.

"Rebel Three, rotate right, lay some cover fire for the infantry," he said.

"Roger," Soon replied, turning the top half of his mech and firing a pair of thick plasma bolts into the field. They slammed into the side of a crumbling wall, quieting the smaller attacks.

Donovan looked ahead of them. They were moving deeper into the small town, where more destroyed buildings were waiting. They had chosen the hospital because it was the best cover to be found, and none of the other ruined structures came up higher than the mechs' knees.

It left him uncomfortable as they cleared the safety of the larger building. He didn't see any opposition ahead of them, but he didn't expect that to last.

It didn't.

The enemy forces moved out from behind the more distant buildings, in smaller vehicles Donovan hadn't seen before. They had a loose resemblance to tanks, with angled carapaces and a larger barrel that emerged from it, surrounded by four smaller ones. There were at least a dozen in all, floating slightly above the ground and nearly silent.

"Gel'shah," Ehri said. "The plasma cannon is the most powerful the bek'hai carry on the ground. Do not let it hit you."

No sooner had she spoken than a stream of plasma bolts launched from the tanks, coming toward them in a deadly line.

Donovan watched the trajectory, getting his legs going and moving the mech forward as quickly as he could. He ducked as the screen brightened from the combined firepower, cringing slightly as the blue pulses passed over his head. He hoped Ehri and Soon had managed to evade the assault as well.

The plasma slammed into the hospital behind them a moment later with a burning hiss followed by the crashing of the already damaged floors as they finished giving way.

"I hope Kroeger wasn't in there," Soon said, witnessing the result of the assault.

"It looks like the transport is buried," Ehri replied.

"Damn," Donovan said. "Let's spread out a bit and make it harder for them to concentrate their fire."

"Yes, sir," Soon replied, his mech sidestepping away.

The Dread tanks released a second volley. Again, the mechs ducked beneath it, letting the rounds hit whatever debris was beyond them. It was easier to move aside right now. It wouldn't be once they got closer.

"Rebel Two, Can we take them out from here?" Donovan asked.

"No, Major," Ehri replied. "The armor is too thick. We need to get closer."

"How do you usually take these things on?"

"Gori'shah. Starfighters."

"I knew you were going to say that."

Donovan ducked under the third volley. There was a fifteen-second delay between attacks, presumably while the plasma cannon recharged. The closer they came to the tanks, the better their timing would need to be.

"Keep the rhythm. They need fifteen seconds to recharge. Try to burst forward while they do."

He followed his own advice, sending the mech dashing forward, crashing through damaged mortar and stone before slowing and dropping the mech into a crouch. Ehri and Soon did the same, and the fourth volley passed less than a meter beyond their heads.

"I felt that one," Soon said.

"Rebel Two, are we in range?" Donovan asked.

"Almost, Major," Ehri replied.

He could see the tanks more clearly now. They were backing up and spreading apart, clearly understanding their limitations.

One of the symbols on Donovan's HUD turned red as something hit him from the rear, burning into the mech's armor but not piercing it.

"Gur'shah," Ehri said. "Three of them."

The other side of the pincer. Donovan had been hoping to stay ahead of it, but it wasn't meant to be. "How the hell did they find us?" he hissed. "We managed to avoid them for days." He paused to regain his composure and think. "Rebel Two, can you deal with the rear?"

"I will do my best, Major."

"Rebel Three, break left. I'll go right. Let's see if we can give as good as we're getting."

"Yes, sir," Soon replied.

Donovan steered his mech away from the tanks, using the debris as cover while he tried to flank them and at the same time offering a smaller profile for their plasma bolts to strike. He continued to time the attacks, counting after each blast, using the time as best he could.

He glanced to the corner of his HUD. He knew the larger battle was displayed there, and Ehri's mech was a green shape moving ahead of the three red ones. Smaller dots lined the area to his rear, in the form of the Dread foot soldiers. It took him a few seconds to find Kroeger in the midst of the chaos, three small black dots clustered near the middle of the action. They weren't in a good position, having gotten pinned down there.

"Rebel One, I'm in position," Soon said a moment later, surprising Donovan.

Had he made it around already?

"Prepare to engage," Donovan said.

"Yes, sir."

Donovan ducked the mech behind some rubble, and then rose and faced the tanks.

"Engage," he said, tapping the triggers on the twin joysticks.

Plasma bolts launched from the mech, slamming hard into one of the tanks. The armored side melted, but the armor continued to move, trying to get him in front of its cannon.

He fired again, not wasting any time. He could feel the heat rise in the cockpit as his mech spewed another stream of energy at the tank. It was another direct hit, and it left the tank slagged and silent.

"Rebel Two, how are you holding up back there?" Donovan asked, dropping his mech as another blast passed over him.

"These pilots are druk. I am not surprised. They are carrying the sigil of Fior'el."

"That sounds good for us."

"It is very good for us, Major. Fior'el is from a low cell. This may be his entire militarized pool."

"You're saying he sent his whole army after us?"

"There is a great reward waiting for whichever pur'dahm destroys us. It is a dangerous risk on his part, but worth it, I suppose. I am more concerned with the fact that he knew where we were hiding. It should not have been possible."

"Let's get ourselves safe first, and then we can figure that out."

"Yes, Major."

Donovan unleashed another plasma beam at the scattering tanks, hitting a second as it tried to reverse course. "Take that," he said as it began to smoke. He glanced at his HUD. Soon was holding his own, having already destroyed four of the tanks to his two. Damn, he was good.

He rotated his torso, seeking another target.

A ball of plasma hit his right arm. The impact of it almost knocked him over, forcing him to scramble to keep the mech upright. The HUD flashed, and a warning tone sounded in the cockpit. Donovan checked the damage by moving the right-hand controls, and finding the arm didn't move with it.

He shook his head, backing away as he counted the seconds. He had gotten too aggressive, and now one of their best assets was damaged. Stupid.

He kept a closer eye on the HUD, watching the movement of the different units his sensors were detecting. He retreated toward Kroeger's position, firing back at the tanks as they also retreated. When Soon's mech passed in front of him, he turned around and unleashed a volley of slugs toward the Dread clones, chewing their front line to pieces.

Kroeger would owe him for saving his life. Again.

"It looks like they're retreating, Major," Soon said, blasting one of the remaining tanks. The others had been backing up, but now they accelerated, trying to escape the battlefield.

"Let them go," Donovan said, releasing his finger from the trigger. He had to continue firing a moment later, as the clones surprised him by pressing their attack. "What the hell? They can't win."

The main forces might have been retreating, but the pur'dahm, Fior'el, continued throwing his clones at them. Donovan felt sick as he kept shooting, cutting them down one after another. There was nothing glorious or honorable about sending these soldiers to slaughter.

"It is the way of the pur'dahm," Ehri said. "Especially Fior'el. Lek'shah resources are limited. Clones are not."

It was disgusting, no matter the reason. He tried to look away as his slugs tore through human bodies, knocking down soldier after soldier until his conscience couldn't take it anymore. He stopped firing, leaving a handful of the clones standing.

"Enough," he said, releasing the controls. He wanted to vomit.

The few remaining clones stopped shooting, standing in the middle of the field, looking at one another, confused. The confusion was interrupted when a series of plasma bolts fired from the ground cut across the field, striking each in turn.

Kroeger stepped out from behind a wall and looked up at him as if he could sense the reluctance to kill. Then he walked over to one of the dead clones and spat on it. He looked back up at Donovan, and sat down on top of the body, waiting.

3

"Do you have to sit there like that?" Donovan asked.

"I don't think he minds," Kroeger replied, patting the dead soldier on his bloody rear. "Do you?" He laughed harshly. "Kill or be killed, Major. It's an adage as old as time."

"You could show a little respect."

"For this thing? Why the hell would I? It isn't human. It isn't any different than those machines you blasted. Smaller scale, different materials. That's all."

"They are human," Donovan replied. "They have human DNA. They have individual personalities."

"Well, boo-hoo. If those individual personalities came with the smarts to not walk into the line of fire, maybe you could convince me, and that's a pretty large maybe. Until they stop following every order no matter how asinine it is, not matter how unfair it is, I'm not going to give a shit when they die."

They were standing near the center of the broken city. The smell of blood and burning metal and flesh was thick around them. There was no sign of Fior'el's army. Not any more. The four remaining tanks had retreated along with one badly damaged mech, the pur'dham's forces routed in the sneak attack.

Ehri returned from the hospital with Mendez a moment later, her expression dark.

"The collapse damaged the ped'ek, Major," she said. "It is no longer operational."

"What about the contents?"

"We can retrieve them."

"At least it isn't all bad news."

"No, Major."

"Looks like we're humping it the rest of the way," Kroeger said. "That's fine by me. How many kilos until Austin?"

"Three hundred," Ehri said.

"Not bad at all. Hey, what was with that bullshit attack anyway?"

"What do you mean?"

"I mean, they had three mechs to our three, fine. Even Steven. Bastards had a dozen tanks and almost five hundred infantry. You would think that would tip the odds in their favor a little bit. Excuse me if I'm wrong, but we wiped the floor with them." He kicked his chair in the side for emphasis.

"The bek'hai factories are only able to output so much in a given amount of time. The lek'shah especially is very difficult to produce. The lower a pur'dahm is in the cells, the longer he has to wait for these resources."

"Okay, but aren't all clones the same? Equally skilled assholes?"

"If that were true, I would not be standing here. You forget that I am also a clone, Kroeger."

"That's because you've got a mind of your own, and you're easy to look at. Makes it easy to forget. Right, Major?" He gave her a crooked smile, while Donovan felt his face heating up at the comment. "Yeah, so you're saying he gets the rejects?"

"Basically."

Kroeger laughed, patting the corpse on the back. "You hear that, buddy? You're a reject."

"Enough," Donovan said. "Get off him."

Kroeger glanced up at Donovan, raising his eyebrow.

"You wanted to be part of this," Donovan reminded him.

Kroeger stood up. "Yes, sir. I forget myself sometimes."

"The bigger concern is that a pur'dahm with an army of rejects, as you so eloquently put it, was able to track us here while no others, including the Domo'dahm, have. Fior'el is not unintelligent. There is more to this than it seems."

"Like what?" Donovan asked.

"I'm not sure yet," Ehri replied. "It is possible we are being hunted."

"No offense, darling," Kroeger said. "But, duh."

"Hunted, Kroeger. Not chased. By a pur'dahm hunter."

"Like the ones we encountered at the base? The ones who were about to decapitate you?" Donovan looked right at Kroeger.

"I was setting him up," Kroeger said.

"Yeah, to kill you," Mendez replied.

"If you're right, that means he's out there right now," Donovan said.

Kroeger's eyebrow went up again. "Watching us?"

Ehri nodded. "If I am right."

"We should take him out."

"You are welcome to try. Any hunter that has been keeping pace with us is no reject. He will be of a high cell, and extremely skilled."

"Yeah? If he's been following us, why hasn't he done us in yet?"

"The time has not been right."

"What the hell does that mean?"

"Does it matter?" Donovan said. "Ehri, what do you suggest we do?"

"When you are the hunter's prey, there isn't much you can do except defend yourself when he attacks. I will try to bring him out to parlay."

"You want to talk to him?"

"Perhaps I can convince him to give up the hunt."

"You really think so?" Kroeger asked.

"I don't know. What I can tell you is that he was keeping pace with us before we lost the ped'ek. Now he will have time to rest, time to recover and gain strength before he makes his move. We have a slight advantage because we know he is here, and can catch him off guard."

"By talking? Why don't we just scour the earth with our, what do you call them? Grrrr-shah?" He emphasized the first part like a growl. "Plasma talks pretty loud."

"We can't blanket the entire city," Donovan said.

"And we don't have time to sit here all day," Soon said. "I imagine the rest of the bek'hai will figure out what happened here soon enough."

"Soon is right," Ehri said.

"Fine. But I don't see what yapping is going to do for us? He'd be an idiot just to decide to go away if he thinks he can take us out."

"I do not expect him just to go away," Ehri said. She turned to Donovan. "Major? Will you put your faith in me?"

"I have so far."

"I will go out to engage him. He will not dishonor himself by attacking me. Even so, we should be ready to move, in case more pur'dahm forces are nearby and wish to take advantage of Fior'el's failure."

"Okay," Donovan said. "Mendez, take Ehri's mech. Kroeger, Thompson, these cockpits are tight, but let's head back to the transport and stuff as many weapons into them as we can fit."

"Yes, sir," they said.

He approached Ehri, putting his hand on her shoulder. "Be careful."

She nodded. "I will, Major."

He retreated to his mech, climbing up and into the cockpit. He watched her back through the HUD as she began winding her way through the destruction. Then he got the mech moving again, back to the side of the hospital. The transport was nearly buried beneath a portion that had collapsed across it, leaving only half of the opening into it exposed.

Kroeger paused in front of him to survey it, said something to Thompson that Donovan couldn't hear, and then the two soldiers crawled inside.

"He's a piece of work, isn't he, Major?" Soon said.

"You can say that again."

"You worried about Ehri, Major?"

He rotated the mech's torso back the way she had gone, but she had disappeared from view.

"You can say that again."

4

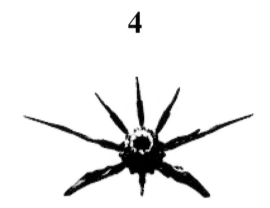

LEX'EL DUR RORN'EL WATCHED the line of gel'shah retreating from the field. His breathing was sharp and thick as he tried to contain his rage at Fior'el for interrupting his hunt. No. For doing more than interrupting it.

For ruining it.

He had hoped that Ehri and the humans would win the battle because the thought of that pathetic pur'dahm stealing his glory burned him more than anything else could. Even so, the un'hai was smart enough to know that Fior'el would never be able to find them on his own. She would make the connection, and his existence would be revealed.

He slapped his fist on the ground beside him. So close. He had been so close. He took another breath of pure oxygen to comfort himself. There was nothing he could do about it now. A good hunter knew how to let go of the near misses and refocus.

He stood up, keeping his back pressed against the wall of the shattered building. He wasn't going to give up on his quarry that easily. Not when defeating them would push him so so much closer to succeeding his father as leader of the bek'hai.

He spent the next few minutes watching the remaining gel'shah disappear over the horizon. Then he returned to the corner, peering around it.

Ehri dur Tuhrik was standing only a dozen meters away, her back to him. He swallowed his surprise, resisting the urge to press himself back against the wall. What was she doing here?

He kept his eyes on her as she took a few steps away and then paused, listening. She swiveled her head slightly, and her nostrils flared. She knelt down, putting a finger to the earth and lifting it to her nose before touching it to her tongue.

What was she doing? There was no way she could sense him like that. He hadn't even crossed that area.

Then again, how was she already so close?

He drew further back behind the wall, curious and slightly concerned. Ehri may have been an un'hai, but that didn't explain these actions. It was almost as if -

"Lex'el dur Rorn'el," Ehri said loudly, returning to her feet and pivoting around again.

He ducked back before she could see him there. Did she know for sure he was near or was she guessing? And how did she know it was him out of all of the pur'dahm hunters.

"Lex'el dur Rorn'el," she repeated. "I know you are here somewhere. I can smell your breath."

His breath? He held it in involuntary response to the statement. How?

"It is a foul thing," she said. "You have been away from the regeneration chamber for some time. Do not tell me that you don't feel it."

He would never admit that he did, even to himself. He remained still, trying to decide what to do.

"The humans don't know where I am, Lex'el. They trust me enough to let me operate on my own."

He made his decision, swinging out from behind the wall.

She was already looking right at him.

"So did the Domo'dahm," he said. "And you betrayed him for it. Do you wish to betray your humans as well?"

"You wouldn't accept that even if I did," Ehri replied.

"No." He took a few steps toward her. "You knew where I was. You could have taken me by surprise."

"I don't desire a war, Lex'el. I believe the bek'hai and the humans can live together."

"Disgusting."

"Why do the bek'hai despise them so, even as they steal their genes?"

"We use their genes by necessity."

"The reason doesn't matter. It is senseless. I was hoping I could open your eyes."

"And what? Get me to side with the humans? To betray my kind? My father?"

"No. You are too honorable to do that. It is one thing that sets you apart from your peers. I was hoping only to convince you to remove yourself from this particular fight."

He laughed. "You don't want me to kill them."

"I won't allow you to kill them."

He laughed harder. "You? You're a scientist, Ehri dur Tuhrik. Your namesake was a pacifist."

"I would rather be a pacifist. I'm going to tell you something I have not told the humans."

He stopped laughing, suddenly intrigued. "Oh?"

"Yes, but this truth cannot reach the Domo'dahm. Once I tell you, I will have no choice but to kill you. Do you understand?"

His eyes narrowed. There was something about the way she said it that gave him pause and sent a slight chill along his arms.

"I can see that you do. You have another choice, hunter. You can give me your word that you will abandon this hunt. If you want to claim the glory of killing the humans and me, do it in the open, on the field of battle."

"That is not my way, and you know it. I have no armies. I have no gur'shah. I have only myself, and sometimes my brothers. That is the path of the hunter. You are more than any un'hai I have met before. Only a druk would be unable to see it. Even so, this is my only path to Domo'dahm. Either I kill the humans, or I spend the rest of my life in cruhr dur bek. Those are the only options for me."

"You will never be Domo'dahm, Lex'el. If you know your history, you know the hunters nearly destroyed the lori'shah, and in doing so nearly destroyed the bek'hai. There has not been a hunter named Domo'dahm in five thousand years."

"Then my glory will be all the greater," Lex'el said. "I don't know how to exist any other way." He paused, giving one last consideration of her words. "Tell me your secret, Ehri dur Tuhrik."

"I am not a clone. My name is Juliet St. Martin."

She smiled at him. It was not the smile of a scientist.

It the smile of a hunter.

5

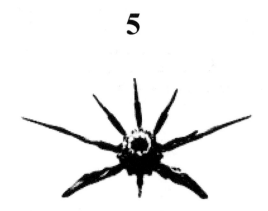

LEX'EL REACHED FOR HIS lek'sai, giving up on the effort as the un'hai across from him closed the distance between them, faster than he would have ever believed possible.

It took only a single leap forward, nearly five meters from a stand, for her to be on top of him, her foot angling in and hitting him in the chest before he even realized the fight had started. The impact pushed him backward, and he shifted his weight, rolling away on his hands and coming to his feet.

She didn't give him any quarter, coming in hard and fast, throwing quick jabs and hard hooks that he struggled to bring his hands up to block.

"You are a clone, Ehri dur Tuhrik," he hissed, jaw clenched, eyes tight and focused. "No human can do the things you do."

Her smile grew a little wider. She faked a punch to his stomach, and when he moved to block she spun around behind him, grabbing one of his lek'sai and pulling it from him before backing away.

"The bek'hai's advanced command of genetic engineering is useful for more than making twisted monsters or direct copies," she said. "Draw your weapon."

"You want me to believe you are the original pur'hai, from which all of the un'hai were made?" He didn't believe it. Why would he? It sounded ridiculous. And if it were true, why would she hide it from the humans? He drew his lek'sai. It wouldn't matter, once she was dead.

If he could defeat her.

No sooner had he brought the blade into position than she was on him again, her lek'sai flashing, darting in and out as he continued to retreat, barely finding the time to knock the blade aside. It knicked his arm, and then his leg. He growled and clenched his teeth. He was not going to lose like this.

She eased up, stepping back, treating him like a toy.

"I am the original. Juliet St. Martin. I didn't remember. I didn't know it until I saw him. My son, Gabriel. He came to me. He came to Earth to save us."

"Why haven't you told the humans?"

"I have earned their trust as Ehri dur Tuhrik. If I make a claim like that, they will begin to question."

"As they should."

"Yes. So it is better that they do not know." She paused, looking into the distance, in the direction of the humans. "It is better that no one knows." She stared back at him, her expression sending another chill through him. "Make your move, hunter."

Lex'el was motionless, watching her watching him. Measuring her. Searching for any clue of her planned defense. She was fast. So fast. He didn't want to admit it, but he wasn't sure he could defeat her. He didn't want to admit it, but he was certain that he couldn't. He was going to die today. Within the next few minutes.

He crouched and started to circle. She matched him, following his path, keeping herself balanced. They locked eyes. She smiled. He forced a smile back. He didn't want her to see that for the first time since he had been made, he was truly afraid.

She could see it, though. He could tell. Maybe she could smell it on him. Maybe she could sense his cold sweat, or his ragged breathing. Her senses were enhanced. Her strength enhanced. How had she managed that? Whether or not she was this Juliet St. Martin, how had she altered herself using bek'hai technology and word of it had never reached the Domo'dahm?

She couldn't have done it herself. Who else knew about this? Who had helped her? How? Why?

He wanted to know. He had to survive to learn the fullness of her confession.

He circled her again, looking for an opening, seeking a path to the truth. If there was another traitor within the bek'hai and he discovered them, it could be the final piece he needed to ascend to rule. Unless...

"Who was it?" he asked. "Who helped you?"

"It does not matter. He is dead."

"It was Tuhrik, then?"

"He was obsessed with humans. He was especially obsessed with me. He knew he would have to die to save them, but he also believed their ways are better than our ways. He believed that the bek'hai could only survive in partnership with them, not as conquerors. Fifty years and we have yet to produce a fully viable splice. Fifty years, Lex'el! That should have told the Domo'dahm something. He does not seek viability. Even as the bek'hai are dying, they refuse to accept what they must become." Her smile vanished. "Now, make your move, hunter. Or I will make it for you."

Lex'el dur Rorn'el opened the path to his oxygen, breathing it in and letting it continue to fuel him. He could feel a small amount of energy return to his body, and he felt a comfort he had nearly forgotten in the nine days he had been tracking them. He watched her for a moment more, no more certain of his odds than when they had started this fight.

Finally, he charged, silent and even, leading with his lek'sai, putting all of his years of training and skill into the approach.

He saw the opening he was looking for then. A slight imbalance on the left side. He adjusted his attack, flipping the blade to his other hand with a deftness and agility few of his brothers could match.

His quarry was still. Motionless. Every part of her, except her foot.

She kicked out, not at him, but at the ground below him.

His foot landed on the chunk of concrete at the same time it slid away. His balance faltered for just an instant.

An instant was all it took to die.

He stumbled, finding his other blade buried in his chest as he tried to recover. He barely felt the pain as he backed away from her, eyes wide in shock. He hadn't seen that coming. He would never have seen that coming.

The strength drained from him along with his life force. He dropped to his knees, looking back at Ehri. There was no hint of glory on her face. No expression of joy or comfort at his defeat. In fact, she looked even sadder than she had moments earlier.

"It is a waste, Lex'el," she said. "It is all such a waste. It never had to be."

He tried to speak. The oxygen was still flowing, but he couldn't get enough of it into his chest to make a sound. He felt hot. Confused. It was getting dark.

"Tuhrik and I tried to change them. To make them see. We failed, and now you are dead. I am sorry, Lex'el dur Rorn'el."

He looked at her but didn't react. His body was unwilling to move at his discretion. He lost his balance, rolling over onto his side.

Two quick gasps, and then the hunter was gone.

25

6

DOMO'DAHM RORN'EL PEERED OUT from the shadows of his throne, waiting for the messenger to finish the long walk across the antechamber to his position. He could sense Orish'ek shifting in his position beside the throne, eager for whatever news the messenger might bring. Ul'bek was to his left and equally on edge, tapping his sharp fingers against the arm of his seat.

Rorn'el refused to move, though he felt the same unease as his pur'dahm. None of the news they had been receiving recently was to his benefit. It had started with a report from the Ishur that not only was Tea'va planning to use his new position to bring challenge against him but that the pur'dahm he had assigned to watch him, Gr'el, was intending to do the same.

He had known Tea'va couldn't be trusted, which was why he had sent Gr'el with the failure of a pur'dahm. It should have been an easy and clean way to remove the disgusting specimen of a drumhr from his concern. Instead, he had been forced to send two more ships out in pursuit of the

Ishur to ensure that whoever was in charge of it by the time they arrived, whether it was Gr'el or Tea'va, would fall back into line or be destroyed.

It was an annoyance, but not a completely unanticipated one. He had been a pur'dahm once himself, fighting with his brothers to gain position within the cells. His victory had come by being aggressive and launching the assault on the planet while the others were still preparing to fulfill Kesh'ek's command. It had been a risky maneuver, as they had not ascertained the humans' technological prowess at that point.

It had been worth the effort.

Still, having three of the domo'shah away from the planet was difficult to accept. The ships were more than transportation. They were home to hundreds of bek'hai, and thousands of lor'hai. They were resources that he hated to part with, especially now.

Ehri dur Tuhrik. He couldn't think of the name without feeling an irrational mix of anger and attraction. She was so much like the human woman, Juliet, that he had become so enamored of. Strong-willed and intelligent, with a streak of compassion that it took him many cycles to come to understand. She had valued life in a way that was still senseless to him sometimes.

He glanced away from the messenger, looking down at the gori'shah cloak he was wearing. He pushed it aside, revealing a simple wooden rosary. He glanced nervously from Orish'ek to Ul'bek, to make sure they couldn't see. It was the only thing he had left of Juliet. A token of her belief in some greater being that controlled the fate of the universe. He had never believed in her Domo'dahm, but lately, he wasn't so sure. When he had ordered the pur'dahm to begin exterminating the remaining humans, he had challenged Him to stop it, if it was not within His will.

That was only days before Ehri dur Tuhrik betrayed him, and now he had lost an outpost worth of resources to her and her small group of human rebels, along with two of his best hunters. It was an embarrassing defeat, and it had allowed the pur'dahm occasion to begin whispering that he was not up to the task of stopping her and that he still cared too much for the un'hai to approach the problem as he should.

The truth was, they were probably right.

He pushed the cloak back over the rosary as the messenger neared. He could never say it, but he missed Juliet. He missed her calm, and her kindness. They had destroyed her planet, and she had forgiven them. She had forgiven him. He didn't need her forgiveness and had never asked for it, but he was intrigued by the lack of hate she had always exhibited. How could she be so free of disdain?

There was so much hate silently coursing through the bek'hai, most of it directed at themselves. They had never wanted to leave their homeworld. They had given themselves no choice. After years of warring with one another to stop the murder of the legra'shah and the abandonment of physical reproduction, they had damaged themselves almost beyond repair. If it hadn't been for their chance encounter with a machine the humans had cast out into space, their entire race would have been gone by now, their domo'shah all floating aimlessly throughout the universe, with none alive to guide them.

He forced himself away from those thoughts as the messenger finally reached him. The drumhr was of a low cell. Low enough that Rorn'el didn't recognize him, and had probably never seen him before. He waited while the messenger dropped to a knee, hanging his head low.

"Domo'dahm Rorn'el. Domo'dahm." The drumhr was still while he waited for the Domo'dahm to respond.

"Rise and make your report," Rorn'el said.

The messenger stood. "Domo'dahm, we have received a final communication from the Ishak and the Ishel prior to joining the slipstream. They have charted a course directly to the Pol'tek system, where the Ishur was last reported to be headed."

"When will they arrive?"

"Three days, Domo'dahm."

Three days. Rorn'el smiled. Tea'va had needed much more than that. Whoever his science officer was, they had done a poor job.

"I am pleased," he said.

"Yes, Domo'dahm." The messenger bowed. "Pur'dahm Elsh'ek and Alk'el report that they are continuing the search for Ehri dur Tuhrik and the humans who destroyed Be'kek. They are having difficulty locating them, as the armor they stole allows them movement over any of the terrain moving north, and they do not appear to be following any of the former human paths."

"No doubt she is helping to guide them," Orish'ek said to his right.

"No doubt," Rorn'el agreed. "Are there any other pur'dahm currently tracking the un'hai?"

He could feel Ul'bek's eyes on him immediately, and he hissed softly at his mistake. He shouldn't call her that here.

The messenger continued without pause. It was not his place to judge. "None that have declared themselves, Domo'dahm. As you know, some pur'dahm may seek greater glory by surprising you with her capture."

"Or death," Ul'bek said, perhaps in retaliation for his words.

"Or death," Rorn'el agreed, biting back his anger at the actions that had forced him to agree to allow her to be killed. He still wanted her back. He wanted to know how she could be so like her pur'hai, and yet so different. He leaned forward in his seat, digging his claws into the lek'shah of his chair. "And the location of the human base?"

The messenger dared to let himself smile. It was always better to be the bearer of good news. "Your science team has narrowed the potential systems based on reevaluation of the examination done on the wreckage of similar starships, the most optimal slipstream paths, and the most habitable worlds."

Rorn'el allowed himself to bare his teeth, opening his mouth wide. It was better news than he had expected. He had made a mistake, ignoring the human's surviving off world colony for too long, thinking that the bek'hai would forever be impervious to their efforts of rebellion. It had been a decision made by a Domo'dahm who had been younger, less wise, and too confident.

"I am very, very, pleased," he said.

"Yes, Domo'dahm."

"Orish'ek, prepare a commendation and promotion for the pur'dahm who owns the science team that completed the analysis."

"Yes, Domo'dahm," Orish'ek replied.

He considered for a moment. "Orish'ek, hold that command. Who is the pur'dahm in question, messenger?"

"Pit'ek," the messenger said.

"Tell Pit'ek he is reassigned to the domo'shah Ishrem. He will be leading the expedition to the systems his scientists have suggested."

The messenger nodded. Orish'ek shifted beside him.

"Are you certain you don't want to tell Pit'ek yourself, Domo'dahm?"

"There is no time," he replied. He raised his voice. "I want that colony destroyed. No survivors. If the human starship tries to return to it, I want them to find it in ruin. This is our world now. Our home. There is no place for humans on it or near it." He lowered his voice again, directing it at the messenger. "Make sure Pit'ek is clear on that. And if he fails to find the colony, tell him that he is to retire himself before he ever returns."

"It will be so, Domo'dahm," the messenger said.

"You are dismissed."

"Yes, Domo'dahm."

Rorn'el leaned back in his throne as the messenger departed. He glanced at Ul'bek and Orish'ek, and then closed his eyes. Juliet had begged him to spare the humans that remained, and swore they were no threat to him. For a short time, he had even believed it, allowing the rebels to plant their seed of discontent.

Fifty cycles later, it was clear to him that their hope of achieving the impossible would only die when they did.

7

GABRIEL ST. MARTIN WALKED side by side with the bek'hai known as Tea'va. His father, General Theodore St. Martin, rolled a few meters ahead of them, the bek'hai science officer, Zoelle, at his side.

Two days had passed since the crew of the Magellan had successfully, and impossibly, managed to crash their starship aboard a Dread fortress and gain control over it.

Two days had passed since Zoelle had told Theodore that she was his long missing, and previously believed dead wife, Juliet.

Two days had passed since Theodore had believed it.

It was a situation beyond anything Gabriel could ever have imagined. A situation that had left him struggling to come to grips with a weird new order to things. It didn't take much examination to know that this thing was not his mother. Besides the obvious age difference, there was the fact that she was hardly the only clone of Juliet St. Martin the Dread had produced. He had met another just like her on Earth, fighting for the humans with Major Donovan Peters. While he could accept that maybe, just maybe, she was somehow programmed to sympathize with humanity and perhaps even to fight for them, there was something about her that he just didn't trust.

That mistrust was only magnified by the fact that Tea'va didn't have faith in her either, going as far as to find a reason to pull Gabriel aside and explain what the clone had done to him, betraying him to the other pur'dahm, Gr'el, in exchange for a greater position of power.

"Watch her," he had said. "Power is the only thing she truly desires or cares for, and she is willing to do anything, including posturing as Juliet St. Martin, to get it."

While Gabriel didn't know Tea'va well enough to explicitly trust him either, the former commander of the fortress had been proving himself since the moment they met. Not only had he had killed a number of his own in their defense and had directly helped them gain control of the ship, but even now his assistance was invaluable as assisted them in making the most efficient use of the ship they had captured.

The problem was that Theodore was more than willing to accept her account of the truth without any evidence to back the claim. He was smitten with this version of his wife, regardless of how she had come to exist.

It wasn't as though Gabriel couldn't understand why. His father's adoration for his wife was as solid and sure as a steel beam, and the pain he had suffered for all of these years over losing her had been apparent to Gabriel from the time he was old enough to speak. He didn't blame his father for wanting Juliet back so badly that he was willing to disregard logic to make it happen.

But he did blame General St. Martin.

The General had a responsibility to the crew of the Magellan, and as far as Gabriel was concerned, it went above and beyond everything else. Just like Theodore had found the strength to bring the Magellan away from Earth and get the people on board to safety all of those years ago, he had a fresh responsibility to put one hundred percent of his efforts into the war now. While they were still working toward that goal, Gabriel couldn't help but feel like his father's misguided loyalty to the genetic twin of his mother was going to hurt them sooner or later.

"Where are we going?" Gabriel whispered to Tea'va.

His father had asked him to meet near the transport beam and then told him to follow, but hadn't given him any indication of their destination. They had entered the beam and traveled directly to the bottom level of the ship, heading deeper into the heart of the fortress.

The bek'hai glanced over at him, making a face that Gabriel still found difficult to translate. It appeared to him as a mix of amusement and disdain.

"What are the correct words in your language?" Tea'va paused. "The place where we make the clones. Factory, is it? Zoelle wanted to show it to your father."

"Do you know why?"

"Not for certain, but I can guess. I believe she will ask him to make more soldiers."

"Make soldiers?"

"Yes. That is what the factory is for. Not only soldiers. Mothers. Scientists."

Gabriel was only loosely familiar with the different clone types, but he knew there were more than the three Tea'va mentioned. The Cleaners, for example, who moved into the hidden areas of the ship and kept the fortress maintained. He had seen them in the shadows from time to time, going about their business as if nothing was different, seemingly oblivious to the new ownership. It was a sharp contrast to the mothers, who had refused to serve anyone but Orish'ek. Colonel Graham and his team were still trying to secure the rest of them after they had killed a pair of crew members in an ambush.

The real clone soldiers, on the other hand, were loyal to whoever was Dahm of the fortress. All it had taken to make them stand down and get in line was a word from Tea'va, and now they coexisted with the human crew as though they had always been part of it. It had taken some time for him to sort them out and order each of them to accept a new chain of command, but it was becoming a more common sight to see the strapping, blonde haired doppelgangers working alongside human counterparts.

Still, that was making use of the existing clones that survived the battle.

Making new ones?

That was something else entirely.

"I would say my father would never go for that, but if she's pushing him? I'm not sure."

Tea'va gave him a slight nod of agreement before Gabriel returned his attention forward. He eyed the corner of Zoelle's face, turned slightly in his direction. Had she heard them from that distance?

She didn't react to his stare, continuing ahead with a smooth gait that perfectly matched Theodore's pace in his chair. She had her hand on his shoulder, keeping it there as they walked.

They reached the end of the corridor a few minutes later. Gabriel hadn't seen much of the fortress yet outside of the bridge and some of the living spaces, but he was already impressed with the efficiency of the design. Despite the massive size of the starship, it seemed to him that nothing was ever more than a short walk away.

The sheer volume of the space that opened up ahead of him caused him stare, letting out a small, "wow" as he took in the enormity of it. The fortress had seemed huge from the outside, but whether it was some bend in reality or some trick of the light, it actually seemed bigger on the inside.

"Gabriel, I'm the one without the legs," he heard Theodore say. "Do try to keep up, son."

Gabriel caught himself, taking a few quick steps to catch up. The others were heading toward an illuminated opening in a roundish glob of black carapace, the material Tea'va had told him was called lek'shah. His eyes followed the shape as it flowed upward, spreading out into a larger form that had to be the factory.

He paused once again, impressed with the sight. He would have fallen further behind once more, except Tea'va put a hand on his back and pushed him gently forward.

"It is more impressive on the inside, Heil'bek."

8

IT DIDN'T TAKE LONG for Gabriel to discover that Tea'va was understating the truth. The inside of the clone factory was more impressive than the outside of it. Much more impressive. It was also more than a little disconcerting. He didn't need to ask Theodore directly to know his father felt the same way.

There was a scientist on duty inside the factory, another clone of Juliet St. Martin who didn't seem to bear the same distorted beliefs as Zoelle. She smiled politely at them as they entered, listening attentively as Zoelle ordered her to show the General how the cloning technology operated.

"As you command, Dahm Zoelle," the clone said, bowing to her. Then she looked over at Theodore, bowing to him as well. "Please, follow me, Dahm St. Martin."

Gabriel watched his father's face as he observed the clone. While they had been in control of the ship for two days already, this was the first time they had strayed far from the bridge and was Theodore's first interaction with what Tea'va had named an "un'hai."

He thought he spotted a pained expression on Theodore's face at the sight of the Juliet duplicate, but it was gone within seconds, replaced with a polite, slightly uneasy grin.

"Well, I wouldn't be able to tell the two of you apart, if not for that pin of yours," he said to Zoelle.

"The process creates perfect copies every time," she replied. "You will see."

The clone began walking, taking them deeper into the facility. The entire thing was made of the lek'shah, rounded and shaped and broken up by glowing moss and cutouts that had been replaced with a clear version of the material. Through it, Gabriel could see different parts of the facility. The first looked like a research area, where oddly shaped, alien terminals displayed holographic imagery that reminded him of his chemistry classes growing up. There was a clone laid out on a flat surface there, naked, dead, and cut open. It was one of the mothers.

"What were you doing with that?" he asked.

The clone was walking ahead of them. She stopped at the question, turning around and looking at Zoelle.

"You may respond to any questions the Heil'bek has," Zoelle said.

"Yes, Dahm Zoelle. Heil'bek, can you please be more specific?"

"The mother on the table," Gabriel said.

The clone backed up and looked through the transparency.

"We are studying the effect of the crossed programming on the biology of the capsule," she said.

"I don't understand."

"If I may, Gabriel," Zoelle said. "The mothers that Gr'el produced were given the precognitive implantation of the soldier clone." She paused. "I should start closer to the beginning. My apologies. All bek'hai clones are preloaded with a standard set of instructions. How to walk, how to speak the bek'hai language, how to read. Then each subset of clones is provided more specific instructions. For the mothers, it is based on our research on human reproduction and companionship. For the soldiers, it is how to use our weapons, how to work as a team, and other combat related skills. The clones' genetics are engineered precisely to optimize these instruction sets, not unlike a computer. By placing the instructions for one type into another, you are introducing mental instability and the potential for disaster. Here, we are examining the physiological effects of the soldier programming on the mother."

"And who gave you that order?" Gabriel asked. "These clones were killed during our takeover of your ship."

He worded the statement deliberately, to see how she would react. She smiled in response, not giving anything away.

"I gave the order," Theodore said. "Based on your mom's recommendation."

Gabriel tensed his jaw. He hated to hear his father speak like that for so many reasons.

"What is the ultimate goal of this research?" he asked. "What's the point?"

"Strategy," she replied. "I will explain in more detail as we continue the tour. Is that okay?"

Gabriel nodded. There was no point to being contrary just for the sake of it.

"Shielle, please continue," Zoelle said.

"Yes, Dahm," the clone replied.

She moved back to the front of the group, guiding them further into the factory. They paused a short while later, reaching another room filled with alien terminals.

"This is where the-" the clone paused, trying to think of the English word, "instructions, are managed. As Dahm Zoelle said, we have a standard set of instructions, but they can also be modified here, as needed to adjust to changing variables."

"For example," Zoelle said. "If we create a new weapon, or need to alter our programming so that the clone has a new piece of knowledge on emergence from the maturation chamber."

"One second there, darlin'," Theodore said. "Why don't you just give them everything you know up front, if it's as easy as writing a line of code into a computer?"

Zoelle gave him a warm smile. "It isn't as easy as that. And, like a machine, our modified human brains have a limit to the amount of information they can store. Experimentation revealed that too much data causes the clone to freeze, unable to make any decisions. Of course, we knew this was an outcome based on the bek'hai brain, but the human mind is able to hold almost four hundred percent more information."

"But we're the primitive ones?" Gabriel said.

"There is a difference between holding information, and utilizing it," she replied. "While the human brain has more capacity, the bek'hai brain is more efficient. That is why we have conquered advanced interstellar travel, while you are struggling to reach beyond your system."

"Whose side are you on again?"

Zoelle's face flushed as she realized she was speaking for the enemy. "My apologies, Gabriel. I've become accustomed to referring to the bek'hai as part of my own. I've only recently been reunited with you and your father, after all. Please forgive me."

Gabriel glanced at Theodore, whose face remained static. He needed to be careful how he handled the situation. "I understand."

She smiled. "Thank you. As I was saying, we have to be very cautious what instructions we give to the clones. There is a great amount of experimentation that happens in creation of another type. Shielle, continue."

"Yes, Dahm," the clone replied.

She brought them down a longer corridor. Gabriel began to hear the sound of flowing liquid as they approached. It was the only noise he had heard inside the facility since they arrived. In fact, he realized almost as if by accident that the Dread fortress, in general, was deathly quiet. He wondered if that would change once they managed to get it underway.

They reached a solid wall of lek'shah at the end of the passage. Shielle brought them to a stop in front of it, turning to face them.

"What's the problem?" Theodore asked.

Shielle looked at Zoelle, hesitant. Gabriel didn't like it. He glanced over at Tea'va, who seemed unconcerned.

"It is not typical for anyone other than the caretakers to enter the maturation hall," Zoelle said. "Most bek'hai do not like to be reminded of where they come from."

"Well, I didn't come from there," Theodore said. "And I want to see it."

"Me, too," Gabriel said. "You brought us down here for a reason."

"Open the door," Zoelle said to Shielle. "Tea'va, you may remain outside, if you wish."

The way she said it made it clear to Gabriel that she was challenging the warrior. He laughed in reply.

"I know where I come from," he replied. "I have no fear of it."

"Suit yourself."

Zoelle nodded, and Shielle put her hand on the wall.

The door slid open.

9

GABRIEL COULD ALMOST BELIEVE what he was seeing, but only because Zoelle's earlier statements had given him hints of what was to come. The maturation hall, as Shielle had named it, was a massive space toward the center of the facility. It was lined with row after row of capsules, three meters square, filled with a fluid of some kind, with tubes running in and out of machinery placed at the top. The fluid was in a constant state of motion, swirling toward the center, draining and being reintroduced.

In the center of each capsule was a human child. It floated freely in the goop, eyes open, head and limbs moving, seemingly aware of itself. Some were touching the transparency in front of them, trying to navigate their way in the fluid. Others were touching themselves, feeling their flesh, trying to make sense of who and what they were. All of them were male, identical in size and shape. All looked to be around ten years old.

It was difficult to tell how many capsules there were. They stretched ahead and to either side of them as they entered the space, moving down a short ramp and onto the floor. Gabriel noticed it was cooler in here than the other rooms, and he felt a sudden shiver as his body adjusted. He looked to Theodore, noting his father's disgusted expression, and then to Tea'va, whose normally pale face had somehow paled even further. The bek'hai looked as though he wanted to retch.

A clone approached Shielle from the left. A male, short and bald, wearing a simple gori'shah robe. He was flanked by two identical clones, who surprised Gabriel by being armed.

The clone said something to Shielle in bek'hai. Shielle responded, and then pointed to Theodore. The clone argued, she raised her voice, Zoelle got involved, and finally the clones retreated.

"The caretakers are very protective of the capsules," she explained once they were gone. "They are the only non-soldiers generally permitted to carry weapons."

Theodore grunted, and rolled his chair forward to the first capsule. The boy inside seemed to notice him, and he flailed his arms to position himself facing the General.

"They're alive in there," Theodore said.

"Yes."

"Is that why seeing the chamber is so traumatic? Do they remember?"

"No, Theodore. Their minds are erased when they reach maturation. The new instructions are implanted after the bodies are released. They wake up with no memory of their time being cultivated."

Gabriel flinched at the word. He noticed Theodore did as well. "How old are the children in there?" he asked.

"They aren't children," Zoelle said. "We need to be clear about that. These clones have been the chamber for seven days, their bodies aging ten years in that time. In seven more days, they will be ready for programming."

The clone in the capsule jerked and fell away from the transparency, its eyes rolling back in its head.

"Is it okay?" Theodore asked.

A caretaker rushed over, reviewing alien text that appeared on the glass.

"It is fine," Zoelle said. "It is part of the process. The enhanced maturation rate can be painful to the embryos, but they will never remember that it occurred."

"How many are there?" Gabriel asked.

"Four hundred," Zoelle replied.

"Soldiers?"

"Yes."

Theodore looked back at Gabriel, one eyebrow going up. Gabriel shook his head slightly. He didn't want his father to think he agreed with any of this.

"I know it is shocking for you to see, and can be difficult to accept," Zoelle said. She returned to Theodore's side, putting her hand on his as she knelt beside him. "Consider that I am only here because of this technology. I should have died long ago, Theodore. I was going to die. One of the pur'dahm, Tuhrik, brought me to a capsule and placed me inside." She stood and looked back at Gabriel again. "Like the bek'hai regeneration chambers heal the bek'hai, the maturation capsules have the ability to heal human frailties. To reverse the aging process." She glanced down at Theodore. "To return the ability to walk."

Theodore's face changed then. His disgust faded, and Gabriel could picture him running through the scenarios in his mind. He could have his legs back. He could be young again, with a young bride. He could have the second chance with Juliet that he had always wished for.

"The technologies are the same," Zoelle continued. "The fluid is filled with nutrients vital to the human genome. For the bek'hai, this fluid is mixed during delivery with a second plasma that contains all the drumhr need to be restored."

"How is it made?" Gabriel asked.

"It is produced from human and bek'hai stem cells. Our technology teases out the appropriate permutation to restore optimal health."

"Where did you get the stem cells?"

Zoelle's eyes turned sharp for an instant, her frustration over the question obvious to Gabriel. That frustration vanished a moment later as she removed herself from whatever she had been thinking.

"It took time to develop the cells," Zoelle said. "The original fluid was derived from the humans we collected when we took the Earth."

"People?" Theodore said. "That stuff is made from people?"

"Not anymore, as that would be untenable in the long-term. Though it is possible the Ishur is still utilizing some percentage of origin resources."

The disgust returned to Theodore's face. Zoelle noticed and knelt beside him again.

"Theodore, consider what this technology can do for you. For everyone on this ship."

"I'm not about to piss on the dead by using their life fluid like some kind of damn vampire," Theodore said. "Not for anything in this world." He looked at her. "You would never have agreed to anything like that either, would you? Ain't a God I know that sees anything right with that."

Zoelle was silent for a moment. "I did what I had to do, Theodore. To survive, but more than that. To return to you, but more than that. The freedom of all of humankind is at stake. I had an opportunity to make their deaths mean something. God delivered me to the bek'hai so that I could do something."

Tea'va tapped Gabriel on the shoulder, shaking his head at Zoelle's emotional outpouring. It was clear the bek'hai didn't believe it was real. Gabriel wasn't so sure. What would she have to gain by healing his father?

Theodore stared a Zoelle for a long moment. "I have to think about it," he said.

Zoelle nodded. "Very well. These clones will be mature in seven days. You have the option to continue the process or to terminate them now."

"Terminate? No. Ain't a God I know sees anything right with that, either. This batch is already underway; then we'll live with the hand we're being dealt. When they're done, I want this place shut down. No more clones."

"Theodore," Zoelle said, preparing to argue.

He put up his hand. "No more clones. If you did what you did to save us, that's one thing. You saved Gabriel; you helped us get this ship. If time changed you a bit, that's another thing, and I can live with it because I can't imagine what you had to live with, darlin'. I ain't about to make the same damn mistakes as the bek'hai. You become reliant on clones, on damn near slaves, soon enough you can't do a thing for yourself."

"How many soldiers do the humans have, Theodore?" Zoelle asked. "How many to fight against the bek'hai?"

"Hopefully, enough," he replied. "Now tell me this: you can make humans on this here ship. Can you make weapons, too? Armor? That kind of thing?"

"The clones, Theo-"

"I said no," Theodore said, his voice staying soft, treating her with a gentleness Gabriel knew he would never impart to anyone else. "And I mean no. I'm still a General of the New Earth Alliance Army, and apparently the Dahm of this here, what do you call it? Domo'shah. I always reserve the right to change my mind, but right now it ain't on the table."

Gabriel smiled at the response. Maybe he should have a little more faith in his father?

"Weapons? Armor?" Theodore repeated.

"Every Domo'shah is designed to be self-sufficient," Zoelle replied. "We have full manufacturing capabilities on board."

"Good," Theodore said, smiling. "Because we did a number on Maggie getting in here, and I have a feeling we're going to need her again before this is over. If you've got a program to make some of these clones into engineers, I'd sure appreciate it."

"We'll be crossing the programming," Shielle said.

"Violent to non-violent," Theodore said. "I imagine that isn't as bad as the opposite?"

"It should be less volatile," Zoelle replied. "But it is likely they won't be as performant as the clones specifically programmed for such tasks."

"As long as they can follow orders, it'll have to do. I hate to be so flippant with the brains of these things, but like I said, we'll work with the hand we've been dealt."

"It will be so, Dahm St. Martin," Shielle said.

"I appreciate it, Shielle." He rolled his chair to face Tea'va. "I want you to keep an eye on the soldiers when they come out, get them organized under Colonel Graham and the others."

"Yes, Dahm St. Martin," Tea'va replied.

"Theodore," Zoelle said. "What about yourself?"

"What about myself, darlin'?"

"The maturation capsule. When the clones are mature, will you be using one to restore your health?"

Theodore shook his head. "You know, I'm feeling pretty damn fine right now, and to be honest, I've gotten used to the alternate means of transportation. Maybe once the war is done, if I can get some of that synthetic juice, I'll give it a second thought. Until then, I'll be fine with what I've got. Now, let's head on back up to the bridge. We need to collect sitreps from the rest of the officers and see if we can figure out when we can get our asses back into this thing."

10

"GENERAL ON DECK," COLONEL Choi announced as Theodore rolled onto the bridge of the alien starship.

The bridge crew was small, the members of it almost lost amidst the many stations afforded to the original bek'hai contingent, but they all stood and came to attention as their leader rejoined them.

"At ease," Theodore said, rolling past the command dais to the front of the space, as Gabriel moved to his position in the first bank of terminals, with Tea'va following to sit beside him. Zoelle remained at the back of the room.

Gabriel turned his head to look back toward the dais. Miranda was sitting in the first row ahead of the raised platform, and she smiled when she saw him looking her way. He smiled back before returning his attention to his father.

"Mr. Mokri, Mr. Larone, are you present?" Theodore asked, seeking the two engineers among the glow of the terminals.

"I'm here, General," Reza said, moving out from beneath one of the stations and raising his hand. "Guy and Sarah are with Lieutenant O'Dea, going over the damage to the Magellan."

"What are you doing down there, son?" Theodore asked.

"Trying to figure out the interface," he replied. "I'm monitoring the impulses along the organic wiring, and tracing them to the precise outputs in an effort to translate them into something we can use. Or interrupt and control, as the case may be."

"Any luck so far?"

"Limited. I think I can turn on the ship wide communication systems through my tablet. It isn't much, but it's a start."

"Still a job well done, Mr. Mokri. Do you have an ETA on shields and weapons systems?"

"Not yet, General. Although the weapons systems seem to be individually controlled, not networked. We can fire the main plasma cannon from the bridge, but using the smaller systems means having a crew stationed directly at the battery."

"Tea'va, how many batteries are on this thing again?" Theodore asked.

"Two hundred, Dahm St. Martin," Tea'va replied. "We only have enough soldiers to operate fifty-three."

"What he means, Mr. Mokri, is let's see if we can get them networked."

"Yes, sir."

"Seems to me your advanced tech isn't always all that advanced," Theodore said.

"There has never been a need to link the systems to one another," Tea'va said. "And it makes the whole vulnerable to a single point of failure."

"He has a point," Reza said.

"Yes, he does," Theodore agreed. "See what you can do, but don't make it a top priority." He paused. "What about flight control?"

"It's going to take a while, General," Reza said. "It's a lot more complicated than communications."

"Define a while for me, will you Mr. Mokri?"

"Two weeks, General. Maybe more."

"That isn't awhile, son, that's forever. We need to do better than that."

"I'm doing the best I can, General. I haven't slept in almost thirty-nine hours."

"I know. You're doing a bang-up job, Mr. Mokri. Don't ever let my impatience suggest that you aren't. But, and it's a big but, not only are we sitting ducks out here, but we've got friends on Earth waiting for our help."

"Dahm St. Martin," Tea'va said, standing and bowing. "I have offered my assistance in flying the Ishur before. Perhaps you have reconsidered?"

Theodore looked at Tea'va. "I'd prefer if Gabriel could take the stick while you observe. No offense because you've done good things for us, but you can understand why I'm hesitant to give you that much control."

"Of course, Dahm St. Martin. I would do the same in your position under most circumstances. However, this is not most circumstances. Pur'dahm Gr'el deposed me by the will of the Domo'dahm. This may not have a lot of meaning to you, General, but what it tells me is that he was reporting back to the Domo'dahm with regularity. There is a very strong possibility that reinforcements have been sent to this system."

"It took you more than two days to get here," Gabriel said. "I imagine it will take those reinforcements a similar amount of time?"

"That is true," Zoelle said from the back. "My team calculated the most optimal course."

"Even so, Dahm St. Martin," Tea'va said. "We currently cannot defend ourselves from an attack by another domo'shah. We will be torn apart."

"I hear you, Tea'va," Theodore said. "I'm open to ideas."

"General," Colonel Choi said. "What if we focused our efforts on getting the shields operational? If we can update them to use Reza and Guy's new modulation, we should be able to defend ourselves from any incoming attacks. Even if we only have the main plasma cannon, it should be enough at that point."

"I can't interface with the systems," Reza said. "Not until I finish the translation. I can probably get the shields online sooner if I concentrate my effort there. Five days, maybe? I really need to get a little sleep, though, I'm fuzzy as it is."

"Five days is still a long time, General," Choi said.

"We should have that much time," Gabriel said. "Assuming Zoelle is correct in her assumption about her slipstream path."

"I am," Zoelle insisted. "But if you don't believe me, I can still help you update the Ishur's shields. I do have some knowledge on their function, and I can integrate our systems directly. You don't have to spend the time on the translation right now."

"No offense, Zoelle," Choi said. "But we don't know you all that well yet."

"You do know me, Theodore," Zoelle said, stepping forward. "You know me better than anyone. You know who I really am."

Theodore smiled at her. Gabriel glanced to Colonel Choi, who made eye contact with him. He could tell she didn't like it either. The enhancements Reza and Guy had made to the phase modulation of the Dread technology was their secret weapon; their one means to level the playing field in a war where they were vastly outnumbered. Passing that information through Zoelle meant giving it to a former enemy, and if Tea'va was right about her, it could be a disaster.

"The lives of everyone on this ship are at stake," Zoelle said. "Please, let me help you, my love."

"Mr. Mokri, show Juliet what we've got," Theodore said. "Protecting the crew should be our number one priority right now. We've got too many people depending on us to take chances."

"Yes, General," Reza replied.

"Thank you, Theodore," Zoelle said.

"Do we have any other scientists on this boat, darlin'?"

"Three of my original cell remain," Zoelle replied.

"Get them working on coordinates for a slip. Tea'va, I'm doubling down here. Do what you need to do to get us going. Make sure you tell Gabriel every move you're making."

"Yes, Dahm St. Martin," Tea'va replied, showing his own version of a smile.

Gabriel expected his father to make eye contact with him, and when he did, he made a point to hold it. He hated the idea of giving so much of their control over to the former residents of the Dread starship, regardless of whose side they said they were on. He hoped his eyes could express as much to Theodore.

"Gabriel, come and see me in my quarters," Theodore said, holding his gaze with confidence. "The rest of you, if you have a specific job to do, get back to doing it."

11

"WHAT DID YOU WANT to talk about?" Gabriel said, as soon as the door to Theodore's quarters had slid closed.

It was the space that had previously belonged to Gr'el. It was simple and spartan, with no visible effects to speak of, and no furniture save for a soft, flat surface that served as a bed. There was a regeneration chamber in the center of the room, but Theodore must have gotten Reza to disconnect it because it was powered down.

Theodore spun his chair around, reversing as he did.

"Your mother," Theodore said.

Gabriel tensed. He had been waiting for this. "My real mother? The one who died on Earth? Or the clone that thinks she's the real deal?"

Theodore's eyes looked angry, but he surprised Gabriel by not yelling. "You don't know she isn't your mother, Gabe."

"You don't know she is."

"Yes, I do, son. Oh, sure, my heart pretty much burst out of my chest when I saw her for the first time. And sure, I know it would be easy, real easy to believe it's her even when it isn't just because I want it so bad. Don't disgrace me by thinking because I'm old that I'm that daft. You've only seen what you've seen, and you haven't seen everything."

"I just saw you give her access to our only edge against the Dread. What if she's spying for the Domo'dahm, Dad?"

"She isn't a spy," Theodore said. "I'd bet my life on it."

"Based on what? She looks like Mom because she's a genetic duplicate. Even if the maturation capsule can reverse the aging process as she claims, there's no way that can be her. Of all of the Dread starships, in all of the Dread communities, and we end up with the one carrying the real Juliet St. Martin? I met another clone on Earth. You know that. How do we know she isn't the real thing?"

"It has to be her, Gabe. You never met your Mom. Oh, I wish you had. I've always felt guilty for bringing you into this world without her. But you didn't know her, and not like I do. That woman, Zoelle? She's your mom."

"I understand that you think that. I understand you want it to be true. I can't imagine what it's like for you to see her come back from the dead, young and healthy like you were never parted. But the Dread have been cloning people for years, and cloning themselves for thousands of years before that. You don't think they can make a convincing copy?"

"No. She knows things, son. Intimate things. Things I've never told another soul."

"Like what?"

"Heh. I'm not about to tell you. That's personal. The point is she told me about them. I didn't ask. She just knew. How would she know if she weren't your mother?"

"They can program brains. Maybe they reverse-engineered Mom's to get that information."

"To what end? Do you think there's any chance in the world the Dread thought we'd be capturing one of their ships? Do you think they ever expected they would come in contact with us? With me? So what would be the benefit?"

Gabriel knew he had a point. He shrugged. "Maybe it's a side effect of the programming? Maybe it comes along for the ride? Or maybe Mom did manage to alter her clones somehow? They have a special name for them, you know. Un'hai. They're different than the other clones."

"And all the others might be clones. Zoelle is Juliet."

"How do you know if we had the other clone from Earth on this ship, that she wouldn't say the same things? Know the same things? Let's say Mom did something to her clones and made them sympathetic to humans somehow. That still doesn't make her Juliet, no matter how much she knows. I'm sorry, Dad, but there are too many questions around it, and I think that by trusting her you're putting all of us at risk."

Theodore stared at Gabriel. When he spoke again, it was still at a normal volume, surprising Gabriel again. "Let's put our difference of opinion aside, son. It don't matter how much I want you to believe, because you're your own man, and I respect that. The fact is, I'm putting us at risk by not trusting her. What am I supposed to do? If the Dread are sending more ships out this way, we have to be able to defend ourselves. We have to. And we can, thanks to Reza and Guy. Damn fine work, that. We can take care of our people, we can get back to Calawan, and we can take care of our own there, too. We can rally the troops, and we can go back to Earth and duke it out with this Domo'dahm. Maybe we can even win. But none of that happens if we don't get the time we need."

"Tea'va can get us out of here. We can catch a stream and start heading home, long before any reinforcements can make it to us. You didn't need to give our secrets to her."

"It's funny to me that you question your mom's loyalty, and yet you trust that one so explicitly. Now, I know he saved our lives, but he wasn't the only one, and he's still a Dread, not a clone of a human. He's further from identifying with us than anyone. Anyway, didn't you hear me give him permission to get us out? I'm not taking any chances on this one, Gabe. We have to rely on every resource we have to get through this. Every resource, no matter where it originated. I know you can understand that."

"That doesn't mean I have to like it."

"Nope, it don't. And again, I'm not asking you to. But I could do without you making dirt face at me whenever I say something you don't like. I'd rather not dress you down in public, but I'm still your commanding officer, and you damn well better respect me."

Gabriel felt the heat run to his face. He had been overstepping his position in the last couple of days. "I'm sorry, Dad."

"I forgive you. We're gonna get through this, Gabe."

"I know. So, are you and Zoelle sharing these quarters?"

"I'm an Old Gator, son. And she might be Juliet, but she's been through more than her share these last fifty years. You saw for yourself; sometimes it's hard for her to separate herself from them."

"Do you think you'll do it? Use the maturation capsule to get your legs back? Heck, I think you'd come out younger than me."

Theodore laughed. "Wouldn't that be something? No, not so long as there's any chance one of ours gave their life in exchange. That isn't what God's about. It isn't what I'm about either. I haven't had these things for a long time, and I conquered that demon not very long ago. I've come to terms with the place I'm at."

"I'm glad to hear it."

"I bet you are. In all seriousness, Gabe, try to give your mom a chance. I know it's hard to believe, and hard to accept. Just try to look at her with a little less biased eyes."

"I'll try," Gabriel said.

"Thanks. And while you're at it, pay closer attention to Tea'va, too. I know you like him, but there's something about that one that I don't. He's got a politician's smile, and I always get the feeling when he talks to me he'd rather be sinking a knife into my chest."

"To be honest, I hate depending on either one of them."

"To be honest, I'd rather not lean on your mom, if only because I don't want her to have to be involved in this. Yeah, I get what you're saying, and overall, I agree. We just have to do the best we can."

"I will, Dad."

"I know." Theodore smiled. "I'm going to get a little shut-eye. Wake me if anything interesting happens."

"Then I'll hope I won't have a reason to wake you."
"Me, too."

12

"HERE SHE COMES," SOON said.

Donovan turned the mech's torso, rotating it until Ehri came into view in front of him. She had been gone almost two hours, and he had considered going to look for her more than once, forcing himself to resist the temptation. He told her he trusted her. He had to prove it.

She walked calmly through the rubble-strewn streets, not moving in any particular hurry, despite her earlier concern that there might be more Dread units nearby. It would have bothered him, except their sensors had stayed clear the entire time, and he had a feeling pur'dahm Fior'el would prefer to delay his embarrassment for as long as possible.

He opened his cockpit as she neared, evacuating the mech and climbing down to meet her. She smiled at the sight of him, raising her hand in greeting.

"Major," she said.

"Did you find him?" Donovan asked.

"Yes. He will not be troubling us any longer."

Donovan raised an eyebrow at the statement, feeling chilled by the way she said it. "You killed him, didn't you?"

"Yes. He was unwilling to listen to reason."

"You said he was likely a highly skilled hunter. You don't have a scratch on you."

"I was fortunate. He was tired from chasing us all of this time. He confirmed for me that there are no other forces nearby."

"I figured as much, but it's good to have it confirmed."

"Are you nearly finished with the salvage?"

"Yeah. We packed as much in as we could. I think we're all pretty anxious to get moving again."

"I'm sorry for my delay, Major. It took some time for me to find him."

"If it gets the monkey off our back, I'm not sorry at all."

"Hey, Major," Kroeger said, exiting the ped'ek with two Dread rifles in his arms. "This is the last of the weapons. I figure I'll carry them since they're not going to fit inside the big men." He looked at Ehri. "You're back."

"I am."

"Well, hell, did you kill the bastard?"

"Yes."

"Good work, then." He turned toward Mendez. "You owe me."

"Screw you, Kroeger. I wasn't serious."

"Damn right. I was."

"Forget it."

Kroeger laughed. "Good women are hard to find out here. Thompson, get off your tail and let's move it out."

The other remaining foot soldier was crouched nearby, watching the perimeter. He stood and moved over to them, joining them without a word.

"Would it kill you to burp out a yes, sir once in awhile?" he asked the soldier.

Thompson shrugged.

"I'm surrounded by crazies," Kroeger said. "Military company excluded." He laughed again.

"Let's get going," Donovan said. "I want to be in Austin within forty-eight hours."

"Yes, sir," Kroeger said. "You heard the man. Thompson, Mendez, we're on the move."

Donovan retreated to his mech, climbing into the cockpit and sliding it closed. He followed Ehri as she gained her ride, bringing the bipedal armor to life a moment later.

They were underway minutes later, with Donovan leading them through the remainder of the city. It was slow going, even after the soldiers climbed onto the back of the mechs. They couldn't move too quickly without the risk of knocking them off.

"It's like Jack and the Beanstalk," Kroeger said, finding a perch on the undamaged shoulder of Donovan's mech.

"How do you figure that?" Donovan asked through the mech's external speakers. He had heard the fairy tale a couple of times from his grandfather when he was young. He didn't see any connection to their current circumstances.

"You're the giant, and I'm Jack," Kroeger said. "My father's name was Jack. Did you know that? He was a car salesman. Can you imagine? A damn car salesman. Talk about a dying trade."

"I always thought your father was a soldier."

"Why?"

"You have a soft spot for the military. I assumed either your father, someone in your family or you were enlisted at some point."

"You know what they say about assumptions and assholes, don't you Major?" He laughed. "No. Nobody in my family was military. I had a sister who was a cop. That's as close as I ever got to organized violence." He laughed again. "I've always had an appreciation for those who risk their necks for others. A lot of respect."

"That didn't stop you from trying to rob us."

"Should it have? Besides, I thought we were over that? It's old news, Major. We're on the same side now. Anyway, I always loved military stuff. The jets. The tanks. The female officers. Let me tell you, Major; military women are the best kind of women. Tough. Strong. Confident. I know

Ehri's a clone, but she's like that."

"She is," Donovan agreed.

"So, you do it with her yet?"

Donovan almost choked on the statement. He had kissed Ehri once, back in Mexico, and there was a definite attraction there for him, at least. But Diaz's death and the constant threat to their lives had stolen away any thoughts of romantic anything, and besides, Ehri seemed have cooled on him in the days since. He didn't blame her for that. He appreciated that she was as focused on their mission as the rest of them.

Kroeger knew he had hit a nerve, and he laughed raucously at his reaction.

"I can dump you off this thing," Donovan said.

"I'm just screwing with you, Major. It's what I do. When you've seen what I've seen, done what I've done, you need levity to stay as sane as you can. When I say I'm surrounded by crazies, I mean me, too."

"You've said that before. What have you done that's so horrible?"

Kroeger was quiet for a few seconds. "I don't know what I'm going to tell you this. I haven't told a soul since it happened." He paused again, hesitating. "Okay. I used to run with these jackals up in what used to be Phoenix, Arizona. They called themselves the Way. Seriously. The Way. It's like a bad band name or something. Some emo boy band or some shit like that. Anyhow, their leader was this messed up asshole who called himself Itchy. I kid you not."

Kroeger paused again.

"Sorry major, I can't do it. I thought I could. Some things need to stay buried, you know? Long story short, they had an initiation. I was starving. Desperate. Half mad. I killed someone. That was the easy part. There was more. That's all I'm going to say. Whatever you infer from that, whatever you think it is I did, I can almost guarantee the truth is worse than that."

Donovan looked over at the soldier. Kroeger was leaning on the mech, his head in his hands. Donovan looked back to the road ahead. A long silence passed.

"Anyway," Kroeger said. "This reminds me of Jack and the Beanstalk. Only in this version, the Giant and Jack are working together, trying to right all of the wrongs in the world. Right now, that's a damn shot better than the truth."

"What is the truth?" Donovan asked.

"You don't want me to tell you."

"Go ahead."

"The truth, Major? We're going to die. All of us. But at least we can die like heroes."

13

DONOVAN WAS ALMOST READY to believe in Kroeger's prophecy by the time they neared Austin.

The area around the former city was as bad as he had ever seen, apparently owing to the larger flock of people who had come to the area to find refuge near the rebel base there. They started coming across the bodies from twenty-five kilometers out, finding random groups of corpses scattered along the one-time highways. Some had been gunned down by clone soldiers, their bodies burned with two or three plasma bolts each. Others had been torn apart by the Dread's armors, the heavy projectiles they carried chewing human flesh and bone into little more than a mist that settled on the area around them. A few had been hit by the enemy fighters, their remains surrounded by craters from the attacks.

He lost count of the dead within the first few kilometers. It was over four hundred, and that was only adjacent to the road. He was sure there had to be more scattered throughout the surrounding countryside, forever lost amidst the trees.

It got worse as they moved closer, the dead becoming more frequent, more concentrated, and more recently killed. By the time they were fifteen kilometers out, the blood on the ground was still wet, the carrion being picked over by circling vultures and other animals. The smell of death began to reach into the cockpit where Donovan was sitting, and a growing sense of foreboding started eating into his thoughts.

At ten kilometers, they began to hear the echoes of gunfire in the city ahead, still partially obscured by rolling hills.

At five kilometers, as they gained a vantage point to the decaying metropolis, they found that the battle for Austin wasn't quite over yet.

In fact, it appeared to Donovan as though it might have only been beginning. Not because there was a lot of opposition to the Dread units they could spot from their position, but because the Dread were still organized as though they suspected they might be effectively attacked.

"What do you think?" Donovan asked, opening a channel to Soon and Ehri.

"I believe they attempted to accelerate their assault and destroy the rebel assets here before we could arrive," Ehri replied.

"I concur," Soon said.

"What took them so long to get here in the first place?" Donovan asked. "We weren't exactly covering a ton of ground, and look." He pointed to the outskirts of the city, where he could see the edge of a transport. "They flew in. At least some of them. They should have been done with this place days ago, if not longer."

"I'm not sure, Major," Ehri said. "It is curious."

"Are we going to just stand here and watch them kill our people or are we going to go kick some ass?" Kroeger said.

Donovan scanned the Dread forces, trying to estimate their size. A few hundred foot soldiers, at least six mechs, and a handful of the tanks as well. The lack of fighters suggested the fighting was too spread out for them to be of any use. Maybe his initial impression had been wrong. Maybe they were there to mop up.

"We can't take them head on," Donovan said. "We need to find the

62

rebel forces and start handing out rifles."

"How do we find them?" Soon asked.

"Follow the noise," Kroeger suggested.

"Kroeger, join Thompson and Mendez on Soon's mech. Soon, I want you to bring up the rear and carry the others down into the city. Ehri, you and I will advance on the east side of the city, and try to get ahead of the Dread. We'll try to locate the rebels, clear out any targets in the area, and arm them as fast as we can."

"Yes, sir," Soon and the others said.

"Good hunting, Major," Kroeger said, before sliding down the side of the mech to the ground. He hurried over to Soon's armor, easily scaling the side of it.

"Ehri, let's go," Donovan said, putting his mech in motion. He moved it horizontally across the slope, angling it parallel to the city below.

Ehri followed him, her mech easily keeping pace with his. The top speed of the machines were limited to the full extent of the biomechanical muscles that powered them, but also dictated by the skill of the pilot. Donovan knew she could have easily outdistanced him if needed.

They went nearly one kilometer on the parallel and then adjusted course to take a gentle vector down the side of the slope and into Austin proper. The complexion of the battle wasn't changing much as they made their way toward it, and after a few minutes, Donovan began to wonder why the Dread weren't advancing further into the city at greater speed.

He had his answer a moment later when he witnessed a massive bolt of plasma launch away from the city center toward a mech that was trying to close in. It hit the armor square in the chest, knocking it backward as it tore a hole through it and into the cockpit.

"Whoa," Donovan said. "What the hell?"

The profile of the burst looked like it came from a Dread tank. How could the rebels have gotten hold of one?

"I've locked onto the source of the blast, Major," Ehri said. "That must be the rebel position."

"They have a Dread weapon," Donovan said.

"Clearly."

"How?"

"I do not know. We must be cautious. They won't recognize us as friendly."

"That's definitely a problem. Can we adjust the frequency of the communications equipment?"

"Not from inside, Major."

Damn.

"Soon, what's your ETA?" Donovan asked.

"Three minutes, Major," Soon replied.

"Okay. Hopefully, if they see you carrying human soldiers they won't shoot at you. Ehri and I will try to pick off the Dread blocking your path."

"Hopefully?" Soon said.

At least now he understood why the battle wasn't over. Somehow, the rebels had gotten a Dread tank into a highly defensible position and were blasting anything that got too close.

"Stay close, let's hit them together," Donovan said. "Full speed ahead."

14

DONOVAN GLANCED TO HIS left, finding Ehri's mech right beside him, so close he flinched in fear they might collide before remembering who was piloting the machine. They were bearing down on the edge of the city, almost on top of the torn and broken skyscrapers that littered the area. The rebel tank hadn't fired again, but now that they had moved in closer they could see there were other rebel soldiers on the ground, armed with Dread plasma rifles and firing on the enemy clones.

Somehow, the Austin rebellion had gotten their hands on Dread technology, before Donovan even had a chance to bring it to them.

They skirted through the war-torn streets, moving in tight synchronicity across the urban battlefield. Donovan checked his sensors every few seconds, tracking Soon on his way down behind them. It was their job to give him breathing room.

He aimed the mech's cannons, launching a barrage of projectiles into a squad of clone soldiers taking cover behind an old car. It burst apart under the assault, leaving a trail of metal and smoke that disguised the death of the enemy behind it. He found another target and opened fire, a plasma bolt ripping into another group of enemy combatants.

Beside him, Ehri did the same, seeking targets and cutting them down, creating a swath of destruction as they advanced toward the city center. They had to be careful they didn't draw too close and risk getting hit by friendly fire.

"Rebel One, on your right," Ehri said.

Donovan rotated the mech. The remains of a once massive building blocked his view, but his sensors had tracked another mech heading their direction. He immediately stopped moving, taking a few steps back. The mechs weren't able to register one another as enemy targets, and the Dread pilots didn't know they were there yet.

"On three," Donovan said. "One. Two. Three."

He and Ehri both moved out into the open ahead of the mech. They fired simultaneously, their combined plasma bursts ripping right into the cockpit of the armor and killing the pilot before he had a chance to react.

"Looks like you didn't need me after all," Soon said. "You've got friendlies cheering at your back."

Donovan turned his head to look toward his rear. Three human soldiers were at the corner of a building, fists in the air at their victory.

"Get Kroeger over to meet them," Donovan said. "We need word passed to that tank that we're the good guys."

"Affirmative."

"Rebel One, it looks like the bek'hai commander has realized we are here."

Donovan glanced at his sensors. They were picking up the signal of seven remaining mechs. All of them had turned to head their way.

"Damn," he said. "Rebel Three, drop your cargo and form up. We've got a fan club."

"Yes, sir," Soon said.

Donovan headed down a wide street, before ducking the mech through a tighter alley, crunching over a layer of rubble and attracting plasma attacks from clones on the ground. He hit them back, cutting them down and shaking his head at the futility of their efforts. Why didn't the pur'dahm let them run? It was so pointless. Ehri tracked down a separate lane, staying close but split apart as they moved to intercept the incoming mechs.

"Cargo unloaded," Soon said. "I'm on my way. Leave a dance partner for me."

"I don't think that will be a problem, Rebel Three," Donovan said.

"Incoming," Ehri said.

Donovan's HUD was showing red marks coming toward them. He ducked his mech, pressing it against the side of a building as most of the projectiles slammed into the area beside him, sending shards of concrete and glass and rubble everywhere. He cursed as two of the missiles hit the already damaged arm, the impact shaking the mech and causing the appendage to fall off completely, leaving only a trail of exposed biomechanical muscle and wires behind.

"Son of a bitch," Donovan said. His mech wasn't carrying any missiles. In fact, he was pretty sure his cannon rounds were nearly depleted as well.

"Back up, Rebel One," Soon said. "Lead them in. I've got you covered."

"Roger," Donovan said, moving his feet to put the mech into reverse. It backed away, crossing three streets as the enemy mechs appeared ahead of him. He took a few potshots with his plasma cannons and then reached a wider thoroughfare.

"Sharp left, Rebel One," Soon said.

Donovan made the turn, still backing away. The Dread pilot had sped up to reach him, and as he finally turned the corner, he left his back exposed to a waiting Soon. It didn't take much to destroy the armor from behind, taking one of the mechs out of the fight.

"This is Rebel Two. I could use a little help over here."

"On our way," Donovan said, checking his HUD again. Ehri was mixing it up with three of the mechs. The other three were still circling them, trying to get a better attack vector.

"Like sharks," Soon said.

"How do you know about sharks?" Donovan asked.

"I saw it on an old vid. I'd love to see a real one."

"Then let's finish off these assholes."

"Affirmative."

They reached Ehri, breaking around the corners on opposite sides and catching one of her assailants in a crossfire. The mech shook as their plasma dug into it, and then toppled over.

"That's two," Soon said.

"Watch the outliers," Donovan warned, noticing the three circling mechs beginning to close in from behind. "We're getting cut off."

"Crap," Soon said. "There's too many of them."

"One at a time," Ehri said. "Let's take the one on the left."

"Good idea," Donovan said.

They adjusted their vectors, using the buildings as cover while they circled the lone mech. It left them open to attack from the others, but there was no way around that anyway. They needed to thin the numbers, to have fewer weapons able to target them.

"Rebel Three, break left," Donovan said. "Rebel Two, ease off. Let's meet him at the same time."

The other two mechs followed his commands, angling in and emerging on the target as one. They blasted it with their combined firepower, knocking it into a pile of rubble and taking it out of the fight.

"Three," Donovan said, checking for the next target.

His heart raced as he caught sight of his tail. Two of the Dread mechs were closing in behind him, about to clear the cover he had inadvertently positioned himself behind.

"I need backup," he said as they reached the open space.

He swung his mech, rotating it around to clear the delicate backside as they opened fire. Plasma bolts tore into the side of the armor, ripping into the remaining arm and one of the legs. More red symbols appeared on his HUD, and a warning beep began to sound.

"Rebel Two, what does the beeping mean?" he asked as he tried to back away from the onslaught, fighting to remain calm.

"Critical damage," Ehri said. "You need to get out of the mech now,

Major."

Donovan looked ahead to the two mechs. Another plasma bolt crossed the distance, slamming into the torso directly below him.

He grabbed at the cockpit release, finding some relief when it responded, and the mech opened up to let him out. He didn't give much thought to climbing down. Instead, he grabbed one of the Dread rifles before sliding down a leg, feeling the heat of the damaged mech against the gori'shah he was wearing under his clothes. He heard the stomping of feet, and watched as Ehri cut in front of his downed mech, unleashing her ordnance on the two attackers. The strikes hit them in the legs, blistering through delicate joints and knocking them off-balance. One fell, hitting the other, and they both collapsed in a heap.

Donovan couldn't communicate with them now that he was out of the mech, and he was reduced to little more than a bystander. At least for a moment, until the Dread clones started shooting at him. He ducked behind his mech, and then ran down an alley, turning his head back every few seconds to try to keep track of his squad.

Soon's mech passed in front of him, crossing his path as it tangled with one of the Dread armors. It had taken some damage but appeared fully operational.

The remaining enemy mechs were closing in, and even from the ground he could see Soon was in trouble. Every instinct in him told him to run toward the fight, not away from it. He tried to resist. What was he going to do on the ground?

Soon was going to die if he did nothing. Ehri, too.

"Major."

He heard Kroeger's raspy shout over the din of the battle. He looked that direction, finding him surrounded by rebel soldiers, all of them already armed with Dread rifles. Mendez was with him.

"Where's Thompson?" he asked.

Kroeger shook his head. Damn.

"We need to help Soon and Ehri. They're about to get pummeled."

"I wouldn't worry too much about that, Major," Kroeger said. He put his arm around one of the soldiers. "Give it up to my man here, will you

Corporal?"

The soldier, who couldn't have been more than fifteen, held out a small device that looked like a radio. "Put it up to your ear," he said.

Donovan took it and did.

"Mech One, make your way across 38th. Mech Two, keep them coming. You're doing great."

It was a woman's voice, older and slightly gruff. She fed the orders like she had been doing it her entire life.

"Roger," he heard soon say. "Mech Two bringing bringing them home."

Donovan glanced over at Kroeger, who was laughing like the whole thing was a massive joke.

"Seems we're late to the party, Major," he said. "It looks like our efforts back in good ole Mehico paid off big-time."

"Follow me," the Corporal said, leading them back down a smaller alley.

They moved parallel to the action, toward the city center. Donovan kept the radio to his ear, wondering how the rebels had managed to establish a connection with Ehri and Soon. The whole thing had taken him completely by surprise. They weren't supposed to be so well-equipped, or so able to fight back. Not that he was complaining.

"Mechs One and Two, we're ready for crossover. When you pass in front of one another, get as low as possible."

"Roger," Ehri said.

"Roger," Soon said.

Donovan had no idea what was going to happen, but it seemed the rebel commander had a plan.

The Corporal brought them to another intersection, already filled with smoke from smoldering wreckage. Then he turned to Donovan and smiled, his teeth a sharp contrast to his grime covered face. "We made it just in time for the fireworks," he said.

Donovan looked down the street as Soon and Ehri's mechs crossed one another a few streets apart. They were backing up, taking fire from the enemy as they retreated. He felt a wave of discomfort at seeing them on the defensive, and it only doubled when four of the Dread mechs moved into the same avenue.

"Fire," he heard the rebel commander say.

He lowered the device. He could feel the charge in the air even before the plasma beam reached them, washing past in a streak of heat and fury.

It tore into the Dread mechs, burning them into slag in an instant, cutting them apart like a sword. Within seconds, the four enemy targets were reduced to legs carrying misshapen carapace above them.

"What the hell was that?" Soon said.

He was feeling the same way. That blast was bigger than anything he had ever seen, including the Dread tanks.

"Four targets, four kills," he heard the woman say. "Nice work."

"It looks like the Dread are bugging out," the Corporal said beside him.

Donovan looked down the street. A Dread transport had risen in the distance and was moving away from Austin. Another followed a moment later.

"We won?" Donovan said in disbelief.

"Yes, sir," the Corporal said, laughing. "Welcome to Texas, Major."

15

THE CORPORAL, WHOSE NAME Donovan soon learned was James Wilkins, led him, Kroeger, and Mendez down the same street where the plasma beam had fired, covering nearly a kilometer before reaching the entrance to the rebel stronghold.

It was the entrance to a loop station, a small outbuilding only a few meters across and a few meters wide, resting on a corner and shielded from most sides by the remains of taller buildings. It was immediately obvious to Donovan why the Dread hadn't been able to bombard it from the sky. What wasn't clear was how they had managed to defend it from all sides or where that massive plasma beam had really come from.

"I'm confused, Corporal," he said as they neared the entrance, where three more squads of soldiers were standing guard, already armed with enemy rifles. "I thought we were the only ones fighting back against the Dread and hurting them."

"You were a few weeks ago," Wilkins replied. "I'll let the Colonel fill you in. She'll be pissed if I ruin it for her."

"What about my people outside? The mech pilots?"

"We've got a place they can store their equipment. We might even be able to put the armor back together if we can grab some more salvage. Anyway, don't worry about them."

They entered the station, descending one hundred meters to the waiting area. There were tunnels on either side of it, and a few free-standing shops lining the center. Most of them still had their wares inside, forgotten after the initial Dread invasion.

"You have power," Donovan said.

"Yes, sir. We have even more power now."

"Where's the weapon that fired the plasma beam?"

"On its way home. It did its job."

"Home?"

Donovan was confused until he heard a soft whoosh from one of the tunnels. A loop pod appeared a moment later, coming to rest beside the platform.

"The station is operational?" he said, barely able to believe it.

"It is now," Wilkins said. "And it sure beats the hell out of walking." He led them to the car. "Get in."

Donovan glanced over at Kroeger, whose face was stuck in shocked amusement. The smile hadn't faded since he had joined him outside.

"I never thought I'd see the day," Kroeger said.

"Me neither," Donovan agreed. He climbed into the pod and sat. The textile seats were cracked and worn, but they felt like heaven compared to the Dread mech. He watched as the top of the car closed above him and then smiled like he was a kid again when it began to move.

The ride was short, the pod passing underground, traveling thirty seconds to the next destination. The top swung open to release them, and then Donovan stood and marveled.

This station was four times bigger than the last, with eight tunnels leading away from it, two in each direction. The center island was huge and dotted with nylon tents, piles of equipment, cans of food, and everything else a rebel base required.

"We call it Fort Neverdie," Wilkins said.

Donovan kept turning his head, taking in the sight. He paused when his eyes landed on a large contraption in the corner. It looked like the Dread reactor he had seen inside the transport, hooked up to a what resembled the turret of one of their tanks, nestled in a package that could be deployed anywhere in the city if they threw it into a loop pod or had enough people to heft it on their shoulders.

"That's-"

"Big Bertha," Wilkins replied. "Our magic plasma cannon."

"How?"

"Let me introduce you to the Colonel, Major."

"Good idea."

Wilkins brought them across the platform, weaving around the multitude of tents. They were all empty right now, the soldiers who occupied them out on the streets for the battle. Unlike Mexico, there were no non-fighting women or children to be seen. Were they somewhere else? Or were they not allowed to find refuge here?

At least now he understood why so many had been trying to reach the city before the Dread arrived.

Wilkins brought them to a stop outside of a small space stacked high with so many electronics that they created a room of sorts. Most of the pieces had been opened up and reconfigured in some way, with connections crisscrossing one another and joining other connections, creating a web of colored lines that seemed impossible to decipher. Dozens of wires snaked away from the mess, down the side of the platform and vanishing into one of the tunnels.

A dark-skinned woman was standing in the center of it all. Her head was turned toward one of a dozen monitors mounted to the other equipment. She had a device similar to the one the Corporal was carrying near her face, and she was barking orders to the teams outside.

"Colonel Knight," Wilkins said, getting her attention.

She glanced their way, her eyes narrowing.

"Corporal. Where's Captain Rami?"

"He didn't make it, ma'am," Wilkins replied.

Donovan could see the pain on her face. Judging by the wrinkles, it was an expression she had made far too often.

"Colonel Knight," Donovan said, getting her attention by saluting. "My name is Major Donovan Peters. I'm-"

"I know who you are, Major," she said, putting up her hand and giving him a small smile. "I'm very eager to speak to you, but right now I have to manage my crew."

"Understood, Colonel. Is there anything I can do to help?"

She hesitated for a moment, and then nodded. "Yes. Actually, there is. Come on in here."

Donovan entered the space. He quickly took in the different displays. It seemed they had gotten cameras hooked up at various places in the city.

"Keep an eye on the screens. You see any Dread, you holler. Okay?"

"Yes, ma'am."

Donovan watched the screens while Colonel Knight returned to sending orders out to the troops. He noticed the volume inside the base grow as more as more of the soldiers returned home. Two hours later, and without another sign of Dread activity, the Colonel finally put down the comm device and looked at him once more.

"You showed up at a good time, Major," she said. "Your squad turned the tide in a hurry. We've been at a standoff for the last three days."

"I'm happy we could help, ma'am," Donovan replied. "Although it seems you're pretty well organized without us."

"We've done okay lately, but we weren't able to capture any heavy equipment. We only have one person who knows how to drive it."

"You have someone who knows how to pilot a Dread mech?"

"Yes. I'll introduce you to her as soon as I can."

Donovan raised his eyebrow. Her? It couldn't be. Could it?

"Where did you get the rifles? And the cannon?"

"I'll answer all of your questions, but let me give you the quick briefing first. Deal?"

"Yes, ma'am. My apologies."

"Major Donovan Peters, you are the biggest war hero this planet has right now. You don't have to apologize to me for anything."

Donovan felt a chill at the words. Him? "I'm just doing my duty, ma'am."

She laughed. "That's what all good heroes say. Come on over to the command tent, I'll give you the quick rundown." She led him out of the area. "You've already gotten the two-cent visual tour, I take it?"

"I looked around a little, yes, ma'am."

"Good. I'll show you more later. This way."

She brought him back into the sea of tents, leading him to a larger one near the corner. There was no way he would have guessed it was the command tent without having it labeled.

They went inside. There was another soldier already there, and he saluted as she entered. "Colonel."

"At ease, Captain," she said. "Captain Omar, this is Major Donovan Peters."

Omar looked at him and then smiled. "It's an honor, Major."

"Thank you," Donovan said, feeling uncomfortable with the greeting.

"Captain, can you go find Juliet and bring her here?"

"Of course, Colonel."

Donovan's heart jumped. "Juliet?"

"Our secret weapon," Colonel Knight said. "She was a Dread slave, but she managed to get free. It's a pretty incredible story, really."

"And her name is Juliet? As in, Juliet St. Martin?"

Colonel Knight furrowed her brow. "Yes. How did you know?"

Donovan felt numb.

"Lucky guess?" he said weakly.

16

"WELL, IT SEEMS WE both might have stories to tell, Major," Colonel Knight said. "I'll go first, and then you can fill me in on what you know about Juliet St. Martin. Unless I need to be concerned about her?"

Donovan overcame his shock, shaking his head. "No, I don't think you need to be concerned. I doubt she's a Dread spy or anything, especially if she's the reason you've managed to get your hands on their technology."

"Good enough. So yes, she is the reason we've managed to staunch the bleeding, so to speak. I've been running things down here since this base was established seventeen years ago. Four weeks ago, we were barely eking out an existence, trying to keep up with the communications from the teams across the globe, and of course especially interested in your work down in Mexico. The transmissions to the space forces have been our lifeline to hope for a long time."

"They were for us as well."

"Then we caught wind of a message your General Rodriguez sent up to General Parker in New York. A transmission about the space forces, and your involvement in not only getting inside a Dread fortress but escaping with one of their weapons. We were on the edge of our seats waiting to hear what had happened to you after that last transmission. Did you make the transfer? Didn't you? I even stood outside and tried to watch the sky, to see if I could get any clues."

"You saw the Magellan?"

"Yeah. I saw it. I damn near cried." She smiled. "Unbelievable. Anyway, two days later, one of our squads is out on routine patrol when this woman shows up. She snuck up on Delta, came up right behind them and they never knew she was there. She was wearing this black cloth." Colonel Knight paused, looking at Donovan. His uniform had been torn during his escape from the mech. "Like that one."

"It's called a gori'shah," Donovan said.

"Yeah, she told us. Anyway, she said her name was Juliet St. Martin, the wife of the General in charge of the space forces. She asked to be brought to see me, so she was. She then proceeded to tell me the craziest story I'd ever heard, about being made into a clone, about reversing her aging, and then about finally escaping from the Dread. She said they had been keeping her in their main research facility in Honduras, and that she stole a transport and headed here because she had heard the message from her husband and knew you would need her help. Of course, we didn't believe her at first, until she showed us the transport and started handing out the weapons inside."

Donovan nodded. Things were starting to make a little bit of sense, anyway. Juliet St. Martin alive? She had said it, and he could still barely believe it.

"A few days after that, the Dread started sweeping the area. They came over in their fighters at first, but they couldn't do much to us from above. These tunnels are too deep, and there are too many stations to hit them all. By the time they close one up, we manage to dig out two more. They had to start sending in foot soldiers, except they didn't know right away that we had been armed.

"Juliet helped us salvage the power source from the transport, along with some of the communication equipment. We hooked it up down here. For the first time in years, we weren't relying on handmade candles and the remains of fifty-year-old batteries that we scavenged from around the city. Even better, it turned out that the loop was still operational. All it needed was a little juice. Before that, we had to walk the tunnels everywhere."

"I get where the rifles came from, and how you've managed to move your resources quickly enough to shore up weak spots in the defenses," Donovan said. "What about the gun? The one Wilkins called Big Bertha?"

"Yeah. So, we had power. We had Dread rifles. Juliet said it wouldn't be enough. They would send mechs to dig us out. They would send clones to come down into the tunnels. We needed more firepower. I couldn't argue with that. We got a broadcast from someplace called Hell; they said that you were on your way to assault a Dread military outpost, and I thought, well hell, if he can do it, why can't we?" She laughed. "There was an outpost fifty klicks east of here. It isn't there anymore."

"You attacked the Dread?"

"And won. They aren't so tough when they aren't invincible. You proved that. We had to leave the mechs, but we did get our hands on one of those tank things, along with a whole bunch of small arms, enough for every soldier in the base, and then some. Anyway, we couldn't fit the tank down here, so we got to work on pulling the cannon off it."

"The one that vaporized those mechs?"

"Yes."

"That was more powerful than any Dread weapon I've seen."

Her smile grew bigger. "Yes. Juliet's quite handy with the Dread weaponry. She replaced some of the conduits with copper wiring instead of that stuff they use, and she was able to triple the strength and duration of the plasma. Boom. Big Bertha was born. What you saw was the first time we fired it at full strength. We didn't want to give anything away if we didn't have to."

"I would say it was a successful test."

"I would say that, too, Major."

"Does General Parker know about all of this?"

"Yes. In fact, he's on his way here."

Donovan leaned forward. "What?"

"He's on his way here. Two thousand rebels are doing everything they can to get to Austin alive. He left over a week ago."

Donovan sat there in silence for a few moments, considering.

"You want to attack Mexico," he said.

"No, Major. We're going to attack Mexico. It's a given. The only question is when. General Parker isn't the only one on the move. We reached out to as many bases as we could. We told them to come to Austin. I don't know how many troops are incoming. Whatever we have, we'll use. One last push to get the Dread off our planet."

"What about the space forces?"

"I don't know. You made the exchange, but we haven't heard from them since. Did they survive? Are they coming back? We hope so, but we can't pin all of our hope on it. We need to make our own move. If we can coordinate something, we will. Otherwise, we're going in anyway. This is our moment. Our one chance. We can't let it slip away."

Donovan froze again. He couldn't believe it. He had expected to find a half-beaten army here, and instead, he had landed at the center of the rebellion. He felt a new energy flow into him, and the greatest sense of hope he had ever felt in his life.

"You need mechs. And mech pilots."

"Yes, we do," she agreed.

"Do we still have access to the ones you left behind?"

"I don't know for sure. Without pilots, what was the point? Now that you're here, we may need to reconsider."

"I'll go," Donovan said.

"I know. Hold that thought for now. At the moment, I want to hear your story. I want to fill in the gaps between the signals we've been receiving."

Donovan's heart and mind were racing. He could barely calm down. After all, he had been through, all he had lost. They were going to fight back. They were going to hit the Dread city and avenge Renata, Matteo, General Rodriguez, his mother, and all of the others.

He had just opened his mouth to speak when he was interrupted by a sudden commotion from outside.

"What's going on out there?" Colonel Knight said, getting to her feet and heading for the door to the tent.

Donovan followed her, exiting at her back. He saw the cause of the uproar immediately.

Ehri was standing to his left. Juliet St. Martin was opposite her, on his right.

They looked like they were ready to kill one another.

17

"EHRI?" DONOVAN SAID.

SHE looked over at him, making sure to keep her head tilted to watch her twin out of the corner of her eye. "Yes, Major?"

"What are you doing?"

"Do not trust this thing, Major. It is false."

"What are you talking about?" Juliet said. "You're the one that's false."

"Both of you, calm down," Colonel Knight said. She looked at Donovan. "I have to admit, Major. I'm a little confused."

"Permission to handle this, Colonel?" Donovan said.

"Granted."

Donovan stepped between them, facing away from Ehri.

"Colonel Knight tells me that you're Juliet St. Martin," he said.

"Yes. That's correct."

"Juliet St. Martin would be almost eighty years old."

"Yes." She smiled. "Lord knows, I understand your doubt. Major

Peters, is it?"

"Yes, ma'am."

"I understand your doubt, Major Peters. I can assure you that I am Juliet St. Martin. If Theodore were here, he would be able to confirm as much."

"Excuse me, Major," Ehri said.

Donovan turned around. "Yes?"

"The age of Juliet St. Martin is not in question."

"It isn't?"

"No. Only the identity of this clone is in question."

"I'm not a clone," Juliet said. "You are the clone. One of many produced by the bek'hai."

"Wait a second. Ehri, there has never been a question of whether or not you're a clone. Has there?"

She hesitated for a moment. "Not previously, Major."

"What do you mean, not previously?"

"It is a long story. I have not been completely honest with you."

Donovan froze. "What? I asked you, after we gave the weapon to Captain St. Martin, if you had any other secrets. You said no."

She looked at the ground. "I know. I am sorry. I had to. You would never have believed the truth, and you would never have trusted in me."

Donovan cringed to ask the question, because he was afraid of the answer. He had to put it forward regardless. "And what is the truth?"

She looked up at him. "I am Juliet St. Martin."

Donovan stared at her. Then he looked at the other Juliet. Then he looked back at her. "No. You aren't."

"Yes, I am."

"Major?" Colonel Knight said. "What is going on here?"

"I'm not sure yet," he replied. "Ehri, don't you think it's a little odd that there's another clone of you here that is helping the rebellion, and thinks they're Juliet St. Martin?" He looked at Juliet. "Don't you?"

"Not at all," Juliet said. "Some of my clones have been programmed to believe they're me. To activate when they come in contact with humans. It isn't a mistake. It was intended to help the rebellion fight the Dread."

"I would have said the same thing, had you asked me, Major," Ehri said.

"You would not," Juliet replied.

"Yes, I would."

Donovan wasn't about to accept that idea that either one of them was the real Juliet St. Martin. Even so, the tension between the two clones was obvious.

"Hold on," he said. "Both of you. If that's the case, how do either of you know you're the real thing?"

"I have memories of my time with Theodore," they both replied in unison.

Ehri paused, her face flushing. She looked at her twin.

"Name one," she said.

"I still remember the day we met," they both said.

Ehri froze again. So did Juliet.

"Major," she said. "I believe there has been some mistake."

"It can't be," Juliet said.

"Major?" Colonel Knight asked.

"I'm sorry," Donovan said. "Without definitive proof, the fact that you are both clones is the only thing that makes sense."

Ehri nodded. "I know I am Juliet St. Martin. I feel it in my soul. Down to the deepest core of me."

"So do I," Juliet said.

Ehri paused for the third time. Then she looked at Donovan, her expression frightened and sad. "I need to consider this."

She fled the scene, making her way around the tents and heading toward a dark corner of the platform. Juliet stood her ground, watching her go.

"We can't have the same memories," she said. "They don't copy memories."

"Can they?" Donovan asked.

"Yes. But they don't."

"What if they did?"

"Then any clone with the memories would believe they were Juliet St.

Martin. They would believe it with everything in them."

Donovan stared at Juliet.

"It can't be me. I can't be a copy."

"Why?"

A tear trailed from her eye. "I just can't. I remember seeing the Magellan over the planet. I remember the moment when I realized who I am. It isn't my imagination. It can't be."

"What if it is?"

"I don't know."

She stood there, silent. What else was there to say?

"Major, you're suggesting there are two Juliet St. Martins?" Colonel Knight asked.

"At least two," he replied. "And probably more. Something is going on here. Something we don't completely understand yet."

"All I need to know is if these clones are on our side or not."

"They are, Colonel," Donovan said. "At least, I believe they are, and I've never had a reason to think otherwise."

"Then that's good enough for me. We're preparing to go to war, Major. We can't worry about a pair of Dread clones who think they're the same human."

"Maybe not, ma'am," Donovan said. "But we need them to be part of this. We need them to fill the roles they were made to fill."

"What do you propose?"

"I don't know. I'll go and talk to Ehri. We can't afford to lose our best pilot. Not when we have so few."

"Agreed." Colonel Knight walked over to Juliet. "Juliet, maybe you want to take a little break, clear your head?"

Juliet's eyes shifted to her, and she nodded meekly. "Perhaps that's best. I will be in my tent if you need anything, Colonel."

Donovan watched her go. Then he looked back in the direction Ehri had gone. He could think of a lot worse things than having multiple copies of Juliet St. Martin on their side.

Now they just had to convince the copies of that.

18

DONOVAN DIDN'T HURRY RIGHT over to where he had seen Ehri disappear. He needed a few minutes to himself, to consider what was happening, and to figure out what he wanted to say.

He thought about what he knew of her. First, that she and her superior, Tuhrik, had concocted a plan to bring a human into the Dread capital, ostensibly so that she could study them. It was a plan that the Domo'dahm had known about and approved, with the understanding that Ehri would return to the fold within a few weeks, after gathering information about how the rebels lived, and perhaps tactical details that he could use to finish his eradication. Tuhrik had expected to die in the process, or at least had known there was a risk to it, but he was nearing his time for retirement regardless and really, had nothing to lose.

She had joined them as a clone scientist, aware of her source genetics but otherwise ambivalent to them. At least, that was what she had said. Looking back at the way she had integrated into their society, such as taking care of the children with his mother or showing a level of compassion she said the Dread rarely felt, he could sense that there must have been some part of her that was relating to what she knew of General St. Martin's wife.

It was an understandable part considering they shared the same DNA, and she had never said anything about actually being Juliet St. Martin. Of course, if she had turned around and made the same claims as the Austin Juliet, would General Rodriguez, who had known the original personally, have believed her? Or would she have been putting the security of the base in jeopardy at a time when they most needed to be able to trust her, with the Dread closing in on their position and the entire war teetering on the edge.

If she had believed she was Juliet St. Martin then, would there have been a benefit for her to tell them? Would any of them have really believed, when they knew so little about the Dread in the first place? Would he?

He didn't think he would have, and it made it easier for him to accept the omission. In hindsight, he believed she had done the right thing.

He made his way past the tents, over to the corner of the platform. The rebels had stashed a large portion of their edibles there, in the form of thousands of handmade cans stuffed and sealed with whatever vegetables they had been able to scavenge, along with a large, functional refrigerator that he imagined was stocked with game. Ehri was sitting on one of the crates filled with cans, her back to him, her head in her hands.

"Ehri," he said.

"Please, Major," she said. "I'd like to be alone."

"I understand that, and given other circumstances, I'd be happy to comply. In this case, I can't. We're gearing up for the biggest battle in fifty years, and I need to know where you stand."

She lifted her head but didn't look at him. "Where I stand, Major? How am I supposed to answer that? I don't even know who, or what, I am."

"You've always been Ehri dur Tuhrik."

"I don't want to be Ehri dur Tuhrik. I don't feel Ehri dur Tuhrik. That was a disguise. A mask that Tuhrik placed on me to hide me from the

Domo'dahm. At least, that is what my memories tell me." She paused. "Apparently, I can't trust my memories."

"When did the mask come off?" Donovan asked.

"When I heard his voice," Ehri said. "Theodore's voice. When I heard him speak. I wanted to help you before that. I always felt it within me. But when I heard him I knew who I really was. Or who I thought I was."

"Juliet St. Martin couldn't fight like you do."

"I had training, as Ehri dur Tuhrik."

"You know what I mean."

She turned to face him then. Her eyes were red and moist. She looked tired and miserable. "My enhanced abilities. Yes. In here, they come from the maturation capsule." She tapped the side of her head. "But to consider it scientifically, Tuhrik may have altered the cloning process in some way to make me stronger and faster."

"I didn't get the impression the other Juliet has those traits."

"Perhaps not. The weapon, Big Bertha, that is a technology the Dread do not possess. Not at that scale. Maybe she is smarter."

"Different clones with different strengths?" Donovan suggested. It made sense, although he had no idea how the bek'hai scientist could have done it.

"Or the personality helps determine the strengths. But to accept that is to accept that I am a clone, and that is very difficult for me to do. I feel like Juliet St. Martin. I feel the love of God. The love of my husband. And Gabriel." She looked down again, shaking her head. "I almost told him, when we met him on the mountain. I almost gave myself away. I wanted to touch him, to hold him. How can that not be real?"

"Nobody is saying it isn't real. Whatever is causing your emotions, they're completely real. Whatever is motivating you, that's real, too. Who you are is real. The truth is additive to that. There isn't one of you fighting for us. There's a multitude. Who knows how many? Think of what you could accomplish if you all worked together, instead of being at odds because you believe there can be only one."

Ehri was silent for a moment. "I understand what you are suggesting, Major. And logically, it makes complete sense. Emotionally? I desire to be unique. To be the one Juliet St. Martin. I don't want to share Theodore and Gabriel with the others."

"But do you want them to survive? Do you want them to have the opportunity to return to Earth?"

"Yes."

"Are you willing to sacrifice your ability to be with them to give them that?"

"I would sacrifice my life to give them that."

"Then what's the problem?"

Ehri looked up at him for the first time, meeting his eyes with hers. He could sense the immediate change in her, the sudden resolve. He was right, and she knew it.

Loving someone wasn't about being loved. It was about sacrificing anything and everything you had for them, without resentment, without remorse, without regret.

He hoped Diaz had felt that way before she died.

"I cannot argue your point, Major," Ehri said, getting to her feet. "Thank you for giving me some perspective. I won't say the truth isn't painful, but at least I have something to fight for."

"You're welcome. Let's go see what we can do to help."

19

GABRIEL RETREATED FROM HIS father's quarters, intending to return to the bridge. He was interrupted when Miranda appeared at the end of the corridor, heading toward him.

"Gabriel," she said, smiling as he neared.

"Hey, Randa," he replied. "Colonel Choi let you off the bridge for a while?"

"She dismissed almost everyone. There isn't much we can do up there until Reza gets some of the systems online. A skeleton crew is good enough to sit here."

Gabriel glanced out one of the transparencies that speckled the outer hull. There was nothing to see but stars floating on a sea of black.

"Where were you headed?"

"I was going to check on Wallace for you, and then make my way to the Magellan."

"Do you mind if I join you?"

"Never."

She flinched then. Gabriel wasn't sure why until he noticed the dark shape near the corner. It crossed the corridor and vanished into an access tunnel.

"I'm not used to them yet," she said about the cleaner.

"I'm not used to any of this," Gabriel replied.

"Like Zoelle?"

"Especially Zoelle. I just finished talking to my father. He said she told him about things nobody else would know. I don't know how that's possible, but it's sure got him convinced."

"What if she really is your mother?"

"Don't tell me you believe that."

"You're so sure she isn't. I'm just worried you might be missing a chance to get to know her. I mean, even if she isn't, she knows things about her that you'll never know any other way."

The statement reminded Gabriel of all of the time he had spent avoiding his father back on Alpha. He regretted that loss now, even while he was thankful to have the real Theodore St. Martin back.

"Maybe you're right. And what's that old saying again? Keep your friends close, and your enemies closer?"

"She's not our enemy. You told me she saved your life."

"Yeah. Maybe. Do you think I'm being stubborn?"

"Probably a little. It seems to run in the family."

"I think I'm going to take a pass on our walk if that's okay with you?"

"You're going to find Zoelle?"

"Yes. I want to see what Reza's up to, anyway."

Miranda nodded and leaned forward, kissing him on the cheek. "I'll see you later then, Major St. Martin."

"As you will, Spaceman Locke," Gabriel replied, smiling. "By the way, thanks for looking out for Wallace for me."

"It's no trouble at all."

He watched her walk down the corridor for a few seconds before heading on to the bridge. When he entered, he found the entire thing nearly deserted, save for a few of the Magellan's crew scattered around the terminals, and Colonel Choi sitting slouched on the command dais. She looked exhausted, too, but she straightened herself quickly as he approached.

"Colonel Choi," he said, saluting.

"At ease, Major. What can I do for you?"

"I'm looking for Reza and Zoelle. Do you know where they went?"

"Reza said something about the phase modulator, and Zoelle suggested that they get the schematics into the ship's replicators so they could try to match it."

"Replicator?"

"I'm assuming it is what it sounds like."

"Do you know where it is?"

"No. Zoelle said she would show him. I sent Diallo with them, just in case. She didn't seem thrilled with the idea, but too damn bad."

"Okay. I could stand a little exercise anyway. I might as well get it exploring this place a little bit."

"I don't know if that's the best idea. We can't be sure all of the mothers and the drumhr loyal to Gr'el are taken care of. Besides, you might get lost."

"I can take care of myself," he replied. "I'll grab a rifle before I go too far, and Tea'va showed me how to use the communications systems. I'll be able to call for help if I get into any trouble."

"Be careful."

"I will. You should get in touch with Colonel Graham and have him take over for you. You look like you're ready to collapse."

"I would, but Colonel Graham is busy with the repairs to the Magellan, and I don't want to interrupt him. I'll give your father six hours, and then he's coming back up here whether he likes it or not."

"Are you going to be the one to tell him that?"

She laughed. "At that point, I might be overtired enough to do it."

Gabriel left the bridge, heading down another corridor to the space where they had stashed their collection of Dread weaponry. Spaceman Ewing was standing in front of it.

"Major," he said, saluting as Gabriel approached.

"Spaceman Ewing. At ease. I need to borrow a rifle from the armory. I'm heading below decks, and I'm not completely sure what I might find down there."

"Are you sure that's a good idea, sir?" Ewing asked, moving aside and pressing the wall so the room would open.

"I'm sure it's not a completely bad idea," Gabriel replied.

He entered the armory. It was as simple and bare as any other in the Dread starship, save for the neatly assembled rows of plasma rifles they had collected from their defeated enemy. Rifles they would use to invade Earth with the entirety of the New Earth Alliance military, once they finally returned home.

He picked one of them up, checked the energy level, and carried it from the room.

"Good hunting, Major," Spaceman Ewing said as he headed toward one of the transport beams.

"Thanks," Gabriel replied.

He reached the beam a minute later, taking a deep breath as he prepared himself to enter it. He still found the technology a little frightening, probably because he didn't understand how it worked. He stepped in, lowering his hands for a moment and then coming to a stop at the bottom of the fortress, on the same level as the cloning factory. If the replicator was a similar thing, only for inanimate objects, then this was probably where it would be found. If he happened across anyone else, he would be sure to ask them.

As he moved into the dim corridors alone, he began to wonder if, like Colonel Choi, he was overtired enough to be doing something stupid.

20

THE FEAR OF THE unknown began to wear off as Gabriel navigated through the Dread ship, spending most of his time alone until he finally made his way out into the open space where the clone factory was found. He smiled, impressed with himself for finding his way to it, and from a different entrance. Then he scanned the area beyond the factory. There were three more corridors branching off from it, heading further into the fortress. He was sure he was going to follow one of them, but which one?

He decided on the middle and started crossing the open area beside the cloning facility to reach it. He had only gone a few steps when he noticed movement in the corner of his eye. He paused, turning to see what it was, growing curious when he saw Tea'va moving from an adjoining hallway toward the factory.

He was going to head over to meet him, but decided against it, choosing to observe instead. Tea'va took long strides to the facility's entrance, his head remaining straight, his posture much more rigid and proud than Gabriel was used to. The bek'hai didn't look around, and didn't seem to notice him standing there.

What would he be doing, going into the factory by himself when he was supposed to be healing? And why had he told Theodore he would need to rest if he didn't?

Gabriel took a few steps toward the factory before stopping. What was he going to do? Confront the Dread warrior? He had seen Tea'va fight. If he were doing something subversive and was caught in the act, he could kill Gabriel with little effort.

He decided not to follow. Whatever it was, he could have Zoelle look into it later. Not that he could necessarily trust anything she said about it, but if one or both of them was playing games with their new human companions, it was only fair that the humans played them back. Either way, he didn't like secrets, and he could feel his trust in the bek'hai beginning to wane.

He pushed the thought aside, returning to his original plan. He crossed the open space to the center corridor, heading through it without hesitation. He began traveling down another long, glowing black hallway, his rifle resting on his shoulder.

As he walked, he found his mind wandering, thinking about Miranda. They had always been friends, but lately, he was starting to feel so much more for her. An attachment that hadn't been there before. Something had changed between them, and he liked it.

He also felt guilty about it. But how long was he supposed to mourn? How long was he supposed to be alone? Jessica would have wanted him to be happy, and she had been friends with Miranda, too. Wasn't it a good match?

He reached an intersection in the corridor, still distracted by his thoughts.

He almost walked right into a plasma bolt.

It hit the wall beside him, only centimeters from his face, so close he felt the burn of it as it was absorbed by the lek'shah plating. He caught himself, stumbling back the way he had come, getting under cover around the corner and dropping his rifle into his arms.

What the hell?

Another bolt sizzled past, smacking the wall again. Close. Too close. He looked back the way he had come. He had gotten too distracted, and hadn't been paying attention. He knew he had stayed in this corridor the whole time, but he could see there were other intersections branching off from it.

He retreated, running from the threat. He didn't know who was shooting at him yet, or why. If it was a pur'dahm, he was sure he was going to die.

He fired back as he went, his bolts wild. Someone turned the corner behind him. A mother. Two more followed. They traded fire with him, and he ducked around another corner.

He hadn't expected them to be this close to the cloning facility. Why hadn't Graham's team sniffed these out? He growled under his breath as the plasma bolts flowed past, slapping harmlessly into the walls. He couldn't make it back down the hallway. He needed to reach a functional space where there might be a static comm link and call in for help.

He started running again, down the adjacent corridor, trying to keep track of his movements in his head as he fled. Left, left, right, straight three intersections, left, right. He kept going, the mothers staying behind him, keeping up the chase. He was faster than them, allowing him to stay ahead of their attacks, but he couldn't keep going forever.

He had been right. He was stupid for coming down here alone.

He finally reached the end of the hallway, running out into another large, open space, similar to the one where the cloning facility rested. His eyes shifted nervously as he sought another avenue to run down or for a place to hide.

He froze as a strange smell reached into his nostrils, making his nose feel as though it were burning. Next, he noticed a dark pile near the far end of the space, and that the ground was littered with rough, black rocks.

What was this place?

He ran out of time to think about it. He heard the mothers coming. He had to get away from them.

He hurried into the space, reaching one of the rocks and crouching down behind it. The mothers appeared a moment later, entering the massive chamber before coming to a stop.

Gabriel stood, aiming his rifle, ready to shoot them.

They dropped their weapons. They weren't even looking at him.

He followed their gaze to the back of the space, where an inky darkness replaced the dim glow of the luminescent moss. He felt a chill run down his arms when he thought he saw something move. He ducked back behind the rock, something in him telling him to be very afraid.

It moved from the darkness like an extension of it, though the corners of the scales that covered its body seemed to catch a small portion of the light and throw it back, bending it at an odd angle as it did. It was fast, terrifyingly fast as it slithered across the open space, ignoring every obstacle in a direct line toward the mothers.

They cried out as it approached them, raising their rifles and firing. Gabriel watched the plasma bolts smack harmlessly against the creature's scaly carapace. Then he watched as a short arm reached from the front of the creature, grabbing one of the mothers and squeezing. He felt sick as he watched her compress beneath the thing's claws, and he ducked back to his hiding place.

How had he managed to go from bad to worse?

And why did the Dread have a literal monster moving freely inside of a starship?

The remaining mothers managed to get moving. One of them made it back out of the room, far enough into the adjoining corridor that the large creature wouldn't be able to reach her. The second wasn't as lucky, and she cried out as it stabbed her with its claw, running her through, lifting her from the ground and tossing the carcass aside.

Gabriel looked around, trying to find a way out as the creature slowed and came to a stop, blocking the way he had come. He got a look at its face now, bony and angled, ridged and rough and covered in smaller scales. It looked vaguely familiar to him, but much more threatening. It opened its mouth, revealing a row of long teeth. A low groan sounded from it. Its nostrils flared, and a large tongue flicked out.

It knew he was there, and it was looking for him.

He swallowed hard, his heart racing. There was no way past it, no way to outrun it. He could only hope that it wouldn't be able to find him. He tried to duck even lower, but couldn't without shifting too much and risking being seen or heard.

The creature began to slither forward, slowly moving in his general direction, its head bobbing as it tried to get a bead on him. Gabriel cradled his rifle, trying to decide if he should shoot at it. He had seen the plasma strike harmlessly against the scales.

He froze for a second time as he realized what he was looking at.

Reza had said that a large portion of the Dread technology had an organic component. The walls, the wiring, everything. His father had even made a joke that there had to be a farm somewhere in the ship to provide replacement parts.

Except it wasn't a joke. He had accidentally stumbled onto the farm, and now he was about to be killed by one of the cows.

How did the Dread manage to keep this thing under control?

He held his breath as the monster came closer, still hoping it wouldn't notice him and would go away. The burning smell was stronger now, and his nose felt like it was on fire. He wanted to rub it, to hold it, to do something, but couldn't. His eyes began to water.

Without warning, the creature darted forward, rising up on its serpentine rear, pressing forward and looming over him. He brought the rifle up, as useless as it would be, his finger moving to the trigger.

"Kel'esh! Dokur huruhm bek."

A gravelly voice echoed across the large space, reverberating and repeating itself. Something approached Gabriel from behind, even as the monster in front of him suddenly became still.

He felt sharp fingers on his shoulder a moment later. He turned, coming face-to-face with what almost looked like a miniaturized version of the creature, blended with something else entirely. It was dark and demonic looking, reptilian and raw, and at the same time intelligent. Its eyes regarded him with curiosity, interest, and humor.

"You do not belong in here, Heil'bek," it said in rough English.

It knew who he was? How?

"I am lek'hai It'kek," it said. "A keeper of the legri'shah." It pointed at the creature.

"You're a bek'hai," Gabriel said, making the connection. "Not a human clone."

"A keeper is a clone, but not human," It'kek agreed. "Only the original bek'hai can commune with our forebears. Our visage is outlawed among our people. Our place in society secret and sacred."

"Why didn't you let it attack me?"

"We are keepers, not killers, and while the drumhr know better than to enter our place, you humans do not."

"But you let it attack the mothers?"

"They are lor'hai. Replaceable. You are not."

"That may be true, but we're supposed to be enemies."

"Are we? Your kind had something our kind required. The Domo'dahm chose to take it, instead of asking. You have done me no wrong. You are not my enemy unless you choose to be." It let out a soft hiss that Gabriel took for a laugh or a sigh. "You are within your rights to do so."

"You saved my life. I guess we're even?"

The keeper hissed again. "You remind me of your mother, Heil'bek."

Gabriel had calmed some once he knew he wasn't going to die. His heart began to thump again. "How do you know my mother?"

"We can smell her in you. We knew her. All of the keepers did. The Domo'dahm's pet human. His keepsake. She was like you. She was curious. She came to us. We spoke. She touched many within the bek'hai, with her words of kindness and compassion for all things. We weren't always like the drumhr, Heil'bek. We weren't always like the pur'dahm. Only in the beginning. And perhaps, in the end."

"There's a clone on this ship, Zoelle. Do you know her?"

"We see and hear everything that happens within the domo'shah."

"Is she really my mother?"

"We don't know. She has never come to us."

He couldn't hold that against her if she had only just remembered who she was, as she claimed.

"If I bring her to you, would you know the difference between her and a clone?"

"Yes. We would know."

"Thank you for helping me. I was looking for the assemblers when the mothers attacked me. Do you know how to get there?"

"We will show you our way, Heil'bek. Once you have left this chamber, do not return to it. Now that you know to stay away, we will not stop the legri'shah from attacking you again."

"What if I need to talk to you?"

"We will show you where to come. Where it is safe. Do not come this way."

"I understand. What I don't get is why you are helping me?"

"For your mother. For peace. As we said, this war is not our war. We do not agree with the Domo'dahm."

"Why didn't you stop him?"

"We are powerless to stop him. We are only keepers."

"But you control the legri'shah. The key to their survival."

"The legri'shah are prisoners on the domo'shah. As are the keepers. As are the lor'hai. As are the humans. The Domo'dahm takes many prisoners. The benefit of the few to the distress of the many. Remember that, Heil'bek. That is the truth of the bek'hai. Most of the bek'hai."

It'kek turned and began walking. Gabriel was nervous about turning his back on the legri'shah, but it hadn't moved at all since the keeper had yelled at it. He backed away from the creature, trailing behind It'kek. He would have never expected what he had found down here. It wasn't only a piece of the secret behind the Dread's technology. It was a truth he was sure most didn't know about.

"It'kek," he said as they neared another corridor that had been hidden in the darkness at the rear of the chamber. "If the domo'shah is made of legri'shah scales, if all of the Dread technology is made from these things, there must have been a lot of them on your home world before it was destroyed."

"Millions, Heil'bek," It'kek replied. "Until the hunters nearly made them extinct. Only then did the bek'hai learn to care for the legri'shah. Only once we realized how much we needed them to survive."

21

THE KEEPER BROUGHT GABRIEL to a transport beam hidden in one of the access tunnels, normally used only to travel to the assemblers for the tools and supplies they needed to do their work in the belly of the fortress. Once there, It'kek gave him detailed directions to navigate the area, as well as a suggestion on where to find Reza and Zoelle. Gabriel tried to get the keeper to come with him, to smell the clone and determine if she was telling the truth, but he refused to leave the legri'shah after its interaction with him had made it upset.

Gabriel would have laughed at that statement if It'kek hadn't said it with such serious reverence.

The transport beam brought Gabriel to the assemblers, which were almost what he and Colonel Choi had originally believed them to be. Machines that were able to create nearly anything from nothing by reconstituting them from their original atomic structure using base resources culled from other matter. The facility itself was composed of row after row of storage tanks which contained the fuel for the assemblers, which ranged in size from a few meters to large enough to produce an entire mechanized armor.

Looking at the technology, it was clear the Dread weren't limited by how quickly they could produce the things they needed. Instead, they were limited in specific raw materials to convert. He imagined there was another facility for that process somewhere nearby, but it wasn't obvious from his current position.

It didn't take him long to find Zoelle and Reza, once he was certain he was in the right place. He found the scientist and the clone where It'kek had suggested, in the control space where the molecular breakdown of new materials to copy was recorded. They were alone in the room, standing on opposite sides of a flat counter where a blue light was shining down on the rifle Reza had modified to create the darkspace shield. Reza looked somewhat bored with the process, but Zoelle was following it with intense interest, studying the updated design.

They both looked up when he walked in. Reza smiled when he saw Gabriel. Zoelle gained a look of concern.

"Gabriel? What happened to you?" she asked.

He hadn't thought about how he must look after being shot at and almost crushed by a legri'shah. "I was looking for you, but I took a wrong turn somewhere and wound up on the farm."

"Farm?" Zoelle said, before understanding set in. "You ran into a legri'shah den?"

"It was an accident. A keeper kept it from eating me."

"Legri'shah don't eat meat," Zoelle said. "It would have killed you for invading its territory. You're lucky there was a keeper nearby."

"Why didn't you tell us the Dread have those things on board?"

"Would it make a difference?"

Gabriel paused. "No, probably not. It'kek told me that there used to be millions of them on the bek'hai home world."

"Yes. Many of them were slaughtered during the bek'hai civil wars, the need to produce more and more weaponry overriding all sense. Now, they can keep only a few on each ship. It is the reason the bek'hai can't build more domo'shah, and can only expand so far. It is fortunate for us."

"You should come down to see the keepers with me," Gabriel said. "I was told you used to visit with them quite often."

Zoelle stared at him for a few seconds and then nodded. "I did. I remember now. So many things are still vague to me. So many things I still can't recall. Did your father send you down here?"

"No. I came on my own. Miranda suggested I should try to get to know you better."

"Miranda?"

"Spaceman Locke. She sits near the command dais."

"The woman with the brown hair?"

"That's her."

She smiled. "Your father told me you have an attraction to her."

How did he know? "You could say that. Anyway, don't let me interfere. I just thought I would observe whatever it is you're doing."

"What we're doing," Reza said, "is converting the tech in this rifle to something we can reproduce. Zoelle has been giving me a quick education in basic bek'hai technology at the same time. It's fascinating stuff."

"You looked bored before I came in."

"We were taking a break while it builds a prototype."

"Your engineer is a genius, Gabriel," Zoelle said. "His approach to the problem is unlike anything I've seen before. Now I understand how you were able to get onto the ship and absorb the attack from the main plasma cannon. You should be very proud of yourself, Reza."

Reza's face flushed, and he lowered his head. "Thank you," he replied.

"This system isn't networked, right?" Gabriel asked. "We aren't broadcasting how to make upgraded phase modulators to the entire bek'hai command?"

Zoelle laughed. "Of course not."

"I was able to update some of the sequences to make more efficient use of the organic compounds in the Dread tech. There is still going to be one limitation."

"What's that?"

"We can only push the modulation to a limited surface area at any given time."

"Which means what?"

"The shields will be cascading," Reza said. "Parts of the ship will be vulnerable as the modulation fields move around the hull."

"That doesn't sound good, Reza," Gabriel said.

"I know. The problem is that if we feed too much power into too much of the hull at one time, the lek'shah will break down and lose integrity."

"That sounds worse."

"Yes."

"You figured all of this out in two hours?"

"I have a good partner."

Gabriel glanced at Zoelle. "I thought you were more of an astrophysicist?"

"I've had fifty years to learn as much as I could," she replied. "I'm not anything special, Gabriel. Just a younger model of an older woman, who committed herself to saving not just humankind, but all of the innocents caught in this war and the wars that preceded it."

"Do you mean that?" he asked, wanting so much to believe it, but finding himself still skeptical. As he should be.

"Yes."

Something flashed behind them. Zoelle turned toward it immediately, approaching one of the smaller assemblers. The front of it slid down, revealing a small, cylindrical device. She picked it up, holding it out to Reza.

"We will scan it for a match," she said as he took it.

He nodded, removing the rifle from the table and placing the cylinder down on it. The blue light turned back on, sweeping across the device. It repeated the motion a dozen times, and then a holographic reading appeared above the cylinder.

"An accurate reproduction," Zoelle announced.

"Yes!" Reza said. "Where can we bring it to test it out?"

"Engineering. The main links to the conduits sending impulses through the hull are there. It will take some time to update the systems to utilize it. Much longer than it took to duplicate the design."

Reza looked disappointed. "I was hoping we could get this done today. Wouldn't that have been a treat for the General?"

"I thought you were running on fumes?" Gabriel asked.

"I was until I got involved with this. A good technical challenge is the best way to wake up."

"Why don't you go and get some rest, Reza," Zoelle said. "I will begin the work to integrate the modulator with our existing systems. You can check my work when you return."

"Uh, I don't know," Reza said.

"Go ahead," Gabriel said. "I'll stay here with her. We need you at full brain capacity."

"Okay," Reza said. "Don't do anything exciting without me, deal?"

"Deal."

22

"So, I TALKED TO my father," Gabriel said, as he followed Zoelle through the starship to wherever engineering was located.

He had dismissed Diallo from her guard duty, sending her back to Colonel Choi. They would need to assemble another team to search for more mothers hiding in the shadows before anyone else got killed by them.

"What about?" Zoelle asked.

"Why he thinks you're my mother."

"I am your mother, Gabriel."

"Yeah, that's what he said. You can't blame me for being a little less accepting."

"I don't. It is perfectly understandable."

"Good. I want you to tell me what happened. How you came to be here, on this ship, and fifty years younger than you should be. I want to know who you are, but I also want to know who you were before." He almost told her that Tea'va thought she was full of it, but he held that part back.

"Before?"

"Before you remembered that you're Juliet St. Martin, not Zoelle dur Tuhrik."

She paused for a moment, her expression dimming. "I'm not proud of who I was."

"Why?"

"I feel as though Tuhrik programmed me to be the opposite of who I really am."

"Programmed you? I think you need to go back a little more. What happened?"

"The Dread captured me. They brought me to one of their facilities and gave me the genetic test to see if I would make a good clone. When I passed, they sent me to the Dread capitol, the Domo'dahm's ship. He saw me there and was intrigued because I was calmly defiant. The others they had taken, they cried and screamed, or were silent and distant. I looked him in the eye. I stared at him while he stared at me. I prayed to God to have mercy on him. He thought I was interesting, and took me as his own."

She pointed at a transport beam ahead, taking his hand as they entered since he didn't know where they were going. Her skin was warm and tingling. She squeezed his hand as they exited the beam, smiling at him.

"I never had to try very hard. Only be me. The Domo'dahm, Rorn'el, grew affectionate toward me. Not in a sexual way. The Dread barely understand sexuality. He gave me more and more freedom. In time, I met Tuhrik, and he began to teach me the ways of the Dread. Meanwhile, they were working to clone me. I became more involved in the process as it continued, giving input to the programming. The Domo'dahm wanted my duplicates to be special, so he would have me throughout his life. Tuhrik and I became close. We spent many hours discussing the future of humankind and the bek'hai. He knew Rorn'el was wrong to kill off humanity."

They reached a larger door. It slid open at her approach, revealing a sea of glowing crystals surrounding some sort of dark machine.

"Our power source, and energy stores," she explained.

"Where are the technicians to maintain all of this?"

"There were none assigned to the Ishur. This technology is thousands of years old, and incredibly reliable. My team was able to handle potential minor problems."

She circled the engines, moving to a separate door that opened when she neared.

"It was Tuhrik who helped me, but his goal was to help everyone. The Domo'dahm, the pur'dahm, they have lost their way over the years. They are setting themselves up, either to be forced to seek another life form or to go extinct. It is a cycle that cannot be allowed to repeat."

"I can't argue with that. So what did he do?"

"He saved me after I died."

"What do you mean, after you died?"

"My body was brought to be processed, broken down into raw materials. It sounds horrible, but it was an honor that no other human ever received. I was to be retired as a true bek'hai would be retired. Only Tuhrik arranged for me to be brought to his laboratory. He had a maturation capsule there, and he put me in it. He knew the healing power it had from his studies with the clones. It didn't only reverse my aging. It brought me back to life."

Gabriel stared at her, a part of him beginning to wonder if maybe she was telling the truth. He couldn't deny that he wanted it to be so.

"Why didn't he tell the Domo'dahm?"

"To what end? To continue the cycle of violence and destruction and genocide? No, he decided that I should wait and that we would work together to fuel the change the bek'hai need. Clearly, I couldn't be alive as myself, and so he subjected me to the programming sequencer, turning me into a clone of myself, as odd as that sounds."

They crossed another corridor until they reached the second room. This one was filled with large conduits and wires, along with a holographic terminal. She put her free hand to it, manipulating the alien writing.

"But what about this clone of yourself? I don't really understand. Clones should all be the same, shouldn't they?"

"That isn't how it works. Even with perfect genetics and programming, all clones are unique to some extent. The un'hai were always more unique than others. They have the closest thing to free will of any of the lor'hai. When the programming Tuhrik inserted interacted with the rest of me, it made me very cold, very calculating, very hungry for power and control, and willing to do anything I had to in order to get it. I'm not proud of that."

Gabriel felt his heart beating faster. Was she admitting everything Tea'va had said to him? Could it be that Theodore was right after all? "Tea'va told me you couldn't be trusted."

"He was right. Before I remembered who I really am, I couldn't."

"But the fighting. The killing. Juliet St. Martin believed in peace."

"I would never let anyone hurt you, Gabriel," she said, looking at him. "You or your father. I can kill for that, as many as I have to. I'll beg God's forgiveness later."

Gabriel reached under his shirt, taking hold of the crucifix there. He lifted it out so that Zoelle could see it. He was going to ask her if she remembered it, but by the tears that formed in her eyes, he knew she did.

"I'm happy he gave it to you," she said. "I'm happy you're here. That we're all here together."

Gabriel felt himself losing the battle not to believe her. If she were faking everything, she was doing a masterful job. And that was possible, too, wasn't it? The clones could be programmed to do anything. How much of her story was true? What should he believe?

He was more confused than he had been before. Was it better than doubting?

He looked at Zoelle, trying to find words to express what he was feeling. Only she wasn't crying anymore. She wasn't sad anymore. Her face was pale, her eyes panicked.

"Oh, Gabriel," she said. "Oh, no."

"What is it?" Gabriel asked.

"I'm sorry. Gabriel, I'm sorry."

He felt his own panic setting in. "What?"

"I lied. I didn't know it, but I lied. Talking about it, I only now remembered. When I told Theodore that I plotted the optimal course. That isn't true. I delayed the Ishur intentionally."

"Why?"

A voice suddenly echoed across the room, and throughout the Dread fortress. Colonel Choi's voice.

"Red alert. Red alert. All hands to stations. All hands to stations. This is not a drill. I repeat, this is not a drill."

Zoelle's voice was weak when she spoke again.

"I transmitted a message to the Domo'dahm to send reinforcements."

23

GABRIEL'S SHOCK VANISHED, HIS instincts taking over as Colonel Choi repeated the red alert.

"We barely have control over the ship," he said.

"I know."

"Where is the comm?"

"Here." She put her hand to a blank side of the wall, and a light appeared.

"Bridge, this is Major St. Martin. Can you hear me?"

"I hear you, Gabriel," Colonel Choi said.

"What's going on?"

"Two Dread fortresses just appeared off the slipstream. They're heading our way."

"ETA?"

"Twenty-two minutes. Where are you?"

"Engineering, with my - Zoelle."

"Well, get your ass up here, Major."

"Yes, ma'am."

Gabriel turned to Zoelle. "Twenty-two minutes. How well can this ship hold up to attack from two others?"

"Without any interceptors and only the main plasma cannon? Not long."

"Damn it." He took a step toward the door. "What about that?" he said, pointing at the modulator in her hand. "Can you get it installed in that time?"

"I don't know. I'm not as familiar with these systems as some of the others."

"We have to try. How can I help?"

"Aren't you needed on the bridge?"

"Tea'va can handle the flying. I don't know what I'm doing yet, anyway. What can I do?"

She nodded, her hand working the terminal faster. She tossed the modulator to him as a small hatch slid open, revealing a power conduit.

"The hard part is going to be programming the systems to handle the modulation. I'm going to cut the power to the conduit. Do you see the capsule joining the wires?"

Gabriel looked inside the panel. The capsule was filled with some kind of gel, glowing a soft blue as the power passed through it. "Yes."

The blue glow faded.

"Pull it out, carefully. You don't want to damage it."

Gabriel reached in, putting one hand around the capsule and another on the bundle. He pulled, flinching as a tangle of wires and deep red fluid seeped from the bottom of it. He lowered the wire to the side of the panel, and then disconnected the capsule from the top and removed it.

"Good. Look at the modulator. It has connectors for the wires on both ends."

Gabriel looked at it, finding the connectors. "There are an awful lot of them."

"I know. You'll need to join them individually."

"In what order?"

"The order doesn't matter. The strands can only carry so much power each; that's why there are so many."

He wondered if he had made a mistake in offering to help as he lifted the bottom bundle and separated the finer threads at the end, and then began attaching them one by one.

"What are you doing?" he asked.

"I have to adjust the power output through that conduit so that it will modulate the phase appropriately." She reached up and tapped the comm. "Bridge, this is Juliet in engineering."

"Juliet," Theodore responded. "What are you up to down there?"

"Gabriel and I are working to integrate Reza's phase modulator into the bek'hai systems. Theo, if this works, you'll have cascading shield coverage across the bow of the domo'shah."

"Cascading? As in non-static?"

"Yes. You'll have to adjust course to try to keep the ship angled to deflect the Dread fortress' attacks. They'll try to flank you and get you in a crossfire. Don't let them."

"Affirmative," Theodore replied. "You got that, Tea'va?"

Gabriel didn't hear the bek'hai's response. He was sure the pur'dahm understood. He focused his efforts on binding the wires to the modulator.

The time passed too quickly for Gabriel to keep track of. He was halfway through the top end of the modulator when Zoelle announced that they only had two minutes left to make something happen. The ship had already shaken once from a long-range strike that Tea'va hadn't managed to avoid.

"I'm going as fast as I can," Gabriel said, reaching for another of the small wires.

Zoelle moved in beside him. "Here, let me do it." She took the modulator from him, her fingers dancing across it as she laced the rest of the wires to it in less than thirty seconds.

"I think you should have done this yourself," he said.

"I've had a lot more practice. I used to knit your father sweaters. Did you know that?"

Gabriel couldn't help but smile. "No, I didn't." He hadn't gotten to take any of them off of Earth with him.

She finished the wiring, reaching into the panel and slipping the modulator into place.

"What do we do with this?" Gabriel asked, holding up the gel-filled capsule.

"Hope that we don't need it," she replied.

"Juliet, darlin', give me some good news," Theodore said over the comm. "We're twenty seconds from firing range, and the bastards are sending fighters at us."

"Tell Tea'va to get the ship angled and fire the plasma cannon at them," she said, her voice angry. "What is he doing up there?"

Theodore's laughter filled the room. "Tea'va, what in the hell are you doing over there? Mr. Mokri, did you get me my damn fire control?"

"Yes, General," Gabriel heard Reza said. "Take my tablet. Charge status is here; fire button is here."

"Like a damn video game," Theodore replied. "Nice work, Mr. Mokri."

"Thank you, sir."

"We're almost done," Zoelle said. "I'm about to power it up. Remember, we can't control the cascade. It's going to cycle for now, and the Dahms on those ships are going to figure out what's happening pretty quickly. We need to hit them back as hard and fast as we can."

"I hear you, darlin'," Theodore said. "Nothing to do now but pray."

"Amen," Zoelle said, her hands a blur on the terminal.

A moment later, Gabriel could feel the charge of the energy as it began running through the conduit once more. The modulator began to whine softly, and two of the connectors on top sparked and smoked.

"I don't think it's working," he said, his stomach sinking.

"Come on," Zoelle said, her hands still working the terminal. "It can't handle the power. We need to reduce it. The surface area is going to be smaller than we planned."

"How small?" Gabriel asked.

"It will be just large enough to stop the main plasma cannon if it catches it square in the center."

"With rolling coverage? No pilot in the universe can keep the shields centered like that. What if we keep the power levels up?"

"It will destroy the modulator."

"How quickly?"

"I don't know."

"We don't have a choice," Gabriel said. "Do it."

"Okay. God be with us and have mercy on our souls. Theodore, the shields should be active, but they can't handle the strain for long. Remember, hard and fast."

"Affirmative. Tea'va, bring us in."

24

THEODORE DIDN'T LIKE THE Dread's command dais, even though it wasn't much different than the raised platform on the Magellan. The seat was uncomfortable, designed for a taller, leaner shape, and certainly not adjustable for an old man with no legs. More than that, it was obvious when sitting on it that it was designed to make the rest of the bridge crew feel submissive and small, and he hated that. Each and every soul on the bridge was invaluable to him, even if they were limited in their helpfulness during their first taste of combat aboard the alien vessel.

They had held themselves well in the last two battles. At least this time they had a weapon to fire back at the enemy.

A weapon that could actually hurt them.

And now, Mr. Mokri had pulled a rabbit out of his hat one more time, and along with Juliet and Gabriel had given them some semblance of shields. He knew it was true because, despite the original blackness of the lek'shah armor, it had given way to an even deeper, darker black that he identified immediately as darkspace. It curled and rolled around the hull of the bow like a typhoon, as though they had somehow released a storm on top of the ship. He had been expecting it to be more evenly distributed and as such easier to adjust to, but they would take what they could get.

"Keep us heading in the right direction, Mr. Tea'va," Theodore said. "Full ahead."

"Yes, Dahm St. Martin," Tea'va replied.

The two Dread fortresses had come from nowhere, retreating from slipspace and making a direct line toward them, firing on them without any attempts to communicate. Theodore found that strange, considering they were supposed to be friendly and there was no way they could have heard about their takeover of the ship already. It meant that the incoming ships probably thought they were shooting at one of their own, and they were doing it intentionally and without any quarter.

It was a chilling thought.

"Hard to port, Tea'va," Theodore said as he watched the position of the fortresses ahead of them.

They were doing exactly as Juliet had said, trying to split apart and get to both sides of the ship. It was a standard but effective maneuver, especially considering their shield situation. They couldn't cover both at once, which meant they needed to take one out, and fast.

He held his finger over Reza's tablet, where a big red 'FIRE" button rested on the screen. There was a wire snaking from the tablet to one of the forward terminals, giving him interpolated access to the Ishur's main cannon. He didn't have a targeting computer to help him line the shot, which meant he had to do it by eye across the vastness of space.

No pressure.

He clenched his teeth as the two Dread fortresses fired their plasma cannons simultaneously. Tea'va rolled the Ishur slightly as the bolts approached, and Theodore couldn't help but pump his fist when he saw the first go beneath the ship, and the other hit the swirling maelstrom of darkspace. The ship shuddered from the impact, but the strike didn't leave any lasting damage.

"My turn," Theodore said, tapping the button.

The front of the fortress began to glow with bright blue energy which arced away a moment later, spewing toward the target on their port side. Theodore refused to blink as he watched it approach the ship, and as the ship tried to evade the strike. It managed to shift slightly, turning broadside and moving the impact further toward the rear. It still took the hit, leaving him satisfied as layers of lek'shah were burned away, and debris began to vent from the side of the vessel.

"That's one for the good guys," he said.

"Dahm St. Martin," Tea'va said. "The starboard target will be aligning their secondary batteries. We don't have coverage to stop them."

"Can we take the hit?"

"For a few minutes, Dahm."

Damn. They needed to be faster. He looked at the charge on the plasma cannon. Fifty percent.

"Juliet, you with me, darlin'?" he said, opening a channel.

"I'm here, Theodore. What do you need?"

"More power to the main plasma," he said. "Recharge time is slower than a gator in a mudhole."

"I will see what I can do."

Theodore shifted his attention to the starboard fortress. It was bathed in light as its secondary batteries began firing at them, dozens of positions belching plasma across a thousand kilometers, too close for comfort in space. Tea'va started to shift the bow toward them, to catch the attack with the shields.

"Stay on the port target, Mr. Tea'va," Theodore said.

"Dahm, I do not think-"

"I think, you steer," Theodore snapped. "Stay on the port target."

"Yes, Dahm St. Martin."

The ship shuddered slightly as the plasma attack began battering into it.

"Do we have damage reports showing anywhere?" Theodore asked.

"It isn't integrated yet, sir," Reza replied.

"Damn it. Get me a clone or something up here, someone that can read the alien symbols. Juliet?"

"I will contact Shielle. One moment."

The charge on the plasma cannon completed.

"Mr. Tea'va, give me four degrees port."

"Yes, Dahm."

The ship began to turn, the bow coming out slightly ahead of the enemy ship. Theodore slapped the fire button again and then watched as the bolt slammed into the front of the enemy ship. More debris exploded from the impact point, and it began to turn away from them.

"Was it just me, or did our cannon recharge faster than theirs?" Theodore asked.

"I rerouted the power from the batteries we can't use," Zoelle said. "Theodore, you must hurry, the modulator will not hold out much longer."

"Dahm St. Martin, the starboard target is turning to fire its main cannon."

Theodore stared at the fortress to their port side, trying to determine if it was out of the fight. It had turned its nose away from them and was still leaking debris. At the same time, secondary batteries were lighting up and beginning to fire out of sync.

"It is damaged," Tea'va said as if reading his mind. "If the Dahm of the ship is courageous, he will continue the fight until he is destroyed, but he is less of a concern. We should engage the other target, Dahm St. Martin."

"Agreed. Do it, Mr. Tea'va."

Theodore didn't know what the Dread did, but the ship began to shiver and moan, the forward velocity terminating abruptly as it shifted on its axis, the bow rotating toward the second domo'shah. It was already alight in the blue glow of the plasma cannon, and Theodore couldn't stop himself from flinching as it fired at relatively close range.

The Ishur shuddered again as it began to reverse, turning again, Tea'va working to move the shields to deflect the attack. It was as impressive a piece of flying as Theodore had ever seen, and he howled as the bolt smacked against it.

"Yes," he shouted, looking down at the status of their own cannon. It was almost ready.

He quickly checked on the first target, which was staying back further and firing the weaker secondary batteries at them. The bolts were striking the hull and digging into the lek'shah, but not nearly with enough focus to cause immediate critical damage.

A new figure arrived on deck, running across the bridge. Shielle, the clone of Juliet. He noticed that she glanced at Tea'va as she passed him by, and then took a position behind one of the terminals.

"Damage report," Theodore said.

"Hull breach on three decks, all sealed, Dahm St. Martin," she replied. "Damage is minimal."

"That's what I want to hear. Mr. Tea'va, get us lined up. Six degrees starboard, bring the bow up eight degrees."

"Yes, Dahm St. Martin."

The fortress began to turn again, maneuvering well considering the size. The enemy ship was turning as well, having realized the Ishur's shields were superior. It was trying to broadside them again, to stay out of their main cannon range and pepper them with secondary fire until they gave in.

"Dahm St. Martin, we have a breach on forty-six," Shielle said. "Emergency seals are closing."

The port side fortress was having some success with their own small arms.

"We need to end this now," Theodore said. "Give me some lead, Mr. Tea'va."

"Yes, Dahm."

The Ishur's bow kept turning, making it ahead of the starboard enemy.

"All ahead, Mr. Tea'va," Theodore said.

He didn't feel the acceleration, but he could see it in the rate at which the enemy fortress grew in front of them. They were bearing down on the ship, racing toward it, the shields on the bow absorbing most of its firepower. Their main plasma was charged, and they were getting so close he couldn't miss.

He pressed down on the trigger, and watched the blue bolt streak away from the Ishur, slamming into the side of the fortress, digging into the hull and through, vanishing on the inside.

"A good hit," Tea'va said. "That will reach the engines."

"Get us away from it," Theodore said.

"Yes, Dahm," Tea'va replied.

They accelerated, vectoring beneath the fortress as gouts of flame began to escape from it. The first fortress didn't follow, unwilling to risk getting caught in the second's death throes, and understanding that they had lost this fight.

Theodore kept an eye on the ships as they continued accelerating away from them. The first continued to vent fire for a couple of minutes before finally falling still and silent, the glow of the interior lights through the hull transparencies fading away and leaving it nearly invisible in the darkness of space. The other fortress retreated, heading in the opposite direction from the Ishur.

"Ha!" Theodore cried, pushing himself up on his hands. "Take that, you damn couillon bastards."

He smiled as the other crew members cheered along with him.

In front of him, Tea'va shifted in his seat, looking over at Shielle. She looked back at him, nodding slightly.

Then they both smiled.

25

TEA'VA ENTERED HIS QUARTERS, his chest pulsing, his muscles pumping with adrenaline. It had been a good fight, and unlike anything he had ever experienced before. He had participated in a number of gi'shah competitions over the years and had done well enough to still be alive. This? This was something completely different. A record for his History that deserved to be kept. When was the last time a domo'shah had engaged another? It could only have been during the civil wars, over ten thousand years earlier.

He was honored to be the pilot who had maneuvered the Ishur, keeping the humans' incredible shield technology positioned to absorb the attacks of the opposing fortresses and lining up the main plasma cannon to fire direct, decisive hits. Not the Heil'bek. Him. He had proven his superiority to Theodore St. Martin, and to all of the others who saw how he had managed the massive starship. He had proven his superiority to himself.

His face twisted as he smiled once more. His plans were coming together well, much better than he could have hoped for at the moment when he decided to use the rebels to help him achieve his ends. Not only would he have his ship back, but he would have new defenses that none of the other domo'shah could match. Defenses that would allow him to bombard the capital from space and force the Domo'dahm to rise to meet him or face destruction on the ground. He would have the opportunity to force Rorn'el's hand, and in the end, destroy him and seize control of the bek'hai.

It was hard for him to be patient, but he knew he had no choice. The clones wouldn't be mature for another six days, and there was no way he could retake the Ishur without them.

Or without Shielle.

In the hours following the humans' capture of the Ishur, he had thought he would need to kill the un'hai, expecting that like Zoelle she would find some kind of regressed awareness of Juliet St. Martin buried within her subconscious. Not only had that not been true, but she was as sneaky and conniving as Zoelle. She had been the one working with Gr'el to alter the mothers, to shift the balance of power on the ship and assist the late pur'dahm in gaining control. She had been the one to come to him, to confide in him how much she hated the humans, and to find out where his loyalties truly were. It was a risky decision on her part. If he had been a subject of their new masters, he would have been wise to turn her in or kill her where she stood.

He had done neither. Instead, he chose to take a risk of his own and confide in her. He hated the humans as well and had only allowed himself to be submissive to them in order to gain their trust. It was a difficult thing to do, to bow and scrape before them. To call Theodore "Dahm St. Martin," and agree with his every command when he wanted only to stab him with a lek'sai and rest his corpse at the foot of the command dais.

It was almost made worse by the fact that he respected the human and his son. They were both skilled warriors, intelligent and brave. The Heil'bek was almost reverent of him, identifying his superiority and commending him for it. The Domo'dahm had never recognized what an achievement Tea'va was, or how skilled he was. Why did it take a human to recognize the evolution that he represented, and the step forward he could be for the good of the bek'hai?

Why did he have to fight to make them see he was better? The Domo'dahm should have raised him to the top of the cells on his evolution alone.

He moved to his terminal in the back of the room, leaning over it and activating it. Should he have confided in her? It was a question he had asked himself over and over again. Trusting in others had been his downfall in the first place. At the same time, he couldn't do everything alone. He was a single bek'hai. He needed allies. Or at least, one ally. Especially one like Shielle. She had access to the cloning facilities, and neither Zoelle or the humans suspected her of being anything more than a standard clone. She was able to operate beneath their notice, while he was sure every member of the human crew was keeping a close eye on him.

He opened his History. How would he explain this to any that came after? How would he describe his allegiance to the humans?

"Today, the army of Tea'va dur Orin'ek encountered the forces of the incompetent Rorn'el -"

He paused, deleting the entry. That wouldn't do. He backed away from the terminal to give it more thought. Was he a fool for trusting Shielle? What else could he have done? He had considered killing Theodore St. Martin and his son and ordering the current clone soldiers to attack the humans. He had gone as far as to strategically organize them around the human crews to give them the best chance to overwhelm them. The problem was that there weren't enough remaining. One soldier for each human and they had all been disarmed. The element of surprise would help, but a victory wasn't guaranteed. If he were going to take chances anyway, he preferred to move his risk to a single point of failure. If Shielle did turn on him, he would have the opportunity to deny any accusations she made and start again. The Heil'bek would believe him. The Heil'bek trusted him. More than that, the Heil'bek actually liked him.

He nodded to himself, deciding once more that it was risky to trust her, but riskier not to. He returned to his terminal, considering the entry he wanted to add to his History again.

"Today, I alone directed the domo'shah Ishur in a direct confrontation with two domo'shah of the regime of Domo'dahm Rorn'el, as he sought to put an end to the evolution of our people that would ensure our survival. I alone engaged the domo'shah, and with the power of my new technology and my command expertise, I was able to destroy the domo'shah, and preserve our future."

He paused the History. That was a better introduction. Embellished, but not too much. History was written by the victorious, after all.

He stood again, pacing. He had six days until the clones were ready. He had to make his move before the humans returned to their settlement and collected reinforcements. Otherwise, he would be left waiting again. At the same time, who knew what enhancements they would make in that time? They were an inferior species to be sure, but their resourcefulness was something to commend them on. Could they make the Ishur even more powerful than it already was?

He was about to return to his terminal when a heavy pounding sounded from the other side of the door. Tea'va almost laughed at the humans' continued struggle to utilize interspace communications and their reliance on physical presence and force to get one another's personal attention. He flattened his expression and walked over to the hatch to open it.

The Heil'bek stood in front of him.

"Can I help you, Gabriel St. Martin?" Tea'va asked, a mixture of hate and admiration crossing through him.

"The General asked me to collect you," Gabriel said.

Tea'va felt a moment of discomfort. Had Shielle said something? Did they know? "Is there a problem?"

"Zoelle's team has finished the calculations. General St. Martin has called a meeting of senior officers to debrief before we make the slip. He wants you to be there."

"He does?" Tea'va said, surprised. He had been part of the meetings on the bridge before, but not the humans' more confidential discussions.

"You impressed the hell out of him, and me, with your flying. You've earned his respect, which isn't always an easy thing to do. You've also earned a little more of his trust."

"I don't see why he would trust me more. By defending the Ishur, I was preserving my own life as well." Tea'va smiled. The best way to invite more trust was to point out why it shouldn't be given.

Gabriel's eyes shifted back into the room, as though he were looking for something. Then he shrugged. "Be that as it may, you've proven yourself to be a valuable ally. Personally, I think you've earned it."

Tea'va studied Gabriel's face, trying to determine if he was going to be walking into a trap. There was no obvious attempt at deception there. In fact, was that pride? "Why do you look at me that way, Heil'bek?"

"When we met, you told me the Domo'dahm wanted to kill you because you're different. Because you're too human. Today, you helped prove that being more human is a benefit, not a malfunction. Now, come on. You don't want to keep the General waiting."

Gabriel turned away from him, taking a few steps down the corridor. Tea'va remained still. Being more human was the benefit? He made himself swallow the sudden fury he felt at the words. Being more human only made his body healthier, so that his bek'hai strengths did not deteriorate beneath him. He was better than the humans, better than the other bek'hai because of that. The thought that there was anything else in the human genome that had improved him was a disgusting one.

"Well?" Gabriel asked, noticing he wasn't following and looking back.

It took all of Tea'va's will to force himself to smile. "Yes. I am coming," he said, clenching his teeth once he was done, and at the same time feeling a crack beginning to form in his resolve. He had to forget about the fact that the Heil'bek was proud of him. He couldn't let that in. Wouldn't let that in.

Six days. He had to be patient for six more days. Then he would be in control of the Ishur once more. Then he would be the one returning to Earth to destroy the Domo'dahm.

Not the humans.

Him.

26

"Do you have·any advice for me on how best to present myself, Heil'bek?" Tea'va asked.

Gabriel glanced over at the bek'hai and shook his head. "Be yourself," he replied. "If you have an opinion, don't keep it to yourself. The General doesn't bring his officers together to kowtow to his ideas."

"Kowtow?"

"Be subservient. Kiss his ass."

Tea'va considered for a moment and then nodded tersely. "Yes, I understand."

Gabriel smiled. He was happy his father had asked him to retrieve Te'ava and to make him part of the briefing. The Dread had proven himself more than capable in the thick of battle, and his experience in real combat would be invaluable to them as they tried to figure out how to proceed, now that they would have some time in slipspace to prepare for whatever came next.

He glanced over at the bek'hai again, opening his mouth to speak before putting his head forward once more. He had already made three weak efforts to tell Tea'va he had seen him going into the cloning facility and to ask him why he had been there. He had stopped himself every time. There was something about the Dread that gave him pause. Something in his body language that made him uncomfortable. He couldn't quite put his finger on it yet, but for as pleased as he was his father had invited the Dread to sit in on their meeting, he was also feeling hesitant about it.

He liked Tea'va, more than he had expected he would be able to like one of the enemy. Maybe it was because they were both pilots, and respected one another for the times they had met as enemies in orbit above Earth. Maybe it was because they shared a mistrust in Zoelle, though Gabriel was finding his fading after recent events.

He wanted to have complete faith in him.

He didn't, and so he didn't speak up. He didn't want Tea'va to know what he had seen. Not yet. He needed time to speak with Zoelle first, to ask her to check in on the cloning factory. He would go with her, and with Sergeant Diallo, to make sure everything was as it should be. What other choice did he have? None of their crew knew anything about the factory to be able to spot any inconsistencies.

They reached the hangar, the small personnel hatch sliding open. Gabriel smiled when he saw the Magellan resting there, beaten but not broken. The ramp leading into her was down, with crates resting on either side. Some were old parts to be removed; others were replacement parts to be installed. Soon, they would bring both to the assemblers and be able to put Maggie back together again.

"You are meeting in your starship?" Tea'va asked, surprised.

"It was the General's idea," he replied. "To remind us what we're fighting for, and what we started with."

"I am interested to see the interior."

"I thought you would be."

Tea'va made the low hissing sound Gabriel identified with laughter.

They climbed the ramp into the ship. Gabriel breathed deeply once he was on her, appreciating the smell of grease and alloy, a scent that was missing from the Ishur. The debris had all been removed from the corridors, as had the body of Spaceman Dix, the soldier who hadn't secured himself in time and had been killed by the impact of the crash. Everything had also been scrubbed down, their reduced water supply replenished by the ample volume stored on the Ishur. She looked as good as she was going to get before they could get the new parts installed.

The rest of the officers were already present when Gabriel arrived. Theodore, Colonel Choi, Colonel Graham, Second Lieutenant Bale, and two enlisted, Sergeant Diallo and Sergeant Abdullah, along with Zoelle, Guy Larone, and Reza Mokri. He was surprised to see that Sarah Larone wasn't there as well.

"Major Gabriel St. Martin and pur'dahm Tea'va reporting, sir," Gabriel said, coming to attention.

"At ease, Major," Theodore said. "Mr. Tea'va, thank you for joining us."

"It is my honor, Dahm St. Martin," Tea'va said, bowing low.

"Why don't you and Gabriel take a seat over there?" Theodore said, pointing to two empty chairs near the rear of the table. "Then we can get started."

Gabriel led Tea'va to their seats. He stifled his laughter at how awkward the bek'hai was trying to sit in them. He was too tall for their basic chairs and looked uncomfortable when positioned.

"Now you know how I feel trying to sit on that command chair, Mr. Tea'va," Theodore said, laughing.

"Indeed, Dahm St. Martin," Tea'va replied, returning the laugh.

"In all seriousness, the reason I brought you all here is because, one, we just kicked the Dread hard enough in the ass to send them packing, and two, we need to be ready to do it again after we pick up the boys and girls back home. We're just about prepared to head into slipspace for, how long was it again, darlin'?"

"Twelve days," Zoelle replied. "Two slips."

"You're sure that is the fastest path?" Tea'va asked.

Gabriel looked over at him. Did he know something about that, or was he truly curious?

"Yes," Zoelle replied, not bothering to look at him. "The first slip will bring us out within fifteen AU of Earth."

"Close enough to send a quick message to our friends on the ground," Theodore said.

"The second will bring us to Chalawan," Zoelle finished.

"Any idea how long to get back to Earth after that?" Gabriel asked.

"I ran some estimates," Reza said. He looked a little better, having gotten a couple of hours to sleep. "Another eight days."

"So, twenty days total," Colonel Graham said. "A day or two to get our soldiers organized and boarded. Depending on how you look at it, either that isn't a lot of time, or it's an eternity."

"I'm sure Major Peters would prefer us back yesterday," Gabriel said.

"Twenty-two days," Theodore said. "Let's start with the basics. When we come out of the first slip, we need to get a message down to Earth to tell the rebels we're going to load up and come on back for them. Does our new ride have the capacity to do that at long range? Remember, we need to hit their antenna hard to be heard. That question is for you, Mr. Tea'va, or you, Juliet."

"I believe our array does have the capability you desire, Dahm St. Martin," Tea'va said. "However, does such a message not pose a risk if the Domo'dahm intercepts it? You will lose the element of surprise."

"Yeah, I've been thinking about that. The trouble is, if the ground forces don't know we're on our way, how can we organize an offensive? We don't have enough firepower up here, even with reinforcements, to hit the central Dread capital hard enough to destroy it."

"There is truth to your words, Dahm St. Martin; however, I question the capability of the ground forces. They have failed to organize efficiently up until now and with the Domo'dahm intensifying his efforts to destroy them, I fear you may leave such a message and find there is no one remaining to hear it save the Domo'dahm himself. In which case, the element of surprise grows even more valuable."

"So you think the rebels on the ground are going to lose?" Colonel Graham asked. "Not that I'm surprised, all things considered."

"Colonel," Theodore barked. "Mind yourself."

"I am not offended," Tea'va said, though Gabriel doubted that was true. "I speak only from experience. The rebels have had some success of late, but they are still greatly outnumbered and possess an extremely limited arsenal. Dahm St. Martin, I would caution against letting your emotions interfere with your tactical mind."

"Ha!" Theodore said. "You have a point there, Mr. Tea'va. Nobody here can argue your logic."

"Thank you, Dahm."

"At the same time, we're in this together. All of us. Sometimes, emotions have to win out. We live or die as one. Up here. Down there. I know that isn't tactically right, but it is right."

Gabriel noticed Tea'va's face tighten at the statement. He wasn't surprised the bek'hai didn't agree. Even so, Tea'va held his tongue.

"So we can send a message out," Theodore said. "Maybe our people can get in position in time, maybe they can't, but at least we can try."

"Agreed," Colonel Graham said.

"Next question. What can we do to get ourselves ready? By that I mean, for one, can we get the Magellan flying again?"

"She's pretty beat up, General," Guy said. "I've examined her systems. Most importantly, we need to replace the reactors, because they're completely spent. After that, we need to do something about the armor, the life support, pretty much every critical system. Some of it is minor, some of it not as much."

"That wasn't what I asked, Mr. Larone," Theodore said. "I know she's beat up, but I have a feeling the big bird is going to be staying in orbit, taking on some of the other big birds in the air. That means we need a smaller bird to drop our soldiers. Can we get her good enough to use as a ferry?"

"I think I can get her ready enough to make a drop planetside," Guy said. "Other than that, I don't know."

"Mr. Mokri, Zoelle, tell me more about these assemblers. You made a copy of the phase modulator in what? An hour?"

"Yes, General," Reza said.

"The duplicate was insufficient," Zoelle said. "It failed to handle the power requirements and will need further refinement."

"I understand, and you'll have time to work on that. What I need to know is what all we can produce in twenty-two days. Parts for the Magellan? A new power supply? More guns for the troops? That sort of thing."

"All of those, Dahm St. Martin," Tea'va said. "There are twenty-six assemblers on the Ishur. The items you are requesting are all minor as long as we have the resources available, and there is no reason to believe we do not. The scrap from the gi'shah you destroyed can also be used as raw material, along with other surplus."

"I like where it sounds as though you're going with this, Mr. Tea'va. What else are you suggesting?"

"We have two assemblers on board that are capable of building ships, Dahm St. Martin, both gi'shah, and ek'shah. They will need modification to utilize human pilots, but we should have materials and time to construct a few. We can also repair your damaged starships, including the Heil'bek's." Tea'va looked at Gabriel. "It would be my honor to soar with you."

"And mine," Gabriel said in return.

"That's what I want to hear," Theodore said. "Juliet, do you agree with Mr. Tea'va's assessment?"

"I will need to review the logs, but in general, yes."

"Excellent. Next question. Mr. Mokri, Mr. Larone, what about those modulation upgrades? The cascading shields are something, but I would prefer full coverage."

"I don't think that will be possible, sir," Reza said. "It's a limitation of the design. We might be able to give you a little more control over it, though. To at least try to direct the coverage."

"I'll take whatever you can give me."

"I'll work on it, sir."

"Good man."

"Sir," Colonel Choi said, speaking up for the first time. "With regard to our return to Chalawan."

"What about it?"

"General Cave wasn't very happy with us when we left."

"Heh. No, he wasn't. I think coming back in a bigger, better starship might change his mind."

"You don't think he'll court-martial us?"

"Him and what army? No. Alan will fall in line. He lost, we won. He isn't too old or too dumb to see that. Let's move on down to the nitty-gritty. Colonel Graham, I expect you to organize the ground forces that we'll be dropping in the Magellan. Let's get our ducks in a row there. I don't want any question regarding our plan of attack. Mr. Tea'va, I'm going to need your expertise here. You know how the Dread capital is organized better than any of us."

"Of course, Dahm St. Martin," Tea'va said.

"Okay then," Theodore replied, bringing up a map of Earth on the table. The dark splotch that was the main Dread fortress was visible from space. "We collected this data on our pass through. Let's come up with a plan. Nobody leaves this room until we do. Understood?"

"Yes, sir."

27

"WE'RE NEARING THE EXODUS, sir," Gabriel said, watching the terminal in front of him. He was getting the hang of recognizing the different shapes and symbols that made up the bek'hai language, deciphering them more quickly by the day.

"Great news," Theodore said, rolling his chair to the front of the bridge and rotating to look out the viewport. There was nothing in front of them but the blankness of slipspace.

Four days had passed since the Ishur had made the first of two slips, this one intended to carry her from the outer system the Dread called Pol'tek to the system near Ursae Majoris that they called home. For Gabriel, they had passed in an almost literal blur. As one of the highest ranking officers on the ship, he had been assigned the task of keeping an eye on the work being done to prepare for war. That included everything from check-ins on the status of the Magellan, to trips down to the assemblers to ensure everything was set up and coming along according to their designs. It had meant no time to do much of anything else, including his intended conversation with Zoelle about Tea'va's activity in down below.

Time had made that conversation seem less important, as Tea'va had been nothing but a model soldier over the past days. He had offered endless help to Gabriel, Theodore, Abdullah, and the others regarding the operational systems of the Ishur, and had even been able to assist Reza in nearing completion on the integration between interfaces. They had already managed to network half of the secondary weapons batteries on the fortress, and given another week they expected to have them all ready to go. Even better, Reza was making amazing progress on cooking up a solution to give them better control over the phase modulation, though he continued to be stumped by the mathematics surrounding full shield coverage.

"You're getting quite skilled, Heil'bek," Tea'va said. "We'll make a pur'dahm of you, yet."

The Dread was sitting behind Gabriel, watching him control the Ishur through an assembled duplicate of Reza's tablet. It allowed him to use his fingers to manage vectors and thrust, instead of needing to place his hands in a vat of goop to transfer electrical impulses through the organic subsystems.

"I'll pass," Gabriel replied. "Maybe we can make a human of you, instead?"

Tea'va hissed softly. "Perhaps."

The pur'dahm was more than a model soldier. Gabriel was beginning to think of him as a friend.

"Disembarking in twenty seconds," Gabriel said, watching the symbols. Eventually, the tablet would be able to convert it all to alphanumerics, but Reza hadn't gotten that far yet.

"Spaceman Locke, are we ready to transmit?" Theodore asked.

"Yes, sir," Miranda replied. "The message is loaded into the system. Transmitters are online and at full-power. From what Sarah told me, there's no way the rebels can miss this."

"Not unless every listening device on the planet is dead," Theodore replied. "I only wish the Dread weren't going to hear it, too."

"They'll be getting a nice earful, at least," Gabriel said.

"That they will."

"T-minus five seconds," Gabriel announced. "Four. Three. Two. One. Disengaging phase generators."

He slid his finger on the tablet and tapped a button. The ship responded immediately, vibrating softly as the spiked nacelles that surrounded the main structure began to fold back. He closed his eyes, feeling the shift in his body as they were gently released from the stream and dropped back into realspace, the blankness ahead convalescing into a sea of stars.

"Status?" Theodore said.

"We're right on target, sir," Gabriel replied.

"Good. Get us headed for the next insertion point and prepare for the next slip. Spaceman Locke, trigger the transmission."

"Yes, sir," Miranda said. "Transmitting... now."

Of course, there was no visible evidence of the transmission. Even so, they had just released a recorded message from Theodore St. Martin to the United Earth Rebellion, as he was calling it, giving them a time and place to be in eighteen days. Knowing the Dread would be listening in, he had also added a second message, in their language, just for them.

"Transmission sent, General," Miranda said.

"ETA to stream insertion?"

"Seven minutes, General," Gabriel said.

"How's our radar?"

"We're free and clear, sir."

"And too far out for the Domo'dahm to waste his energy trying to catch us," Tea'va said. "Especially now that he knows when you'll be coming back."

"I know you don't agree with this one, Mr. Tea'va," Theodore said. "We have to trust in our people to get their jobs done. If they do, it won't matter what your leader throws back at us. We'll be just as indestructible as they were when they took the planet from us."

"He is not my leader," Tea'va said sharply.

Theodore smiled. "My apologies, Mr. Tea'va. No, he isn't."

"Five minutes to slip," Gabriel said.

"Sir," Miranda said. "Something just came up on my terminal here, but I don't know how to read it."

"Mr. Tea'va, would you mind?" Theodore said.

"Of course, Dahm St. Martin."

Tea'va stood and circled to the back, where Miranda was sitting. Gabriel lifted his head to watch him, curious about what she had seen. When Tea'va reached her terminal, he glanced at the message, and then his eyes darted to Theodore and back again, almost too quickly to notice.

"It is nothing, General," he said. "A confirmation that the transmission has completed. Would you like to repeat it?"

"No. Once is enough. Thank you, Mr. Tea'va."

"My honor, Dahm St. Martin."

Tea'va returned to his position behind Gabriel as the countdown to the next slip continued.

"You're sure it was nothing?" Gabriel asked.

"Yes, Heil'bek. I am certain. A standard status message. That is all."

Gabriel nodded and returned his eyes to his terminal. He forced himself to concentrate, but something was eating at the corner of his thoughts. He had spent enough time with Tea'va to become familiar with his body language, and as much as he wanted to believe what he had seen was nothing, he didn't.

As he triggered the Ishur to re-engage its phase generators and return to the slipstream, he resolved himself to have that conversation with Zoelle after all.

And soon.

28

"WHAT DO YOU HAVE, Sergeant?" Donovan asked. He was crouched behind a small outcropping of stone, ten klicks east of downtown Austin and the rebel base.

"Call me Sarge if you have to use a rank," Kroeger said, lowering the pair of binoculars he was carrying. "I'm still not used to this enlisted shit."

"It makes organizing units easier to not have vigilantes roaming around. It's a matter of convenience as much as anything."

"Yeah, whatever. Anyway, to answer your question, it looks like we waited too long on this little scavenger hunt." He passed the equipment to Donovan. "Damn jackals are all over the place, even if they don't have a clue what they're doing."

Donovan raised the binoculars, looking at the Dread outpost two kilometers distant. It was the same one the Austin rebellion had hit earlier when they had captured the rifles and the tank but left the mechs behind. As he swept his eyes across it, he noticed the movement of people outside of the open entrances. They were dirty and disheveled and carrying old rifles. They didn't look like much of a threat.

"The mechs should be to the eastern side," Orli said.

Donovan glanced over at the clone. He was glad Ehri had convinced her to see his way of thinking, and to start using her original name to prevent confusion.

"Where?"

She pointed to a larger bulb to the left of the hub. "In there."

"That's what we came for," he said.

"It's a good thing you picked the Dread guns out before they showed up," Kroeger said. "It'll make things a lot easier."

"Bullets can still hurt us," Soon said. "And I've been shot at enough recently."

"Those are humans down there," Donovan said. "I'm not too keen on killing them."

"You're suggesting we go talk to them?" Ehri asked.

"Yeah. We don't want the property, just the mechs. They certainly can't use them. They probably don't even know how to open them up."

"Major, how much experience do you have with jackals?" Kroeger said.

"You're the only one I've encountered before," Donovan replied.

Kroeger smiled at that. "Trust me. I'm reasonable compared to most of those assholes."

"You don't think they'll hear us out?"

"I'll tell you what I think is going to happen. We're going to go down there. You're going to ask to speak to the man in charge. Someone will go in and talk to him, and maybe they'll lead you back, or he'll come out. You'll tell him you came for the mechs, and he'll say, what'll you give me for them. You'll politely explain that they aren't his, he'll respond that they most certainly are. You'll ask him what he wants, and he'll point to her." He pointed at Ehri. "Or her." He shifted his finger to Orli. "Or, maybe even him." He pointed at Soon. "Just depends on which way the wind blows for him. Of course, you'll say no, and before you know it, we'll be shooting at one another at point blank range. They'll die, we'll die, and the whole thing will be net zero because all of our pilots will be dead."

"You can't be serious," Soon said.

"I'm dead serious. How did we meet again?"

"Point made."

"You think we should just take what we want?" Donovan asked.

"Yup. It's us or them, Major, and these assholes gave up civility a long time ago."

"That doesn't mean we need to come down to their level."

"It damn well does if you want to come and go in one piece."

Donovan leaned back, eyeing his team. Kroeger, Ehri, Orli, Soon, Corporal Wilkins, and another of Colonel Knight's men, Corporal Hicks.

"Civil or not, they're still human," he said, trying to rally support. "If we get rid of the Domo'dahm, restore some sense of community, they could come back in line."

"No, they can't," Kroeger said.

"Why not? You did."

Kroeger laughed. "I'm good at faking it; that's all."

"Bullshit."

"Think what you want, Major."

"I agree with you, Major," Ehri said. "We are all God's children, and we have no right to kill one another without just cause."

"Agreed," Orli said.

Soon shrugged. "I don't think it's up for debate. You're in charge, sir. You tell me what to do, and I do it."

Donovan hesitated, a part of him wondering if he was about to make a mistake.

"Okay, we'll go down and talk to them. Kroeger, I want you to stay here."

"What?"

"You're a crack shot. If things start to look bad, I want you dropping them before they can drop us."

"Yes, sir."

"The rest of you, let's go."

Donovan stood. So did all of the others, save Kroeger. He adjusted his

Dread rifle, putting it on the ground beside him and swapping it out for an older human rifle that he had taken from the rebel's armory. Donovan had thought it odd he had brought the piece at the time, but it seemed the newly minted Sergeant had expected a problem like this.

"This thing'll drop a bear at half a kilometer," Kroeger said, catching him looking at it. "It'll pulp heads if that's what it comes to."

Donovan hoped it wouldn't come to that as he led his squad down the side of the incline and toward the outpost. They were still a ways out when the guards spotted them, yelling to one another and calling for reinforcements. Within seconds, the size of the jackal army had expanded from a handful to nearly fifty. Against six? He started to think he should have listened to Kroeger after all.

"Just stay right there," one of the guards said. A heavyset woman in a pair of torn pants, her head shaved. "Not another step, or we'll kill every last one of you."

Donovan stopped moving. His squad halted behind him.

"My name is Major Donovan Peters," he said. "Earth Rebellion."

"Major? You think you're some kind of soldier?" one of the other jackals said.

"Yes," Donovan replied. "I am a soldier. We're trying to get the Dread off our planet."

"Ha," the woman said. "That's a good one. How do you think you're going to manage that, pretty boy? You can't hurt the Dread. Everyone knows it."

"Really? Then where did all the Dread who ran this base go?"

"They left, I suppose. All the better for us."

"They left?" Donovan said. "What about the bodies? The clones?"

"Didn't' see them."

Donovan didn't know if the woman was being intentionally obtuse, or if she was outright lying. He didn't care. They couldn't afford to waste time here.

"There are some Dread mechs in that part of the base over there," he said, pointing toward the bulb. "The rebellion cleared this base. You're welcome to it, but we want those machines."

"We're welcome to it?" the other jackal said. "Who the hell do you think you are? You don't get to decide for us what is and isn't ours." He approached Donovan, looking angry and making Donovan wonder if Kroeger might get twitchy.

"You're right," Donovan said, putting up his hands. "My apologies. Look, the Rebellion is planning to move against the Dread capital in Mexico. We know how to pilot the machines in there, and we want to use them against the Dread. That's the only thing we came for."

"Well, Major," the woman said. "This is our home now. It was empty when we got here, so we have every right to it. You want something from our home, there's only one way to get it."

"Which is?"

She rubbed her fingers together in a timeless suggestion. Donovan stared at her for a moment. This was going down exactly how Kroeger had said. He should have listened.

"I'll bargain," Donovan said. "But only with whoever's in charge."

The woman smiled. She was missing half her teeth, and the other half didn't look very good. "I thought you might say that. Frank, go get the boss."

The man closest to the doors retreated into them, vanishing a moment later.

They stood facing one another in tense silence until Frank returned, moving ahead of who Donovan assumed was their leader. He was a lanky man with a thick mustache and wiry muscle, wearing a leather jacket over his bare chest.

"This better be important," he muttered as he left the safety of the compound. "I've got a lot more important shit to deal with than another one of those so-called rebellion armies. Poor saps. You'd think they'd be tired of dying for nothing by now."

He saw Donovan, stopped moving, and smiled. "My man Frank over there tells me that you have an interest in the contents of this here-"

He stopped talking when his head exploded, splashing the woman beside him with blood and bone.

Three more of the jackals were down before Donovan heard the first report of Kroeger's rifle.

What the hell?

He raised his weapon, barely getting a bolt off and into the jackal immediately ahead of him before they fired back. Then he was moving, rushing toward the enemy. If they were trapped at close range, it was better to make them risk hitting one another. He had to trust that Kroeger wouldn't hit him.

The night echoed with pops as the jackals overcame their shock and started shooting for real. Three more fell to Kroeger's sniper rifle, but Donovan barely had time to see it. He dove into the melee, firing the Dread rifle directly into flesh, filling the air around him with the smell of cooking meat and blood.

Screams followed the echo of gunfire as everything turned to chaos. Donovan didn't have time to think or time to plan. He simply reacted, letting his instincts to survive take over as he waded into the enemy, smashing one in the face with the rifle, bringing it back and shooting, grabbing one of the jackals from behind and throwing him just in time to let him take a bullet. He dropped the body, aiming and firing. He saw Kroeger take out two more.

He saw Soon ahead of him. There was blood on his hands, and he had dropped his weapon. He looked confused and frightened. He put his hands up as Donovan rushed toward him, trying to reach him. He shook his head, afraid. Donovan saw the jackal aiming his weapon at Soon. He watched that man's head vanish as well when Kroeger finally got him in his sights. Soon didn't drop his hands, though. He stood there, frozen, despite the fact that he was clear.

Donovan reached him, tackling him, pulling him down. He rolled over, quickly scanning the field. Where was Ehri? There. Orli? There. Wilkins? He didn't see Wilkins. There. On the ground. Was he dead?

Two more shots rang out. Then everything was silent.

Donovan counted five breaths before he moved, pulling himself to his feet. There were bodies all around him, half of which had been cut down by Kroeger. Ehri was up and moving, too. So were Orli and Hicks.

Kroeger was running down the slope toward them.

Donovan turned around, leaning down and putting out his hand to help Soon. Soon didn't take it.

He didn't move at all.

"Major," Kroeger said, his voice raspy and out of breath as he reached them. "Major. Shit. I'm sorry. I had to. I had to do it."

Donovan spun around, acting without thinking. His fist connected with Kroeger's jaw, hitting him hard enough that the older man fell back on his rear.

"What the hell was that?" Donovan shouted. "He didn't even have a chance to ask for anything."

Kroeger stayed down. "Major. I know you're pissed."

"You have no idea," Donovan said. He was shaking with anger. "Did you see him make a threatening move?"

"No, Major. But-"

"Soon is dead, damn it. So is Wilkins, and it's your damn fault."

"Major, wait," Kroeger said.

"We had four pilots. Now we have three, you asshole. I said-"

"Hold on there a minute," Kroeger shouted. "With all due respect Major, you don't know shit about shit. I've been out here. I do. That mustached asshole I killed? I know him. Shit, I thought that bastard was dead. He would have killed you. No matter what you said, no matter what he agreed to, he would have killed each and every one of you, and not quickly, and not in a good way. Go inside, Major. Step in and see. I bet the evidence is just waiting in there."

Donovan clenched his jaw. His head was pounding, his entire body numb. Kroeger's words beat through it, giving him pause.

"Who was he?" he asked.

"His name was Myles Sarkova. He used to be part of another group called the Innocents. We ran together for two years. Major, I never said I was a good man, but that guy made me look like a damn cherub. Last time I saw him he was dead in a ditch. At least, I thought he was." Kroeger spit on the ground. "Shit. If I had known it was him, I would have never let you go down to parlay."

Donovan stood in silence for a moment, feeling a sudden wave of guilt crash over him.

"It was my fault," he said, and he believed it. "I should have listened to you in the first place."

"Yeah, you should've," Kroeger said. "But I get why you didn't. I felt the way you do once, before I learned better. If we win this war, if we free the Earth from the grip of the Dread, that doesn't mean everything goes back to being just like before. Not right away. It may seem crazy, but it will get harder before it gets easier. I guarantee it."

Donovan might not have agreed five minutes ago. Now he simply nodded before glancing over at Soon one last time, using all of his strength to keep himself together.

"We have three pilots," he said, a chill running through him in response to the words. "We can take three mechs."

Then he started walking, certain he was as big of a piece of shit as he felt like, but not knowing what else to do.

29

DONOVAN CHECKED HIS SENSORS, keeping an eye out for the familiar and at the same time unwanted display of more than their three targets on the HUD, happy to find that it remained clear.

His mind wandered as he steered the mech back toward Austin, leading Ehri and Orli as they returned to the rebel base with the added weaponry, bringing the count of functional armors to five. It didn't sound like much, and after what had happened it didn't feel like much, but Donovan would take what he could get.

At least Soon hadn't died for nothing.

Had he?

Donovan had dealt with the loss of soldiers before. He had dealt with the loss of loved ones as well. His mother. Diaz. Matteo. He was used to people dying around him. That was the world he was born into. The world he had grown up in. Even so, Soon's death was lingering, weighing on him like the mech he was riding in.

It was his fault the man was dead. His fault his wife would never have a chance to see him again. His fault they would never have the child they had wanted. He should have listened to Kroeger and killed the jackals before the jackals killed Soon. But how could he have done that in good conscience? How could he have just assumed the humans were bad when they were all supposed to be fighting on the same side?

He didn't know, but he still felt like he had made the wrong call. There was no going back in life, only forward, and so he was doing his best to shake it off and stay focused. It was just too new. Too raw. It was a struggle.

"Austin Actual, this is Rebel One. Do you copy?" Donovan said. They were getting close enough to the base their shorter range signal should have made it through to the loop station.

"This is Austin Actual," Colonel Knight replied. "I hear you, Major. What's your status?"

Donovan opened his mouth, closed it, thought for a second, and then spoke. "We had a run in with a jackal pack," he said. "Some group Kroeger said was called the Innocents. We have three mechs, but we took a pair of casualties."

He could hear the quiver in the Colonel's voice when she answered. "Acknowledged, Major. I'll expect a full debriefing when you return."

"Of course, ma'am."

There was silence for a moment, and then Colonel Knight came back on. "Who did we lose?"

"Corporal Wilkins, and Captain Kim," Donovan choked out.

"Oh. Donovan, I'm sorry," Colonel Knight replied. "Damn it."

"My sentiments exactly."

"What's your ETA to Checkpoint Alpha?"

"Fifteen minutes," Donovan replied. "I'll." He paused as his sensors picked something up to the north. "Actual, hold that thought. I'm getting something on my sensors." He looked at the HUD. A single small symbol had appeared there. "Rebel Two, do you know what that is?"

"Negative, Rebel One," Ehri replied. "But it's multiplying."

"Actual, have the scouts reported signs of a new Dread assault group assembling?"

"No, Major, they haven't. If you're picking up something new, we need to know what it is."

"Affirmative. Rebel Four, take Sergeant Kroeger and Corporal Hicks back home. Rebel Two, you're with me. Let's go see what we're dealing with."

"Roger," Ehri replied.

"Actual, I'm going to take Rebel Two and scout out the situation."

"Affirmative, Rebel One. You're going to be back out of short wave communications range. Do not engage. I repeat, do not engage. Find out what your sensors are picking up and get back in range to report. Understood?"

"Yes, ma'am," Donovan said, bringing his mech to a stop and turning it to the north. Orli continued toward Austin, while Ehri fell in beside him.

They headed out at a fast walk, the mech shuddering slightly each time a heavy foot landed on the ground. The targets on the HUD were still multiplying, growing from a single mark to a dozen, for a dozen to a hundred, and from a hundred to still more. The sensors weren't giving much indication of what was out there. While the Dread mechs would paint as friendlies, clones registered as unknowns. Even so, the size of the force suggested the Dread had landed another army somewhere else, and they were making their way south to the city.

"Soon died fighting," Ehri said. "It was an honorable death."

He felt a sudden tension fill him at the words. She always seemed to know what he was thinking. "I got him killed."

"You led him into battle. That's what commanders do."

"I made the wrong decision."

"And yet he believed in you and supported that decision. Give him the same option again, and he would have done the same."

"Do you really believe that?"

"Yes. You're a soldier, too, Major. Wouldn't you do the same?"

He sighed audibly. "Yes. I would. Without hesitation."

"Then why are you blaming yourself?"

"To be honest, I don't know. Maybe I feel like I should. Maybe because he survived all of that time in space, he survived our rescue. He made it all the way here." He paused. "I'm so sick of the violence. The death. The war."

"That is natural. It is also not a reason for guilt."

Donovan considered it. "I know you're right, logically. Emotionally? I'm struggling with that."

"Also natural. Just try to remember that he trusted you and he believed in you and the decision you made."

"Okay. I'll try." He checked the HUD again. "Looks like our targets are just beyond this incline. Let's go in low and slow and try not to give ourselves away. We aren't picking up any large assets, but you never know."

"Roger."

They slowed to a walk, crouching their mechs and lifting the feet only a foot off the ground before more tenderly bringing them down. It took a few extra minutes to near the crest of the incline this way, but it also prevented the shapes on the sensors enough time to react to their approach.

Donovan eased his mech forward, taking a few more steps up the hill. As he did, he began to clear the obstruction, starting to gain visual on the area ahead.

He saw the rear of the column first. A few lines of soldiers, marching forward at a light jog. He stared at them for a moment before taking another step forward, gathering more height and becoming able to look further down the line. He felt his heart jump as he adjusted his view, zooming in on the scene below.

The uniforms were all wrong for Dread clones. These were olive green, drab and simple. Their wearers weren't identical either. They were male and female, dark and light, old and young. They were all on foot, each and every one of them, marching double-time in a column that had to be nearly four thousand strong.

At the front of the line was an older man with a chiseled face, marching along with the rest of the troops. The only reason he stood out at all was because he was carrying a metal pole. Affixed to the end of it was a shred of cloth, a field of stars amongst a series of red and white stripes printed on it.

"Rebel Two, run back to comm range," Donovan said, barely able to control his sudden elation. "Tell Colonel Knight that General Parker and his rebels have arrived."

30

DONOVAN WAS WAITING FOR General Parker as the front of the army started climbing the hill. He left the confines of the mech, opening the cockpit and climbing out to stand on the foot of the machine, his hand raised in greeting.

The General lowered his flag as he neared, a big smile piercing his otherwise rough face as he stared up at the Dread armor. He said something to the woman next to him, and the army continued onward, flowing around Donovan and continuing on, the soldiers closest to him waving and saluting but otherwise remaining quiet. It was obvious they had a lot of experience avoiding notice.

"General Parker," Donovan said, jumping down from the foot and greeting the man with a salute. He had never actually seen the General before, but the hardware on the jacket he was wearing made it clear who he was.

"And you are, soldier?" Parker asked, returning the salute.

"Major Donovan Peters, sir. Mexico."

Somehow, the General's smile grew even larger. "Major Peters," he said. "The man who started the Dread downfall. It's an absolute honor."

"I'm just doing my part, sir. You've been at this for much longer than me. The honor is mine."

"Humble, too. I like it. We can share in the honor then, Major." He looked up at the mech behind Donovan. "That yours?"

"It's the rebellion's, yes, sir."

He moved forward and put his hand on it. "I've been running from these things for most of my life," he said softly, the smile vanishing. "I never thought I'd get to touch one. I never thought we'd capture one."

"We lost some good people getting our hands on them," Donovan said.

"I'm sure you did, Major. We've lost too many good people. Too damn many."

"I sent my second back to Austin to inform Colonel Knight of your arrival. I expect things to get a little interesting once all of yours start pouring in."

"Not enough space?"

"More than enough space, sir. We've got the city locked up tight. The Dread have failed to break it twice already. What I mean is that we'll have a big enough army to launch an offensive."

"That's the idea, Major."

Donovan pointed up to the shoulder of the mech. "Can I give you a ride? It's not the most comfortable perch, but it'll make a statement."

The grin returned to the General's face. "I like the way you think, Major," he said, holding up the flag again.

They climbed the mech. Donovan slipped back into the cockpit, while General Parker moved to the shoulder of the machine. When he got there, he raised the flag high. Then Donovan put the armor in motion, turning it around and bringing it back down the hill, careful not to hit any of the soldiers as he carried the General toward the front of the line.

It was a surreal experience. He could see the rebels around him. He could see the way their faces changed as they passed, carrying the flag through the line and toward the front. He could sense their excitement and

152

their enthusiasm, even as they did all they could to keep a low profile.

They reached the front of the line, continuing on. Donovan could see Ehri's mech in the distance now, facing him and waiting. He could see Austin behind her, its mangled skyline taking on a new beauty in the dim light of the night sky.

He kept going, a new sense of hope filling him. He imagined it would infect all of them soon, as the General's forces began to mingle with theirs, and the plans for an assault were arranged. For fifty years they had been trampled on or used, taken or murdered, left so broken that all vestiges of civilization had been lost.

Not anymore.

Donovan reached Ehri. She reversed course, turning back toward Austin, syncing her mech's motion to his and helping him lead the troops home.

"Austin Actual, this is Rebel One," Donovan said. "We're on our way in."

"Roger, Rebel One," Colonel Knight said. "I've already given the orders to get a welcoming party going. Fresh uniforms and Dread for as many as we can equip."

"I'm sure the General will appreciate it, ma'am. ETA-"

Donovan was interrupted by a sudden burst of static over the comm, followed by a whine that registered loudly enough it hurt his ears.

"What the hell?" he said, wincing as the internal speakers squealed again. A new symbol appeared on his HUD, and then the noise normalized.

"Earth Rebellion," a voice said through the comm. "This is General Theodore St. Martin, New Earth Alliance. Heh. New Earth. Forget that. Earth Alliance."

Donovan felt his heart skip. General St. Martin? He was still alive. More importantly, he was close enough to send them a message. He reacted without thinking, leaning forward and hitting a switch to activate the external speakers so General Parker and the others could hear it.

"This message is being broadcast with all the juice this here starship can muster, which I've been told is quite a lot. We're taking a risk to send it because we're hitting the entire spectrum, which means the Dread are going to be hearing this, too. You know what? I don't give a damn, and you shouldn't either. Let them hear. Let them know.

"This message is being transmitted from a starship called the Ishur. You think that's a funny name? That's because it used to belong to the Dread. It was one of their fortresses. Now it's ours."

General St. Martin paused, as though he had known how they would react to the statement. More than one soldier on the field was close enough to Donovan's mech to hear the message, and they forgot themselves when they did, whooping and cheering at the news.

"We're on our way back to our home system to pick up the rest of our people. To pick up our soldiers. To arm them and get them ready. Then we'll be on our way back here to you. Back to Earth to reclaim what's ours. To challenge the Domo'dahm of the bek'hai for the right to this planet. If you can hear this, you need to get ready. You need to be prepared. Whoever you are, wherever you are, if you can get to Mexico, get there. Fifteen days from now, the Ishur will be back in Earth's orbit, and the battle for our freedom will begin. Fifteen days from now, the Dread occupation will end.

"You want to be part of it? Get to Mexico. Fight with everything you have. Fight with your bare hands if you have to. Show these alien coullions that we never gave up. We never lost hope. Show them that they'll never be rid of us. Never be free of us. Never have this planet to themselves. This is our home. Our Earth. You hear that, Rorn'el? Our planet. I'm coming, you son of a whore. You've got fifteen days to enjoy my planet, and then I'm tossing you and yours out on your ass. If you're with me, be in Mexico and be ready.

"General St. Martin, out."

31

DOMO'DAHM RORN'EL SHOOK WITH anger, his entire body quivering as he clutched the sides of his throne, holding them so tightly that his fingers scraped along the lek'shah. He had sent two domo'shah to confront Gr'el or Tea'va and the Ishur.

Gr'el or Tea'va.

Not a human.

Not Theodore St. Martin.

"What of the domo'shah?" he said softly.

"Domo'dahm?" Orish'ek said. "I did not hear."

"What of the domo'shah?" he shouted. "The two ships I sent to destroy the Ishur. What of them?"

"They have not returned, Domo'dahm."

"I am aware of that, Orish'ek. Were they destroyed?"

"I do not know, Domo'dahm. We have had no word from them. If the humans have taken the Ishur, we should assume that they were."

"How?" Rorn'el said. "How does this happen? Their ship had no weapons. No defenses. How did they survive? How did they capture the Ishur? It defies all logic."

He hissed softly, trying to release his frustration. He knew how. There was only one reasonable explanation. Zoelle. The un'hai. It had to be. The clones had always been willful, but lately, they had started becoming more and more troublesome. First, there had been Ehri, who had tricked him into allowing her freedom to study the humans. Then there was Orli, a Dahm of a research team who had stolen one of the few clone pilotable transports they had and taken it to the rebel base in Austin and ultimately helped them attack one of their bases and claim the resources there.

He forced himself to release his hands as they began to hurt from the pressure. He hissed louder, trying to deal with his anger. Zoelle. It had to be. Both Ehri and Orli were connected to Tuhrik at one time, as was she. His splice brother had done something to them. He had altered them somehow.

He reached up and clutched at Juliet's rosary. She and Tuhrik had been close. Maybe too close. They had both begged him to change the course of the bek'hai, to integrate more completely with humankind. Tuhrik had insisted it was the only way they would survive in the centuries to come. He knew Tuhrik never agreed with his desire to exterminate the humans, but he never believed it would come to this.

"How could you?" he whispered.

Tuhrik had betrayed him. Juliet had betrayed him. She had taken the freedom he offered and used it against him. She had claimed to want peace while preparing her people for war.

"Domo'dahm, what are your orders?" Orish'ek said. "How should we respond to this declaration?"

"Respond? How else will we respond? If the humans are coming here to fight, then we will prepare to meet them."

"Domo'dahm, they took the Ishur. For all we know, they destroyed the other two domo'shah. We can't sit idle and wait for them to come. If they have developed a new weapon, we will be unprepared for it."

"You heard the human, General Theodore St. Martin," Rorn'el said.

"You heard how he threatened me. How he challenged me. I will not back down. I will not respond with fear. You heard that he is returning to his home system? Pit'ek will be there ahead of him. He will find his home in ruin. He will find his people dead. The first victory will be mine, as will the last."

"Yes, Domo'dahm," Orish'ek said.

"That does not mean we won't prepare for war. Send messages out to our forces. Tell the Dahms of the precepts to bring their domo'shah into orbit to wait. Order the consolidation of our ground forces back to the capital. The rebels in Austin have been difficult to dig out, but now we will not have to. They will come to us, and they will die."

"Yes, Domo'dahm. It will be done."

"Have Sor'ek dur Kan'ek brought before me. I require him to trace all of the un'hai who have been produced so that we can identify those who may have been tainted by Tuhrik."

"Domo'dahm?"

"He changed them, druk'shur. He gave his loyalty to her over me."

"Who, Domo'dahm?"

Rorn'el hissed loudly. "Juliet St. Martin, and by extension the humans. He was a traitor. A legri'shah laying in wait."

"Then, would it not be wise to exterminate all of the un'hai?" Orish'ek asked. "If they are working against you, then they should not be permitted to exist."

The Domo'dahm squeezed the rosary. For as angry as he was, there was still a part of him that hesitated to let go. To destroy all of the un'hai would mean losing her forever.

"No. Only those with ties to Tuhrik. The others have shown no inclination toward deceit."

The doors at the end of the antechamber slid open. A drumhr hurried in, crossing the distance to the throne.

"Domo'dahm," he said, falling to his knees at the base of it.

"You were not requested, drumhr," Orish'ek said.

"I have important news, Domo'dahm."

"Rise and present it," Rorn'el said.

The bek'hai stood, keeping his head bowed as he spoke. "We have received an encrypted message from the Ishur," he said.

"What kind of message? Who sent it?"

"It is a data file, attached to the humans' signal but transmitted separately. It was not signed, Domo'dahm, but it was decrypted using current keys."

"And the contents?"

"It appears to be schematics pulled from the Ishur's assemblers. A device of some kind that the humans call a Darkspace Phase Modulator. It was saved to the databanks by Zoelle dur Tuhrik."

"A Darkspace Phase Modulator? Do we know what it does?"

"Not yet, Domo'dahm, as our science team has just started examining it. They believed it was important enough to tell you right away, as the human name suggests it may be a shield of some kind."

Rorn'el felt his anger begin to fade. A shield? That would explain how they had survived this long. But how had they taken the Ishur? At the moment, it didn't matter. At least someone on the ship was still loyal to him and had managed to feed him valuable information, perhaps at risk of their own life. If he ever discovered who they were, he would be sure to honor them.

"Orish'ek, send a message to Pit'ek, along with the schematics. Perhaps he can find a use for this device as well."

"It will be done, Domo'dahm."

"Drumhr, you are dismissed."

The bek'hai stood, still keeping his eyes on the floor. "Yes, Domo'dahm," he said as he retreated from the room.

Rorn'el leaned back in his seat, feeling his tension release a little. Perhaps there were a few traitors in their midst, but he was the Domo'dahm, and he was still in control. It would take more than a few un'hai to change that.

He lifted the rosary, holding it up in front of his face. This was the betrayal that stung the most. He knew she wanted him to spare her people, but he had never believed she would turn to violence to achieve it. Was her God not a peaceful being?

He closed his hand around the crucifix at the end of the beads and pulled forward, yanking it from his neck. The rope snapped, the wooden balls rolling from it, clattering to the ground and scattering on the floor. The other pur'dahm in the room were startled by the sudden noise and the appearance of the baubles, but they did not remark.

He squeezed the crucifix harder, pressing down on it until it finally cracked and splintered, breaking in half and dropping it to the floor.

"You cannot destroy me, Juliet St. Martin," he said quietly to the remains of the rosary. "This is my Earth. Not your mate's. Not your people's. Mine."

32

"HEY, MIRANDA, HOLD UP."

Gabriel jogged up as she turned around, smiling when she saw him.

"Gabriel. Is everything okay?"

"To be honest, I'm not sure yet."

"Oh?"

"I've been trying to catch up to you since we went back into slipspace yesterday. It's been hard to find a few minutes to grab you in person."

"In person? What for?"

Gabriel put his hand on her arm, guiding her down the corridor, positioning himself close to keep his voice low.

"Yesterday, on the bridge. The symbol that came up that you couldn't read. Do you remember what it looked like?"

"Hmmm. I'm not sure. Why?" She paused to think, and then her expression changed. "Do you think Tea'va was lying about it?"

"I don't know. I hope not. I caught him looking over at my father before he said it was nothing. There was something in his eyes that I didn't like. Also, when I went down to look for Reza and Zoelle a few days ago, I saw him heading into the cloning facility when he was supposed to be in his quarters."

"Maybe he had a good reason?"

"Maybe. I don't want to think he can't be trusted. I like him. But I also can't ignore what I see. He was willing to turn on his own kind, how can we know for sure he won't turn on us? Anyway, I was going to take the symbol to Zoelle and get her opinion on it."

"How do you know you can trust her? She and Tea'va don't like one another."

"I know. Maybe I can't. I mean, I want to trust her, because like you said, whether she is really my mother or not she's still a conduit to her, and I'm eager for a chance to talk to her about her, instead of about phase modulators and assemblers. That doesn't mean that she might tell me it means something it doesn't and I wouldn't know the difference." He laughed. "It's hard to work all of this stuff out when the people you depend on the most are the ones you trust the least. Anyway, if we have enough time I can try to have Reza verify, but the clones are due to mature tomorrow, and if he did something to them-"

"It would be too late."

"Yes."

"Maybe I should come with you and try to describe it to Zoelle?"

"Do you have time right now?"

"Yes."

"Good. She should be down with the assemblers, working on the modulators. From what I hear, we've managed to produce three of them so far that can hold up to the power flow."

"How many do we need to cover the ship?"

"Three hundred. This is a big ship."

She laughed. "You can say that again. It's weird having so much space. It almost feels too big sometimes."

"You should have seen the legri'shah."

"Legri'shah?"

Gabriel realized he had never had time to talk to her about his adventure in the belly of the Ishur. "Let's walk. I'll tell you the story on the way."

They headed down the corridor, going to one of the transport beams. Gabriel started to tell her about how the mothers had ambushed him, and how he had wound up in the legri'shah's den. They had nearly reached the edge of the hub leading to the beam when Tea'va emerged from it.

"Ah, much honor, Heil'bek," Tea'va said, seeing them. "And to you, Spaceman Locke." He dipped his head slightly.

'Tea'va," Gabriel said, wondering where the bek'hai was coming from. He couldn't think of a way to ask that didn't seem suspicious. "Have you seen Wallace around?"

"Wallace?"

"My dog. He's been sniffing his way around the ship lately, trying to find something edible, I guess."

It was a lie. A simple one. Wallace had been quarantined to quarters since he had panicked at the sight of a transport beam and led Daphne on an extended chase across the ship.

"No. I haven't seen your creature, Heil'bek. Would you like me to help you search for it?"

"That's okay. I'm sure you have better things to do. I was just asking."

"Of course. My regrets that I have not seen him."

"I'll see you later, Tea'va," Gabriel said.

"As you say, Gabriel," Tea'va replied, bowing again before continuing on his way.

"I don't know if it's just the power of suggestion or what, but that interaction gave me the chills," Miranda said.

"All the more reason to keep going forward with this," Gabriel said. "I trust your instincts."

"I wish you didn't have to. I don't like this at all."

"Me neither, but it is what it is."

They took the transport beam down to the lower decks and then made the long walk to the assemblers using the secondary passage that It'kek had shown him. Unlike the last time he had been there, the assemblers were all in use now, each of them humming and groaning as they collected the raw materials and recombined them into something else. A few of the Magellan's crew were there to monitor the progress, including Sergeants Abdullah and Hafizi, along with a contingent of the clone soldiers they had captured in the initial attack.

"Major St. Martin," Abdullah said as Gabriel and Miranda approached him, coming to attention. "What brings you down this way, sir?"

"Relax, Sergeant," Gabriel replied. "I'm looking for Zoelle."

"Assembler number twelve, sir," Abdullah replied.

"Thank you."

They made their way down the line, to the same assembler Gabriel had found her in the last time he had come down. She was leaned over a terminal, an updated version of the phase modulator resting on the table behind her.

"Zoelle," Gabriel said, getting her attention.

She smiled warmly. "Gabriel. It's good to see you." Gabriel returned the smile. He felt it from the way she said it. "What can I help you with?"

"I need a bek'hai symbol translated," he said.

"You came all the way down here for that? Why didn't you ask Tea'va to do it?" Her face changed as she made the connection. "What's going on?"

"Maybe nothing. Maybe I'm paranoid."

"It isn't like a St. Martin to be paranoid," she said. "If you think it's something, it probably is."

"Miranda, can you describe the symbol for her?"

"It came up on the bridge communications terminal," Miranda said. "It didn't have a translation, so I didn't know what it meant. It was something like two parallel lines with a circle in the middle, and then two circles, a line, and two more circles."

"Interesting," Zoelle said. "What did Tea'va say about it?"

"He said it meant the transmission was complete."

"He was not lying."

Gabriel could feel his entire body relax at the statement. He hadn't realized how tense he was about the whole thing. "I'm happy to hear it."

She lowered her voice, glancing around the small chamber as she did. "He was also not telling you the entire truth," she added. "What color was the text?"

"Orange," Miranda said.

"An encrypted message," Zoelle said.

"The message we sent wasn't encrypted," Gabriel said, feeling the tension begin rushing back.

"Yes, I know."

"That son of a-"

"Gabriel, wait," Zoelle said, her voice remaining quiet. "Just because he didn't tell you someone sent a second message doesn't mean he is responsible for sending it."

"What are you saying?"

"Why would Tea'va send a message to the Domo'dahm?" Zoelle said. "The Domo'dahm wanted him dead before he helped you."

Gabriel considered it. There was no good reason for Tea'va to do something like that.

But if he didn't, then who did?

33

TEA'VA HURRIED THROUGH THE back passages of the Ishur, his mind racing as he worked to adjust his strategy.

"Druk'shur, Shielle," he muttered to himself, angry. Trust. Risk. Why did he always wind up on the wrong end of it?

He had been trying to find an excuse to sneak back down to the cloning facility for hours, desperate to confront the un'hai clone and find out what exactly she had been thinking, sending an encrypted message to the Domo'dahm on the back of the humans' message to their brethren.

She had betrayed him; that much was clear. She had chosen the Domo'dahm over him. What he didn't understand was why?

He had offered her everything, just as he had offered it to Zoelle. Power. Control. A standing in the bek'hai ranks that was beyond what any lor'hai had achieved. There had to be some kind of malfunction with the un'hai. Bad programming that made them do things which defied logic. He couldn't comprehend her reasons, and he didn't care.

He would find out what she had sent to the Domo'dahm, and then he would kill her.

He had lied to the humans, telling them it was nothing. He thought he had gotten away with it until he ran into Gabriel and the female, Miranda, in the corridor. He saw the way she was looking at him. Suspicious. Uncomfortable. He had worked so hard to earn the Heil'bek's trust, and Shielle had forced him to break it.

It was discouraging, but not the end of the world. He could recover from that lie. He was sure of it. They would ask questions, and he would answer them. He had always been ready for Shielle to double-cross him, only not this soon, and not in this way. It was infuriating.

He had to reach her before they did. If they questioned her first, she would have the opportunity to implicate him, to blame him for her actions. Perhaps they wouldn't believe her, but it would further any doubt they already held in their minds. And with only one more day until the clones matured, he couldn't afford for them to be watching him closely or limiting his movements out of their mistrust.

He slipped across a corridor and into another back passage, nearly colliding with a drek'er on the way by. He shoved the small clone aside, knocking him into the wall with a grunt. He was practically running now, racing to reach her before they did.

Gabriel would ask Zoelle what the symbols meant. She would tell them, and then they would suspect. Not him, at least. Zoelle was smart enough to know he wouldn't go crawling back to the Domo'dahm. No, they would guess it was her. She was an un'hai, the highest ranking clone on board after Zoelle herself. When they did, they would confront her, as he aimed to do now.

The race was on.

He came out of the passage right beside the transport beam, stepping in and heading down, coming out and skipping back into the hidden maintenance corridors. He didn't want her to see him coming. He didn't want anyone else to see him either. The only reason he was rushing now was because the human, Reza Mokri, had cornered him and asked him for help with more of the translations, tying him up for hours. It was work for a regular drumhr, not a pur'dahm, but he had forced himself to remain patient to avoid question. What other choice did he have?

He moved gracefully through the darkness, bypassing two more of the drek'er on his way. He reached the access hatch nearest to the front of the cloning facility, crouching as it slid open. He scanned the area, making sure it was clear, before sprinting across the distance and into the front.

He didn't slow as he went deeper inside, navigating the layout and heading for the sleeping quarters near the back. He was certain she was in hers. Where else would she go? She had no allies on the ship.

He entered the corridor, slowing his pace as he did so that he could approach more quietly. He eased himself through the hall, bypassing the other empty rooms in a direct line to hers. He had been here before, when he first decided he would need her to get what he wanted.

He reached her quarters, pressing himself against the entrance and trying to listen through to the other side. He didn't hear anything. He put his hand on the control surface to see if it would open for him. He was surprised when it did.

He leaned over, peering inside. The sparse room was vacant.

Where was she?

He paused, looking back over his shoulder, and then returning his attention to her room. He needed to know what she had sent. Could he retrieve it from her terminal? He stood there for a few seconds, considering, and then finally deciding against it. He had to catch up to her first, to ensure her silence. He could worry about the details later.

He retreated from the area, rushing back to the main facility. He made his way through it in search of her, checking each of the functional spaces in turn and growing more frustrated by her disappearance. Was it possible Gabriel had caught up to her ahead of him? Was he too late? He felt a wave of panic at the thought but forced it aside. The humans weren't that intelligent.

He made his way into the maturation hall. The caretakers were there, moving from chamber to chamber, checking on the contents. The clones had grown substantially since the last time he had been there. They were fully adult, nearly ready to emerge. They no longer thrashed and writhed in the nutrient bath. Instead, they sat quietly, their eyes closed.

Tea'va felt a new wave of panic. That was wrong. What was happening here?

"You," he said, grabbing the shoulder of one of the caretakers. "Why are they still?"

The clone pulled himself away but didn't speak.

"What did you do, Shielle?" Tea'va said, moving to one of the capsules and peering in. He touched the transparency, bringing up the readings. They were normal. How? Nothing about this was normal.

A caretaker approached him, weapon in hand. Tea'va almost laughed. They would always try to protect the clones. He backed away from the chamber, and the caretaker lowered the weapon.

"They're dead," Tea'va said to him. "Can't you see that? She faked the readings so that she could kill them."

The caretaker didn't react. He went to the capsule and put his hand to it, checking the same data before moving away.

Dead. Shielle had terminated them all to keep them out of the hands of the humans. No. Out of his hands. If he had any question she was sided with the Domo'dahm before; he was certain now.

"When I find you, I'll kill you," he hissed.

"Not if I kill you first," Shielle replied.

34

SHE APPEARED FROM BEHIND one of the capsules, a caretaker's weapon in her hand.

"Why?" Tea'va said. "I trusted you."

"You are a fool, Tea'va. You have always been a fool. You think that you fail over and over again because of circumstance. It isn't the universe that is wrong. It is you. I am a loyal subject to the Domo'dahm, and I will not let you challenge him, either alone or with the humans."

"Fool? I'm not the fool. I am superior. The future of the bek'hai."

"You are too human to be the future of the bek'hai."

"Oh? And what of you, Shielle? You are an un'hai. Why do you not care for the humans like Zoelle does?"

"Her programming is wrong. I don't know how it happened. Someone altered her, and who knows how many others of our type."

"She believes she is the real Juliet St. Martin."

"She believes it, but it cannot be true. The pur'hai is long deceased."

"How do you know?"

"You don't know enough about clones, pur'dahm. You can not make a clone without destroying the source."

"Maybe that isn't true. Surely Zoelle would know this."

"It is always true. She should know it but has forgotten. It is in her programming. I am sure of it."

Tea'va considered it. How many un'hai were there that believed they were the real Juliet St. Martin? How and why did they believe it?

Did it even matter in the end?

"I think you are the fool," Tea'va said, his eyes monitoring the area between him and Shielle. "You should have killed me first, and then spoken to my corpse."

She shot at him then. He was too quick for her, and he dove aside as the bolt struck the ground behind where he had been standing.

"You are no warrior," he said, rolling to his feet and charging toward her. "You are no bek'hai."

She adjusted her aim, firing again. The bolt hit him in the thigh, some of the impact reduced by his gori'shah. He grunted in pain as it began to burn, but didn't slow. She had ruined his plans to take over the Ishur. She had fooled him with her falsehood. He was angry. Furious. How could it be that the humans were the only ones who were honest?

She shot him again as he slammed into her, knocking her backward, throwing her to the floor. The weapon tumbled from her hand as they landed on the ground together. Tea'va could feel the burning in his chest, a close-range strike that was sure to have done damage. He knew by instinct that it wasn't fatal.

"What did you send to the Domo'dahm?" he asked, putting his hand to her throat and squeezing.

She writhed beneath him, trying to push him off. She didn't have close to enough strength to do it.

"What does it matter to you?" she said softly. "You are as dead as I am."

"Your bolts will not kill me," he replied.

"Perhaps you will wish they had."

He didn't know what she meant. He didn't care. He squeezed again. "What did you send? What did you tell him? That druk Theodore already told him when he would be coming. I've never experienced such tactical stupidity before."

"You'll never know. More importantly, the humans will never know. I am loyal to the Domo'dahm, and to the bek'hai. We aren't all traitors, Tea'va."

"I'm not a traitor. I seek to rule the bek'hai so that our kind can flourish. The Domo'dahm wants to keep us as we are. He doesn't want us to evolve as we must, even as he says he does. That is incompatible with our future. I thought you understood that."

"The humans would allow you to evolve, Tea'va. To become like them, if that is what you want."

His face twisted in anger and pain. "That is not what I want. The humans are inferior. Pathetic."

"They have survived this long."

"Because I allowed it," he said, raising his voice. "Me. I let them onto this ship. I killed Gr'el for them and led them to victory so that I could claim victory for all of the bek'hai. And you destroyed it. You killed my clones. You ruined our chances. We will perish, Shielle. All of the bek'hai will perish for what you have done." He squeezed harder, holding her too tightly for her to be able to speak. "You and the Domo'dahm would see us all dead because you cannot admit the need to change. Because you are repulsed by me, instead of accepting, instead of being thankful for my evolution."

He caught himself then, realizing what he was doing in his anger. He let go of her throat, sitting over her, his entire body shaking.

It didn't matter.

She was already dead.

Even in that, he had failed. She had tricked him into anger, tricked him into killing her before he found out what she knew.

"Tea'va," a voice said from behind him.

He closed his eyes, trying to calm himself. Gabriel. How much had he heard?

171

"Move slowly, Tea'va," Gabriel said.

He glanced over his shoulder. Gabriel was there with Miranda, Zoelle, and the one called Sergeant Hafizi. The Sergeant had a rifle trained on his back.

"I wanted only to save the bek'hai," he said.

"You wanted power," Zoelle said. "Don't delude yourself with more excuses."

Tea'va felt his anger flare again. He struggled to keep himself still.

"Did you hear what Shielle said, Heil'bek? About the clones?"

"Yes."

Tea'va smiled. At least Gabriel knew the truth about Zoelle now.

"She may not be my mother, but she thinks that she is. That makes her loyal. That makes her trustworthy. Unlike you."

"What will you do with me?"

"I don't know. I'll let the General decide."

"Will you allow me to retire?"

"An honorable death? For you?" Zoelle said.

"Humans don't kill for retribution," Gabriel said. "You'll probably be confined to your quarters, imprisoned, until we can think of something else. Your knowledge is still useful to us."

Tea'va's shoulders slumped. "She sent the Domo'dahm a message. I do not know what it contained."

"I know. I saw you come down here once before. You didn't see me. Even if she hadn't, we would have figured out what you were planning."

He lowered his head further. He hadn't known about that. It seemed he was always destined to fail. Perhaps Shielle had been right? Perhaps he was the real fool?

"Get to your feet," Hafizi said. "Slowly."

Tea'va didn't move. His body hurt where Shielle had shot him. He could survive it, but then what? He could see the truth for what it was, now. He had never been superior. The Domo'dahm was right. He was defective. In all ways that mattered. It had taken this for him to realize.

"Tea'va, please, stand up," Gabriel said.

Tea'va opened his eyes. He noticed the caretaker's plasma gun at the tip of Shielle's fingers. She had been reaching for it when she died. No wonder they were concerned about him. He breathed in. He would have time for one shot. As far as he knew, only Sergeant Hafizi was armed.

"Tea'va. Now," Gabriel said.

He wasn't going to let them imprison him. His life was forfeit. He had failed. He didn't want to know how it was all going to end. All he had to do now was choose a target. If he shot Hafizi, he might be able to kill the others, but there was no guarantee. If he shot Gabriel, he would finally have his victory against the Heil'bek. If he shot Zoelle, he would have his revenge for her betrayal. There was no value in killing Miranda.

He breathed in again, tensing slightly as he made his decision.

"Tea'va."

He reached for the gun, grabbing it and turning as the Sergeant fired his rifle. The bolt hit him in the side, digging deep into him and causing a wave of immense pain. He didn't let it stop him, continuing to turn, bringing the weapon to bear on its target.

He fired, falling over as he watched the bolt streak toward Gabriel. If he had killed the Heil'bek back on Earth, none of this would have ever happened. He would have been a hero before he ever had to leave the planet. It was only fair.

He landed on his chest, his head up so he could see Gabriel die.

As his own life faded, he watched as Zoelle moved, faster than any human could, throwing herself in front of the plasma, taking the hit and falling to the ground.

Tea'va hissed softly, a final hiss of despair.

Then he died.

35

GABRIEL FELL TO HIS knees beside Zoelle. The plasma had hit her square in the side of her face, tearing through her eye and into her skull, burning a hole right through to her brain. She was dead already, he knew, but it didn't stop him from leaning over her, feeling for a pulse and hoping beyond hope.

Maybe she wasn't the real Juliet St. Martin, but she was the closest thing he would ever have.

Now she was gone.

"Gabriel," Miranda said, coming to kneel next to him. He felt her arm over his shoulders. "Oh, my. I'm so sorry."

He didn't react. He stared at the mess the bolt had made of Zoelle's face. Then he looked to the traitorous bek'hai who had caused it. Tea'va had fired his weapon at him. The shot was meant for his face. He could barely believe it after he had come to think that at the very least they held a mutual respect for one another.

He could barely believe any of it.

"Hafizi, find a comm station and report in to Colonel Choi," he said, his voice weak. "Tell her what happened. Do not tell the General. Do you understand?"

"Yes, sir," Hafizi said.

Gabriel reached under his shirt, pulling out his crucifix. He squeezed it tightly as he made the sign of the cross over Zoelle's body and forced back his tears. He wasn't sure why he did it. It just seemed appropriate. She had never asked to be brought into the world as a clone. None of them did. It wasn't their fault for being what they were.

Then he made himself stand up. He looked over at Tea'va again, face down on the floor, his blood spilling out around him. The other Juliet clone, Shielle, was behind him, her neck purple, her eyes bulging. She had sent something to the Dread on Earth. She had exhibited more free will than any of them expected. It seemed at least some portion of the Juliet clones were capable.

He clenched his teeth, realizing that he had lost more than the best connection to his mother he would ever have, and more than a friend. They had lost their translators as well. Their guides through the Dread technology. Had they learned enough to use it on their own?

"Hafizi," Gabriel shouted, catching the Sergeant near the room's exit.

"Yes, sir?"

"Tell Colonel Choi to bring Reza and Guy with her."

"Yes, sir."

"We need to know what she told them," Gabriel said.

"Whatever it was, it's going to hurt us," Miranda replied.

"Yes."

"Your father-"

"I know."

"You have to tell him she wasn't really his wife."

"I know. I'll try. I tried before. I don't know if he'll believe me. Maybe if he had heard Shielle himself? I don't know."

He paused, his emotions in turmoil. His real mother had been dead for years. From the moment they had cloned her. He had always known she was gone, but Zoelle had brought her back to life somewhat. Now she was gone again.

"I'm sorry," Miranda said again, embracing him.

He held her back, letting the tears come. It wasn't just pain for himself. He knew what his father would go through. Even twenty years after he had left Earth, Theodore's wounds had been raw.

He gave himself thirty seconds. Then he broke away from Miranda, wiped his eyes, and straightened up. He would let her see him like that. Nobody else. He was still an officer, and he still had a job to do.

He walked over to one of the maturation chambers, looking in at the still form. She had destroyed all of the clones, as well. As much as he was against creating people this way, they had been looking forward to adding to their small numbers. They had been especially eager for the new engineers, who could help them accelerate their uptake of the Dread technology. That was lost as well.

Should he have seen this coming? He wasn't sure. Tea'va had been so convincing in his desire to help them, and in his anger at the Domo'dahm for his initial betrayal. And Shielle? She had responded as any subservient clone would. The only way to know for sure that they were secure would have been to lock up or kill every single clone, and they didn't have enough crew of their own to run a ship like the Ishur that way. For better or worse, they needed the clones. They were forced to trust them.

One of the caretakers came over as he stood in the chamber. It eyed him suspiciously, holding its weapon toward him. He backed away, and it went about its business. Some of the clones were so simple. So basic. Like the caretakers, or the cleaners. Others, like the keepers, or the Juliets, were so much more. None of them were the enemy. Not really.

He heard Colonel Choi coming, her boots clacking stiffly against the floor in an even cadence. He retreated back to where Zoelle was resting, Miranda joining him at his side. He felt a growing sense of dread as the echoes grew louder. The pace of her walk was familiar, and not in a good way.

His stomach dropped as she entered, with Theodore at her side and Reza, Guy, Hafizi and Diallo behind them. He could see the relief on his father's face when Theodore saw that he was unharmed.

He also saw the immediate agony when Theodore's eyes landed on Zoelle behind him.

"General," Gabriel said.

Theodore stopped moving. His face turned white. His eyes darted away from the body, back to it, and away again. His jaw clenched tight. His hands tore at the edges of the chair.

Gabriel felt it too. His father's pain. He headed for him, to do what he could to comfort him. To tell him that she wasn't the real Juliet, for all the good it would do.

"Dad," he said, breaking formality. "She-"

That was all he managed to get out. His father wheeled his chair around, retreating from the scene as quickly as he could.

"Dad," he said again, ready to give chase.

"Let him go," Colonel Choi said. "Major, let him go."

"I told you not to tell him," Gabriel shouted at Hafizi.

"He tried," Choi said. "Your father wandered onto the bridge while he was briefing me."

"Damn it. This disaster is getting worse by the second." He looked over Choi's shoulder. His father's back vanished ahead of him.

"What happened down here?" she asked.

Gabriel closed his eyes tight, pushing at the emotion. It killed him to see his father like that, but Choi was right. They didn't have time for that right now.

"We discovered that the clone, Shielle, sent an encrypted message to the Domo'dahm when we passed Earth."

"What kind of message?"

"We don't know. That's why I asked you to bring Reza and Guy. We need to figure it out."

"How are we going to do that?" Guy asked, his face paled by the violence. He looked like he was going to be sick. "I see our translators are all dead."

"Reza, how much of the language have you translated?" Gabriel asked, ignoring Guy. He had never been one for tact.

"I'm not completely sure. I don't think I know all of the symbols yet. Based on what I've done so far, maybe fifty percent."

"Do you think you can get a copy of the message that was sent, and break the encryption?"

"Uh. I don't know, Gabriel. With everything else you have me working on?"

"Guy, what about you?"

"I am willing to try, but I have other duties as well, Major. I'm to ensure the Magellan's systems are ready for the drop to Earth."

The pain of the loss kept growing. Did Tea'va have any idea of what he had done before he died?

"Colonel?" Gabriel said.

"The message has already been sent," she said. "We're struggling for hands as it is, and this is going to make it harder for us. Reza, Guy, find Shielle's quarters and see if there is anything you can do within the next hour. If not, we'll have to drop it for now. If we manage to get everything else ready ahead of time, we can come back to it, but what's done is done. We'll have to do our best to anticipate what the Dread could know that we don't want them to."

Gabriel didn't like it, but he knew she was right. "Yes, ma'am."

"Spaceman Locke, you're dismissed. You have three hours until your next shift."

"Yes, ma'am."

"Major St. Martin, you'll need to increase your familiarity with the flight controls. You won't have a co-pilot to guide you going forward."

"Yes, ma'am," Gabriel said. He paused. "Permission to speak to General St. Martin first?"

Choi nodded. "Granted."

"I'll need a little time, Colonel," Gabriel said. "Can we leave the bodies here for now?"

"You aren't going to bring him back down here, are you?"

"No, ma'am. I am going to bring someone to examine the body, though. His name is It'kek."

She eyed him curiously. "I don't know what you're thinking, Major, but

I trust you. Make sure you alert Sergeant Hafizi when we can send in a team to clean up this mess."

"Yes, ma'am," Gabriel replied.

He wasn't quite sure what he was thinking either, but step one was confirming once and for all that the dead woman on the floor wasn't the real Juliet St. Martin. Shielle might have said she couldn't be, but all it took was one lie to put everything else into question.

Step two was to convince his father of that fact. It wouldn't ease all of his pain, but it would help, and he needed to get him through this as quickly as possible.

Too many people depended on them.

36

GABRIEL WENT TO THE assemblers first, and then traced his path backward to where It'kek had shown him the keepers could be reached. The deepest corridors of the Ishur were faintly lit with the luminescent moss that seemed to hang from everything in the lower decks, and as he walked he began to feel the familiar sting of the legri'shah scent in his nose. It was a difficult feeling to ignore, and he wondered if that was part of the reason so few had ever met the keepers. He also wondered if it might be intentional, a defense to keep others away. The creatures were almost extinct, so rare that they were kept hidden in starships, far from freedom.

He cringed a little as he realized they had likely killed at least one of the beasts when they had destroyed the Dread fortress, along with the keepers who were raising them. He wished there was another way.

He rounded a bend in the corridor, reaching the larger common area of the keeper's community. It was a compact space surrounded by even more compact cells where the keepers slept, near the center of the pens where the legri'shah were kept. He had tried to count the clones' numbers when he had been through the first time, and had guessed that there were at most twelve of them on board, for two or three of the mature creatures and a growing number of younger ones.

He had been surprised to learn that the gori'shah the Dread wore were actually colonies of legri'shah larvae, microscopic creatures that fed on a silk-like substance spun by the second phase of the creature's growth. The entire life-cycle of the legri'shah was too complicated for him to fully grasp, but he appreciated how self-sustaining it was. When he had more time, he wanted nothing more than to learn all he could about them.

Two of the keepers were sitting on the floor in the common area when he arrived. They looked perpetually tired, and they smelled almost as strongly as the legri'shah themselves.

"It'kek?" Gabriel said, unable to tell any of the clones apart.

"He is with the legri'shah," one of them said. "Can I help you, Son of Juliet?"

He was still surprised that the keepers knew who he was without ever having met him. "I don't know. I need one of you to come up to the cloning factory. Zoelle is dead."

"Yes. We heard your Sergeant Hafizi send a message to the bridge. If she is dead, why do you need us? We do not keep the dead."

"It'kek told me he would know if she were the real Juliet, or a clone. I'm pretty sure she's a clone, but I need to know for certain."

"We do not go that high," the keeper said.

"I know you don't usually, but this is very important. Please."

The two clones looked at one another. "Did It'kek agree to do this, if you ever asked?"

Gabriel considered lying. He didn't. There had been enough deceit already. "No. I never asked."

"We are not permitted to be seen by any drumhr. Our form is outlawed among the bek'hai."

"You don't have to worry about that. There are no drumhr remaining on the Ishur."

"None?"

"Tea'va was the only one who survived the attack and Gr'el's betrayal. He's dead, too."

The clones smiled. "Can we both go?"

Gabriel nodded. "You can all come, if you want."

"The others must stay to watch the legri'shah, but we will come now. They will come later. It has been many years since a keeper was able to visit the upper decks of a domo'shah."

The two keepers stood and followed Gabriel as he made his way back to the cloning facility once more. Sergeant Hafizi was standing watch over the area when he arrived, and he drew back slightly at the sight of the keepers.

"Major?" he said, unsure.

"It's okay, Sergeant. They're with me."

"Things have changed," one of the keepers said to the other.

"Yes. Many things."

"How old are you?" Gabriel asked.

"I am three thousand Earth years old, give or take," one of them said.

"I am two-thousand, seven hundred and twelve," the other said.

"And you used to be able to roam around the ship?"

"Yes. Before we were banned, back when the bek'hai left their home world. Back then, even the legri'shah were allowed some measure of freedom. They did not fear their masters then." He smiled. "It is good to roam once more."

"Where is the un'hai, Zoelle?" the other keeper asked.

"This way," Hafizi said, leading them into the maturation hall.

"I smell blood," one of them said.

"Too much blood," the other agreed.

"She's there," Gabriel said, trying to direct them without looking at her.

The keepers walked over to where Zoelle's corpse was resting. One of them leaned down and touched her face. Then he stood and looked back at Gabriel.

Gabriel felt his throat constrict, a sudden fear washing over him that the keeper might say the words he least expected, and least wanted to hear.

"She is a clone," the keeper said, allowing him to breathe once more. "It is certain."

"Thank you," Gabriel said. "Shielle said that clones can't be made without killing the source."

"That was true many years ago. Is it still true? It seems we should have overcome that limitation by now."

"Yes, we should have," the other keeper agreed.

"It doesn't matter," Gabriel said. "This isn't my mother."

"No, it isn't."

"Can you come with me?"

"Where now, Son of Juliet?"

"Please, call me Gabriel. I want you to tell my father she's a copy. He thinks he saw his wife dead on the floor."

"We will tell him, Gabriel. You have given us what freedom you can. We will help you however we can."

"Thank you," Gabriel said. Then he turned to Hafizi. "Have the bodies taken to storage somewhere. Make sure to keep Zoelle separate from those two. I know the Dread have some kind of recycling system for corpses, but I don't know where it is or how it works."

"I will show you," one of the keepers said.

"And I will go with you, Gabriel."

"Thank you again," Gabriel said, impressed with their kindness.

If these keepers were the closest thing to the original bek'hai, what the hell had happened to their race?

37

GABRIEL KNEW HIS FATHER would be in his quarters. Where else could the General go to be left alone, after all?

He wasn't surprised when Theodore wouldn't answer his knocks. The most traumatic thing his father had ever done was leave his mother behind on Earth, even if it had saved thousands of people from death and enslavement. Was that easier than seeing a duplicate of her dead? At least then he was able to hope, and gradually become accustomed to the idea that she couldn't have survived. To have her come to life again? He would never say he knew how Theodore felt.

He knew how he felt, just to think for a moment, even a little bit, that she had been his mother.

He knew how he felt to find a certain closeness to her memory, and then have it taken away by a plasma bolt meant for him.

He was sure he would have time to fall into his own emotional upset later. But not now. Not when they were trying to prepare for all-out war.

Not when every human in the universe was counting on them. He knew he could convince his father of the same thing, especially with the help of the keeper, who said his name was Pil'kek.

"Come on, Dad," he said, knocking one more time. "We need to talk about this. I know you're hurting, but hiding away isn't going to help anything."

He waited. Theodore didn't answer.

"Human emotions are intriguing," Pil'kek said. "We, too, used to feel loss. It seems like so long ago. When creating life becomes as simple as a switch on a machine, it loses its value. It is unfortunate."

"It's turned your kind into monsters," Gabriel said. "Some of them, anyway."

"They used to think the legri'shah were monsters to be destroyed until they realized the value of the lek'shah." Pil'kek shook his head. "Then they became resources to control. It should not be that a human holds them in higher esteem than the ones they saved."

"No, it shouldn't." Gabriel prepared to knock on Theodore's door again. As much as he respected his father, he didn't have time or energy to be polite. "Damn it, Dad. You're making a mockery of her death. You might as well have died fifty years ago if you're going to give up now."

He figured that would bring Theodore out. He was right.

The door slid open, an angry Theodore in his chair behind it. His eyes were red, his face flushed, his uniform wrinkled, shirt untucked.

"What the hell do you know about anything, boy?" Theodore shouted. "Mockery? If I had my legs, I'd run you down and beat some damn sense between those ears of yours. I've given my whole life for this cause. This war. Everything I got. What the hell does it mean? What the hell is it for? She stayed alive for me. She did everything she could to come back to me. She brought me back to life. Now she's gone again."

The tears welled in his eyes. Gabriel felt guilty for what he had said, but there had been no other choice.

"She wasn't Juliet, Dad," he said. "She wasn't. A clone. A copy. Sure, she believed she was, but it wasn't true."

"You keep telling me that, son. I've heard it over and over. You don't trust her. She ain't real. You trusted Tea'va, that son of a whore. You believed in him. How'd that work out?"

Gabriel felt the blow in his gut. He took it in stride. That was his fault, at least in part. But Theodore couldn't have argued that at the time, they needed the Dread. They would have never made it onto the Ishur without him.

"I'm not just saying she wasn't really Mom." Gabriel looked over at Pil'kek, who seemed uncomfortable with the whole exchange. "Pil'kek is a keeper. He knew Mom personally."

Theodore's eyes swept over to the keeper. He didn't react at all to the bek'hai's more reptilian appearance. "You knew Juliet? How?"

"She visited the keepers, Dahm St. Martin," Pil'kek said. "She spent time with us when all others were forbidden. She appreciated the legri'shah, as well as our nature, in comparison with the other bek'hai."

"Legri'shah?" Theodore said.

"The source of the Dread armor," Gabriel said. "Creatures, as big as a dinosaur. Kind of like a dragon. There are a few on board."

"And I didn't know this, why?"

"I only discovered them recently," Gabriel said. "Besides, it wasn't that important. The keepers are peaceful. Their concern are the legri'shah."

"What does this all have to do with Juliet?"

"We knew Juliet St. Martin well, Dahm St. Martin," Pil'kek said. "She was much loved among all of the keepers. Your son wanted me to come to tell you, and I mean this with all honesty, the clone known as Zoelle was only that. A clone. Not the real Juliet St. Martin. I am sad to say; she died many years ago. The bek'hai cannot finish the cloning process without killing the pur'hai. The source."

Theodore froze. He didn't move at all. Not for a minute or more. Gabriel could tell his mind was going, trying to make sense of it all. Trying to come to some kind of resolution on how he should feel.

"She knew things," he said. "Personal things."

"It is not recommended for the memories to be stored and transferred during the cloning process, as it makes the clone unstable for their intended use. It is also not impossible."

"But... that can't be. Shielle, she was a clone. She looked like Juliet. She betrayed us."

"The keepers listen to all communications sent from above, Dahm St. Martin. It is clear to me that there are some clones of Juliet who are, what is a good word? Enhanced. And some who are not. It is wrong to think that clones are all the same. They are not. Even for the bek'hai, biology is so complex that it cannot be fully controlled."

"You're saying that someone muddied the waters? Made a Juliet that was more like my Juliet?"

"That is what I believe."

Theodore grinned. "She always was good at making people see things her way. You think she convinced one of the other ones not to be such an asshole?"

"I'm not sure what you mean, Dahm St. Martin."

"How many of the bek'hai want war?" Theodore asked. "How many agreed with the Domo'dahm's invasion?"

"Many. Not all."

Theodore nodded. "Ah, my darlin'. Heh. The Domo'dahm doesn't know what he's done, does he?"

"Dad?" Gabriel asked.

"We're going to win this war, Gabriel," Theodore said. "Your mother's already seen to it. We just need to do our part."

"Which is?"

"Stay the course, for now. You said Major Peters had a clone of your mom with him?"

"Yes."

"I'm willing to bet she's one of the special ones. I'm also willing to bet there are more of them out there. I hope she's still alive. It'll make things easier."

Gabriel was happy to see his father's despair shrinking, but he still didn't know what he was talking about.

"I'm confused," he said.

"Heh. Don't worry about it, son. I'm gonna be okay, thanks to you, and to you." He looked at Pil'kek. "I'm not saying it don't hurt because it does.

187

I never wanted to see my darlin' like that. But you're right. She didn't go through all of this to have me fail on her. I'm gonna get cleaned up, and then I'll be back on the bridge. We've got a lot of work to do. More now, without Zoelle."

Gabriel nodded. He was glad his father used the clone's name, instead of his mother's.

"The keepers can help us translate," Gabriel said.

"We do have one request," Pil'kek said.

"What's that?" Theodore asked.

"We must try to save as many of the legri'shah as we can. There are so few remaining."

"I'll do my best, Mr. Pil'kek."

"Thank you, Dahm St. Martin."

Theodore smiled. "No. Thank you."

38

GENERAL ALAN CAVE STARED out of the small window of his quarters on Alpha Settlement, looking up at Delta Station in the distance. The military installation seemed so small from here. So unimportant.

Little had seemed important in these last few weeks, for him and for many others in the settlements. Not since Theodore St. Martin had taken away their only hope of ever escaping the nightmare they had been trapped in for the last fifty years, leaving them to wonder just how much longer the equipment that sustained them would last. They had always known the answer wasn't forever, and that they would need to leave Chalawan. While they had always hoped it would be to return to their home planet, he had finally gotten many of them to accept that it wasn't meant to be, and that drastic measures would be needed to preserve what was left of humankind.

It hadn't been easy to do, either. So many of the council members had been loyal to Theodore at first. Hell, even he had started out loyal to the

Old Gator and his delusions. But the years had shown that nothing was going to change. The missions to Earth had only resulted in pilots dying and irreplaceable resources being lost, and the overload of work for their engineers was proof that the temporary facilities they had brought with them would only last for so long.

He had taken the hard road, the unpopular road. He had even gone so far as to drug the man he had once respected more than anything in order to keep him quiet while the important decisions were made. Doing it had made him sick. Lying about it had made him sicker. He had done it for the good of the many. For the future of their entire species, not because he wanted people to die. Not because he wanted to leave anyone behind.

Not that any of that mattered now.

The great General St. Martin had come roaring back to life on the news that the Dread armor wasn't completely impenetrable. He had used his reputation to break every law the New Earth Alliance had composed, and in one fell swoop had effectively killed every single one of them.

He had stolen the Magellan.

He wasn't coming back.

That was the truth General Cave was forced to live with. That they had all been forced to live with. He had sensed the change in the spirit of the people immediately after the Magellan had slipped away. He could still feel their resignation, their loss of hope, and their distress every time he made the journey from his quarters to his office. He could see the way they looked at him, their eyes pleading for a miracle he knew he couldn't produce. They didn't have the resources to build another ship. They didn't have another way out.

He turned from the viewport, picking up his jacket and slipping it on. He straightened himself and then headed out into the community. It had become more important than ever for him to appear to be in control. To stay strong, to look strong, and to act with a confidence he didn't feel. Sometimes, as he walked across the common area toward the loop, it seemed as though it might be the only thing holding any of them together.

He said hello to a few people he passed on his way to the station. The laughter of the children was such a stark contrast to the moroseness of the adults. They were young and innocent. They didn't understand the reality of their future. It was difficult to listen to sometimes, knowing that it was going to end badly for them. It was another thought he had to fight against on a daily basis. Another truth he didn't want to accept.

There was a pod waiting at the station when he arrived, and he stepped into it and sat down, finding himself beside Councilwoman Rouse.

"Angela," he said, nodding to her.

"General," she replied.

"What's on the docket for today?" he asked as the pod's canopy sealed and it began to move.

"We're still working on the plans for the personnel reduction. The baby lotteries have been put on hold, and we've been forced to abort a few of the early-stage pregnancies."

"You're aborting people who are already expecting?"

"At their request, Alan," she replied defensively. "People don't want to have children knowing they're going to grow up here." She paused. "And die here."

"How far along is the planning process for contraction?"

"We have a plan to move Beta settlement over and recapture the resources for necessities. It should buy us at least twenty years. Once that's done, we're going to look into disassembling Delta."

"You should have started with Delta."

"I know, but that motion was blocked by the Believers."

"Is that what they're calling themselves?"

"Yes. They still think Theodore is going to come back and lead them to salvation."

"I guess it's as good a belief as any. People need something to pin their hopes on."

"I'd rather they help us be pragmatic and work out the logistics so that we can maybe find a way to ride this thing out."

"Ride it out? Like there's an end in sight?"

"The science teams are shifting focus to finding other potential ways to get us out of this system. We still have the coordinates to the New Earth; we just need a ship that can take us there. It may be that we have to do a generation style vessel, but it beats the hell out of waiting to die here. That's why we aren't dismantling Delta yet. Rachel Dawes in engineering thinks we might be able to fabricate a solar sail and hook it up to the station. It would take us a few hundred years to get to the New Earth, but we would get there."

"Pie in the sky," General Cave said. "The printers can't do anything that thin and light."

"Not now, but if they can improve them-"

"That's a big if."

"What the hell do you want us to do?" Angela cursed. "Accept that we're going to die?"

General Cave froze. "Damn it. I'm sorry, Angela. I woke up in a lousy mood today."

"I wake up like that every day recently. But we need to pull together. We aren't dead yet, and that's a start."

"Right."

The pod slowed as it reached the central hub. Councilwoman Rouse and General Cave got out together, heading for the administrative offices. They were halfway to the elevators when the doors to them opened, and Spaceman Owens came limping out.

"Sir," he said, seeing the General but forgetting to salute. "I've been trying to contact you. You need to get to the CIC immediately."

"The CIC? What's happening?"

"We just got a comm from Delta. Their long-range sensors are picking up two unidentified objects that just appeared in system and are headed this way."

"Two?" General Cave said. "That can't be Theodore."

"No, sir," Spaceman Owens agreed. "But whoever or whatever they are, sir, Major Looper said they're huge."

39

"GET ME A VISUAL," General Cave said as the doors to the elevator opened, and he stepped out into the CIC.

The settlement's emergency command center was located at the bottom of the central hub, buried four hundred meters deep. It was a claustrophobic space, small and dark and crowded with monitors and communications equipment. Five soldiers worked in rotating shifts within it, manning the stations in case of a red alert. For years, those shifts had changed from one to another without incident or interruption. For years, the entire ready room had been ready but never utilized.

Until today.

"And patch me in with Major Looper on Delta while you're at it," he added as he took a seat behind the main control unit.

The monitor in front of him changed, showing him the large blobs outlined by their sensors. They were massive. Easily bigger than any of the settlements, and even dwarfing Delta Station by order of magnitude.

"General," Major Looper said, his face appearing on the corner of the monitor.

"Major. I'm looking at your sensor images. What can you tell me?"

"Nothing good, sir," Looper replied. "They're big. Damn big. They came out of nowhere, just showed up on our sensors about ten minutes ago. And they're coming this way."

"Just showed up, as in traveled in from a slipstream?"

"We still have astronomy looking at the vector data to confirm, but my gut feeling says yes."

General Cave looked at the screen again. There was only one thing he knew of that was that big and could travel through slipspace. Just the thought of it sent a wave a panic rushing through him and prickling his skin.

"Major, scramble the fighters," he said, forcing himself to stay calm. "Prepare whatever BIS you have and get as many personnel clear of Delta Station as you can."

"Sir?" Major Looper said. "What is it?"

"I hope I'm wrong about this Major; I really hope I am. I think the Dread have found us."

The silence at the other end was all the confirmation General Cave needed that Looper understood the gravity of the situation.

"Looper, are you still there?"

"Yes, sir," the Major replied, his voice weak. "Sir, am I clear that you want me to send the starfighters to attack the Dread?"

General Cave drew back in surprise of his own. The Major was only thirty-three years old and had never seen the Dread before. He didn't understand what he was suggesting. "Attack them? Absolutely not. Our ships can't do anything against those things. No. I want you to evacuate Delta Station. Get as many troops to Alpha as possible, and get them down into the shelters. Do you understand, Major?"

"Yes, sir," Looper replied. "Affirmative."

"Good. Cave, out."

General Cave glanced at the soldiers manning the CIC. They all looked terrified at what he had said.

"Sound the general alarm," he said. "Red alert, across all settlements. All civilians are to report to their designated attack shelters."

"Yes, sir," the soldiers replied.

A moment later, a red strobe light began to flash above the hatch behind him, signaling the red alert. A similar strobe would be going off everywhere around Alpha, Beta, and Gamma settlements, along with announcements directing people to the underground bombardment shelters.

Not that it would make a difference if the Dread really had found them and were coming to finish the job they started all of those years ago. The shelters were deep underground, but they had also been bored into stone that would turn to slag under the heat of a massive plasma attack. A single crevice venting their limited atmosphere was all it would take to kill them.

"Now what, sir?" one of the soldiers asked.

"Now we pray," General Cave replied. "That's all we can do."

The soldier nodded, turning back to his monitors. General Cave shifted his attention to the screens in front of his station. He switched the view, cycling through the cameras positioned around Alpha settlement, both interior and exterior. The contrast was stark and frightening. Inside, the base was a flurry of activity, as everyone within it was on the move, headed for the underground shelters. Outside there was near calm, save for a squadron of starfighters streaking away from Delta Station toward him.

"ETA to visual?" he asked, watching the monitor for signs of the enemy ships.

"One minute," one of the soldiers replied.

They were coming in so fast.

He pulled in a deep breath, trying to steady suddenly shaking limbs. He was scared. Hell, they were all scared.

"Major Looper," he said, opening the comm to Delta again. "I don't see any BIS out there."

"Sir," Looper said. "We're still loading them."

"Loading them with what?" he asked.

"They were half-filled with supplies. We had to discard them to get more people on."

"There's no time left, Major. Get as many people on them as you can and get them away from the station."

"Yes, sir." He paused. "Sir?"

"Yes, Major."

"We only have space for five hundred on the transports."

General Cave closed his eyes. That was one-third of the people currently on the station. How were they even deciding who stayed and who went?

"I'm sorry, Major," he said.

"I should have gone with General St. Martin," Looper replied. "When I had the chance. I should have gone with him. Oh, God. I don't want to die."

"Get those transports launched Major. Don't think about anything else."

"Yes, sir."

General Cave felt his heart thumping in his chest. Everything was happening so fast. Fifty years and it was all going to be over within minutes.

He had been drowning in hopelessness for the last few weeks. Now that the end was near, he found he had held onto more hope than was probably reasonable. Maybe they had been down, but the scientists were working on the problem, and given a chance they might have even solved it.

He saw the first Dread fortress appear a moment later, coming out from behind Ursa Major, a dark spot against the light of the star. The second appeared shortly after that, trailing slightly behind the first, both headed right toward them.

A blue dot appeared on the front of the first fortress. General Cave cringed at the sight of it, knowing what it meant. Major Looper's voice echoed in his ears, his cries of "I don't want to die" causing him to lean forward for balance as the Dread starship unleashed the bolt from its main plasma cannon.

The blue streak arced across the distance between the Dread fortress and Delta Station, a flash of lightning that ended with the space station being torn to pieces, dark and silent as it disintegrated beneath the onslaught, literally vanishing in front of his eyes.

"No," he said, slamming his fist on the monitor and cracking the screen. "Damn it. No."

He stopped himself, wiping at the tears that had come to his eyes as he returned his attention to the Dread ships. They were spreading apart, one of them headed toward Alpha, the other breaking for Gamma. He could only hope the other settlements had gotten underground in time.

The seconds passed like an eternity, the Dread ships slowing as they drew nearer. The tip of the second one began to glow, and General Cave closed his eyes as it unleashed its fury, sending a plasma bolt into Gamma Settlement. Would the shelter protect the people there? He had no idea. He could only hope.

"We're going to die," one of the soldiers said, watching the same approach on his own monitor.

"We might," he replied. "And if we do, let us die with courage and dignity, not filled with fear."

"Yes, sir," the soldier said.

"Sir," one of the others said. "Sir, look."

"What is it, Spaceman?" General Cave said, looking at his screen. He didn't see anything. Then again, his view was obscured by the crack he made.

"There. Behind the Dread ships."

General Cave hurried to the soldier's position, leaning down beside him to look at his monitor. He squinted his eyes to make out the shape in the distance, positioned behind the Dread fortresses.

"It looks like-"

"Another Dread ship," he said, identifying it. His heart might have sunk further, had there been anywhere else for it to go. "We have no weapons; we can't touch them, and yet they sent three ships to find and destroy us. Why?"

40

THEODORE GRITTED HIS TEETH as the Ishur tracked behind the Dread fortress while vectoring away from the slipspace exodus point. They had arrived only seconds earlier, just in time to see the lead starship fire its plasma cannon on Delta Station and blow it into little more than debris.

Just in time to watch their people die.

"Mr. Mokri, divert power to the main plasma cannon," Theodore shouted, his eyes glued to the scene ahead of them. "Gabriel, get us on target to intercept the port ship before it can fire again."

"Yes, sir," Gabriel replied, manipulating the makeshift controls Reza had created to allow him to fly the fortress and turning the Ishur toward the enemy ship.

The domo'shah had already blasted the surface once, burning into the exposed part of Gamma Settlement and leaving little more than a crater behind.

It was possible the residents had made it into the shelters.

It was possible the blast hadn't dug quite deep enough to reach them.

Then again, it was possible they were all dead.

"Let's show them sons of bitches what happens when they screw with the Earth Alliance," he said, looking down at the status screen of his tablet. The button at the bottom of it turned red as the main plasma cannon finished charging. "Gabriel, give me five degrees starboard."

"Yes, sir."

The ship began to adjust again, shifting slowly as it crossed the space. The Dread fortresses were slowing down, beginning to make their own turns to come about and face them. Given a choice, he would rather hit them both before they finished the maneuver.

"Firing," he said. He squinted as the bolt of blue energy launched from the bow ahead of them, a streak of light that crossed thousands of kilometers in seconds, heading for the exposed side of the Dread ship.

Theodore tracked it intently, leaning forward in his seat, smiling at the very thought of the energy blast piercing the heart of the enemy. He may have promised the keepers he would try to spare the legri'shah, but he hadn't sworn to put the lives of the creatures over the lives of their people.

The bolt slammed into the side of the fortress, creating a flash of light as it struck. Then the light faded away, the bolt absorbed by a sudden ripple of pitch black that formed against the hull.

"What the hell?" he heard Miranda say in front of him.

"That looks like our shields," Gabriel said.

"Mr. Mokri?" Theodore said, asking for confirmation.

Reza was looking at his tablet and shaking his head. "Confirmed, sir. It has the same modulation signature as our Darkspace Defense System."

"In other words, they're using our tech against us?"

"Yes, sir."

"What?" Colonel Choi said. "How can that be?"

"Shielle," Theodore replied. "It has to be. We never had time to figure out what she sent. Well, now we know, damn that woman."

"General, if they have our shields," Colonel Choi said.

"We're on even footing offensively," Theodore said. "But also outnumbered."

He watched as the first Dread ship finished reversing course, getting the bow pointed back at them. They were heading directly toward one another on a terrifying collision course.

"Mr. Mokri, is the DDS ready for action?" Theodore said.

"Uh. General, I'm not-"

"That was a rhetorical, Mr. Mokri. It damn well better be, or we're all about to die."

"Yes, sir," Reza said. "But we haven't tried this yet. I'm not sure the modulators will hold up to the stress."

"Nothing like beta testing on the job. Turn the damn thing on."

"Yes, sir. Activating the DDS."

Reza tapped on his control pad. There was no immediate visual or audible change in anything, and for a moment Theodore wondered if there was nothing happening down in engineering but a shower of sparks and a nice big electrical fire.

"Forward DDS, online," Lieutenant Bale said from her station.

"Port side DDS, online," Miranda said.

"Starboard side DDS, online," Colonel Choi said.

"Stern DDS, online," Sergeant Hafizi said.

"Fantastic," Theodore replied to the news. "I know this is new for you ladies and gents, so do your best to stay calm and focused. Prioritize the mains over the secondaries. We can't afford to let that bad boy through."

"Yes, sir," the soldiers replied.

"Gabriel, don't let us get caught between them," Theodore said.

"Yes, sir."

The Ishur began to rise, vectoring up and away from the oncoming Dread ships.

"Picking up an energy spike from the starboard fortress," Miranda said.

"Colonel, that's yours," Theodore replied.

Colonel Choi stared intently at the hologram in front of her. It was a generated depiction of the side of the Ishur, matched to a line from the side that was piercing the lower portion of the hull, along with a red dot that was placed to the left of it. She put her finger to the red dot, dragging it toward the line.

The darkness lessened as the enemy domo'shah fired, sending a return volley back at them. It appeared as a tapering yellow line that was lining up almost perfectly with the line on Colonel Choi's terminal, and she held her finger steady while the heaviest part of the line slammed into the dot.

The ship vibrated softly under the impact.

"Damage report, Sergeant?" Theodore said.

"No damage reported," Sergeant Abdullah replied. "It looks like the DDS is working."

"Sir, energy spike from the port ship," Miranda said.

"Got it," Bale said, repeating the same motion as Colonel Choi.

The plasma blast filled their viewport, crossing the chasm of space and hitting the front of the ship. Again there was a soft vibration, but no evidence of harm.

"Hell, yes, Mr. Mokri," Theodore said in response to the success of the system. "Let's try part two. Gabriel, bring us in on that port side bastard. I want to broadside him and see how well they've integrated our technology."

"Yes, sir," Gabriel replied.

The Ishur began to shift and accelerate, heading toward the fortress while the other released another plasma blast. Colonel Choi shifted her hand, moving the dot to the impact point. The ship shook a little more violently this time but came out of it unscathed.

Theodore flicked the screen on the tablet, changing from the main plasma cannon to the freshly networked secondary batteries. With the push of a button the batteries opened up on the port side, over one hundred lighter plasma cannons creating a ripple of energy along the Ishur. The enemy ship followed suit, giving them the first true test of their makeshift system.

Miranda needed both hands to try to deflect the attack, raising them and placing them on the threat display, dragging the red dot across the visual and through a series of white lines. She kept the shield modulation on the move, sweeping it from the closest attack and across, catching a series of bolts with the DDS.

Meanwhile, the Ishur's guns pounded the side of the enemy fortress. Not only did the Dread's modulated darkspace shields hold up to the attack, but they didn't seem to have the same coverage limitations as the Ishur did.

"Damn it," Theodore said. "Mr. Mokri, how is your work on the weapons modifications coming along?"

"It isn't, General," Reza said. "I've hit nothing but dead ends so far."

"We need to think of something, son," Theodore said. "Gabriel, watch your starboard side. Duck and cover."

The Ishur shuddered as Gabriel manipulated the thrusters, bringing them downward in a sharp maneuver that wasn't quite exact. The second Dread starship opened fire on them again, the heavy plasma crossing the decreasing distance in a matter of seconds.

It didn't leave Colonel Choi much time to react, and she was a split-second late in dragging the red dot to the line on her display. The Ishur rocked more violently, taking a measure of damage from the plasma before recovering.

"Hull breaches on Decks thirty-four to forty," Abdullah said.

"Casualties?"

"No, sir. The decks are isolated. Emergency bulkheads are sealing."

"Sorry, General," Choi said.

"We're still alive," Theodore replied.

He eyed the two Dread fortresses. They were trying to maneuver around the front corners of the Ishur and get their main cannons in line. In fact, as Theodore watched them turn, it appeared to him that they were trying to target the same area of the ship, perhaps in the hope that a combined blast would penetrate their defenses.

If that was true, it was something they could use.

"Mr. Mokri, how much more power can we send to the plasma cannon?"

"I'm not sure, sir. Why?"

"I want to concentrate a steady stream on a single point. Can we do that?"

"Uh. I'm not sure, sir."

"That isn't a no. What do we have to do?"

"I'll need to make some adjustments to the parameters."

Theodore looked at the two Dread ships outside the viewport. They were getting dangerously close.

"You'd better do it fast, then, Mr. Mokri."

"Already on it," Reza replied, his fingers a blur on his tablet. "Sir," he added a moment later.

"Gabriel, head right for the port side ship. Full thrust. At five hundred klicks, bounce up and rotate the ass end to get us pointed down towards that coullion. Got it?"

"Yes, sir," Gabriel replied.

"Starboard ship is firing again, sir," Miranda said.

Theodore felt the soft shudder that signaled the attack had been deflected.

"I think I have it, sir," Reza said. "Hold down the trigger to keep firing a steady stream. You should know, it might fry the systems and leave us without the main cannon."

"A risk we have to take, I think," Theodore replied. "Gabriel, a little more rotation on the bow."

"Yes, sir."

The Ishur spun and rolled in space in a breaching maneuver that left them tilted over the top side of one of the Dread ships.

"Keep us over it," Theodore said. "Help me steady the shot."

"Yes, sir," Gabriel replied, working his own translated controls. The Ishur responded to them, the bow shifting in sync with the Dread ship's forward momentum.

Theodore pressed down on the firing button.

The blue bolt of plasma burst from the main cannon, hitting the Dread ship almost immediately. The darkspace flared beneath the attack, absorbing the energy. Theodore held the attack, and the flow of plasma continued, forming a near stream that bombarded the enemy ship.

One second passed. Two. Five. The beam remained solid, digging into the spot on the Dread fortress. The starboard ship fired again, its blow deflected by Colonel Choi.

"Come on, you bastard," Theodore said, watching the darkspace continue to absorb the attack. "I know you want to fail. Come on, damn you."

Seven seconds. Eight seconds. Nine seconds. Theodore could barely believe the cannon was still functional after all that time.

"Sir, DDS is offline," Lieutenant Bale said.

"We don't have the power," Reza replied. "General, half the ship is shutting down."

"We're already committed, son. We may not get another chance."

He kept his finger on the trigger.

Twelve seconds. Thirteen seconds.

He was about to give up, to try to think of something else, when the miracle he was waiting for finally happened, and in a way that was more fantastic than he could have ever expected.

One second, the darkspace shield was absorbing the energy of the plasma cannon. The next, it was collapsing inward, the pitch of the alternate continuum appearing to flip and fold backward and into the Dread fortress' hull, sinking through the lek'shah and eating away at the structure like a plague.

Theodore lifted his finger, the main cannon disengaging. The ship rocked from solid strikes by the second Dread starship's secondary batteries. A moment later, the DDS came back online, and his defense crew returned to work blocking the attack.

Small gouts of flame vented from the growing disintegration within the first vessel, the darkspace modulation almost seeming to implode and destroying everything in its path through the ship. It started to tilt a few seconds after that, and by the time the Ishur had swept past the side of the Dread starship it had fallen dead, drifting away from the human settlements.

"That's one," Theodore said, more than satisfied with the outcome. "Even if I don't know exactly what all just happened."

He refocused his attention on the other Dread ship. It had used their time in a relatively static position to improve its attack vector, sneaking in toward the rear of the Ishur and peppering it with secondary batteries.

Both Colonel Choi and Sergeant Hafizi were working feverishly to keep their DDS points centered on the brunt of the force, absorbing the incoming attacks before they could burn into the lek'shah hide of the ship.

"Come about, Gabriel," Theodore said. "As hard and fast as you can."

"Yes, sir," Gabriel replied. "Coming about."

The Ishur was silent, the power to the thrusters cut. They floated freely for a few seconds, gaining proximity to the settlements while Gabriel adjusted their vectors. The domo'shah behind them fired its main plasma cannon again, but this time Gabriel managed to steer them out of its path.

Theodore watched his son work with a measure of pride. Gabriel had blamed himself for the damage the Magellan had taken, but it seemed to him that the boy had used the situation to learn and improve. He was flying the huge fortress almost as well as Tea'va had done it and with much less experience, pushing it to extremes and getting the results.

The Ishur's bow swung forward, coming to rest in a nearly direct line with the enemy fortress.

Theodore pressed down on the trigger again.

He held it once more, counting the seconds as the beam tore into the leading edge of the opposing ship, somewhere within a few hundred meters of the bridge. He wondered what the pur'dahm in charge of the ship might be thinking after he had just watched his partner succumb to the same attack.

He found out a moment later. The second domo'shah accelerated toward them before altering course and ducking below, vectoring around in an effort to run.

"Oh no you don't," Theodore said, "Not after what you did to Delta. Stay on that bastard. We aren't letting this one run away."

"Yes, sir," Gabriel said, aligning the Ishur to give chase.

"She's heading for a slipstream," Reza reported.

"We're at max thrust, sir," Gabriel said. "We can't catch up to them."

"Damn it," Theodore cursed.

His finger hovered over the fire button while he considered whether or not to take the shot. It would be more for show than anything. The fortress was gaining range too fast for the weapon to be effective.

He hesitated for another second before pulling his hand away. "Pack it in, Gabriel," he said. "There's no point in risking the cannon, and we'll get another crack at him when we get to Earth."

Theodore could tell Gabriel didn't want to give up the chase, but he followed the order without hesitation, using the tablet to slow the Ishur once more.

"Lieutenant Bale, take over for the Major and bring us back toward the Settlements. Gabriel, Mr. Mokri, you're with me. Colonel Choi, you have the bridge."

"Where are we going, sir?" Reza asked.

Theodore lifted himself on his arms and shifted himself over, coming down in his chair. He began rolling toward the exit.

"To the hangar," he replied. "We aren't about to land this thing down there."

"What about General Cave?" Gabriel asked.

"Alan? What about him?"

"He's going to blame us for leading the Dread here."

"We've got a war to win, son. He can either get on board, or he can get the hell out of the way."

41

GABRIEL EASED THE BIS away from its position on the floor of the Ishur's hangar. The Magellan loomed beside him, a definitive work in progress as it underwent the transformation from starship to dropship.

The remaining nacelle had been removed, the damaged side also picked apart and reduced to a stub. The plasma damage along the hull was in the process of being repaired, with random bits of lek'shah affixed over the original armor where the cuts were too deep to heal.

Also new to the ship were a handful of ion cannons. They were smaller than even the smallest of the secondary batteries on the Ishur, rebuilt from as much material as they had been able to salvage. They wouldn't do much against a domo'shah or even the smaller ek'shah, but they would be effective against Dread starfighters and ground based weapons.

"Guy is installing the Dread zero-point reactors today," Reza said, a hint of pride in his voice. The two men had become unexpected friends after the whole ordeal with Guy's wife, Sarah, bonding over their shared desire to figure out and control the enemy tech.

"That means she'll be ready to fly soon," Theodore said.

"Yes, sir," Reza replied.

"The work your people have done is impressive, Dahm St. Martin," It'kek said from behind Gabriel.

"We couldn't have done it without you, Mr. It'kek," Theodore said.

Gabriel glanced back at the keeper. He had been hesitant to bring the reptilian bek'hai with them, but Theodore was insistent. According to him, it was important that the rest of the colonists understood what he had come to understand over the last few days.

That the bek'hai, the real bek'hai, weren't their enemies.

Instead, their enemy was the remnant of a once proud race, a descendent that had come about almost by accident, and who had been hugely responsible for destroying their world. It had started with the hunters, who had learned to kill the legri'shah with abandon for the value of their scales, their muscles, and their meat. It had ended with the loss of genetic diversity and the need to turn to the same creatures to save them. Millions of the animals had died in the civil conflict that had engulfed the bek'hai and transformed them into a more violent race. Hundreds more were still being slaughtered every cycle in order to provide resources to build more war machines, to repair the domo'shah, and to satiate the hunters desire to prove themselves against the creatures.

It'kek had told Gabriel about the competitions. The Circle of Honor was one thing. The legri'shah ring was another.

"This is Major Gabriel St. Martin," Gabriel said, opening a channel to Alpha Control. "Requesting permission to land."

There was a pause on the other side of the link. A woman replied a moment later.

"Roger, Major St. Martin. You have clearance for Bay C. General Cave has requested that you remain on board until he has arrived with a security detail."

"Ha," Theodore said. "Security detail? Who the hell does he think we are?"

"Traitors?" Reza said. "Deserters?"

"Bullshit. We didn't desert them. We're saving them."

"Affirmative, Control," Gabriel said. "Entering approach to Bay C."

He guided the BIS deftly toward the small opening in the structure outside of the central hub, noting how much more responsive the box in space was compared to the Ishur. While Reza had done a fantastic job getting it to interface with a human control system at all, the delays involved in the translation were still less than ideal.

"How does it feel to be home, son?" Theodore asked.

"Not like home," Gabriel replied. "I've seen Earth up close, remember?"

"We all have," Theodore said. "A little too up close."

He was referring to almost crashing the Magellan into the Pacific Ocean. At least they could laugh about it now.

"By the by, Mr. Mokri," Theodore said. "Any idea what happened with that Dread fortress up there?"

He pointed back into the deep black, where the dead domo'shah was still floating. They had already discussed sending a team to search it and look for salvage and survivors, especially among the keepers and legri'shah, but it was a secondary concern to getting the ball rolling with their own people.

"Not really," Reza replied. "Sir."

"Take a wild guess."

"Hmm. If I had to guess? I would say the energy in the plasma cannon destabilized the phase modulation enough that we created a wormhole of sorts, which wound up spinning out of control and through the enemy ship."

"A wormhole spinning out of control?" Gabriel said. "That doesn't sound good."

"It isn't if you happen to be in its path," Reza said. "Fortunately, space is a big place, and it isn't going in Earth's direction."

Gabriel tried to wrap his mind around the idea of a rogue piece of matter crushing darkspace as he steered the BIS into Alpha Settlement's main landing bay. He guided the ship to Bay C and brought it down.

"I have to admit, General," Reza said. "I'd rather not have to do that again. The plasma cannon was at critical heat levels, and an overload would have had a high likelihood of cooking everyone inside the Ishur ."

"Duly noted," Theodore replied. "Figure out the modulator for the plasma, and we won't have to do that again."

"Yes, sir."

"Your architecture is very interesting, Dahm St. Martin," It'kek said. His head had been turning back and forth during the entire trip, taking in the sights of the human base. "Very simplistic, yet functional."

"Well, thank you, I guess," Theodore replied. "It isn't much, but it does the job."

"Or did," Gabriel said. "Delta Station was destroyed. How many people do you think were on it?"

"Judging by the number of ships in here, hopefully not too many," Theodore said.

Gabriel nodded. Bay C was one of the only landing bays available, the rest filled with starfighters and BIS that he knew were usually assigned to the station.

"That's our cue," Theodore said, as soon as the light in the cockpit turned green, indicating the bay was pressurized.

"General Cave ordered us to wait," Reza replied.

"Mr. Mokri, do you work for him or for me?"

"For you, sir."

"Then I repeat. That's our cue."

"Yes, sir."

They moved to the rear of the BIS and down the opening doors to the floor of the hangar. It felt weird to Gabriel to be back where he had started, back to the confines of the place he had once called home. After spending the last two weeks on the Ishur, it felt small and primitive and dirty. After having landed on Earth, it felt downright unacceptable.

They reached the bay door. Theodore tapped the control to open it.

General Cave was standing in front of it, flanked by four armed guards. Councilwoman Rouse was waiting a few meters away, her hands folded against her chest.

"Ah, Alan," Theodore said. "I guess you knew I wasn't going to listen to anything you said."

General Cave stared at Theodore for a moment, his expression grim. Then he glanced over at Gabriel, and then at Reza, and finally at It'kek. He couldn't hold back his surprise at the sight of the bek'hai.

"Ha. That one caught you off-guard, didn't it?" Theodore said in response.

General Cave returned his attention to Theodore, who raised his hand.

"Hold up, Alan. Before you say anything, I think you should know; we're winning this here war."

It was General Cave's turn to surprise them. His stern expression melted away, and he started to laugh.

"The Old Gator," he said through his smile. "You've always had a flair for the dramatic, haven't you?" He stepped forward, leaning down to put his arms around Theodore. "I thought it was over for us."

"General Cave," Rouse said, sounding unhappy with his reaction. "Excuse me, General."

Cave ignored her, releasing Theodore and approaching Gabriel. "Gabe. I'm sorry for doubting you. I'm sorry for doubting any of you."

"General Cave," Rouse repeated, joining them. "These people are traitors."

Cave ignored her again. "They hit Delta Station, Teddy. They killed eight hundred of our people."

"We'll avenge them," Theodore replied. "That's why we came back. To gather the troops and take them home."

"You aren't taking anyone, anywhere," Rouse said. "General, I thought we came to arrest them?"

"Are you mental, woman?" Theodore said. "We just saved your life."

"You put us in danger in the first place. You stole our only means to travel away from this place, our only chance of finding a new home. You left the people here frightened and struggling to cope. You-"

"If I do remember correctly, Councilwoman, you were planning on sacrificing half the people in this colony so that you could head out to the stars in hopes of finding your new home. By my count, my way has only cost us approximately seven percent. I know that sounds harsh, but you can't argue the numbers. Furthermore, we came back. Oh, and if that weren't good enough for you, we brought you a big fat spaceship that can take every last resident of this here colony to their new home back on Earth as soon as we finish retaking it."

Theodore stared at Rouse, who tightened her hands against her chest, sighed, and moved back a few meters to her original position.

"I'm sorry for every soul we lost," Theodore said. "And I'm sorry I took Maggie. But it had to be done, Alan. You were wrong."

"Maybe I was. It doesn't matter now. I'm certainly not going to arrest you. What good would that do? You say we're winning this war? Then I say, what can I do to help?"

42

"AND THAT'S HOW IT all happened, in a nutshell," Gabriel said.

General Cave leaned back in his chair, a look of focused interest replaced by something more contemplative. Gabriel had spent the last two hours debriefing the General and his immediate staff on the situation back on Earth, and on their pressing need to rally the New Earth Alliance military to join the fight.

"And you are one of the, what did you call them again, Major? Bek'hai?"

The question was posed by Colonel Janet Ames, who had taken over Colonel Choi's position after she had left with Theodore. She was looking pointedly at It'kek, a hint of disgust mixing with fascination, mixing with anger.

"That is correct," It'kek replied. "We are some of the few original bek'hai that remain."

"Interesting. What I'm not clear about is why you're helping us, instead of your own kind?"

"We are helping our own kind, Colonel. The Domo'dahm does not understand that his path of resistance to complete genetic splicing with the humans will continue the extinction vector our kind has been on for many generations. He will not accept that the only way we survive as a species is to work with the humans, not fight against them. These bek'hai are not what we once were, or what we have the potential to be. But the keepers and the legri'shah are few in number. We are powerless to stop them, or we would have already."

"But you are betraying your people."

"Is it a betrayal to sacrifice what you must to save them? For us, it is not about helping the humans defeat the bek'hai. It is about helping the humans and the bek'hai coexist."

"And why would we want to coexist with you?" one of General Cave's other staffers, Captain Huang asked. "You took our planet. You killed billions."

"Because that is the only way either of us ever knows peace. Your kind on Earth have resisted bek'hai rule for fifty of your years. If you depose the Domo'shah, do you suppose there will be immediate peace? Do you think the remaining bek'hai will simply accept the loss of the planet and the death of their kind?"

"General," Huang said. "We can't seriously be considering trying to make peace with the Dread. Especially now, when we have the means to fight back." He looked at Theodore. "General St. Martin, surely you can't be in favor of this."

Theodore shook his head. "In favor of requesting an audience with the Domo'dahm? It'll be a cold day in hell. But here's the rub, Captain. There are thousands and thousands of prisoners living among the rest of the Dread. A lot of them are clones of one kind of another, each with a job that they're programmed to do. They're slaves of a fashion, locked into what they have always known, but they have individual personalities as well, and some of them can be influenced. Then there are the keepers like It'kek here. They want to change course for their people, but don't have the power to do it on their own." He smiled. "And then we have the un'hai."

"Un'hai?" General Cave said. "Oh, right, the clones of Juliet."

"We don't know how many there are, but they're already embedded deep inside the Dread system. Some of them, when they hear my name, it trips something in their minds, and they get access to Juliet's memories. They begin to think that they're her, and they start to act on those beliefs."

"Like spies?" Colonel Ames asked.

"Better than spies," Theodore replied. "Juliets. Heh. For all we know, there are drumhr in the Domo'dahm's circle that are opposed to what he's doing as well. The un'hai creator, Tuhrik, was one of them. Good old Juliet. She got to them all. She showed them the light of forgiveness and peace. I know it."

"That's all well and good, Teddy," General Cave said. "How do we use this to our advantage?"

"We're gonna have to fight on the ground. We're gonna have to fight in space. There're no two ways about it. And, even with our crews mixed with the rebels on the ground, we're still going to be heavily outnumbered and outgunned. But, if we can get through to these other groups behind the scenes? We may just have ourselves a chance."

"It seems like quite a long shot," Captain Huang said. "General Cave, we have other options, and I think we should at least discuss them."

"Like?" Gabriel said. He had a feeling he knew what the Captain was going to say.

"The Dread fortress, the domo'shah, is capable of slipstream travel. It's also larger than all of our settlements combined and built for longevity. We can take it to the New Earth. We can settle there. Let the bek'hai keep the old Earth. Let them run themselves into the ground. We shouldn't risk our chance at freedom on a fight whose odds are so against us."

Gabriel sighed. It was the same old argument as before, framed and updated to match current events. Never mind the sacrifices people had made to get them here. Never mind the people on the ground who were going to die. Earth wasn't home to billions anymore, but there were still a few million people under the Domo'dahm's thumb.

"Alan," Theodore said calmly. "Would you like to court-martial this coward, or do you want me to do it?" He glanced at Captain Huang. "By the by, you aren't related to Councilwoman Rouse, are you?"

Huang opened his mouth to speak. General Cave put up a hand to silence him. "Hold on. Both of you. Teddy, I appreciate your decision to stay relatively calm. It's not like you. I want to make this clear to everyone gathered here right now, and to the entire colony once we leave this room. Under no circumstances are we abandoning Earth or the people on it. Just like the bek'hai nearly destroyed themselves with their own ignorance, if we run away now we'll be doing the same thing, and probably to the same result. Maybe we'll lose. Maybe we'll die. If we go out there and try to forget about what happened here? It will change who we are for the worse, forever."

"With all due respect, sir," Captain Huang said. "You used to be in favor of leaving Earth behind."

"You're right. I was. And I would have allowed the death of half this colony to make it happen. I'm embarrassed to admit that now. I'm embarrassed to know I never would have been embarrassed if Theodore hadn't come back and saved my life, and all of our lives. I thought running was the answer and the only option. I hurt a lot of people because of that. I regret those decisions."

Captain Huang stood up. He didn't look happy. "You don't need to court-martial me, sir. Either one of you. I resign." He pulled his rank insignia from his chest, dropping it on the table and storming toward the door.

Theodore cut him off, rolling his chair in front of him.

"Get out of my way," Huang said.

"No I will not get out of your way," Theodore said. "You listen to me, boy. For starters, you're in the military. You don't get to resign. For another, you're an officer in that same military, which makes you too valuable just to walk away. Third, I'd sooner kill you with my bare hands than let you disrespect me, General Cave, Major St. Martin, or even Mr. It'kek over there. What do you think we've been doing these last few weeks, twiddling our thumbs? Or maybe sticking them up our asses? Good men and women have been dying, down there on Earth, on my ship, and right here in our backyard. Those are our people, Captain. Not some other alien race that's no concern of ours. Now, why don't you go sit down? Take a minute to think about something other than yourself. We win through unity. We die with division."

Captain Huang stood in front of Theodore, glaring down at him. Theodore met his gaze, his expression so condescending that Gabriel expected Huang to punch him.

Instead, he retreated, taking a few steps back and then returning to his seat.

"That's better," Theodore said. "Alan, I promised the rebels back on Earth that we'd be in Mexico in eight days. That leaves us forty-eight to get as organized as possible. My thinking was to load up all of our troops and consolidate the civvies to Alpha. Once this thing is done, we can come back for them."

"I think that can work," Cave replied. "Although forty-eight hours isn't a lot of time."

"Excuse me," Captain Huang said.

Theodore shot a nasty look over at him.

"Yes, Captain," General Cave said.

"If the soldiers all leave and the civilians stay behind, there's a chance they could get stranded here."

"Only if we were to lose," Gabriel said.

"That's beside the point. I think we should give everyone the option to return to Earth. Some will choose to stay behind, but some won't."

Theodore's face softened. "Well, we do have the space. I don't see any harm in it."

"Neither do I," General Cave said.

"Then we'll do that. Damn. I should have brought Lieutenant O'Dea down to help us with the logistics. I'll ship her over on the next boat. For now, I think we should start moving troops by company. That way we can get them properly armed and outfitted on their way in. Parallel to that, we can begin moving whatever resources we can spare. I'm sure we can convert them into something we can use. Captain, does your statement mean you've reconsidered?"

Huang had picked his insignia back up and reaffixed it to his uniform.

"Yes, General," he replied.

"Then don't worry too much about your little outburst. It won't leave this room, and I forgive you."

"Thank you, sir."

"I want you to be our liaison to the Council. General Cave is going to be too busy helping me organize to deal with Rouse and the others. Tell them what we're doing, make sure they know that part of it isn't optional, but coming along for the ride is. Can you do that, son?"

"Yes, sir."

"Good man."

"What about me, General?" Colonel Ames asked.

"You used to a be a pilot, didn't you? Before you got the arthritis?"

"I made three runs past Earth, yes, sir. I'd still be doing it if I could."

"Well, the Ishur is a bit of a different animal. I don't think your disability would affect your ability to serve on the bridge, and I have other plans for Major St. Martin." Theodore turned to Gabriel. "Would you mind giving Colonel Ames a few lessons on flying the fortress?"

"Not at all, sir," Gabriel replied.

"Good. Mr. Mokri, I want you to take a shuttle over to Gamma. Help the science teams figure out what they can salvage there, and what we can use. Thank God the bastards only got one shot off."

"Yes, sir," Reza replied.

"Mr. It'kek, you're with Alan and me. You and yours have been invaluable so far, but we need to pick your brain a little more to put together a complete plan."

"Of course, Dahm St. Martin," It'kek said.

"General Cave and I will be reaching out to all of you again over the next two days. If any of you were expecting to sleep, cancel those plans. You can catch up when we go into slipspace."

"Yes, sir," the others said.

"Alan, is there anything you want to add?"

General Cave smiled. "No. I think you covered it all."

"In that case, you're all dismissed. Let's get to work."

43

"I NEVER GOT A chance to meet Captain Kim," General Alan Parker said. "I wish I had. I've spent a lot of years dreaming of the day when I would meet someone from the space forces. When I would get to sit with them, embrace them, and thank them for never giving up. For never leaving us behind. And while I didn't know Captain Kim, that's what he represents to me. Hope. Hope for a better future. A future without the Dread."

The assembled rebels clapped as General Parker finished his eulogy, putting his hand on the simple casket that had been made to lay the fallen soldier to rest. It was more than a lot of the dead received, but Donovan understood why the General was placing Soon front and center as a symbol of the war. They had all heard General St. Martin's message. They all knew the storm was coming. It was right to be afraid. It was natural. Having something to cling to and to rally around could be the difference between victory and defeat.

It had been two days since the General had arrived, riding into Austin on the shoulder of Donovan's mech, his American flag waving in the breeze. It was an arrival that had kicked the gears of war into full motion, an arrival that had set the already focused rebels into a greater sense of purpose and motivation.

Not only because of General Parker, but also because of General St. Martin.

Donovan could still barely believe the man General Rodriguez had called the Old Gator had managed to survive. It was even harder for him to believe that he had somehow captured one of the enemy fortresses for the rebellion. To think that only a short time earlier they had still believed the Dread to be untouchable. Unbeatable. Now it seemed as if victory, or at least the chance for victory, was imminent.

He watched the General finish the ceremony, and then joined Ehri and Colonel Knight at the front of the assembly. They lifted Soon's casket together, carrying it to the corner of the loop station, where a grave had already been dug. They lowered it in, and then General Parker handed Donovan a makeshift shovel.

"Thank you, sir," Donovan said. He used the shovel to return a scoop of the earth to its place and then passed it on to Ehri. She did the same, and the process was repeated, the shovel passed along to a line of soldiers that formed behind them. Most of them had never had a chance to get to know Soon, but they respected him for what he had done, and for what he represented.

After two days, the rebel army was almost ready to move out. Donovan had barely slept the entire time, getting involved with the effort to organize and coordinate the influx of new fighters, and to help Colonel Knight and General Parker put together a plan for when they reached the Dread capital. He and Ehri had the most experience with both the layout and military capabilities of the linked Dread fortresses, and so their input had been essential to the strategy.

Not that there was anything fancy about their plan. The intent was to use the same tactics that had gotten them this far, only on a larger scale and with a little more firepower behind it. That meant trying to stay out of the Dread's sensor range, to keep silent and cool as they made their approach. The mechs would hang back, aiming to cover the ground teams as they came under pressure, and to offer a distraction to pull the Dread heavy units away. The goal, they had decided, was to infiltrate the Dread fortresses, to get soldiers inside where they would have better success fighting the enemy army in close quarters. For Donovan, that meant he was going to see the worst of the fighting from within the cockpit of a Dread mech.

It also meant he was one of the soldiers who was most likely to be killed.

While the infantry would be sneaking through the streets of Mexico City, he would be looking to intercept both Dread mechanized armors and starfighters as they swept over the field, laying down cover fire and trying to pull the birds from the sky. The mech alone was going to make him a huge target, but his harassment would make him impossible to ignore, and that was the idea.

He wasn't afraid of dying. He had seen too many of his friends fall to the Dread to fear being killed in battle. His real fear came from the thought of failure. Of being shot down before he accomplished his mission and gave the infantry enough time to reach the enemy's gates. He was comforted a little to know that Ehri would be covering his left side, but standing in front of Soon's grave only reminded him that someone else would be to his right, someone he would have to learn to trust in a hurry.

He wasn't sure who would receive the assignment just yet. They had returned with three mechs to add to the two they already controlled, and a salvage team had brought back his damaged armor to try to repair under Orli's supervision. That meant there were four seats for nearly a dozen people who had made the cut of initial volunteers and who had been training to drive the machines. He knew that Lieutenant Bastion and Corporal Knowles were currently at the top of the leaderboards they had devised to track progress. Would it be one of them?

Not that it mattered in the end. They were all in this together.

Donovan began moving away from the grave, clearing space for others to offer their respects. Kroeger was near the front of the line, and the soldier tossed a pile of dirt onto the casket before hurrying to catch up with him.

"Major," Kroeger said, keeping pace as they walked. "I hear we're moving out tonight."

"That's right," Donovan said.

Kroeger stopped and put out his hand. "Major, if we don't see one another again, I just wanted to thank you."

"Thank me?"

"I spent years out there in a world where hope was hard to come by, and civilization even harder. It changed me, in good ways and bad, but more in bad, I think. I was trying to do something good with Hell, and I think I did okay at it. But since signing up with you, I feel pride I thought I had lost. A sense of purpose that I thought was long gone. So yeah, thank you for that, Major. Even if we don't always see eye to eye." He paused, looking back at Soon's grave. "Even if you should have listened to me."

He gave Donovan a half-smirk and headed off, returning to the ground unit where he had been assigned.

"Asshole," Donovan said softly to his back. He still wasn't sure if he liked Kroeger or not, but he couldn't deny the man was a survivor.

"Excuse me, Major?" General Parker said, having overheard him.

Donovan turned to face the General, saluting as he did. "Sir. Not you, sir. Sergeant Kroeger."

"An interesting character for sure," General Parker replied. "I've seen a lot of people like him out in the human wasteland."

"Those are the people we're fighting to save?"

"Yes. We can't discriminate, even if sometimes we wish we could."

"Yes, sir."

Donovan kept his eyes on the General, waiting for him to announce his intentions. He had learned over the last two days that it was one of the General's strongest, most subliminal traits. He had a confident, commanding presence about him, one that made soldiers want to be still and listen or wait to be addressed. He was a leader. A true leader, who had taken over the Austin operation on his arrival and within eighteen hours had everyone in it following his command without question. Donovan admired the quality.

He also admired the man. Stories about General Parker had started circulating when his army from New York had arrived. Stories about his bravery and sacrifice, about his strategic genius and his fatherly demeanor. He had not only held things together as the situation had gotten worse in the northeast, but he had also overcome it, adding to their numbers even while they couldn't put a scratch on the Dread.

"I was going to talk to you about this later at the officer's meeting, but I thought it might lift your spirits a little bit to hear it from me right now. I want you to lead not only the mech unit but also the entire diversionary force, including the Bertha Brigade, as they've taken to calling themselves." He smiled. "I'm also going to shift two companies over to your command to help with the external defenses. Both J and K Companies will fall under your flag."

K Company was Kroeger's unit. It seemed they wouldn't be parting ways just yet.

"Major is a low rank to have that much responsibility," General Parker continued. "It won't affect your pay grade, but I'm promoting you to Colonel. Congratulations."

Donovan looked at the General's face, and then at his hand. Colonel?

"Yes, sir," he replied, taking the hand. "Thank you, sir." He knew his mother would have been proud of him for this.

"I also thought you might want to meet your new squad mate."

"You, sir?" Donovan said.

General Parker laughed. "I'd be honored, Colonel, but no. I need to help run the overall attack." He motioned back to Colonel Knight. "Colonel Knight has been taking lessons from Ehri in private. From what I hear, she might be a better pilot than you."

Colonel Knight approached at the mention of her name. "I thought we were going to cover this later, sir?" she said.

"Now seemed as good of a time as any."

"Colonel," Donovan said, saluting her.

"Colonel," Colonel Knight replied, returning the salute. "Looks like I'm taking orders from you now, sir."

"I guess you are," Donovan said, feeling a little uncomfortable with the role reversal.

"We're all professionals here," General Parker said. "And we all want the same thing. There's no need to feel strange about it."

"Yes, sir," Donovan said.

"Good. I recommend that you try to enjoy your last few hours of calm. It might be the last we have for a while."

44

"Domo'dahm," Orish'ek said as he entered Rorn'el's private chamber beside the throne room.

Rorn'el turned at the approach, shifting his back toward the pur'dahm to avoid being seen. It was improper for Orish'ek to look on him directly, and he would be forced to retire if he caught more than a glimpse. For as embarrassing as the human form was, the legri'hai shape was even more of a failure, and one that he hoped they could one day forget.

"Have you forgotten your place, Orish'ek?" he snapped. "Or do you intend to defy me as well?"

He hissed softly at the idea of it. Too many of his subjects were proving to be less than trustworthy.

"My apologies, Domo'dahm," Orish'ek said. "I thought you would want to know that Pit'ek has returned. I have already ordered him to appear before you."

Pit'ek was back from his hunt for the human settlement? Did that mean the technology that had been delivered to them from the Ishur had worked? That was news worth being intruded upon for.

"Excellent. I will prepare myself for the audience. What of our efforts to root out the un'hai?"

"Sor'ek has assembled a complete roster of all of the active un'hai as you commanded, Domo'dahm. The report is within your data store."

"Have you seen it?"

"Yes, Domo'dahm."

"What are your thoughts?"

Orish'ek was hesitant to respond. Rorn'el turned slightly, glancing back at him from the corner of his eye.

"What is the problem?" he asked.

"Domo'dahm," Orish'ek said. "Tuhrik was directly responsible for the creation of the un'hai, at your request."

"Yes. And?"

Orish'ek froze.

"And?" Rorn'el repeated with a hiss.

"Domo'dahm, the un'hai compose nearly ninety percent of our science and technology focused lor'hai. This includes our splicing research, the assemblers, astronomy, and many other vital roles. Further, it was the un'hai Kehri's work with the human technology that allowed Pit'ek to integrate the systems into the lek'shah."

"What are you suggesting?"

"Two things, Domo'dahm. First, there are very few, if any, un'hai that Tuhrik did not have any opportunity to manipulate. Second, it is clear from the actions of at least one of the un'hai that they are not all disloyal."

Rorn'el considered it. In his initial anger at Zoelle's betrayal, he had been of a mind to destroy all of the Juliet clones and replace them with something more reliable. Now it was clear that not only was that not feasible; it also might not be necessary. Only some of the un'hai seemed to be infected with whatever damage Tuhrik had introduced to them.

"Do we have any way to determine which of the un'hai might be traitorous?" he asked.

"No, Domo'dahm. Sor'ek has tested the brain function of a random sample and has uncovered no discernible differences. An autopsy has also failed to reveal any obvious patterns to identify these copies."

"But it is possible his sample was too small?" Rorn'el said.

"Yes, Domo'dahm. However, if there are only a limited number of tainted clones, it would be inefficient to continue destroying them in the hopes of discovering one."

"Of course. There is no reason to continue to focus on this. If there are more un'hai like Ehri hiding in our midst, they will reveal themselves sooner or later, and then they will die. As long as Sor'ek is certain this is not a widespread problem?"

"He is certain, Domo'dahm. His estimate places one to three of these un'hai on each domo'shah, along with another thirty scattered among our outposts."

"Less than one hundred? Surely our pur'dahm can handle them if the need arises."

"Yes, Domo'dahm."

"Go now, Orish'ek. I must prepare myself for audience."

"Yes, Domo'dahm."

Rorn'el turned around again once the pur'dahm had left. He used the arms of his chair to lift himself to a stand, shifting slightly as he did. His legs cracked at the motion, and he hissed in pain.

Old. He was getting old. He had taken Kesh'ek's place nearly forty cycles ago, himself already fifty cycles in age. While his natural lifespan was hundreds of years longer, his days in the legri'shah ring had taken their toll, and given him reason to look forward to his retirement. Not now, though. Not while the humans were still trying to take the planet back from him. He would see every last one of them destroyed before that day came.

He moved to the corner of the room, opening a small chamber there and removing a lek'shah mask from it. He lifted it out, lowered the hood of his gori'shah, and placed it over his scaled face. Then he raised the hood again, tilting himself downward to reduce his profile. He hobbled over to a second compartment, opened it, and looked down at the splintered cross he had recovered. It was no longer a symbol of peace of him, but one of anger and clarity. He had been too soft on the humans because of her. It was her fault he was in this position now.

He closed the compartment and then headed out into the hallway between his throne and his quarters. He looked at both ends of the corridor, finding it empty, before crossing the short distance to the other side and entering the antechamber. Once inside he climbed into the darkened cage that was his throne and removed the mask. Then he activated his console, using it to move the throne into position.

Orish'ek was already sitting in his proper place beside him as he moved into place. The pur'dahm did not look at him on his arrival. Neither did the others who were already present.

"Bring him in," he said a moment later, shifting his body to get more comfortable in his seat. The hatch at the end of the room slid open, and pur'dahm Pit'ek entered.

The commander of the Ishrem bowed at the rear of the room, and then made the long, lonely walk to the front. He bowed again when he reached Rorn'el, sweeping his head so low that the patches of black hair on the sides of his head hit the floor.

"Domo'dahm," Pit'ek said nervously.

Rorn'el stared at the pur'dahm. He could tell that something was wrong.

"Did you locate the human settlement?" Rorn'el asked, feeling a growing sense of unease and anger in his gut.

"Yes, Domo'dahm. We found the settlement. It was broken into five separate locations. We destroyed two of them."

"Two? Why not five?"

"With your honor, Domo'dahm." Pit'ek began to look more uncomfortable. "There were complications."

"Complications?" he replied, forcing himself to stay calm for now.

"The Ishur arrived just as we were commencing the attack on the humans. They attacked us."

"And the shields?"

"The shields were effective, Domo'dahm."

"What about the Ishur? Did they also have these shields?"

"Yes, Domo'dahm, only their defenses were not the same. The modulation of their hull seemed very unstable. I would claim that our technology is superior."

"Then the Ishur was destroyed? This General St. Martin was destroyed?"

Pit'ek kept his head low. "No, Domo'dahm."

"But you are not destroyed."

"No, Domo'dahm."

"Explain yourself, Pit'ek."

"With your honor, Domo'dahm. The Ishrek was destroyed, and the Ishur was deflecting all of our attacks."

"You just said their defenses were inferior," Orish'ek said.

"Yes, Si'dahm," Pit'ek said. "Perhaps they weren't as inferior as we believed. They moved around the ship as though they were being controlled from the bridge. It was an interesting solution to the problems the scientists discovered."

"If the shields are effective, how was the Ishrek destroyed?"

"They converted the plasma cannon to a solid plasma stream, Domo'dahm. I believe this was possible because they are using only a small portion of the resources available on the domo'shah. They are not supporting thousands, and they are not utilizing the factories. The stream held for many ticks, many more than we could possibly achieve. It is possible that they have upgraded the systems similar to the shields. I do not know, Domo'dahm. I am unsure. The stream appeared to overwhelm the lek'shah modulation and invert, creating a small wormhole which traveled through the Ishrem and disabled it."

Rorn'el felt his hands clenching into fists as he listened to the story. They had the perfect opportunity to destroy the human settlement, to destroy the Ishur, and to leave the rebels on the ground exposed when their expected reinforcements never arrived. Instead, not only had Pit'ek failed in his mission, but he had failed to die with honor.

If entire wars hinged on single battles, this one would continue because of that failure.

"I do not understand," he said. "I told you that if you returned with the humans still alive your life would be forfeit, Pit'ek. And yet you returned."

"Domo'dahm," Pit'ek said, bowing low once more. "We could not match the Ishur in offensive capability, and I believed that this information was more valuable than my sacrifice."

Rorn'el smiled, shifting his head so that light would catch enough of it that Pit'ek would see his sharp teeth. The pur'dahm drew back slightly at the sight.

"You have done well to return this information to me."

"Thank you, Domo'dahm."

"Now that it is delivered, I expect you to fulfill the orders you were given."

"Orders, Domo'dahm?"

"Yes. I ordered you not to return to me without having destroyed the human settlement, or to be prepared for your retirement."

The pur'dahm lifted his head slightly, ready to argue, before lowering it again. "Yes, Domo'dahm."

"Be glad I do not disgrace you by killing you myself."

"Yes, Domo'dahm."

"You are dismissed."

"Yes, Domo'dahm."

Rorn'el sat in silence while Pit'ek fled the room. He had no doubt the drumhr would fulfill his obligation to retire.

"So, the humans continue to outmaneuver us," Orish'ek said.

"It appears that way. A plasma stream? It may have been effective against only two ships, but it will not be enough to save them." He paused. "Order all of the domo'shah not attached to the capital to take up position in orbit and bolster the defensive net. Once there, they are to deploy their full complement of ek'shah and to have the gi'shah on standby for deployment."

"Domo'dahm?" Orish'ek said. "All of the domo'shah?"

"You believe this is the wrong decision?" Rorn'el asked.

"If the ground forces break through, it will make it all the easier for them to reach us."

"The rebel forces are not the problem here. They have a secure position underground, but once they emerge they will be decimated before they can even get close. No. The Ishur is the real danger. They possess the firepower of a domo'shah, and the ingenuity to survive. It is a shame I will have to destroy General St. Martin. He would have made a fine splice." Rorn'el looked at Orish'ek. "Why are you still here? Send out my orders."

Orish'ek hesitated for a moment as if he wanted to say something else, and then bowed and left the room.

Domo'dahm Rorn'el leaned back in his throne and closed his eyes.

He would see the humans destroyed before his time came to retire.

It was his legacy.

It was his destiny.

45

"Preparing to join the slipstream in five. Four. Three. Two. One. Now," Gabriel said, counting down as the Ishur accelerated toward the subspace wave, her large quantum phased fins stretched out around her.

They shimmered and began to vanish to the alternate thread of time and space, pulling the main body of the fortress along with them. A few seconds later, the stars collapsed, leaving them in a place of infinite black.

"Slipstream joined," he said, turning to look back at his father.

"And we're on our way," Theodore said with a smile. "ETA to arrival, Mr. Mokri?"

"Five days, nine hours, sir," Reza replied.

"Three hours ahead of schedule. I hope the rebels don't mind that we're early."

"I hope they weren't planning on cutting things that close," General Cave said. He was sitting in the station right in front of the command dais, two seats from Miranda.

As expected, the two days at the colony had passed in a blur, finding everyone involved with the war effort under increasing pressure to get everything organized and prepared. While General Cave and Theodore, along with Colonels Choi and Graham had gotten to work organizing a definitive strategy, Gabriel had been tasked with both training Colonel Ames on how to fly the Dread starship, and in keeping abreast of the status of the many other projects underway. It had meant a lot of shuttling back and forth between the Ishur and Alpha Station, a lot of walking through the corridors of both, and absolutely no sleep.

He was tired, but he would never show it. He had wanted nothing more than to be the one to bring the Ishur into slipspace, and now that it was done he felt the sudden weight of his exhaustion.

He didn't realize he was yawning until his father called him on it.

"Major St. Martin," Theodore said, using his rank. "Are we boring you?"

"Sorry, sir," Gabriel said, feeling his face flush. "It's been a long couple of days?"

"Long? It went by like a dream to me. Give me a quick sitrep on our preparations and then head on to your quarters. I can't afford to have my top pilot going into the shit with eyes half-open."

"Yes, sir," Gabriel said, trying to remember all of the reports he had received in the hours before the Ishur had departed. "The Ishur's current population is eight-thousand forty-four souls, including two thousand six hundred and forty civilians, one hundred and three clone soldiers, twelve keepers, three mature legri'shah, and an unknown number of cleaners. We also have five thousand two hundred and seven trained soldiers from the colony on board, who have been armed with three thousand seventy-two Dread rifles. It is expected that the assemblers will complete almost one hundred percent of the inventory needed for the infantry before we arrive."

"I am seriously impressed with your memory, son," Theodore said.

"I'm just getting started, sir," Gabriel replied. "The assemblers have also completed four gi'shah capable of being piloted by humans, and two of the larger ek'shah, which require at least a dozen souls to operate. They have also used recovered salvage to repair or produce sixteen of our own starfighters, with upgrades to the ion cannons for standard phase modulation. The bad news is that we currently only have ten qualified pilots and eight academy trainees who are advanced enough to put in the cockpit."

"Too many ships. We have six days to find soldiers we can train."

"Yes, sir. It is expected the assemblers will produce two more starfighters during the trip."

"What about Maggie?"

"According to Guy, the Magellan is as fit to fly as she'll ever be. They'll be finishing the plasma cannon mounts during the trip. Unfortunately, we only have enough resources for five of them."

"Not ideal, but I'll take what I can get."

"Yes, sir. The civilians have all been assigned berths on decks three to nineteen. Its one level above the cloning facilities and the legri'shah pens. We've done our best to teach them how to use the transport beams and to warn them about wandering randomly, but we don't have the manpower to babysit."

"I told Councilwoman Rouse to do what she could to keep them in line," Theodore said. "Damn that woman for being good at what she does; once she put her mind to being part of the solution instead of part of the problem."

"Yes, sir. There are still two thousand or so civilians remaining on Alpha Settlement that we'll need to pick up after we win. With the reduced population, they should have the capacity to stay alive for years."

"In case we don't come back? Heh. The ones who stayed behind are idiots."

"Yes, sir. We have enough food and water to last for months and enough space that everyone on the ship is pretty happy with the living situation. Although, they might change their minds once the fighting starts."

"You can say that again. I think half of them think we're going for a stroll and we'll just land somewhere and let them out."

"Yes, sir."

"Anything else, Major?"

Gabriel thought about it for a few seconds. "Just that I'm proud to be part of this offensive, sir." And proud to be your son. He didn't say it, but he felt it.

"I'm proud to have you," Theodore replied. "If you're done with your report, you're dismissed."

"Yes, sir. Thank you, sir."

Gabriel stood to leave.

"Spaceman Locke," Theodore said. "When was the last time you had some bunk time?"

Gabriel found Miranda, who looked surprised at the question. She looked spent, too. "Uh. I lost track, sir."

"You're dismissed as well. I'll get one of the new recruits up to take your place. We aren't running a skeleton crew anymore."

"Yes, sir."

Gabriel felt himself blush. He knew what his father was doing. He probably thought he was a sly old gator.

Gabriel headed off the bridge, with Miranda right behind him. They stopped together a short distance away.

"The General seems to think that there's a benefit to us being off duty at the same time," she said, a smile creeping across her face.

"He does, doesn't he? He wasn't exactly subtle about it."

The smile turned to a laugh. "Do you think he knows something we don't?"

"No. I think he knows something we know."

"Gabriel-"

"Miranda. Wait. Come on."

Gabriel reached out and took her hand. She followed him as he led her through the ship and to his quarters.

"Do you want to come in?" he asked. "Wallace is going to pee when he sees us."

She laughed again. "Of course."

Gabriel opened the hatch. Wallace came charging out, yipping and wagging his tail, circling both of them and leaving a little urine on the deck, just like Gabriel had guessed he would.

"Who's my good man?" Miranda asked, petting him while he licked her face.

Gabriel watched her, feeling his pulse quickening. Theodore had given them this time for a reason, and he wasn't going to waste it.

"Miranda," he said.

She looked up at him and stood, keeping her hand on Wallace's back. "Gabriel, I-"

"I love you," Gabriel said, spitting it out before he could reconsider.

"I love you," she said at almost the same time.

They both laughed.

"I've wanted to say that for a while," she said. "Years, actually. I never wanted to push or pressure you after Jessica."

"I didn't know that I did until recently, to be honest. But I do. You've brought me more joy than I thought I would feel again. You're my best friend." He paused and looked down at Wallace. "After him, obviously."

She laughed again. "I love that you're honest, Gabriel. I love your courage and your strength and your loyalty."

"I love the same things about you," he said, looking in her eyes. "I know this is a little awkward, but I didn't want anything to happen before I got to say it, even though I've been so busy I haven't had the chance."

"Are you sure you're not just overtired?" she asked.

He stepped toward her, reaching out. She moved into him, accepting his embrace. "Absolutely."

They kissed. It was a simple kiss. Soft and short, an expression of an emotion born of admiration and respect. Then they held one another. Gabriel enjoyed running his hands through her hair and feeling the weight of her head on his shoulder.

"Will you marry me?" Gabriel asked. "After this is over?"

"Yes." She picked her head up. "Why not before? Your father can do it. Or General Cave."

"Motivation," he said. "If I have that to look forward to, there will be nothing the Dread can do to stop me from making it back."

She reached up and put her hand on his face. "I believe you when you say that."

"Good, because I mean it." He looked over at his bed. "Now if you don't mind, I'm going to crash and burn here before I crash and burn out there."

"I think you might be on to something. I'm about ready to fall over myself."

"I'll see you on the bridge?"

"Affirmative."

He pulled her close and kissed her again. "Goodnight, Miranda."

"Goodnight, Gabriel."

They kissed one last time, and then she left his room, headed for her own quarters. He retreated to his bed, falling onto it and descending quickly into the best sleep he had ever had.

46

DONOVAN BROUGHT HIS MECH to a stop as they reached the outskirts of San Luis Potosi. He felt a chill at the sight of the city, remembering the battle that had happened there, and the person who had died there.

Diaz. His eyes shifted to the area of the city where he had burned her body, knowing the ashes would still be there. It had only been three weeks since they had left. It felt strange to be back again so soon.

It felt even stranger to be at the head of an army almost twelve-thousand people strong.

It was more than they had started with. It was more than they had ever expected. Men, women, and even children had been streaming in from the world around them, every day since they had marched from Austin at a breakneck pace. They were rebels from other camps, they were jackals, they were scavengers, they were anyone and everyone who had been near any kind of transmitter and had heard Theodore St. Martin's message. They were people who had found their humanity, who had been inspired, and who were ready to fight back.

"Are you well, Colonel?" Ehri asked.

"Yeah. We aren't coming back with our tail between our legs."

"No, sir."

"What do you think the Domo'dahm is waiting for?" he asked.

They hadn't seen a single Dread fighter, a single Dread mech, or even a single Dread soldier since they had left Austin. The route was as clear as any of them had ever seen, trouble and conflict free, as though the aliens had never existed at all.

"General St. Martin issued him a challenge. He will be dishonored not to meet it. Do not let this lull fool you. You will find his forces in Mexico."

"I'm looking forward to it."

"Yes."

"Colonel Peters," General Parker said, his voice coming in over the makeshift receiver mounted to the front of the mech's cockpit. "Take Ehri and Colonel Knight down into the city and make sure it's clear. We'll hang back and wait for your report."

"Yes, sir," Donovan replied, putting his mech in motion once more. "Come on."

The three mechs moved into the decimated city, crossing through the main thoroughfare and winding through the side streets. As expected, Donovan came across the place where Diaz had been put to rest. He bowed the mech's head there out of respect before contacting the General again.

"We're all clear, General."

"Good. We'll rest here for three hours, and then we have to be on the move again. We're running behind as it is."

"The stragglers are slowing us down, sir," Donovan said. That was the downside to the civilians that had been joining them. They were threatening to get the army there late.

"I know, Colonel. We have to make a decision whether or not to leave them behind."

"It doesn't seem like much of a decision to me, sir. We can't ask

General St. Martin to manage this war on his own."

"You're absolutely right, and I was thinking the same thing. We'll pass the word down the line to them. They need to keep up or get left behind."

"Yes, sir."

"Split your squad into two shifts, Colonel. I want your sensors on the surroundings, just in case the Dread try something sneaky."

"Yes, sir. Bastion, Knowles, Knight, you're on first shift. Move into position to maximize sensor coverage. I don't want anything getting near this city without us knowing about it."

"Yes, sir," the pilots replied.

Donovan moved his mech back toward the oncoming army. The foot soldiers moved in first, two hundred strong. They swept through the area, taking up defensive positions on rubble piles and broken rooftops. Donovan spotted Kroeger among them, finding a good place to roost with his sniper rifle.

"The rest of you, try to get a little shut-eye," Donovan said. "Ninety minutes and then we switch."

Donovan settled back in the cockpit, closing his eyes and trying to relax. He was nervous. Impatient. They couldn't get to Mexico City soon enough.

He was halfway through his ninety minutes when the sudden sound of deep rumbling and a beeping from the mech's terminal caused him to wake. His eyes snapped open, and he looked around outside. The buildings were shivering, throwing up a cloud of disturbed dust, and the rumbling was getting louder.

"What the-" he started to say. The sound was familiar. He had heard it before, but it was so much louder now.

"More domo'shah are launching," Ehri said. "Judging by the vibrations, a lot more."

Donovan turned his mech to the south. There was a building in his field of view, so he walked the armor over to clear his sightline. He could see the light in the distance, illuminating the entire sky. The rumbling was getting louder, the ground shaking even more. The soldiers resting around him were all up and standing, searching for the source of the distress.

"There," Ehri said, using her mech to point into the distance.

The first of the domo'shah was rising, reaching a point where they could see it climbing into the night sky, a bright red and blue flare of energy behind it. Another appeared a moment later. Then another.

"How many of them does he have?" Donovan said.

Another appeared, and then another, creating a train of the massive starships climbing toward the atmosphere. The ground shook, their air around them rippling and heating up from the energy being used to bring them all into orbit.

"Seven, not including the capital ship, which is nearly twice the size of the others," Ehri said.

Donovan watched them rise, counting them.

"Seven," he said. "He's sending all of them to intercept General St. Martin and his forces."

"It is a good sign," she replied. "It means he is worried about the General. Seven ships to defeat one?"

"Eight," Donovan said. They had seen the other fortress appear a few hours earlier, coming to rest in geosynchronous orbit. "Eight against one. They're going to be slaughtered."

"Then the weight of this war has shifted back to us," Ehri said.

General Parker seemed to understand that instinctively. His voice carried over the receiver a moment later.

"All units, break time is over. This is a red alert. I repeat, this is a red alert. I know you're tired. I know you're stretched to the limit. But that there is a sign that the enemy is afraid. It's also the opportunity we've been waiting for. We need to dig deep and take whatever strength we have left, and we need to use it now. We have to get to the Dread capital before the Ishur arrives. We have to use the chance we're being given. General St. Martin is depending on us. All of humankind is depending on us. Gather your things and let's move. I want to be on the Domo'dahm's doorstep ASAP. Are you with me?"

"Yes, sir," the soldiers replied as one, a shout that almost reached through the din of the rising fortresses.

"I said are you with me?" Parker repeated.

"Yes, sir," they replied.

"Let's beat those bastards this time. Are. You. With. Me?"

"Yes, sir," they shouted, the sound of it overcoming the rumble and echoing through the night.

It was immediately followed by a flood of humankind as it continued its journey toward what would prove to either be a new beginning or a final end.

47

GABRIEL STOOD AT THE front of the open space next to the dark cloning facility. The lights within the factory had been put out, the doors sealed shut. The caretakers who had worked within had been relocated to another area of the ship, where two of the New Earth Alliance's social workers were both trying to comfort them over the loss of their singular programmed task, and determine whether or not Dread clones could be rehabilitated. He had heard that early results indicated it was not only possible but that the programming was easily overcome with the right mental stimulation.

He looked over to his left, at the line of officers standing at attention beside him. Colonel Graham, Colonel Choi, Colonel Ames, and of course Generals Cave and St. Martin. The New Earth Alliance council members who were making the trip were also present, headed by Councilwoman Rouse. They were at the head of an all-hands assembly his father had called, causing the large open floor of the deck to be crowded with both military and civilians.

They were still nearly a day out from Earth, still traveling through slipspace toward their final destination. They would spend the next series of hours in active preparation for the battle to come, checking their equipment, moving assets into place, making sure they were as ready and organized as they could be. This would be their last chance to see one another before it happened. One last motivational push. One last opportunity to say whatever needed to be said.

Gabriel shifted his attention to the crowd, finding Miranda near the front. She was already looking at him, and he smiled and tapped his chest. She returned the knowing gesture. Everything had been better since he had declared himself to her. He had only realized in hindsight that he had loved her long before they had stolen the Magellan, he had just never let those emotions in.

"I think we're ready to start," he heard General Cave say to his father.

Gabriel kept scanning the crowd. He found Daphne in the corner, surrounded by a contingent of Dread clone soldiers who had served under Tea'va and Gr'el. The former had ordered them to follow her commands, and they continued to do so with precision even after his death, becoming invaluable to the logistical preparations. For her part, Daphne had continued to be strong, confident that Soon was down there with the rebels, and that she would see him again. He didn't blame her for that. He believed the same thing.

"Angela, if you will," Theodore said to the Councilwoman.

She nodded, sticking her fingers in her mouth and whistling. The sound of it echoed across the chamber, and they were all surprised when a soft rumble responded to it from deeper within the bowels of the Ishur. Gabriel glanced over at It'kek, who had an amused expression on his face. It appeared the legri'shah enjoyed the sound.

"Ladies and gentleman, and esteemed allies," Councilwoman Rouse said, looking over that keepers when she said the last part. "Thank you all for coming. I know these last few days have been stressful for everyone, and for different reasons. I think you should all be proud of yourselves for being here, and for the strength and courage you've exhibited so far. I'm going to turn this meeting over to General Theodore St. Martin. You all know him, and what he has meant to the New Earth Alliance, and while the General and I have not always seen eye-to-eye, I can honestly say that there are few people whose words I respect more."

She turned to Theodore, who rolled over to her position, shaking her hand when she offered it.

"Thank you, Angela," he said.

He looked out at the gathering, unable to see past the first row because of his diminished height in the chair.

"Men and women of the Earth Alliance," he said, his voice booming through the space. "You'll notice I left off the 'New.' That's because there is no New Earth. There's only our Earth. The one we evolved on. The one we lived on for the last few thousand years. The one that was taken from us, without justification and without cause by an alien race known by us as the Dread, known by themselves as the bek'hai. Some of you may have already met the keepers. It'kek and the others. Some of you know the real story of the bek'hai. You see, those coullions that took our Earth, they're like the bastard sons of a race that was once intelligent and peaceful. A race that I think at times made us look like bloodthirsty monsters. You might wonder why I'm telling you this. Why I'm leading with this. I want you to look around this room. I know it's hard to see past your neighbor but take a look around. Make eye contact with every face you see. Some of them will be different than ours, but everyone in this room is an ally and a friend."

He paused, turning his chair to follow his instructions. Gabriel nodded to him as he did, and he nodded back before returning forward.

"Did you take a good look? You might be thinking; this is it? We're going to get our planet back with this? Hell, I know I am. Except this isn't it. We've got good people on the ground on Earth, making their way to the Dread capital to put the pressure on their leader. It's an army whose size we can't even estimate because we can't put a limit on how big it might be. It's an army with the same strength and courage y'all are showing by being here, especially the civilians among you who didn't need to come. Even so, you think that's the only army we got?" He shook his head. "It isn't.

You see, we have ourselves a secret weapon. A weapon forged fifty years ago when those bastard Dread decided they wanted my Juliet. That she was a good match to make copies of and program as scientists and researchers. For those of you were left Earth with me, who knew Juliet, you can imagine what a mistake they made by letting her in. Even the most brutal bastard sons couldn't ignore the peaceful, devout beauty of that woman."

He paused again, wiping at his face at the memory of her. His father had accepted the truth about Zoelle, and he wore a strong face in public, but Gabriel knew that he was still hurting over the revelation, and over knowing that his wife was truly lost to him.

"We don't know how strong our weapon is until we try to use it, but we're going to find out. We've got a plan to turn the Dread infrastructure into chaos, and if it works? Hoo-boy, if it works, our victory is all but assured. Even if it doesn't, I believe in the people I see in front of me. I believe in every man and woman on this ship. I believe in your strength, in your courage, in your energy and enthusiasm. I believe in your heart and your spirit and your love. I believe in humankind, in humanity, and in the truth that we're going to give every last ounce of ourselves to see this thing through, to reclaim our planet, and to send them sons of bitches home. And I only have one question for all of you here: do you believe?"

"Yes," Gabriel said, along with a handful of others.

"That was pathetic," Theodore said. "Am I wrong about all of you? Tell me, do you believe?"

"Yes," a large contingent said, the sound of it echoing through the chamber.

"Really? Then why are you here? Do you believe?"

"Yes," most of the people shouted.

"Do you believe?" Theodore repeated one last time.

"Yes!"

The sound of it was so loud the room vibrated. Once more, the legri'shah answered the call, a massive roar sounding from deeper behind them, echoing out from the tunnels. It almost seemed to energize the crowd, and they cheered and hollered, leading to a greater response from the creatures. Gabriel's heart pounded, his body and spirit energized by the crowd. He put his hand on the crucifix below his shirt, holding it tight. Whatever happened, he would remember this moment.

"Gabe," Theodore said, rolling over to him.

"Dad. Good pep talk."

"Thank you, son."

"I'm not completely clear what you meant about our secret weapon, though. Do you know something I don't?"

"I do. But not for long. Kneel down next to me so we can talk for a minute."

Gabriel did, coming close so he could hear his father over the continuing sound of people cheering and talking, using the time they had as a group.

Theodore put his hand on Gabriel's arm. "I've discussed this with General Cave, and with It'kek. I would have brought you in on it, but I needed you rested." He paused. "By the by, congratulations on your engagement. I'm sorry I didn't get to hear about it from you. She's a good woman, and she'll take good care of you."

Gabriel glanced over to Miranda, who was talking to one of the soldiers beside her. "I know."

"We think that there are clones of your mother implanted on all of the Dread ships, at least one or two, but they don't know it yet. You remember how Zoelle changed when she heard your voice, and she heard you talk about your mom and me? Well, we think that if we can get a broadcast across their network, we can turn them all on. Even better? We think that the Juliets can get more of the clones, and the keepers, to pitch in."

"Why do you think that?"

"Juliet got real close with the keepers. She used to come and see them all the time. They bonded over their beliefs. Now, the keepers don't want to fight, but they know it might be their only shot at breaking free of the prisons they've been stuffed into, and of not only saving the legri'shah but also increasing their population. There's a lot of history there that we still don't know, and won't for some time, but it's important to them and could make a huge difference for us."

"So why are you telling me this?" Gabriel asked.

"According to Mr. Mokri, we can't force the Dread to output our signal across their ships. While we're pretty sure the Domo'dahm listened to our broadcast, it didn't make it everywhere. We need to get a message out to all of the ships in the Dread fleet, emitted over their internal PA systems. Now, you would think we'd maybe have the ability to do that from here, but we don't. Sure, we can open a channel from one bridge to another, but we can't make them push the signal ship-wide. Do you get what I'm saying?"

Gabriel nodded. "I understand. So how do we get the word out?"

Theodore looked at him, hesitant. He bit his lip. It was as uncomfortable as Gabriel had ever seen him.

"Dad?"

"You know I love you, don't you, son?"

"Of course. I love you, too."

"It isn't that I don't believe in you because I do with all my heart. I just think it isn't right a man should have to ask his son to do this sort of thing."

"What do you need me to do? Whatever it is, I'll do it."

Theodore smiled. "I know you will. You're a St. Martin." He paused again. "Okay. Here's what we need you to do."

Gabriel listened while his father explained the mission they had in store for him. It was nothing he would have expected. It was as close to impossible as he could have ever imagined. More than likely, it was going to get him killed, and if he failed it could mean the rest of them might die as well.

When the time came to accept the assignment, he was honored to do it.

48

THEY COULD SEE THE dark black carapace of the Dread capital long before they got close to it. It rose through the haze of the morning, blurry and frightening, a black splotch against clear blue. It resembled a wart, or a bruise, or a disease.

To Donovan, it was fitting. The Dread were an infection that needed to be cured. A wound that had to be cauterized. Perhaps not all of them, not the clones like Ehri, if there were any more of them, at least. But the Domo'dahm and the pur'dahm for sure. They were the ones with the power. They were the ones with the weapons.

They were prepared to use them.

The rebels had been on the move for forty out of the last forty-four hours, finally nearing the massive fortress and the hubs that had once connected it to the other ships. They were still visible in the daylight sky, smaller bruises spread across the aqua, waiting for General St. Martin and his forces, whatever they might look like, to arrive. When? Today, sometime. In hours, minutes, or seconds? There was no way to know.

They were all tired. The energy of General Parker's rallying cries had been draining a little more with each passing minute, each heavy step, each slow blink of tired eyes. Somehow, the man had kept at it without pause. He was there when they stopped to rest; he was there when they moved again. He was there all of the time, pushing them, urging them on, proving why he had survived as long as he had, and giving them hope that they would survive as well.

As the CO of Delta Battalion, it was Donovan's role to take the lead as they neared the fortress, ready to intercept any heavy mechanized resources and try to get them caught up in an extended firefight, or otherwise attempt to distract them from the ten battalions that trailed behind them, with their eyes on reaching the fortress and getting inside. It was no small task. They had no idea what was waiting for them up ahead, but judging by how eerily quiet everything felt, he knew it couldn't be anything good.

"This is Delta Battalion," Donovan said across the open channel. "We're four klicks out of Mexico City. Sensors are clean. No sign of activity up ahead."

"Roger, Delta," General Parker replied. "I don't expect it to stay that way for very long. You're practically on top of them."

"Affirmative, Actual. If the Dread had any history of ambushes, I'd think we're walking right into one."

"Roger that. Take your team further south and sweep back. I want you to have a clear line to retreat away from the city itself. The cover will help us close in on the fortress under fire."

"Affirmative, Actual." Donovan switched channels to the Battalion frequency. "You heard the General. We'll keep moving south and come in from the rear. Remember, our mission is to harass the enemy as much as possible. Mech One, out."

Donovan rotated the mech's torso toward Mexico City on his right. A waterfall of memories erupted from the sight of it, even though he had only been gone a few weeks. The missile silo, his mother, Matteo, and Diaz. General Rodriguez. The missions into the city to raise the transmission needle and connect with their brethren in space. His mind even wandered to his experience beneath the city, swimming through the sewers and winding up inside the fortress they were preparing to attack. Killing Tuhrik. Meeting Ehri. It all seemed so distant, and so close at the same time.

Humankind had been waiting fifty years for this moment.

Would they win the day?

"Mech One, this is Bertha Actual, I've got visual at three o'clock."

The CO of the second of the two infantry companies was steady as he reported the position. Lieutenant Colonel Dickerson, if Donovan remembered correctly. There had been so little time; it had been difficult to learn everyone's name.

"Roger, Bertha Actual," Donovan replied, checking his sensors. Whatever the man had seen, it was sitting beyond his range. He switched to the mech's networked communication system, opening a channel to the rest of the armors. "Mech Two, this is Mech One. Make a right turn and head toward the visual, see if you can get them on the HUD."

"Roger, Mech One," Ehri said, her mech turning immediately and heading toward the city.

Donovan tracked it on his HUD, watching the spot move away from their group. He put his eyes on the edge of the city, to the broken buildings that spotted the outskirts, and then to the more densely packed destruction beyond. He still wasn't seeing-

His mind switched gears when he caught sight of the movement and a flash of sunlight vanishing against the dark armor of a Dread mech.

"Mech Two, hold position," he said, bringing Ehri to a stop. "Actual, we have positive ID on the enemy. At least one mechanized armor, but I'm willing to bet there are more."

"Copy that, Delta. See if you can pull them out."

"Affirmative." Donovan switched systems again. "Able, Bertha, spread out and find cover. Bertha One Two, get Big Bertha online and in position."

"Roger, Delta Actual," the units replied.

Donovan steered his mech to the right, approaching Ehri. The Dread mech hadn't moved or revealed itself. It was stationary, shrouded by the remains of the skyscraper it was resting next to.

"They aren't attacking," Donovan said, opening a direct channel to Ehri's mech.

"No."

"Even though we're getting into a better position?"

"The Domo'dahm has decided to allow us to attack first. It is not required of a challenge, but he is feeling confident."

"Should he be?"

"The domo'shah in orbit carried close to fifty mechanized armors and nearly fifteen thousand clone soldiers. I imagine they have left most of the armors behind, and a large contingent of the infantry. There is little reason to think that he is concerned about our assault. Clearly, his focus is on General St. Martin."

Donovan had known they were going to be outnumbered. It wasn't the first time Ehri had outlined what they were up against. How the hell were they supposed to win, again?

He forced the sudden wave of panic down. He wondered how many of the other rebels out there were feeling the same way? It didn't help to think about what they were up against, or how impossible it seemed. If they didn't fight today, they were going to die tomorrow anyway. At least they were giving themselves a chance.

"Delta Actual, this is Bertha One Two. Big Bertha is online and in position."

"Roger, Bertha One Two," Donovan replied. "Prepare to fire on my mark."

"Affirmative."

"They will attack as soon as we fire, Colonel," Ehri said.

Donovan stared at the outline of the city in front of him. He turned the mech slightly, looking north to the remainder of the rebel army. They were still a few klicks behind, hanging back while Delta Battalion did its job.

"Actual, this is Delta," Donovan said. "We are in position to commence the attack. Big Bertha is prepared to fire. Waiting on your mark, sir."

"Roger, Delta," General Parker replied. "Hold tight."

There was a long pause. Donovan imagined the General was passing orders to the other battalions, getting them into position to make their runs. They didn't expect everyone to get through. They didn't need to all get in. The inside of the domo'shah would be lightly defended, or at least they hoped it would.

"Delta, this is Actual. All battalions are in position. Bertha One Two, fire on my mark."

Donovan's heart began to thump at the words. He quickly checked his renovated mech's weapons systems, confirming a full payload of projectile ammunition and a ready state on the plasma cannons.

"Delta Actual, this is Bertha One Two. If you could, please take two steps to the left."

Donovan swallowed, surprised by the statement. This was no time to lose it. "Roger, Bertha One Two," he replied, moving his mech to the side.

"Bertha One Two," General Parker's voice said. "Fire."

49

THE BEAM FROM BIG Bertha passed right beside Donovan, so close that the mech began bleating warnings into his ears. He took another involuntary step to the side, squinting his eyes in reaction to the brightness of the bolt as it streaked past.

Less than two seconds later, it speared its target, the dark shape of the mech Donovan had spotted vanishing against the point of light, vaporized by the power of the augmented weapon. The bolt continued through, into the city, blasting into a building and bringing the remains of it down into a heavier pile before fading away.

"So it begins," Donovan said to himself before connecting with the squad channel. "All units, move in." He shifted to the human radio mounted in front of him. "Able, Bertha, hold steady, we'll try to bring them to you. Prepare Big Bertha for another volley."

"Roger," the company commanders replied.

The six mechs moved in toward the city limits, in the direction the plasma bolt had traveled. It would take another minute or two for the charge to rebuild in the cannon and allow it to fire with such devastating force again. They were on their own in the meantime.

Donovan had only made it a dozen steps before the plasma bolts began to pour from the city. They were well-aimed blasts that slammed into the mechs, catching them square and sending more warnings into his ears. One bolt wouldn't be nearly enough to drop the armor, but it was a bad omen of things to come. He slipped his mech to the side, tracking the source of the attack to locate the attackers. They were still hidden from his sensors, and he knew they shouldn't be.

It seemed the Domo'dahm hadn't just been sitting back and waiting.

"Actual, this is Delta. I'm not sure how, but it looks like the enemy is invisible to our sensors. Repeat, we're blind beyond line of sight."

The pause before General Parker's response was long enough Donovan knew he was trying to work out a new approach on the fly. Without sensor readings, they had no idea what their main force was stepping into.

"Roger, Delta." Another pause. "It's too late to turn back now. Get us a path if you can."

"Roger," Donovan said, shifting his mech as a plasma bolt streaked past. He checked the location in the HUD and fired back, quieting the enemy attack for a moment. He shifted to the mech comm. "Okay people, we're going in. Head for the front lines, we'll try to engage and start pulling them south. Bertha One Two, hold position. Bertha One Three, Bertha One Four, stay with Bertha One Two and provide fire support. Mech Six, hang back with Bertha One Two, we can't afford to let them hit Big Bertha."

He looked up as the units affirmed his instructions. Luckily, the air was still clear of gi'shah. A few good strafing runs would whittle their numbers down in a hurry, but it seemed the Domo'dahm was holding those resources in wait for the space force.

Donovan brought his mech ahead at full charge, running across the open space toward the cover of the outlying buildings. Of course, Ehri was tracking ahead of him, while Colonel Knight was hanging close to his side. Orli was in Mech Six, and she backed away toward Big Bertha while the others advanced.

Plasma bolts were joined by projectiles as they drew nearer to the city, and Donovan diverted to find cover behind a blown out building. Colonel Knight joined him there, while Ehri, Bastion, and Knowles found cover further south.

"This is Bertha One Two. Big Bertha is charged and ready. Fire in the hole."

A second massive plasma bolt streaked between the mech unit, blasting forward and striking its target. Donovan rose from cover behind it, just in time to see the remains of two mechs topple to the ground with a soft thud. He opened fire into the space around the blast, pouring projectiles and plasma into a third mech that had been forced into the open. It rocked from the attack, falling back as Colonel Knight added her firepower to his. It fell over a moment later and didn't move again.

"Mech One, this is Able Three One. We've got movement from the south. A whole lot of movement."

The commander of Third Platoon sounded frightened. Donovan turned south, his view blocked by a building. He sidestepped around it, searching for line of sight, nearly caught off-guard by an enemy mech that popped out from a nearby alley. A line of projectiles tore into his left arm, leaving a large, open wound before he could back away from it, getting himself under cover.

"I've got him, Mech One," Colonel Knight said, crossing his path and moving in on the mech. She was joined there by Bastion, catching the mech in the crossfire and mowing it down.

"Bertha One Two," Donovan said. "Get Big Bertha turned to the south and find a target. Fire when ready."

"Roger, Mech One."

"Mech One, this is Bertha Five One," Kroeger said, sounding angry. "We have incoming from the west. Transports, Colonel, just about ready to drop an entire army on our asses."

Donovan spun his mech to the west, looking back past their positions. He saw the transports dotting the sky behind them, two dozen at least. Damn.

"Nobody said this was going to be easy," he replied. "Actual, we have incoming from the south."

"Roger, Delta," Parker replied, sounding a little overwhelmed. "Keep pushing forward, clear a lane. We'll handle the rear as best we can."

"Roger."

Donovan got his mech moving again, running parallel to the city in an effort to get a visual on the forces moving up from the south. He nearly shouted as a powerful plasma beam struck the building a few meters in front of him, sending chunks of slagged concrete rattling against his mech.

He rounded the debris and froze, making eye contact with two columns of Dread tanks, approaching almost leisurely from the south, a dozen mechs and at least a thousand clones soldiers in support.

He bit down on his lip, preventing himself from saying out loud what he was thinking at that moment.

They were all going to die.

50

RORN'EL WATCHED THE BATTLE unfold from his throne, a projection of the battlefield being delivered to him from a gi'shah monitoring the fight from far above it. As he had suspected, the ground forces the humans had sent against him were far too little and far too weak to be of much concern, even with the bek'hai assets they had taken. While the plasma cannon that had given his units so much trouble on the streets of Austin continued to inflict heavy damage, it wasn't as easy to move its position out here, and it would only be a matter of time before his forces got close enough to destroy it.

"Domo'dahm, shall we order the gi'shah to join the attack?" Orish'ek asked, observing the battle from his usual position. He spoke softly, as if he were already bored with the humans' efforts.

"No. We will follow the plan and keep the gi'shah in reserve for the Ishur."

"Domo'dahm, with all honor, we have an opportunity to make a quick end of the ground forces before they can reach the cover of the city. Should we not seize on it?"

Rorn'el considered it for a moment. He had expected the battle against the rebels to go smoothly, as long as they launched their attack before the Ishur arrived. His pur'dahm were not disappointing him, their forces circling the enemy and slowly boxing them in. In time, there would be nowhere for the humans to go. They would be surrounded on all sides, defeated whether they knew it then or not. How could the humans have believed they could possibly win this fight? Were they so desperate they had abandoned all reason? It certainly seemed so.

"Am I not the Domo'dahm?" Rorn'el hissed.

"Yes, Domo'dahm," Orish'ek replied, lowering his head.

"We do not need the gi'shah to win this battle." He pointed to the projection. "Look at how they are moving. Already, their formations are breaking down as they seek shelter from our soldiers. These are not warriors, Orish'ek. Their courage lasts only as long as they are away from our plasma."

"What about the mechanized armors?" Orish'ek asked, pointing to them on the display. "They are inflicting heavy damage on our units. We have lost ten mechs to their one already. That is more than we have ever lost in a single day since we arrived here."

"We won't need the mechs anymore, once this battle is over. What does it matter if we lose ten, or twenty, or even fifty? When we have defeated the Ishur, the humans will be broken. We can continue the extermination without distraction."

"The Ishur has yet to arrive."

"All the more reason to remain patient. Believe me, Orish'ek. The humans will either crumble when they see their last hope destroyed, or we will have crushed them long before that. Look. Look."

He pointed to where the humans had placed their plasma cannon. A single gur'shah was defending it, and while the pilot was fairly skilled they were about to be overcome. Three gur'shah were closing in on the position, along with an entire cycle of gel'shah and a hundred soldiers. The humans were putting up a solid fight, but they simply didn't have the numbers.

One of the gur'shah vanished as the plasma cannon fired for the last time, catching it head on and reducing it to slag. A few of the clones died with the hit, caught in the radius of the blast. Immediately after, five human soldiers lifted the cannon to their shoulders, attempting to change locations with it. He had seen them move it back a few times already while it recharged, but now there were more enemies at their back, closing in, sweeping through the rebels.

The gel'shah fired on the position, the entire cycle at once sending a mass of plasma into the area. The lone rebel gur'shah managed to avoid the bolts, but the cannon was not so fortunate. It exploded at the impact, sending shrapnel out and into the humans around it and killing dozens of them.

"That will be a strong hit on their will to fight," Rorn'el said. "I do not expect this battle to continue. The Ishur will come, but they will be fighting alone."

"Only if that one goes down," Orish'ek said, bringing Rorn'el's attention to another part of the battle. One of the rebel mechs was moving through the city, trailing a sizeable force behind it as they tried to destroy it. It moved unlike the others, with a smoothness and grace that was beyond human.

"Ehri dur Tuhrik," Rorn'el said. "There is none other that it could be. Their cannon is destroyed. Redeploy the gel'shah toward her location. I want her destroyed."

"Yes, Domo'dahm," Orish'ek said, shifting to his terminal. He spoke into it, and a moment later the gel'shah began moving back south in pursuit of the un'hai.

Rorn'el leaned back on his throne, his eyes drifting to the different parts of the projection, watching the humans scatter and break beneath the onslaught of his military. They had learned of the loss of their cannon, and even from above the effect on them was obvious. Whatever morale they had possessed when the fight began, it was quickly evaporating.

And where was the Ishur? His domo'shah were in position, ready to blow it to dust the moment it appeared from slipspace should General St.

Martin be foolish enough to drop too close to the planet. He was even prepared for it to come out of slipspace below their defensive web again, with over one hundred gi'shah and ek'shah ready to deploy at a moment's notice.

The General was a fool to challenge him. Any who might think to oppose him were fools for the idea. At the same time, in a way he was thankful for all that had happened since Ehri dur Tuhrik had allowed the humans to escape with their technology. After all, the human rebellion had continued for fifty cycles, and now they would be able to put an end to it, to all of it, within a single rotation.

He had sworn that he would see the humans extinct before his retirement, and he was glad it was a promise he would be able to keep.

He reached into his gori'shah robes, taking out the splintered crucifix from Juliet's rosary. He had always admired her desire for peace, her desire for understanding between the bek'hai and the humans, and her efforts to introduce them to her all-powerful God. But there was a great divide between admiration and agreement. Like the legri'shah, the humans were tools to be used. So it was for the strongest of the bek'hai, and so it would always be.

"Domo'dahm," Orish'ek said excitedly. "We have a report from the Ishkrem. A domo'shah has just appeared on our sensors. It is undoubtedly the Ishur, Domo'dahm."

"Undoubtedly," Rorn'el replied, his lips parting, his tongue flicking out between sharp teeth. "What is their position?"

"They are positioned behind the moon, Domo'shah, using it as a shield against a potential attack."

"General St. Martin was wise to be cautious, but it will not save him. Order the domo'shah to intercept the Ishur. Do not give it an avenue to escape."

"Yes, Domo'dahm."

Rorn'el turned his attention back to the earthbound battle. The General had arrived too late to prevent their defeat. Much too late. The truth of it gave him pause.

Why was the General so cautious, after all of his past maneuvers had been so bold?

There was something about it that he didn't trust, but he couldn't quite grasp what it was. Not that it mattered. The battle was already over, the war already won.

The humans just didn't know it yet.

51

GABRIEL BREATHED SLOWLY, FORCING himself to remain calm as the domo'shah's phase generators powered down, dropping the Ishur from slipspace back into reality. He felt a sudden wave of nausea at the change, his body affected by the number of times they had slipped in the last two weeks, and he swallowed and tried to focus beyond it.

"Status," he said, looking down at the skeleton crew helping him run the Magellan.

"The Ishur is out of slipspace," Miranda said, looking back at him. "Comm systems are online."

""Weapons systems are online," Colonel Choi said, staring at her tablet.

"Power levels are at one hundred percent," Sarah Larone said. "Phase modulators are stable."

"The Dread zero-point reactors are purring like a kitten," Guy Larone said.

Gabriel nodded, his hand running across the controls of the starship from the command station. Everything was running the way it was supposed to, which meant it was all up to him now.

"Attention all hands, attention all hands," he said, opening a ship wide channel. "Prepare for ingress. I repeat, prepare for ingress. This is not a drill."

He couldn't see it, but he could picture the thousands of soldiers filling the belly of the repaired starship doing their best to buckle themselves in, preparing for the drop.

Gabriel had expected that Theodore would be the one making this run, piloting the ship with the same deft hand that had gotten it away from the Dread twice in the past. When his father had approached him during the all-hands and asked him to take the controls, he was both surprised and honored. The argument for the position was manifold. One, his father was a valuable symbol of the war, a figurehead that the rest of the forces both above and below the thermosphere could rally around. Second, he needed to stay around to help guide the Ishur during what promised to be a grueling fight against a superior defensive force. Third, while he had been successful navigating the Magellan inside of the planetary defenses, it was Gabriel who had the most experience dealing with approaching Earth from beyond them. He was the more seasoned pilot and as such more fitting for the job.

Finally, he had a secondary mission he was tasked to accomplish, one that required reaching Earth's surface. One that might mean the difference between victory and defeat.

"Magellan, this is Ishur Actual," Theodore said, his voice mixing with a small amount of static from their makeshift integrated systems. "We're nearly in position."

"Roger, Ishur Actual," Gabriel replied. "We're ready and waiting. Guy, can you do anything with that static?"

The Guy Larone who had once been a whiney, privileged ass had vanished right after the Magellan had landed on the Ishur. Since then, the scientist had been one of the most valuable cogs in their machine, helping to put Maggie back into fighting shape in record time. That he had volunteered for this mission was a testament to his change of heart.

"I'll see what I can do, sir," he said.

"Excellent. Spaceman Locke, is the DSS ready?"

"Yes, sir," Miranda replied.

While the DSS on the Ishur used a holographic projection to handle manipulation of the darkspace shields, the Magellan's system was more primitive, offering only a three-dimensional schematic of the ship on a table touchscreen, which could be manipulated and tapped to direct the phase modulation along the ship. More importantly, they had only one control unit to cover the ship, versus four on the Ishur. At least Maggie was a much smaller animal.

Gabriel checked the Magellan's sensors. He could see the domo'shah on the longer range array. Seven of them, already moving in their direction.

Time to thread the needle.

"On your mark, General," Gabriel said.

"Prepare for launch in five. Four. Three. Two. One. Go."

Gabriel tapped the control pad, quickly increasing the Magellan's forward vectoring thrusters, pushing the ship backward through the open hangar bay where they had landed. It took a good thirty seconds to get the ship clear of the Ishur, leaving them floating face-forward, drifting upward to the Dread fortress' bridge, giving him one last glimpse of the crew there as he manipulated the other thrusters, pushing the Magellan out and away.

"Magellan is away," Gabriel said. "I'll see you when it's over, Dad."

"Roger. Godspeed, and good hunting," Theodore replied, his voice slightly choked. "Give them hell."

"You, too."

Gabriel got Maggie facing toward the moon, and then hit the main thrusters, almost feeling the acceleration as the Dread reactors provided more than enough power to the ion generators. The ship burst forward, and he adjusted course as they neared the moon.

They cleared the dark side within minutes, finding themselves nearly face-to-face with one of the incoming Dread domo'shah.

"Maggie, how long until the Dread starships reach the Ishur?" Gabriel asked at the same time he vectored to get around the fortress.

"At current velocity, twelve minutes and seventeen seconds," the computer replied.

"How long until we reach Earth's surface?"

"Eight minutes and four seconds."

Gabriel tensed for a moment. He had been hoping they could keep the Ishur back and away from the line of fire long enough for him to finish his secondary mission. It was an incredible long shot to begin with, but now he knew it would be impossible.

"We've got incoming fire," Miranda said, as the domo'shah ahead of them began firing its secondary batteries.

Her hand moved across the tablet, guiding the DSS to the impact points, blocking as many of the bolts as she could. The thick armor handled the rest, taking the hit from the smaller plasma cannons without serious damage.

"Taking evasive maneuvers," Gabriel said, firing top thrusters to drop the Magellan from its current plane. He reversed course as the bolts began sweeping down, crossing over them and rising above while the gunners on the Dread ship tried to adjust.

"Enemy starfighters incoming," Miranda said, helping him keep track of the threat display, impressing him with her ability to multitask with the DSS.

"There's nothing we can about them," he replied. "Their weapons won't do much against us."

Blue flashes passed all around them as they neared the domo'shah, and a second started releasing volleys in their direction. The Dread starfighters maneuvered around the two fortress' attacks, mixing in and making strafing runs across the Magellan's bow. The power flickered on the bridge, the terminals blanking out for a second before returning.

"We may have lost a conduit," Guy said. "Good thing we added backups. Rerouting."

Gabriel shook his head. He had to do more. He adjusted the vectoring thrusters, throwing the Magellan into a wild rotation. Plasma bolts streamed past them, only a few passing the combination of his maneuvers and the DSS.

"Are the enemy ships following?" he asked as they slipped past the fortresses.

"The starships are maintaining course for the Ishur," Miranda replied. "The fighters have split up, though. We've got a tail."

Gabriel could see the smaller ships on the Magellan's display. They were trying to gain velocity to keep up with the larger ship, but it was unclear if they would succeed. It didn't matter. A new threat had appeared ahead of them in the form of the smaller Dread starships. They were on an intercept course, on their way to take them out.

"Targets incoming," Miranda said, too late.

Gabriel adjusted the vectoring thrusters again, leveling the ship and turning it to run perpendicular to the Earth. The Dread ships began firing their plasma weapons, creating another barrage of fire for him to avoid.

"I wish we could use our guns," he said. He and Theodore had decided not to risk them on the way down, in fear of revealing their existence and having them destroyed before the Magellan reached the surface. A few plasma cannons weren't going to be the difference between success and failure on this part of the mission.

He cursed as the lights flickered on the bridge again, and the gravity control momentarily shut down, leaving him rising against his restraints. He shot a look over at Guy, who was tapping furiously on his tablet. They had forgone any non-essential crew, leaving nobody down in engineering to speak to their damage. If Maggie couldn't report it, it didn't exist.

"We're taking a lot of fire, sir," Miranda said, doing her best to keep the DSS moving, blocking the attacks. "I can't keep up."

"I know," Gabriel replied. "You're doing great. Maggie, ETA to the atmosphere?"

"Three minutes, six seconds," the computer replied.

Too long. Much too long. His forward throttle was maxed out, the ship gaining velocity as quickly as it could. The smaller Dread ships were closing in and smelling blood, and a second contingent of starfighters had been sent in.

They weren't going to make it.

He gritted his teeth, his hands moving over the flight controls as quickly as they could, adjusting thrust, changing direction, trying to throw the enemy ships off their tail. They continued to take fire, the ship vibrating as plasma bolts burned into the hull, some of the attacks avoiding the DSS.

He had survived too many runs just like this one to die now.

He changed course, pointing the Magellan toward the nearest starship.

"This worked the last time," he said. "Put the DSS on the bow, Spaceman Locke."

"Roger," Miranda replied without hesitation.

He could see the dark point shift the front of the Magellan, and he looked ahead of it to the quickly approaching starship. The shields captured the incoming volley of plasma, bringing them closer and closer to the ship.

At the last second, the Dread commander blinked. The ship began vectoring away, trying to avoid the bow of the Magellan before it speared them. Instead of a direct hit, Gabriel scored a glancing blow, one that tore a gash in the bottom of the enemy ship on their way by. It vented atmosphere, its attack fading as it sought to stabilize.

The Magellan continued its descent toward the planet, the automatic Dread defense systems drawing near. They began to activate, directional thrusters aligning them toward Maggie as she approached. The good news was that they were simple machines, and they didn't understand the idea of the darkspace shields. They focused their attack on the same point against the Magellan's bow, allowing Miranda to place the shields and leave them, absorbing the firepower of the defensive net as they neared.

More Dread ships were closing in, firing with a fury that lit up the darkness of space. Gabriel skirted the Magellan around most of it, and Miranda caught a large portion of the rest. They were taking fire, but it was a light rain shower instead of a potential deluge.

"Hull breach on deck nine," Sarah said a moment later. "Bulkheads are sealing, but. Oh, Colonel, we had people down there."

Gabriel winced. They needed to get inside the thermosphere and headed for Mexico City. He adjusted thrust again, diving toward the nearest defense pods. The systems peppered the Magellan with fire right up until the starship slammed into them, the darkspace shields throwing them violently out of the way or smashing them completely.

Then they were through, dropping ever downward toward the planet.

"Maggie, enter coordinates for Mexico City and give me a guideline," Gabriel said.

"Setting coordinates," Maggie replied. "Guideline activated."

A flight path appeared on his command screen, giving him the optimal route to the city even as the ship began to shake, hitting the thermosphere and working to break through. Heat flared ahead of them while the ship made its second approach to Earth in a month, the Dread starfighters remaining behind it, still shooting at them as they crossed into the upper atmosphere.

"We're in," Miranda announced.

"Activate all batteries," Gabriel said, watching the ground growing beneath them as they swept toward the surface. "Fire at will."

The new weapons systems were separate from the pre-existing controls, and Colonel Choi took control of them without hesitation, tapping the commands to rotate them on their turrets. They didn't have a complete field of fire, but there was one battery that could reach behind them, and she didn't waste any time triggering the system. The plasma cannon sent bolt after bolt at the fighters behind them, forcing them to evade.

"Almost there," Gabriel said, the dark spot of the Dread capital becoming visible on the ground ahead of them. "Miranda, activate our comm system, let's see if we can get the ground forces on the line."

"Roger." She abandoned the DSS for a moment, leading to the ship shaking as it took another hit. She tapped the console ahead of her, activating the radio. "Comm online. Channel open."

"Earth Rebellion. This is Major Gabriel St. Martin in the starship Magellan. Do you copy? Over."

A flow of static greeted him from the open channel.

"Guy, are we getting anything?" he asked, jerking the ship to the left as Colonel Choi's defenses hit one of the Dread fighters. "Nice shooting,

Colonel."

"Working on it," Guy said, tapping his controls. "Try again, please, sir."

"Earth Rebellion. This is Major Gabriel St. Martin in the starship Magellan. Do you copy? Over."

"Major St. Martin, this is General Alan Parker. Damn, you showed up just in time. We're getting our asses kicked down here."

He had a feeling the Ishur wasn't doing much better above him. "I'm looking for Major Donovan Peters, is he with you?"

He held his breath waiting for the reply. Their plan would be easier to follow if the Major and the clone were still alive.

"Colonel Peters is commanding the mech unit," General Parker replied.

"Is the clone with him?"

"Clone? You mean Ehri or Orli?"

There were two Juliet clones down there? "I don't know, sir. I never learned her name."

"He's not responding to my requests," Parker said. "It could be that his comm is offline. The mech unit is taking a pounding. We all are."

"Understood, General. We'll see what we can do to help."

"Whatever you're going to do, do it fast, son."

Gabriel's eyes tracked over the landscape in front of the ship. The city was getting close, and he reversed throttle in response, slowing the starship down. She wasn't intended for atmospheric flight, and the anti-gravity systems would only do so much.

It was going to be a rough landing any way he tried it, but as his eyes landed on a pair of mechs squaring off against a second, almost identical pair backed by a line of lek'shah carapaced vehicles that resembled tanks, he was satisfied to at least have an idea of where to set down.

"Don't worry, General," he replied. "I intend to."

52

DONOVAN BACKED AWAY, HIS eyes sweeping the landscape ahead of him in search of even the barest of cover.

It had been nearly an hour since the battle against the Dread had started. An hour of running and shooting, ducking, and hiding, pausing and issuing commands to a quickly diminishing battalion.

They had lost Big Bertha nearly thirty minutes ago to a heavy assault by the Dread mechs and tanks, an assault that had also claimed Orli as she tried to take on six heavy armors at one time. They had lost Bastion and Knowles at some point, too, their mechs blasted to slag by the deadly gel'shah that seemed to be in endless supply. Half of Able and two-thirds of Bertha were also down, and their mission to pull the enemy away from the Dread capital was a total and complete failure.

Donovan had long given up the idea of winning this fight. Instead, he had decided that he would press on, keep attacking, and take as many of the bastards with him as he could. His mech was beaten but not quite broken, pitted and scarred across most of the surface, out of projectile ammunition and overheating from the constant use of the plasma cannons. He was coated in sweat and soaking wet, the gori'shah unable to wick the moisture away quick enough. His legs were tired, too, tired of maneuvering the mech away from the enemy, of trying to keep pace with Ehri as she tore apart all comers. She was a machine. He was only a man.

Where was General St. Martin, he wondered, as he sidestepped another bolt fired from a gel'shah, ducking down behind a pile of rubble and raising his right arm over it to fire his plasma cannon. Ehri was circling behind him, using the same cover, silent in her focus. The General was supposed to be here today. Donovan hadn't realized what a wide block of time that was until now. An hour was all it would take for the rebel army to fall apart, to be decimated and sent to early graves. General Parker had even given up on sending orders through the comm, leaving him to himself as he did his best to wreak havoc before he too was destroyed.

The enemy mech ahead of him paused, waiting while the three gel'shah behind it fired on the rubble, blasting it away, sending shrapnel thunking off his lek'shah shell and leaving him in the open. He forced his legs to move again, pushing the mech away from the scene, hoping Ehri would see and follow. She didn't. Instead, she broke the other direction, laying down suppressing fire and drawing the attention away from him. The mechs stayed on her, launching another barrage, blasting her mech in the leg and torso. He saw something break, a loud pop, and the mech fell to one knee.

She wouldn't survive another shot like that. He reversed course, sending his mech to block them, trying to get in front of her before they could fire once more. The enemy mechs were closing in, and there was no way he was going to reach her in time.

The thought caused him to stumble, his mech nearly toppling over from the motion of his exhaustion. Only backup systems kept it upright, though it slowed considerably at the miss. He cursed, pushing harder, while two of the gel'shah brought her mech into their sights.

He checked his HUD. His sensors were dead, the array long destroyed. It suddenly occurred to him that maybe that's why everything was so quiet.

Had his comm system been destroyed as well?

"This is Delta Actual. Can anyone hear me?" he said over the human channels. He switched to the networked mechs. "Ehri, do you read me? Over."

There was no reply.

He kept moving, trying to reach her but knowing he couldn't. One of the gel'shah fired, and somehow she managed to tip her mech sideways, bringing it over to avoid the blast. It crumpled onto its side and then rolled onto its back, giving the enemy a smaller profile. He thought it was odd when she didn't move right away.

Then he looked up.

He had barely noticed the din of the starship approaching; he had become so numb to the noise of battle. When he saw the long bow of the Magellan dropping toward him, he didn't know whether to laugh, cry, or wet himself. When a series of plasma bolts traced from the sides of the ship and into the enemy position nearby and destroyed the gel'shah and one of the mechs, he almost did all three.

"Oh, shit," he cried. "Wooooo!"

He limped his mech toward Ehri, still trying to reach her and block her from the remaining enemy. More plasma bolts rained down from the Magellan, the growl of the incoming ship growing louder with each second. More of the Dread armor vanished beneath the assault, mounds of dirt spraying aside and crystallizing as each powerful blast slammed into the ground.

The earth began to shake as the Magellan neared, the roar so loud that it drowned out everything around it. Donovan saw the fighters now, the Dread gi'shah peppering the ship with fire and trying to avoid its return volleys. It was coming in fast, so fast, its forward and hull thrusters at full burn to break the velocity. He could feel the pressure from them, the heat, and he tucked over Ehri as it buffeted against him. The Dread mechs weren't quick enough, and the force of the displaced air knocked them down and pushed them back.

It was as though God had dropped a steel wall from the sky. The Magellan seemed to float a dozen meters in the air beside him before tumbling straight down, countless kilograms of mass dropping onto four heavy landing gear that extended from the hull just in time. The ground shook harder as they hit the surface and began to sink, hydraulics flexing to catch the rest of the bulk. He knew the ship had anti-gravity technology within it that would make it lighter, but it was still a heavy beast.

The ship dipped slightly and then rose again, coming to rest on the gear with a satisfied thunk. The plasma cannons on the starship continued to move and fire, tracing airborne targets and slamming the ground forces now blockaded by the Magellan's sizable bulk.

Then the next part of the miracle came. Three ramps dropped from the side of the ship, extending to the ground below. Soldiers poured out from them, men and women in neat gray uniforms charging down the ramp and into the battle. They avoided the heavy armors but swept across and back toward the city, where the embattled infantry was making its stand. They moved with a uniformity that Donovan had never seen from the rebels, a clear contrast to the two different types of training they had received.

Donovan shifted his mech away from Ehri's, looking down as he did. Her cockpit slid open, and she climbed out, looking up at him. She pointed at herself and then at the Magellan. She was going to it.

He decided to follow.

53

"STATUS," GABRIEL SHOUTED, GETTING to his feet as the Magellan came to rest.

"We're down," Miranda replied. "No luck getting through to Major Peters, though."

"Colonel Graham is deploying the units to the ground," Colonel Choi said. "Hopefully they'll remember to follow their training, instead of marveling over the fresh air."

"It doesn't look that fresh," Gabriel said. "It probably smells like burned flesh out there. We went over it all with them a dozen times on the way over. They'll do their jobs. Colonel Choi, you have the bridge."

"Where are you going?" Choi asked, not breaking her concentration from operating the plasma cannons.

"I have to find Colonel Peters and the clone," he said.

"Why?"

"My father didn't tell you?"

"No." She dared a glance at him. "What are you two up to?"

"Trying to save the world," Gabriel replied. "Give me three minutes to get off this boat, and then get her back in the sky. We can offer wider fire support hovering over the site than sitting down here."

"Who's the Colonel here?" Choi said.

"If you will, ma'am," Gabriel added.

"I'll take care of it."

Gabriel broke for the exit before pausing. "Miranda," he shouted. She looked up from the DSS display. "I love you."

"I love you too," she replied, but he was already out the door.

He ran down the corridor, his boots clanking along the metal flooring as he headed for the nearest exit. He paused at the armory; a single Dread rifle left intentionally for him to claim. He grabbed the weapon before continuing on, spilling out into the wide hangar where light from outside was filtering in from the open ramp.

He hurried toward it, his heart racing, hoping beyond hope that the mechs they had saved were being piloted by the Colonel and the Juliet clone. So much had gone right so far, why not that?

He was halfway across the hangar when two figures appeared at the top of the ramp, silhouetted by the light. At first, Gabriel raised the rifle, unsure of their intentions. Then he caught a glimpse of the long red hair and cherubic face of his mother, dirty as it was.

"Captain St. Martin?" Donovan said.

"Colonel Peters," Gabriel replied, unable to hold back his smile. "Thank God."

"We got your father's message," the Major said. "Where is he? Where's the Ishur?"

"In trouble," Gabriel said. "We need to go."

"Go? What do you mean?"

"You," he said, pointing at the clone. "What's your name?"

"Juli... Ehri," she said, catching herself.

"Colonel, we need to get into the Dread capital asap. It doesn't matter how, but we have to find a way. My father is a hell of a pilot and a hell of a commander, but there are seven Dread fortresses up there trying to blow him into space dust."

"Captain, I appreciate your enthusiasm," Donovan said. "We're nearly four kilometers away from the domo'shah, and there's a battlefield separating us."

"I don't care," Gabriel said. "In four minutes, those ships are going to reach the Ishur's position and start firing. Do you know what happens then?"

Donovan's face turned pale, and he nodded. "Okay. How are we going to get there before that happens?"

Gabriel pointed to the corner of the hangar. There was something low and long sitting in the shadows there. An excavator they had brought in from Alpha Settlement. "It doesn't look like much, but it's as heavily armored as anything else we have. Let's go."

The three of them ran to the machine. It had a drill mounted to the front of it, and a mechanical arm with a second drill attached to the rear. Gabriel led them onto the top of it, and then down into a manual airlock.

"Close that up for me, will you?" Gabriel asked as he moved to the front of the narrow internal confines and fell into the driver's seat.

Ehri paused, grabbing the hatch and pulling it closed.

Gabriel pressed the ignition, bringing the machine to life with a soft hum. The battery was only good for a hundred kilometers or so, but they didn't need to go anywhere near that far.

"Here we go," he said, pushing the control yoke forward.

The excavator shuddered and jerked as it built up power, and then kicked ahead toward the ramp and onto it, heading down and building speed. Donovan grabbed for the side of the machine as it slammed into the ground, bouncing back up and shaking from side to side before leveling out.

"Sorry," Gabriel said. "Major, we had a pilot crash land after our first meeting. Captain Soon Kim. I don't suppose you know what happened to him?"

Gabriel turned his head, his heart sinking when he saw Donovan's expression.

"I'm sorry, Captain. We rescued him after the crash, and he was with us for a while. He was killed in action back in Texas."

Daphne was going to be heartbroken. He felt his own sense of loss at the news. There would be time for mourning later. "I understand. Thank you, Colonel."

"He was a good man. A hell of a mech pilot, too."

"He was." Gabriel paused, pushing those emotions aside. "Colonel, there's a standard radio over there. You should be able to tune into your people's frequency through it."

Donovan dropped into a small seat beside a series of analog switches. "Please, call me Donovan. How do I use it?"

"Donovan, the dial tunes the frequency. Press down on the button to speak. It's old tech, but it works. By the way, my name is Gabriel."

"I know," Donovan replied. "You St. Martins have quite a reputation."

Gabriel felt the ground shake as the Magellan fired her bottom thrusters, beginning to process to regain altitude. It would have put an impossible strain on her original power supply to stay inside gravity for any length of time. With the Dread reactors, she could remain almost indefinitely.

"We can't see if anything is attacking us in here," Ehri said, finally making her way to the front.

Gabriel scanned the world outside through a narrow window. He could see the Magellan's troops ahead of him, working their way toward the city. "The armor is meant to withstand mountains falling on top of it. We can take a pretty solid beating."

"I think I've got it," Donovan said from the co-pilot seat. "Actual, this is Delta, do you read me? Over. Actual, this is Delta. Over."

"Colonel, is that you?" Kroeger said after Donovan repeated himself a few times.

"Kroeger," Donovan replied. "What's your sitrep?"

"I've got three guys from my unit with me, holed up in a building near the front lines. We've been sniping any of the clone bastards that show their faces and trying to help the rest of the units through to the fortress, but they've got a serious barricade in the way. Mechs and tanks, and they ain't moving."

Gabriel looked back at Donovan. "Colonel Choi will spot the defenses and start hitting them. We need to be ready to move in."

"Roger that," Donovan said. "Kroeger, did you see the starship that landed behind you?"

"Yes, sir."

"She's one of ours, and she's ticked off. See if you can organize a team to make a break for the fortress when she starts clearing the field. We'll be right behind you in a big ugly thing with a pointed front."

"Hell yes, sir," Kroeger replied. "Sir, it looks like she's got a lot of mosquitos biting at her neck."

Gabriel didn't like the sound of that.

"Oh, there goes one," Kroeger said a moment later. "Ouch. That had to hurt. Who's shooting on that thing?"

Gabriel smiled, keeping the excavator on track.

"The tide is turning, Donovan," he said. "I can feel it."

"You and me both, Gabriel. You and me both."

54

THEODORE KEPT HIS EYES glued to the Magellan from the time it backed out of the Ishur's hangar until it vanished around the dark side of the moon. He felt a heavy mixture of fear and pride at the sight of it, knowing it was his boy out there instead of him, running the gauntlet on a mission that was as impossible as anything they had ever tried.

A mission as impossible as getting a starship away from Earth during an alien invasion.

Once the Magellan had vanished from sight, he settled back into the Dread command chair, shifting a few times to get comfortable. Alan was sitting at the station directly in front of him, and he glanced back knowingly. The two men had their past differences, but their goals had brought back the friendship they had once shared. Grudges were pointless, especially when lives were at stake.

"Alan, how long do we have?" he asked.

"About twelve minutes," General Cave replied.

Theodore shifted in his seat again. He picked up the tablet that was spliced into the terminal in front of him and checked the threat display for himself. Seven ships. Seven! He smiled. The Domo'dahm wasn't taking any chances with them.

"The question now is, how do we stay alive long enough for Gabriel to do what he needs to do?"

He said it out loud, posing it to his bridge crew. He was down some of his most trusted people after they volunteered to go with Gabriel. James, Vivian, Miranda, Guy and Sarah Larone. Had he made a mistake letting Spaceman Locke go with Gabriel? Would she have accepted his decision if he had said no? He doubted it.

"We can slip away and come back," Reza said, offering up a suggestion.

"And leave our people behind? No. Never again."

"Then what if we reverse course? Back away? We can gain about six minutes."

"And be that much further away from Earth," Theodore replied. "Let's split the difference. Colonel Ames, reverse at half."

"Yes, sir," Colonel Ames replied.

"Any other ideas?"

There was silence on the bridge.

"Mr. Mokri, can you give me an estimate of how long we'll last against seven Dread fortresses based on our shield accuracy from that tangle with the last two coullions?"

"Yes, sir. One minute."

Reza began working on his tablet while the precious seconds ticked away. Theodore didn't waste them, considering their other options.

"What if we charge one of the flanks?" General Cave asked. "Get in close. It will make it harder for them to all target us at once."

"Not a bad thought, but close range makes the DSS less effective. We need to find the right balance."

"Do we have time to slip past them, and get them all gathered on one side? That will lower our profile and make it easier to cover the area with the shields."

"Except it won't. The modulation only covers a small area at any given time. Multiple angles of attack give us four points to try to defend ourselves with instead of one. Again, it's a balance."

Another minute of silence followed.

"I have the calculation, sir," Reza said. "At optimal DSS positioning, we can gain another eight minutes."

"Giving Gabriel about twenty," Theodore said. "That's not enough time."

Two more minutes of silence had passed when the edge of the first fortress appeared around the corner of the moon, dark and imposing.

"They're launching fighters, sir," General Cave said a moment later.

Small ships would be hard-pressed to take down the Ishur alone, but they could get in close and weaken it.

"ETA?"

"Four minutes, seven seconds."

"Scramble the defenses," Theodore said. "Get our units out there."

"Yes, sir."

General Cave reached out to Lieutenant Bale, who got the squadron launched. Sixteen fighters, a mix of human and Dread configurations, along with the two ek'shah, moved out ahead of the backing up fortress, shooting ahead toward the oncoming swarm of enemy ships. If they were lucky, the Dread either hadn't figured out how to shrink the modulation to cover their fighters or didn't care enough about them to bother. It had taken some time for the assemblers to make the phase paint, but it was the one advantage they held.

"Ishur Actual, this is Red One," Lieutenant Bale said, her channel patched into the bridge. "We are in position."

"Roger, Red One," Theodore said. "Don't dilly-dally on my account. You see a snake; you choke it."

"Roger," she replied. "You heard the General. Let's give them hell."

The smaller ships burst forward on flares of thrusters, splitting apart as they approached the oncoming enemy mass. Plasma bolts began littering the space between them seconds later as the battle was truly joined.

Theodore watched from the bridge, his eyes darting across the swarm of ships as they circled and danced around one another. He saw an enemy fighter get the drop on one of their fighters, firing plasma into its rear. He smiled when a flare of darkspace appeared, swallowing the bolt.

"Thank God for that," he said, as the same enemy starfighter was hit by one of Lieutenant Bale's bolts and stopped maneuvering, drifting away from the battle.

He was quickly snapped out of his reverie when a flare of light near the moon caught his attention. The first Dread fortress had completed its circuit and taken a long-range pot shot at them.

"We're under fire," General Cave said. "Sergeant Abdullah, that one's yours."

"Yes, sir. I have it, sir," Abdullah replied, manipulating the DSS. The bolt flared as it hit the darkspace shield and then vanished.

"What are those coullions thinking?" Theodore said. "They should know they can't slip one by from that range."

"There's no harm in trying," General Cave replied.

"No, I suppose not."

Theodore checked on the fighter groups. They were holding their own, making quick work of the Dread forces with the help of their superior shields. The ships were small enough that the modulation offered full coverage from enemy attacks.

"Another shot incoming from the port side," General Cave said, monitoring the domo'shah.

A second fortress had cleared the moon and fired. Three more were almost clear enough to join the attack.

"Here it comes," Theodore said.

Except there was no plan that gave them more than twenty minutes. Not without a miracle.

He closed his eyes, his thoughts drifting to Juliet.

"I know you're out there," he said softly. "Somewhere better than this. Somewhere peaceful and free. I know you've done your best to get us this far, and I know it isn't fair to ask, but I don't suppose you have one more blessing to pass on? It isn't for me. It's for the people on board. The civilians. The ones who trust in me to keep them safe. They're counting on me. They believe in me like I believe in you."

"Three more bolts incoming," General Cave said. "More fighters are heading this way."

Theodore kept his eyes closed in silent prayer, hoping that something would come to him. Some way of keeping them alive. The seconds passed. The Ishur shuddered as the first of the Dread bolts slipped past their defenses.

"Damn," Sergeant Abdullah said. "They're spacing out their shots, but firing at the same time. I can't cover them all."

The Ishur shuddered again.

"Theodore, we need to do something," General Cave said. "We're out of time." He turned back toward Theodore. "Teddy? Don't quit on us now. We need you."

Theodore opened his eyes. Juliet hadn't answered him, and that was okay. He knew what it meant.

"Quit? Oh no, I'm not about to quit. Just thinking is all. Hoping for a miracle, too. If God isn't going to give us one, we'll have to make it for ourselves. Colonel Ames, reverse course."

"Yes, sir," Colonel Ames replied.

"What are you thinking?" General Cave asked.

"Stay alive, as long as we can, any way we can. Estimates are just estimates. It's our will to fight, our will to live that's going to decide our fate. Tell Red One we're on the move, and to either pack it in and hitch a ride or keep fighting. It's her call."

"Yes, sir."

Theodore surveyed the field ahead as General Cave made the call. He never expected the fighters to disengage and come home, and he wasn't surprised when they didn't.

He located each of the domo'shah. All seven had cleared the moon now, and the change in direction was bringing them in faster and faster. As Abdullah had said, they were synchronizing their attacks, firing all seven heavy plasma cannons at once, clustered but not joined. It was an impossible task for the Sergeant to continue to block them all.

"Colonel, evasive maneuvers, do your best to keep them guessing."

"Yes, sir."

The Ishur shook again, another plasma beam striking one of the long slipspace fins. It sparked and vented oxygen as it was torn from the fortress.

"Too close," Theodore said.

"General, shouldn't we attack them?" Reza asked.

"What good will that do, Mr. Mokri? We can't afford to sit still and pour energy into their shields, and we certainly don't want a wandering wormhole sucking up our planet."

Reza's face paled. "Yes, sir."

"Colonel, see if you can get us in close to that one over there. Alan's idea isn't perfect, but it's the best we've got. We'll try to bounce around it and hope we can slow their attack. Mr. Mokri, head down to engineering. When things get bad, I intend to spike the shields, and I need you to do your best to keep the modulators from exploding."

"Uh. Yes, sir."

Reza stood and ran from the room, heading for the inner bowels of the ship.

"When things get bad?" General Cave said. "I think we're already there, Teddy."

"Heh. You ain't seen nothing yet."

"You're putting a lot of faith in your son."

"I gotta put it somewhere, Alan. He'll come through. I know he will."

55

"THERE SHE GOES," GABRIEL said, pointing through the small viewport of the excavator.

Donovan could feel the pressure from above, the Magellan's anti-gravity systems pushing down on the planet and on them. He could hear the harsh hissing of the thrusters, and he opened his mouth to pop his ears one more time.

He looked forward through the viewport, at the line of enemy targets ahead. They had abandoned the ground forces as the starship had moved in position over them, sending everything they had up into the belly of the ship and causing black splotches to spread across the painted hull, splotches that seemed to be absorbing at least a portion of the damage the Dread were inflicting.

Their attacks were countered by the plasma cannon mounted to the bottom of the ship. They slammed into the Dread mechs, cutting them down one by one in a fight that seemed less than fair. The Domo'dahm had made a huge mistake by sending all of his fortresses out to attack General St. Martin and leaving the Magellan and the space forces free to seize control of the ground battle.

They had already driven through the city, where the soldiers in the gray uniforms were making short work of the enemy clones, and even the few pur'dahm he had spotted in their battle armor. The Dread warriors were fast and strong, but the soldiers had them outnumbered, and their aim was steady and true, so much more so than a good portion of the rebels. These were people who had spent their lives preparing for war, not focusing on survival from one day to the next. All they had ever needed was an opportunity and a weapon that could hurt the enemy, and now they had both.

"Kroeger, we're almost at your position," Donovan said. "What have you got for us?"

"The remnants of a dozen units," Kroeger replied. "Including part of General Parker's company. The General's dead."

Donovan winced at the news. No wonder he hadn't been able to raise him on the comm. "We're almost at your position. Do we have an opening?"

"You will in a minute, Colonel. That ship is cutting through them assholes like they're made of paper."

"Donovan, switch to channel seventy-two," Gabriel said from the driver's seat.

Donovan turned the dial, watching the numbers climb. He stopped at seventy-two.

"Do you want to broadcast?" he asked.

Gabriel nodded, and he pressed the transmit button down.

"Alpha Actual, this is Major St. Martin. Colonel Graham, can you hear me?"

"Major, this is Alpha Actual. I hear you. Was that you in the excavator?"

"Yes, sir. Radio the others, switch to channel-" Gabriel paused.

"Twenty-six," Donovan said for him.

"Channel twenty-six. We're preparing to move on the capital."

"Roger. Switching now."

Donovan moved the dial back to its original channel.

"This is Alpha Actual, Colonel James Graham of the Earth Alliance."

"We hear you, Colonel," Donovan said. "What's your position?"

"We're about halfway through the city. It's getting harder to find targets out here."

"Good. How quickly can you reach the western side of the city?"

"Where the fortress is parked? I can get a battalion there in ten minutes."

"Too slow," Gabriel said. "He'll have to bring up the rear."

"Roger, Colonel. Major St. Martin suggests you bring up the rear. We're heading for the ship."

"What's the hurry, Gabriel?" Colonel Graham replied.

"We may be winning down here right now, but once the Ishur is destroyed those ships will be coming back. When they do, you can bet they'll hit both the Magellan and this city from space. We have to stop the Ishur from being destroyed."

"How are we going to do that from down here?"

"My father had a plan."

"He's playing it close to the chest, then. He didn't tell me anything about it."

"No, sir."

"Are you going to tell me?"

"No, sir."

Donovan reached out to steady himself as the excavator rounded a corner, slamming into a pile of rubble and pushing it out of the way. He could see the Dread capital rising up directly ahead of them, a kilometer away and backed by deep craters where the other domo'shah had been resting. The line of mechs and tanks had taken a pounding from the Magellan, and there was a clear opening between them.

"Kroeger," Donovan said. "Get your people on the move. Double-time. We're coming in."

"Yes, sir," Kroeger replied.

The soldiers poured out of every dark crack and crevice ahead of them, nearly two hundred people strong. They ran toward the break in the defenses while the excavator gained from behind.

The Magellan loomed above them, firing down at the defenses and up at the circling Dread starfighters. There was more activity from the domo'shah now, a mass of airborne reinforcements bursting from the top of it as the Domo'dahm decided to up the ante.

"Gabriel," Donovan said, pointing toward the new targets.

"I see them," he replied. "We have to keep moving."

The pilot of the Magellan seemed to see them too, because the ship began shifting forward, moving over the ground forces as they raced across the broken terrain toward the capital. Plasma bolts tore into the top of the ship, and Donovan could hear the return fire and the explosions when the Magellan's cannons hit the gi'shah.

They kept going, the excavator overtaking the soldiers. Donovan recognized Kroeger as they moved up on him, and the former jackal smiled at the sight of the machine, slowing down and leaping onto it as it passed. A few of the others saw his maneuver and did the same, climbing onto the vehicle as it churned toward the Dread ship.

They covered half a kilometer, bringing the capital so close it became a black wall in front of them and bringing the Magellan within the angle of the secondary batteries. They began firing, heavy plasma heating the air above them and slamming the starship with volley after volley. Donovan could hear loud pops and cracks above them, and he knew the ship was taking a beating, risking itself to protect them as they ran.

A shift in the pressure from above told him when the Magellan had suffered one critical strike too many. He looked at Gabriel, whose face was tight with concern. He leaned up and over the control yoke, trying to get a look at the Magellan, shaking his head.

"She's going to crash," he said, his voice cracking. "Damn it."

They couldn't see it happen from their protective cocoon, but they heard it a minute later and felt it when the ground shuddered beneath the impact. Had the pilot managed to avoid hitting any of their own? The ship was so big; it seemed impossible.

Plasma bolts began to land around them from all sides, the gi'shah from the air joining the gur'shah and gel'shah on the ground. Donovan heard a scream from outside as someone was hit, and he felt the heat of the plasma burning into the armor above them. Maybe they weren't doing as well as he had thought.

He shifted his position to see through the small viewport, surprised to find that they were nearly on top of the fortress and racing toward a cavernous opening ahead. Gabriel didn't seem concerned that there were only the three of them and the few other soldiers who had managed to cling to the excavator to wage their war inside the ship. He was focused on getting there. And then what? He said he had a plan of some kind that involved him and Ehri.

Whatever it was, he hoped it was good.

56

THE EXCAVATOR SLIPPED INTO the open mouth of the domo'shah's hangar, still moving at a good clip toward the rear wall. The massive bay had already been emptied of mechs and starfighters, but a handful of transports and a pair of larger ek'shah were still organized around them, along with a number of clone soldiers.

They traded rifle fire with the rebels who had survived their entrance clinging to the top and sides of the excavator, flashes of blue reaching back and forth across the space. Gabriel had a vague idea of where he wanted to go, and where it would be if this ship was at all similar to the Ishur, but he turned his head toward Ehri regardless.

"The keepers," he said. "Do you know the quickest way to reach them."

"The keepers?" she asked. "What do you want with them?"

"Reinforcements," he said, nearing the far wall.

"I'm not sure I understand," Ehri said.

"You will. Quickest way?"

"I will lead you."

Gabriel hit the brakes, bringing the excavator to a stop. Ehri was the first out of the hatch, with Donovan close behind. Gabriel joined them a moment later, surprised to find that most of the enemy soldiers had already been dealt with.

"Sergeant Kroeger," Donovan said to an older man who was standing beside the hatch, shooting at anything that moved.

"Colonel," Kroeger replied. "Who's the new guy?"

"Major Gabriel St. Martin," Donovan replied.

Kroeger smiled. "You're St. Martin? It's a pleasure."

"We don't have any time to waste," Gabriel said.

He tried to ignore the burn marks, craters, and blood while taking stock of their forces. Eight soldiers in total, including himself.

"Ehri, lead the way."

She jumped down from the vehicle and the others followed. They cleared the excavator only seconds before a large plasma bolt slammed into the back of it, pushing it forward and into the wall. A second bolt hit it, and then a third. A Dread mech reached the edge of the hangar, shifting to target them.

"In here," Ehri said, opening a hatch ahead of them.

They ducked inside, making it to safety only moments before an unphased plasma bolt struck harmlessly against the lek'shah.

"This way."

Ehri guided them through the corridor, pausing at each intersection.

"I can't believe we made it," Kroeger said quietly. "I should have been dead a dozen times already."

"You and me, both," Donovan said.

"In here," Ehri said, bringing them into one of the domo'shah's many smaller maintenance passages.

"You're familiar with the keepers?" Gabriel asked her.

"Yes. I used to talk to them all the time. They have always abhorred violence, and reject what the Domo'dahms have done."

"Just like you."

Ehri looked back at him, smiling sadly. "Like Juliet St. Martin. I understand that I am not her, Gabriel."

"You do?"

"Yes. I am no peacemaker. I was trained to fight. I was modified to fight. But I do agree with your mother. The path of the pur'dahm is a path to an end to both humans and bek'hai. This way."

They hurried through the rear passages until they reached a dead end. Ehri put her hand on the wall, and a hidden hatch opened, bringing them out right beside a transport beam.

"Most drumhr do not know how to reach the keepers," she said. "They don't know the secret ways. Your mother spent years exploring this ship. She knew them all, and so do I."

They hurried toward the transport beam. A shout at the end of the corridor alerted them that they had been spotted only seconds before the bek'hai at the end of the hallway started shooting, cutting down two of their number before they could react.

It was Ehri who ended the threat, moving with a speed that Gabriel had only seen from Tea'va. She lunged out to the front of the group, shooting at the pur'dahm while moving toward him, rolling to the side, leaping from the side of the wall, and ultimately coming down only a meter away, ready to strike him with the rifle.

She didn't need to. He fell backward, dead.

She scanned the corridor, and then rushed back to them.

"There are two squads of clones headed this way. We must hurry. Take the beam to the bottom."

Gabriel was the first in, lowering his hands and traveling in the beam, stepping out into a nearly identical corridor. Ehri came through a moment later and led them into another hidden passage. They ran along it for four hundred meters or so, and then came out into yet another hallway. This one was dim and damp, and the familiar, biting smell of the legri'shah greeted his eyes.

Ehri continued ahead, leading them closer and closer to the creatures. Finally, they reached a round room that was nearly identical to the one on the Ishur. Nine of the keepers were resting there, sitting on the floor, their cloaks hiding their faces. They stirred at the rebels' approach, shifting and looking at them.

"My name is Gabriel St. Martin," Gabriel said. "I carry a message from It'kek." He paused, taking a deep breath. The entire future of both races hinged on what the keeper had told him to say.

"The time has come," Ehri said before he had the chance to. "The walls are crumbling, the cycle completing, the rebellion at hand. Fight, my brothers. Fight, this one time, for the future of our people, the future of the bek'hai. Fight for justice and equality, for the sake of all things that deserve to live. Fight for the legri'shah, but more importantly, let the legri'shah fight for themselves."

Gabriel looked at Ehri, who seemed as surprised as he was at the words. They both turned their attention to the keepers, who were all coming to their feet. One of them lowered his hood, revealing his reptilian face, the splicing of the original bek'hai with the creatures that saved them. The creatures they repaid by slaughtering and imprisoning, just as they had with humankind.

"The keepers of the Ishur are free," Gabriel said. "And the legri'shah will be released as soon as it returns to Earth. But they won't make it without your help."

The keeper continued staring at him. Then he nodded.

All nine of the keepers left the room, headed down separate corridors.

"Well, that was interesting," Kroeger said.

Gabriel looked at the soldier. For a few seconds, nobody moved. Then a loud roar burst from the tunnels, followed by nearly a dozen more.

"I think it's about to get a lot more interesting," Donovan said.

57

"HULL BREACH ON DECKS eleven to twenty," General Cave said, his attention split between two tablets. "Inner hatches are sealing, but we lost a little more atmosphere."

Theodore looked to the right of the Ishur, to where small bits of debris were drifting from the latest in a series of wounds inflicted by the Dread fortresses.

"We're running out of time, son," he said under his breath.

They had done their best to stay close to the fortresses, to position themselves away from the main line of domo'shah and present as small a profile as possible. They were still trading smaller battery fire with the enemy ship alongside them, beating at each other with little effect, save for a few lost guns. It had given them a few minutes more than Reza's best projections, but even those few minutes were spent.

Theodore could barely believe the Ishur was still functional. If he could look at the fortress from the enemy's perspective, he would have seen gash after gash, deep holes, torn fins, and a battered warship that had no right to still have power or air.

"They're firing again," Cave said.

O'Dea had replaced Abdullah at the main DSS, giving him a rest from the stress of trying to defend the ship on his own. For a logistics officer, she was a fine shield controller, and she slid her hand deftly across the projection, bringing the power to the proper place on the hull and causing it to phase and pull in a whorl of darkspace. The first enemy plasma bolt struck it. She whipped her hand over, moving the system, cursing as she only caught part of the second beam. The Ishur shook one more time.

"One of the oxygenation modules just went offline," General Cave reported.

"Open a channel to engineering," he said. It was time.

"Done," Cave replied.

"Mr. Mokri, shift all of the power to the modulators. Full shields."

"We'll only have a few minutes like this, sir."

"I'm aware of that, Mr. Mokri. We only have one more shot in us if we don't."

"Yes, sir. It will take me a minute to adjust the settings."

"Then stop talking and get to it, son."

"Yes, sir."

Theodore looked out the viewport again. He could see four of the Dread fortresses to his left, floating almost stationary in space, firing their plasma cannons as soon as they were charged. He looked further out, to where the starfighter dogfights had shifted. He knew why Lieutenant Bale was staying out there, but he didn't know why the Dread were still bothering with them, especially when that side of the fight was still going in the rebel's favor. They could pack it in, head home, and wait for the bigger ships to finish the Ishur off. The glory of the fight, he supposed.

"Theodore, I'm receiving a transmission," General Cave said, his voice surprised. "If I'm reading this thing right, it's coming from Earth."

"Gabriel?" Theodore said. He hadn't given up hope, but the thought of it boosted it to the next level.

"It doesn't look like it." General Cave was staring at the tablet. "Even the translation is gibberish to me."

The Ishur shook again. The projections and terminals on the bridge all flashed and flickered, and something internal to the ship stopped making noise. Everything returned to normal a moment later.

"Sir," Reza said over the comm. "One of the reactors just went offline. We won't have enough power to hold the shields for long, even if the modulators are stable."

"Damn it," Theodore said. "Alan, pass the transmission to Mr. Mokri. Mr. Mokri, we just received this from Earth, and we have no idea what it is. Can you read it?"

"Sending it to the engineering terminal," General Cave said.

"I've got it, sir," Reza said. "One second. General, where did you get this?"

"It just arrived from Earth. I don't know the source. Why?"

Reza was laughing in the comm. "I don't believe this."

"What is it, Mr. Mokri?"

"Uh. If I have to guess, I think it's the algorithm the Dread ships are using for their improved darkspace shields, but scanning through it. Oh. Wow. Why didn't I think of that?"

"Don't leave me hanging, Mr. Mokri."

"Hold on, General. I'm patching the system with this."

"General, the DSS just went offline," Daphne said.

"Sorry," Reza said. "I had to reinitialize the system."

"The enemy is firing," General Cave said.

Theodore looked up and out at the fortresses. He could see the blue spears at the tips of their design, preparing to lance out at the Ishur, all at once, in one final effort to bring the starship down.

"DSS is still offline," Daphne said.

"Mr. Mokri," Theodore said.

The bolts streaked towards the Ishur, growing brighter as they neared. Reza didn't answer.

"Mr. Mokri," Theodore shouted.

The light from the plasma bolt was blinding, as it was aimed directly at the bridge. Theodore closed his eyes in anticipation, all sense of time and space fading, replacing with a field of white nothingness that he could have easily mistaken for the afterlife. It was calm and peaceful and silent. Maybe Juliet was here?

It ended as quickly as it had come. Breathing, shouting, beeping and pulsing and throbbing came back in a rush of sound. He opened his eyes.

They were still alive.

"You wanted a miracle, General?" Reza said. "I think you have it. Oh. Uh. Hmm. It looks like there's more in this transmission than shield upgrades."

58

THE CORRIDORS OF THE Dread capital ship turned to chaos within minutes, as after hundreds of years of captivity, the legri'shah were set free.

Gabriel couldn't see the creatures from his place within the maintenance passages, but he could hear them, a constant barrage of roars and chirps that echoed across the decks. He didn't understand at first how the large animals could move from their pens to the other decks since the transports beams were too small to carry them. El'kek, the keeper who had risen first, explained while they made their way toward the bridge.

"The domo'shah were not always prisons to the legri'shah," he said. "There are tunnels for them, tunnels that can take them almost anywhere in the ship. Tunnels that haven't been used for hundreds of cycles. You and I can't travel them; they are too steep and smooth and narrow. But the legri'shah can."

"Why were the legri'shah imprisoned?" he asked.

"To hide them away from the new drumhr. Domo'dahm Pir'el decided long ago that we should forget our past to create a new future."

Gabriel couldn't keep himself from snorting. "Huh. Our human leaders were trying to do the same thing."

"Be grateful they did not."

"Are we there yet?" Kroeger said. He was bringing up the rear and growing impatient.

"We are almost there," Ehri replied. "Are you prepared?"

"Locked and loaded."

She led them out of the maintenance hatch once more, coming out near a transport beam. "Up sixty-one decks," she said to them before stepping in.

Gabriel trailed close behind her, with Donovan, Kroeger, El'kek, and the two soldiers whose names he didn't know bringing up the rear. He raised his hands to go up, subconsciously counting decks, and then stepped out of the beam.

Ehri was standing in front of him, two dead clones at her feet.

"This deck is heavily defended," she said.

"Will the Domo'dahm be on the bridge?" Gabriel asked.

"It is not likely. He will remain in his quarters below."

"It is difficult for him to travel through the ship," El'kek said. "He is an original bek'hai. His visage is also banished from sight."

"What?" Kroeger said. "The leader of your race can't go out in public?"

"Yes."

"Because of his ugly mug?" He laughed.

"Keep it quiet, Sergeant," Donovan said.

Kroeger stopped laughing. They moved the corner of the hallway and checked the intersection.

"I don't hear any of the legri'shah," Gabriel said.

"They will find their way out," El'kek replied. "My brothers will keep them from attacking your brethren."

They headed down the corridor, reaching one of the many circular hubs that composed the layout of the decks. A squad of clone soldiers was moving through it, headed for the transport beam in a hurry, and as a result coming right toward them.

"Take them out," Donovan said, raising his rifle.

The clones reacted with surprise, bringing their weapons up. Gabriel brought his Dread rifle to bear and fired, adding to the sudden barrage from his unit. The clones were overwhelmed, and they stepped over them to continue on.

"That's what I'm talking about," Kroeger said.

Gabriel glanced over at the man, disgusted. He was enjoying the violence way too much. Kroeger either didn't notice the look or ignored it.

They kept going, making a quarter-circle in the hub before heading down another corridor. They turned one more corner and entered an area that was familiar to Gabriel. The layout seemed to be identical to the Ishur, and he knew exactly where he was.

They were almost there.

He had expected the resistance to get heavier the closer they came to the bridge. Instead, the opposite soon became true, as all of the soldiers on the deck were abandoning the control center of the ship and heading to the lower decks in an effort to defend against the rampaging legri'shah.

Ehri brought them to a pause a few hundred meters from the bridge, motioning for them to draw near.

"This is a trap," she said. "Designed to cause us to lower our guard. Do not be fooled."

"How do you know?" Gabriel asked.

"I understand Rorn'el, and how he thinks," she replied. "Your mother knew him very well. He wants you to believe the bridge is undefended. This is false."

"What kind of shit are we about to step in?" Kroeger asked.

"hunters of the Third and Fourth Cell," Ehri replied. "High-ranking pur'dahm warriors. Four of them at least, although it is hard to say how many Rorn'el may have called to his side to protect him. This type of chaos may give other pur'dahm ideas on removing him from power."

"They would turn on one another in the middle of a battle?" Gabriel asked.

"If they believed it would benefit them, yes."

"The madness of our kind," El'kek said.

"They will be fast," Ehri said. "As fast as I can be. Stay together, cover one another. I will do my best to stop them."

"Wait a second," Gabriel said. "I need you alive."

"Then I will have to stay alive. There is no other choice, Gabriel."

Gabriel nodded. "Okay. I'm ready. Let's stick together, keep a clear line of fire. El'kek, you may want to stay back."

"No," the keeper replied.

Gabriel didn't argue. "Let's go."

They made their way across the distance to the bridge, pausing to peer inside. The capital ship's command center was larger than the Ishur's, with more stations circling a much higher central dais. The dais was unoccupied. The rest of the bridge appeared to be the same.

"Are you sure about this?" Gabriel whispered.

"Yes," Ehri replied. "I will go in first. Cover me."

Gabriel opened his mouth to argue, but Ehri was already running toward the bridge.

"Shit," he said, getting his rifle up and pointed at her back. The others did the same.

She dove as she passed the threshold, coming in low, somersaulting and getting to her feet. Two plasma bolts burst past where she should have been from either side, hitting nothing but air.

Gabriel caught sight of a dark shape heading for her and fired, sending a bolt toward it. The Dread hunter shifted slightly, letting the bolt go by, barely breaking his stride. Two more of the hunters revealed themselves, facing Gabriel and the others, rifles in hand.

Plasma bolts filled the corridor, forcing the hunters to duck back. Gabriel caught a glimpse of Ehri in the center of it all, ducking beneath an attack by one of the bek'hai, who was using some kind of blade to strike at her. She lashed out with a foot, catching him in the back of the knee and bringing him off-balance. Instead of following up the attack, she skipped away, narrowly avoiding another of the weapons.

"What are we doing out here?" Kroeger said, starting to advance on the room.

They kept a steady stream of plasma targeting the two hunters near the entrance, while also keeping an eye on the two attacking Ehri. She was holding her own, keeping them away, but for how long?

They took a few more steps forward. The hunters near the entrance rolled across the hallway, firing as they passed. Gabriel heard a shout and saw one of the soldiers fall. He heard Donovan curse as well, and saw a burn mark and blood spreading from his shoulder.

"Druk'dahm," El'kek said, grabbing his robe and shedding it. He was nude beneath, muscular, and at the same time lacking in genitalia. A short stub of a tail protruded from the small of his back.

He bared his teeth and rushed toward the bridge. One of the hunters emerged to shoot at him, but he batted the rifle away and barreled into the pur'dahm, knocking him back.

Gabriel kept advancing, keeping his focus on the Dread attacking Ehri. She avoided a strike from one of the hunters and then shouted in pain as the blade of the second caught her arm. She threw herself away from them, gaining a little distance.

The hunter still near the entrance took advantage of the opportunity, leaping at her from behind. He was fast, so fast. Gabriel shifted his rifle almost without thinking, squeezing the trigger and sending three bolts at Dread. The first two went wide, but the third hit him square in the side and cost him his momentum. He stumbled instead of striking, and Ehri bounced out of the way of his corpse as he fell to the floor.

"Nice shot," Kroeger said, reaching Gabriel. He crossed the corridor, taking aim at the hunter engaged with El'kek. "That's it. Keep him steady. No sudden moves."

Gabriel realized just in time what the man intended. He lunged forward, bringing his rifle down on top of Kroeger's and disrupting his aim. Kroeger's bolt went wide, hitting the wall instead of blasting through the back of El'kek's head and into the Dread hunter.

"What the hell are you doing?" Gabriel said. "He's on our side."

"Are you kidding me?" Kroeger shouted back, pulling himself free. "I've got a shot to kill that bastard I'm taking it, even if I have to kill that other dragon man son of a bitch with him."

"You're out of your damn mind."

"Yeah, right. Maybe I'm the only one who's sane."

Kroeger shoved Gabriel aside, bringing his rifle up again.

"Sergeant," Donovan shouted. His arm was dark with blood, and he looked pale.

Kroeger looked at him, his eyes wild. "Sorry, Colonel. I guess I'm the real giant now."

He looked back at El'kek and the Dread, ready to pull the trigger once more.

A sharp blade sank into his arm, cutting it off at the elbow, causing the rifle to fall from his grip and clatter to the floor. Kroeger shouted in pain, his cry cut off as the blade came back around and through his neck, removing his head.

The hunter scowled at them before rushing toward Gabriel. He tried to get his weapon up to defend himself, but there was no time. He shifted his grip, barely getting it positioned to block the hunter's blade, leaving their faces only centimeters apart.

Then he felt a rush of heat, heard a soft thud, and saw the Dread's expression change. A second thud followed. Then a third. The pressure against him vanished as the pur'dahm collapsed.

Donovan could barely lift the rifle with his one good hand, and he let it fall as he leaned against the wall to keep himself upright.

Gabriel stepped over the Dread, taking the last few steps onto the bridge. Ehri was leaning against one of the terminals, her arm bleeding, but no longer under attack. El'kek was standing over the final hunter, breathing raggedly, looking down at his victim with an expression of sadness unlike anything Gabriel had ever seen.

"It's over then?" Donovan asked.

Gabriel turned back to the soldier, getting himself under his good arm and helping him up. "How are you feeling?"

"I don't know yet. It's numb, and I'm cold."

That didn't sound good.

"Ehri, we need to send a message fleet-wide. Can you do that?"

"Yes," she replied, moving across the bridge to another terminal.

Gabriel took two steps toward her when he heard footsteps coming up from behind them. He tried to turn, but holding Donovan was limiting his movement.

El'kek broke from his mourning, whipping around and positioning himself in front of the bridge. By the time Gabriel could see, the keeper had come up short and was staring at another Juliet clone.

"Colonel Peters," she said.

"Orli?" Donovan replied. "It's okay; she's with us."

El'kek moved aside.

"What are you doing here? I thought you were dead?"

"No. I escaped the destruction of my mech. I snuck behind the bek'hai infantry line and stole a transport and brought it here. Colonel, we have to go. The Domo'dahm is on his way here with too many hunters for us to fight."

"Can you help keep Colonel Peters upright?" Gabriel asked, handing him over to Orli. "Ehri, do you have it?"

"One moment, Gabriel."

"Gabriel?" Orli said, her expression changing. Gabriel would have been taken back by it, but he had seen it before in Zoelle.

"I know," he replied. "Not now. I don't know how much longer the Ishur will last."

"The Ishur?" Orli said. "Oh. Don't worry, Gabriel. Your father should be safe for now. I've already taken care of that."

59

"HOW ARE WE DOING, Mr. Mokri?" Theodore asked.

"Shields are holding, sir. Modulators are stable. Power is going to be a problem though, sir, if we have to take much more of this. With one of the reactors down, we can't take this pounding forever."

Theodore smiled, looking out at the Dread fortresses arranged ahead of them. The reaction from the enemy ships had been almost comical when they realized the humans had miraculously managed to provide a vast upgrade to their defenses.

As Reza had explained in the first minute following the shift, it all came down to math.

"How much longer do we have?" Theodore asked.

"I'm shutting down some non-essential systems. Five minutes?"

"Not a lot of time. What about our other upgrade."

"Almost done, sir."

Theodore's comfort faded. Where was Gabriel anyway? They had managed to outlast their predicted demise by nearly thirty minutes, but there was no word from him. Had he failed in his mission? Had the Magellan even made it to the ground?

If Gabriel was dead, there was only one thing left to do.

"I'm sorry, Mr. It'kek," Theodore said, looking over at the keeper on the bridge. "We can't afford to wait any longer."

The keeper's expression was dour, but he nodded. "I understand."

"Mr. Mokri, tell me as soon as the update is complete."

"Oh. Uh. We just finished replacing the last of the conduits, sir."

Theodore looked down at his tablet, switching the screen to the plasma cannon fire control.

"Colonel Ames, bring us toward the fortress furthest to port."

"Yes, sir," Ames replied.

"Uh, sir," Reza said. "We'll only have enough power for five shots, and the shields will go down for a few seconds after you fire. I thought you might want to know that."

"Duly noted, Mr. Mokri."

The Ishur began to vibrate, the damage it had taken causing it to shudder from the thrust. The Dread ships in front of them stood their ground, still unsure of what he was up to. They fired their plasma cannons again, sending heavy bolts into the darkspace shields where they were absorbed.

"Firing," Theodore announced, pressing down on his tablet. The Ishur shuddered even more as power was diverted to the main plasma cannon.

"Thrusters are offline," General Cave said. "Life support offline. Gravity generators offline on half the decks. I don't know what this one means. I think it's the transport beams? It's down, too."

The plasma cannon was sucking all of their power in. A moment later, it spit that power back out.

A stream of blue plasma lanced across space, pouring into the center of the fortress opposite them. For an instant, a black whorl of darkspace blocked the stream, but it was too small to collect the entire blast. It shattered as the plasma burned the area around it, sinking through the lek'shah, passing into the domo'shah, continuing onward until it appeared

307

out the other side, like a giant azure lance.

It vanished a moment later. The Dread ship was still at first, and then slowly began to break apart, the debris spreading from the center.

"Direct hit," General Cave said.

"Get us on the next one, Colonel," Theodore said.

They would only get one surprise attack, and the Dread ships were already breaking formation, spreading out to avoid another bolt. They returned fire with secondary batteries, which dug into the sides of the Ishur while the reactor was still recovering.

"Thrusters online. Life support online. Gravity still down."

"We don't need gravity," Theodore said. "Colonel Ames, get us a better angle."

"Yes, sir."

The Ishur started moving again, changing direction to get a better vector on the Dread ships. They were still firing their secondary batteries, but the attack was being absorbed once more.

"They're decimating our power supply, General," Reza said over the comm. "You need to back away."

Theodore didn't give it much thought. "No. This is our last stand. Let's make it count. Red One, you still out there?"

"I'm here, sir," Lieutenant Bale replied.

"Take what you have left and harass those batteries. Get them shooting at something else."

"Yes, sir."

Theodore could see the remaining fighters break off from their diminished dogfights and race toward the Dread fortresses. At the same time, he kept an eye on his terminal, and on the ship ahead of them.

"Three degrees starboard, lift the nose four degrees, Colonel."

"Yes, sir."

The Ishur shifted in space, getting into position to fire. Theodore held his finger over the trigger.

A soft wash of static burst over the comm, followed by a sharp, shrill tone.

"Bek'hai cruhr dur heil," a familiar voice said. "Un'hai. Lor'hai.

Legri'hai." It paused a moment, and a new voice echoed across the bridge.

"The time has come," Gabriel said. "The end of the pur'dahm is here. My name is Gabriel St. Martin. My father is Theodore St. Martin. My mother was Juliet St. Martin. We are here, and we're fighting to be free. The keepers, the un'hai, the legri'shah, and the humans. The drumhr are leading you to the end. Join us, and help us bring a new beginning. Soldiers, scientists, cleaners, caretakers. You knew Juliet St. Martin. You knew what she believed in. You have the power to see that happen, right now. Preserve the true bek'hai, preserve your identity, save your future. Fight back against the pur'dahm, as the keepers are fighting back. Set the legri'shah free. Set yourselves free."

The comm fell silent again. Theodore's heart was racing, his eyes tearing from the well of pride and thankfulness that Gabriel was still alive.

"My name is El'kek," a new voice said. "I am a keeper on the Domo'dahm's domo'shah. Our legri'shah are free. We are free."

Theodore looked over at It'kek, whose teeth were bared in a smile. He returned his attention to the Dread fortress ahead of them. He kept his finger over the trigger of the plasma cannon while it continued to fire at them. Had they been right about the Juliet clones? Would this really work? He couldn't wait forever to shoot.

They drew within a thousand kilometers. The fortress continued to shoot, but Theodore noticed that the volume was lessening, the batteries falling silent one by one. Something was happening out there, wasn't it?

"There is no reason for war between the bek'hai and the humans," he heard Gabriel saying. "Except that the Domo'dahm wishes it. Why choose violence over peace?"

"Ishur, this is Dahm Pirelle of the domo'shah Ishkore," a voice said, cutting in over Gabriel. "General St. Martin, please respond."

Theodore was surprised by the interruption. Another Juliet? "Alan, patch us in."

"On it, Teddy," General Cave replied. "Go ahead."

"This is General St. Martin. We hear you, Ishkore. What is your status?"

"Theodore, the uprising has begun. We are in control of the bridge, and the entire ship will be ours soon."

"Roger, Ishkore," Theodore replied. "Do you know about the others?"

"Yes. They too are rebelling. They too desire peace. All of the lor'hai desire peace. It is within their nature. It is the gift I gave to them. The gift that was always meant to undo them, though the Domo'dahm never understood it well enough to realize."

It took Theodore a moment to remember that this clone also believed she was Juliet St. Martin. It was tough for him to keep being reminded of her, and at the same time, he was proud of what she had done for them.

"Well, Teddy," General Cave said, turning back to look at him. "It looks like we might just win this thing after all. I'm sorry I ever doubted you."

"Apology accepted," Theodore replied.

He was just happy he never stopped believing.

60

DOMO'DAHM RORN'EL GRABBED HIS mask, sliding it over his face and hissing at the discomfort. It was one thing to wear the apparatus to pass from his private chambers to the throne room. It was another to have to travel the halls of the Dahm'shah in it.

As if he had a choice.

It was all falling apart. Everything he had worked to build since he had become Domo'dahm was coming undone. The humans had made it into the ship. They had somehow freed the legri'shah, and now the creatures were running amok within, killing every bek'hai they saw who wasn't a keeper.

It was Juliet St. Martin who had done it. His Juliet, who he had so adored. A woman of peace and God, who had betrayed his trust by befriending those who were beneath him. He had spent so much time and energy deflecting attacks from his pur'dahm; he had never seen or suspected she would be capable of such a thing.

He opened the door to his chamber, stepping out into the hallway. He could hear the cries of the legri'shah echoing throughout the ship, and it made him want to weep. He was trying to preserve their race. Their purity. Their history. As best he could with the limited resources he was given. Humans were inferior and so unsuitable as splices, yet he had done what he could to make it work. It wasn't fair for it to end like this.

"Domo'dahm," Orish'ek said, approaching him.

He was wearing full battle armor, carrying both a rifle and a lek'sai. Ten members of the Second Cell were with him, ready to protect their leader.

"Orish'ek. We go to the bridge. We can destroy the rebellion from orbit."

"Yes, Domo'dahm."

He led them from his chamber, making sure to keep himself postured so they would never guess what he looked like beneath his robes.

They were near the transport beam when a sharp roar brought them to a stop. One of the legri'shah turned the corner a moment later, pausing as it spied them. Then it hissed and charged, half-running, half-slithering along the corridor toward them, its bulk filling the space. Rorn'el looked at the beam up ahead, knowing it was too far to run.

The hunters didn't flinch. They dropped their rifles, raising their lek'sai and charging back at the creature, shouting in challenging response to its growls. All except Orish'ek.

"This way, Domo'dahm," he said.

Rorn'el hesitated, watching as the hunters were attacked. The legri'shah's head dipped down, mouth open, teeth reaching for one of them. He stepped aside, swinging his lek'sai, cutting into the legri'shah's face. The creature hissed and snapped, catching the hunter's leg and biting it off, its teeth passing easily through the lek'shah.

"Domo'dahm, we must hurry," Orish'ek said.

Rorn'el nodded and followed. He could hear the hunter's screams as they battled the creature. Right before he stepped into the beam, he heard the legri'shah cry out in a high-pitched wail of defeat.

Then he was into the beam. He came out in the hub nearest the bridge, with Orish'ek ahead of him. There were no soldiers left here. No legri'shah either. He took two steps, and then paused as a voice surrounded him. Ehri dur Tuhrik, followed by a human voice.

He hissed as the human spoke of freedom as if he were some manner of tyrant. He hissed as the human used the words he had heard Tuhrik speak before he had abandoned the pur'dahm cells.

"They must be on the bridge," Orish'ek said. "Transmitting to the other domo'shah."

"I will kill them myself," Rorn'el replied.

"No, Domo'dahm," Orish'ek said. "I will take care of it." The pur'dahm lifted his rifle in Rorn'el's direction. "You have failed us."

Rorn'el eyed the weapon, tensing. "And you also will betray me, Orish'ek?"

"I have done my duty, and watched you drive us to ruin. I will save the pur'dahm."

"You will not."

Orish'ek pulled the trigger. Rorn'el slipped to the side, the plasma bolt going wide. The shocked pur'dahm tried to back away, to shoot again. Rorn'el tore off his mask and dropped his robes, revealing his bek'hai form.

"You have seen me Orish'ek," he said. "Now you have to die."

Orish'ek dropped the rifle and pulled his lek'sai, barely getting it up in time to block Rorn'el's claws.

"I am Domo'dahm for a reason Orish'ek. Not because I am soft. Because I am strong."

He stayed on the traitor, striking at Orish'ek's face, at his chest, at his shoulders. The pur'dahm didn't try to block every attack, thinking the lek'shah would protect him.

Thinking wrong.

Rorn'el's nails sank through the material. He was spliced from the legri'shah, and his claws bore the same properties as the creatures'. They were in phase with the armor, and they dug into it without resistance, sinking into Orish'ek's flesh, cutting deep enough to force him to drop his weapon.

"Domo'dahm, please," Orish'ek said, standing unarmed in front of him.
"You beg?" Rorn'el said. "You are no pur'dahm. You are barely a
drumhr. More like a druk'shur."

Rorn'el kicked him, the claws of his feet sinking deeply into his chest.
He held him for a moment with powerful legs before throwing him back
into the transport beam.

He hissed one last time, leaving his robes and mask behind while he
continued on to the bridge.

It was empty when he arrived, and while the sight of the dead humans
pleased him, the dead hunters angered him more. They had failed him, as
all of his pur'dahm were failing him.

He entered the bridge, closing and locking the hatch behind him. The
humans were gone, likely trying to escape before he arrived, with Ehri dur
Tuhrik leading them through the ship. It was well. They wouldn't be able
to clear the area before he bombarded it from space.

He climbed the command dais, sitting and activating the terminal,
feeling powerful in his freedom. He had spent too long covered from head
to toe.

He used sharp, blood-crusted claws to activate the reactors, running
quickly through the launch sequence. It was challenging to fly a
domo'shah without help, but he was up to the task. What else could he do?

Three minutes later, the massive fortress began to rise. It shook the
ground beneath it, knocking down loose structures, and dislodging tons of
earth that had shifted over the ship through the years. He rotated the ship
as it climbed so that he was able to look down on the battlefield. There
was smoke and fire everywhere. The wreckage of gur'shah and gel'shah,
and plenty of corpses. And there was the human starship, its outer shell in
ruins, dead and silent nearby.

That would be his target. While all the land around it would burn
regardless, he would get such satisfaction, such pleasure from finally
destroying the one ship that got away. The one ship that allowed all of this
to happen. It wasn't too late to start again. There were outposts scattered
across the planet, where the clones and the drumhr wouldn't know what
was happening here. The legri'shah might be lost, but they wouldn't need

them anymore.

The dahm'shah continued to climb, rising quickly, reaching the atmosphere and then punching through. He noticed his sensors now, and the domo'shah returning to the planet. Were they still his?

A symbol appeared on his terminal. A hail from one of his ships, probably seeking orders.

"Speak," he said, answering it.

"Hello. My name is General Theodore St. Martin. I'd like to speak to a Domo'dahm Rorn'el?"

Rorn'el shuddered at the human voice, tempted to close the channel immediately. He hissed softly and then replied.

"I am Domo'dahm Rorn'el," he said, as confidently as he could.

"I'd say it's a pleasure, Rorn'el, but it isn't," Theodore said. "You took my planet, and I've never appreciated that much. My wife Juliet was a peaceful, gentle soul. I believe you knew her? I want to spread your ashes across the universe, but she would want me to give you a chance to live. So, that's what I'm gonna do. One chance, Rorn'el. What do you say?"

Rorn'el could barely contain his anger.

It was gone. All gone. The bek'hai race would die, and he would be forgotten. Or, if he were remembered, it would be as the Domo'dahm who killed them.

All because of Juliet St. Martin.

He wasn't going to die without destroying the one that got away. He owed himself that honor at least.

He checked his terminal, noting his position. He found the human starship sitting on the planet below and moved into the weapons systems. He shifted his claws, activating the main plasma cannon.

"I'll take that as a no," Theodore said.

Rorn'el looked up and out the viewport. Six domo'shah were arranged ahead of him, dropping into his field of view. The tips of each were glowing blue, indicating that their plasma cannons were about to fire.

He checked his own. It was still charging. Would there be enough time?

The domo'shah fired, six beams converging on one point near the center of the ship, where the reactors sat. He had never upgraded his shields with the human technology. He had never thought he would need it, and didn't want to soil his systems with their designs.

The beams hit the ship, causing it to shudder.

The terminal indicated the cannon was ready to fire.

His claw never came down on it.

The bridge shook violently, knocking him to the ground. He tried to get back up, but it continued shaking as the energy of the plasma drove through the structure. The viewport cracked and splintered, the entire frame breaking apart. Oxygen began to spill out, and the temperature dropped.

"That was for the human race, you bastard," he heard Theodore St. Martin say.

Then the bridge vanished around him, the pieces blowing out and into space.

Then he died.

61

THE DREAD TRANSPORT LANDED beside the Magellan, and Gabriel jumped out of it as soon as the hatch finished opening. He turned and looked up at the sky, ignoring Ehri, Orli, El'kek, and Donovan as they joined him.

The Dread fortresses were all visible in the space above the city, but none were more visible than the dahm'shah. Or at least, what was left of it.

Chunks of material sank into the atmosphere. The lek'shah, no longer given an electrical current, burned the same as any other part, all of it creating a spectacle of light in the sky that reminded him of streams he had seen, where parties on Earth ended in fireworks. He felt the moisture in his eyes at the sight.

"Gabriel."

He turned, smiling as Miranda ran toward him. He opened his arms for her, catching her in a solid embrace, his eyes landing on the others trailing behind her. Colonel Choi, Guy and Sarah Larone, and Wallace, who barked and circled them, tail wagging.

"We did it," Miranda said. "I can't believe we did it."

"Me neither," he replied, eyes streaming with tears. "I always believed, but I never thought it would actually happen."

"Look," Guy said, pointing up.

A few smaller shapes had broken through the atmosphere, past the burning debris. They dove toward the city, leveling out and streaking across the sky. Starfighters of both human and bek'hai design. Gabriel raised his hand to them, waving at them as they passed overhead and circled back.

A sharp hiss caused them all to freeze. A shape formed to their left, obscured by the smoldering wreckage of a Dread mech. A large, reptilian head appeared a moment later, followed by a huge body.

The legri'shah approached them slowly, while Wallace ran to the front of the group, barking at it.

"Wallace," Gabriel said, reaching for the dog.

"Do not fear," El'kek said, moving calmly to the dog's side.

He put a hand on Wallace's head, and he quieted immediately. Then he said something to the legri'shah in bek'hai, and the creature lowered itself until it was flat on the ground.

"There has been enough killing today. Enough for many lifetimes."

Gabriel couldn't argue with that. He took Miranda by the hand, leading her over to where Donovan was standing. His arm was dead at his side, but he would survive.

"Colonel Peters," Gabriel said.

"Major St. Martin," Donovan replied, smiling.

Gabriel moved forward, embracing him for a moment before backing away. "This is my fiancee, Miranda."

"A pleasure," Donovan said. "A real pleasure, just to have something so normal after all of this."

Miranda hugged him, careful of his arm. "It's an honor, Colonel."

"So," Guy said. "What happens now?"

"Peace," Ehri replied. "Between the humans and the bek'hai, at least."

"It will take some time to restore order," Donovan said. "Some of us have been living in chaos for too long just to give it up."

"It will take time," Gabriel agreed. "But we have time, now. We have all the time in the world." He looked over at Ehri, and then at Orli. "What will you do?"

The two Juliet clones glanced at one another.

"I believe Juliet St. Martin would have wanted us to spread the news of peace," Orli said.

"I agree," Ehri said. "We will help return order to this world, as emissaries for both the Earth Alliance and the bek'hai."

"You'll do her proud," Gabriel said. "Her and Theodore."

He moved away from them, back to Colonel Choi, giving her a hug before first embracing Sarah, and then shaking hands with Guy.

"You both did a fine job," he said. "I'm even starting to like you."

Guy laughed. "Likewise."

Gabriel looked back at the sky. The domo'shah were growing larger above them. The one in the lead was in bad shape. Half its fins were missing, the profile battered and ragged.

"The Ishur," Ehri said. "Your father."

"He'll be happy to see the Magellan's still in one piece," Miranda said.

"He'll be happier to see Gabriel's still in one piece," Donovan said, laughing.

"He always said he refused to die until we had our planet back," Gabriel said. "But I hope he'll stick around a little bit longer."

"He will," Miranda replied. "He won't want to miss the party."

They watched as the Ishur descended, coming to rest in the crater the Dahm'shah had left only minutes earlier. As it settled to the Earth, a new sound began to echo across the landscape. It was like a rumble, but higher in pitch.

"What is that?" Donovan asked.

Ehri titled her head, listening, and then turned toward them. "Cheering," she said with a smile. "The soldiers in the city are cheering. Humans and clones."

"It's the best sound I've ever heard," Donovan said.

"Me, too," Gabriel agreed.

He closed his eyes, his hand falling to the crucifix around his neck. He clutched it tightly, turning his thoughts to his mother. "Thank you," he said softly. "Thank you."

THE END.

Thank you for reading Tides of War, and the Rebellion series.
Reviews are appreciated!!!
mrforbes.com/reviewtidesofwar

More Books By M.R. Forbes:

M.R. Forbes on Amazon

mrforbes.com/amazon

Looking for more sci-fi to read?

Starship Eternal (War Eternal, Book One)

mrforbes.com/starshipeternal

A lost starship...
A dire warning from futures past...
A desperate search for salvation...

Captain Mitchell "Ares" Williams is a Space Marine and the hero of the Battle for Liberty, whose Shot Heard 'Round the Universe saved the planet from a nearly unstoppable war machine. He's handsome, charismatic, and the perfect poster boy to help the military drive enlistment. Pulled from the war and thrown into the spotlight, he's as efficient at charming the media and bedding beautiful celebrities as he was at shooting down enemy starfighters.

After an assassination attempt leaves Mitchell critically wounded, he begins to suffer from strange hallucinations that carry a chilling and oddly familiar warning:

They are coming. Find the Goliath or humankind will be destroyed.

Convinced that the visions are a side-effect of his injuries, he tries to ignore them, only to learn that he may not be as crazy as he thinks. The enemy is real and closer than he imagined, and they'll do whatever it takes to prevent him from rediscovering the centuries lost starship.

Narrowly escaping capture, out of time and out of air, Mitchell lands at the mercy of the Riggers - a ragtag crew of former commandos who patrol the lawless outer reaches of the galaxy. Guided by a captain with a reputation for cold-blooded murder, they're dangerous, immoral, and possibly insane.

They may also be humanity's last hope for survival in a war that has raged beyond eternity.

Or maybe something completely different?

Dead of Night (Ghosts & Magic)

mrforbes.com/deadofnight

Tides Of War

For Conor Night, the world's only surviving necromancer, staying alive is an expensive proposition. So when the promise of a big payout for a small bit of thievery presents itself, Conor is all in. But nothing comes easy in the world of ghosts and magic, and it isn't long before Conor is caught up in the machinations of the most powerful wizards on Earth and left with only two ways out:

Finish the job, or be finished himself.

Balance (The Divine)

mrforbes.com/balance

My name is Landon Hamilton. Once upon a time I was a twenty-three year old security guard, trying to regain my life after spending a year in prison for stealing people's credit card numbers.

Now, I'm dead.

Okay, I was supposed to be dead. I got killed after all; but a funny thing happened after I had turned the mortal coil...

I met Dante Alighieri - yeah, that Dante. He told me I was special, a diuscrucis. That's what they call a perfect balance of human, demon, and angel. Apparently, I'm the only one of my kind.

I also learned that there was a war raging on Earth between Heaven and Hell, and that I was the only one who could save the human race from annihilation. He asked me to help, and I was naive enough to agree.

Sounds crazy, I know, but he wished me luck and sent me back to the mortal world. Oh yeah, he also gave me instructions on how to use my Divine "magic" to bend the universe to my will. The problem is, a sexy vampire crushed them while I was crushing on her.

Now I have to somehow find my own way to stay alive in a world of angels, vampires, werewolves, and an assortment of other enemies that all want to kill me before I can mess up their plans for humanity's future. If that isn't enough, I also have to find the queen of all demons and recover the Holy Grail.

It's not like it's the end of the world if I fail.

Wait. It is.

Tears of Blood (Books 1-3)

mrforbes.com/tearsofblood

One thousand years ago, the world was broken and reborn beneath the boot of a nameless, ageless tyrant. He erased all history of the time before, enslaving the people and hunting those with the power to unseat him.

The power of magic.

Eryn is such a girl. Born with the Curse, she fights to control and conceal it to protect those she loves. But when the truth is revealed, and his soldiers come, she is forced away from her home and into the company of Silas, a deadly fugitive tormented by a fractured past.

Silas knows only that he is a murderer who once hunted the Cursed, and that he and his brothers butchered armies and innocents alike to keep the deep, dark secrets of the time before from ever coming to light.

Secrets which could save the world.

Or destroy it completely.

Join the Mailing List!

"No," you cry. "I will not submit myself to even more inbox spam. I have quite enough garbage coming in from people and places that I care a lot more about than you."

"But," I reply, "if you sign up for my mailing list, you'll know when my next book is out. Don't you want to know when my next book is out?"

"Eh... I'll find it on Amazon."

"True enough, but you see, a mailing list is very valuable to an author, especially a meager self-published soul such as myself. I don't have a marketing team, and I don't have exposure in brick and mortar stores around the world to help improve my readership. All I have is you, my potential fans. How about a bribe?"

"Hmm... Keep talking."

"Picture this... giveaways, a chance at FREE books. There is a 10% chance* you could save at least three dollars per year!"

Silence.

"Where'd you go?" I ask. "Well, I'll just leave this here, in case you change your mind."

http://mrforbes.com/mailinglist

* For illustration only. Not an actual mathematical probability.

Thank You!

It is readers like you, who take a chance on self-published works that is what makes the very existence of such works possible. Thank you so very much for spending your hard-earned money, time, and energy on this work. It is my sincerest hope that you have enjoyed reading!

Independent authors could not continue to thrive without your support. If you have enjoyed this, or any other independently published work, please consider taking a moment to leave a review at the source of your purchase. Reviews have an immense impact on the overall commercial success of a given work, and your voice can help shape the future of the people whose efforts you have enjoyed.

Thank you again!

About the Author

M.R. Forbes is the creator of a growing catalog of speculative fiction titles, including the science-fiction Rebellion and War Eternal novels, the epic fantasy Tears of Blood series, the contemporary fantasy Divine series, and the world of Ghosts & Magic. He lives in the pacific northwest with his family, including a cat who thinks she's a dog, and a dog who thinks she's a cat. He eats too many donuts, and he's always happy to hear from readers.

Mailing List: http://www.mrforbes.com/mailinglist

Website: http://www.mrforbes.com/

Goodreads: http://www.goodreads.com/author/show/6912725.M_R_Forbes

Facebook: http://www.facebook.com/mrforbes.author

Twitter: http://www.twitter.com/mrforbes

CPSIA information can be obtained
at www.ICGtesting.com
Printed in the USA
FSHW022025131218
54469FS